DIAGNOSIS:

DIAGNOSIS:

TERMINAL

AN
ANTHOLOGY
OF
MEDICAL
TERROR

EDITED BY
F. PAUL WILSON

A TOM DOHERTY ASSOCIATES BOOK / NEW YORK

DIAGNOSIS: TERMINAL

A Forge Book
Published by Tom Doherty Associates, Inc.
175 Fifth Avenue
New York, NY 10010

Forge® is a registered trademark of Tom Doherty Associates, Inc.

Design by Lynn Newmark

Library of Congress Cataloging-in-Publication Data

Diagnosis : terminal / edited by F. Paul
  Wilson.
      p.   cm.
    "A Tom Doherty Associates book."
    ISBN 0-312-85972-4
    1.   Medicine—Fiction. 2.   Horror   tales,
American. 3.   American   fiction—20th
century.   I. Wilson, F. Paul (Francis Paul)
PS648.M36D53   1996
813'.0873808356—dc20   96-1407
                                        CIP

First Edition: August 1996

Printed in the United States of America

0 9 8 7 6 5 4 3 2 1

COPYRIGHT ACKNOWLEDGMENTS

CONTENTS

ANGEL OF MERCY   Bill Pronzini   13

DR. JOE   Chet Williamson   23

FRIENDLY WAGER   Matthew Costello   42

PROSPER BANE, 05409021   Billie Sue Mosiman   57

SINISTER   Steven Spruill   80

BAD TOUCH   Richard Lee Byers   115

GET IT OUT   Thomas F. Monteleone   124

THE CUBAN SOLUTION   Tina L. Jens   143

ALL OVER BUT THE DYING   Ridley Pearson   170

PETIT MAL   Jack Nimersheim   219

WIND OVER HEAVEN   Bruce H. Rogers   245

OFFSHORE   F. Paul Wilson   263

SURVIVAL   Ed Gorman   291

FINAL CUT   Karl Edward Wagner   341

DIAGNOSIS:

Bill Pronzini is best known for his Nameless detective novels, but he's also an accomplished short story writer and a respected editor. He won the Shamus Award and has been nominated for multiple Edgars.

I was hoping someone would offer a story set in the past and Bill came up with this little gem. And since I've set up the contents in rough chronological order, Mercy is our first practitioner.

Angel of Mercy

Bill Pronzini

Her name was Mercy.

Born with a second name, yes, like everyone else, but it had been so long since she'd used it she could scarce remember what it was. Scarce remember so many things about her youth, long faded now—except for Father, of course. It seemed, sometimes, that she had never had a youth at all. That she'd spent her whole life on the road, first with Caleb and then with Elias, jouncing from place to place in the big black traveling wagon, always moving, drifting, never settling anywhere. Birth to death, with her small deft hands working tirelessly and her eyes asquint in smoky lamplight and her head aswirl with medicines, mixtures, measurements, what was best for this ailment, what was the proper dosage for that one. . . .

Miss Mercy. Father had been the first to call her that, in his little apothecary shop in . . . what *was* the name of the town where she'd been born? Lester? No, Dexter. Dexter, Pennsylvania. "A druggist is an angel of mercy," he said to her when she was ten or eleven. "Your name comes from my belief in that, child. Mercy. Miss Mercy. And wouldn't *you* like to be an angel of mercy one day, too?"

"Oh yes, Father, yes! Will you show me how?"

And he had shown her, with great patience, because he had no sons and because he bore no prejudice against his daughter or the daughter of any man. He had shown her carefully and well for five or six or seven years, until Mr. President Lincoln declared war against the Confederate States of America and Father went away to bring his mercy to sick and wounded Union soldiers on far-off battlefields. But there was no mercy for him. On one of those battlefields, a place called Antietam, he was himself mortally wounded by cannon fire.

As soon as she received word of his death, she knew what she must do. She had no siblings, and Mother had died years before; Father's legacy was all that was left. And it seemed as though the next thing she knew, she was sitting on the high seat of the big black traveling wagon, alone in the beginning, then with Caleb and then Elias to drive the team of horses, bringing *her* mercy to those in need. Death to birth, birth to death—it was her true calling. Father would have been proud. He would have understood and he would have been so proud.

Miss Mercy. If it had been necessary to paint a name on the side of the wagon, that was the name she would have chosen. Just that and nothing more. It was what Caleb had called her, too, from their very first meeting in . . . Saint Louis, hadn't it been? Young and strong and restless—there driving the wagon one day, gone the next and never seen again. And Miss Mercy was the only name Elias wrote on his pad of white paper when the need arose, the name he would have spoken aloud if he hadn't been born deaf and dumb. She had chanced upon him down South somewhere. Georgia, perhaps—he was an emancipated slave from the state of Georgia. Chanced upon him, befriended him, and they had been together ever since. Twenty years? Thirty? Dear Elias. She couldn't have traveled so long and so far, or done so much, if it were not for him.

In all the long years, how many miles had they traveled together? Countless number. North and east in the spring and summer, south and west in the fall and winter. Ohio, Illinois, Minnesota, Iowa, Montana, Kansas, Nebraska, Missouri, Oklahoma, Texas . . . maybe all the states and territories there were. Civilization and wilderness frontier. Ranches, farms, settlements. Towns that had no druggist, towns that had druggists with short supplies or too little understanding of their craft. Cities, now and then, to replenish medicines that could not be gotten elsewhere. Saint Louis and . . . Chicago? Yes, Chicago. Oh, she could scarce remember them all.

And everywhere they went, the people came. The needy people with their aches and pains, ills and ailments, troubles and sorrows. First to marvel at her skill with mortar and pestle and her vast pharmacopoeial knowledge; at the cabinets and tight-fitted shelves Elias had built to hold the myriad glass bottles filled with liquids in all the colors of the rainbow, and below the shelves the rows upon rows of drawers containing ground and powdered drugs, herbs and barks, pastilles and pills. And then to buy what they needed: cough syrups, liniments, worm cures, liver medicines, stomach bitters, blood purifiers. And so much more: two-grain quinine tablets, Bateman's drops, castor oil, Epsom salts and rochelle salts and siedlitz powders, paregorics and rheumatism tonics, bottles of Lydia E. Pinkham's Vegetable Compound and Ford's Laxative Compound and Dr. Williams' Pink Pills for Pale People. And, too, in private, with their hands and eyes nervous and their voices low, embarrassed, sometimes ashamed: potency elixirs and aphrodisiacs, emmenagogues and contraceptives, Apiol Compound for suppressed and painful menstruation, fluid extract of kava-kava or emulsion of copaiba for gonorrhea, blue ointment for crab lice.

Mostly they came during the daylight hours, but now and then someone would come rapping on the wagon's door after nightfall. And once in a long while, in the deep, dark lonesome night—

"Oh, Miss Mercy, I need help. Can you find it in your heart to help me?"

"What is your trouble, my dear?"

"I've been a fool, such a fool. A man . . . I was too friendly with him and now I'm caught."

"You're certain you're with child?"

"Oh yes. There's no mistake."

"He won't marry you?"

"He can't. He's already married. Oh, I'm such a fool. Please, will you help me?"

"There, now, you mustn't cry. I'll help you."

"You'll give me something? Truly?"

"Truly."

"Apiol Compound? I've heard that it's rich enough in mucilage to bring on—"

"No, not that. Something more certain."

"Oh, Miss Mercy, you're true to your name. You're an angel of mercy."

And again, as always, she and Elias would be back on roads good and bad, empty and well traveled. Another town, another state—here, there, no pattern to their travels, going wherever the roads took them. Never lingering anywhere for more than a day or two, except when storm or flood or accident (and once, an Indian attack) stranded them. And as always the people would come, first to marvel and then to buy: morphine, digitalis, belladonna in carefully measured doses, Dover's powder, petroleum jelly, spirits of camphor and spirits of ammonia, bone liniment and witch hazel, citrate of magnesia, blackberry balsam, oil of sassafras, throat lozenges and eye demulcents, pile remedies and asthma cures, compounds for ailments of kidney and bladder and digestive tract.

And then again, in one of their stopping places, in the deep dark lonesome night—

"Miss Mercy, you don't know what your kindness means to me."

"I do know, child. I do."

"Such a burden, such an awful burden—"

"Yes, but yours will soon be lifted."

"Just one bottle of this liquid will see to that?"

"Just one. Then you'll have no more to fear."

"It smells so sweet. What does it contain?"

"Dried sclerotia of ergot, bark of slippery elm, apiol, and gum arabic."

"Will it taste bad?"

"No, my dear. I've mixed it with syrup."

"And I'm to take the whole bottle at once?"

"Yes. But only at the time of month I tell you. And then you must immediately dispose of the bottle where no one can ever find it. Will you promise?"

"Yes, Miss Mercy. Oh yes."

"And you must tell no one I helped you. Not even your dearest friend. Will you promise?"

"I promise. I'll never tell a soul, not a living soul."

And again, as always, she and Elias would be away at the break of dawn, when dew lay soft on the grasses and mist coated the land. And sitting beside him on the high seat, remembering the poor girl who had come in the night, she would ask herself once more, as she had so many times, what Father would have said if he'd known of the mixture of ergot and slippery elm, apiol and gum arabic. Would he still think of her as an angel of mercy? Or would he hate her for betraying a sacred trust? And the answer would be as it always was: No, he could never hate her; she must have no real doubt of that. He would understand that her only aim was to bring peace to those poor foolish girls. Peace and succor in their time of need. He would understand.

And she would stop fretting then, reassured of Father's absent pride, and soon that day would end and a new one would be born. And there would be new roads, new settlements and towns, new needs to serve—so many needs to serve.

And one day she saw that it was fall again, the leaves turning crimson and gold—time to turn south and west. But first there was another town, a little town with a name like many others, in a state that might have been Kansas or perhaps Nebraska. And late that night, as Miss Mercy sat weary but strong at her mixing table, her hands busy with mortar and pestle while the lamplight flickered bright, a rapping came soft and urgent on the wagon's door.

Her name was Verity.

Names and faces meant little to Miss Mercy; there were too many to remember even for a minute. But this girl was different somehow. The name lingered, and so she knew would the face. Thin, not pretty, pale hair peeking out from under her bonnet—older than most of the ones who came alone in the night. Older, sadder, but no wiser.

Miss Mercy invited her in, invited her to sit. Verity perched primly on the stool, hands together in her lap, mouth tight-pinched at the corners. She showed no nervousness, no

fear or embarrassment. Determined was the word that came
to Miss Mercy's mind.

Without preamble Verity said, "I understand you're willing to help girls in trouble."

"What sort of trouble, my dear?"

"The sort that comes to foolish and unmarried girls."

"You're with child?"

Verity nodded. "I come from Riverbrook, Iowa. Do you
recall the town, Miss Mercy?"

"Riverbrook? Iowa? There are so many places . . ."

"You were there four months ago. In June. The second
week of June."

"The second week of June. Well. If you say I was, my
dear, then of course I was."

"A girl named Grace came to see you then. Grace Potter.
Do you remember her?"

"So many come to me," Miss Mercy said. "My memory
isn't what it once was. . . ."

"So many girls in trouble, you mean?"

"Sometimes. In the night, as you've come."

"And as Grace came."

"If you say so. As Grace came."

"You gave her something to abort her fetus. I'd like you
to give me the same . . . medicine."

"If I do, will you promise to take it only at the time of
month I tell you?"

"Yes."

"Will you promise to dispose of the bottle immediately
after ingestion, where no one can ever find it?"

"Yes."

"And will you promise to tell no one that I helped you?
Not even your dearest friend?"

"Yes."

"Then you shall have what you need."

Miss Mercy picked up her lamp, carried it to one of Elias's cabinets. When she handed the small brown unlabeled bottle to Verity, the girl removed its cork and sniffed the neck. Then Verity poured a drop onto her finger, touched her tongue to it.

"It tastes odd," she said.

"No odder than sweetened castor oil. I've mixed the compound with cherry syrup."

"Compound. What sort of compound?"

"Dried sclerotia of ergot, bark of slippery elm, apiol—"

"My God! All those blended together?"

"Yes, my dear. Why do you look so shocked?"

"Ergot contracts the womb, tightens it even more. So do dried slippery elm and apiol. All mixed together and taken in a large dose at the wrong time of month . . . cramps, paralysis, death in agony. This liquid is pure poison to a pregnant woman!"

"No, you mustn't think that—"

"I do think it," Verity said, "because it's true." She had risen to her feet and was pointing a tremulous finger at Miss Mercy. "I've studied medicine. I work in Riverbrook as a nurse and midwife."

"Nurse? Midwife? But then—"

"Then I'm not with child? No, Miss Mercy, I'm not. The truth is, I have been three months searching for you, ever since I discovered a bottle exactly like this one that Grace Potter failed to dispose of. I thought you guilty of no more than deadly quackery before tonight, but now I know different. You deliberately murdered my sister."

"Murdered?" Now it was Miss Mercy who was shocked. "Oh no, my dear. No. I brought her mercy."

"You brought her death!"

"Mercy. Your sister, all of them—only mercy."

"All of them? How many others besides Grace?"

"Does the number truly matter?"

"Does it truly—! How many, Miss Mercy?"

"I can't say. So many miles, so many places . . ."

"*How many?*"

"Thirty? Forty? Fifty? I can scarce remember them all. . . ."

"Dear sweet Lord! You poisoned as many as *fifty* pregnant girls?"

"Unmarried girls. Poor foolish girls," Miss Mercy said gently. "There are worse things than death, oh much worse."

"What could be worse than suffering the tortures of hell before the soul is finally released?"

"Enduring the tortures of hell for years, decades, a lifetime. Isn't a few hours of pain and then peace, eternal peace, preferable to lasting torment?"

"How can you believe that bearing a child out of wedlock is so wicked—?"

"No," Miss Mercy said, "the lasting torment is in knowing, seeing the child they've brought into the world. Bastard child, child of sin. Don't you see? God punishes the unwed mother. The wages of sin is death, but God's vengeance on the living is far more terrible. I saved your sister from that. I brought her and all the others mercy from *that.*"

Again she picked up the lamp. With a key from around her neck she unlocked the small satin-lined cabinet Elias had made, lifted out its contents. This she set on the table, the flickering oil lamp close beside it.

Verity looked, and cried out, and tore her gaze away.

Lamplight shone on the glass jar and on the thick formaldehyde that filled it; made a glowing chimera of the tiny twisted thing floating there, with its face that did not seem quite human, with its appendage that might have been an arm and the other that might have been a leg, with its single blind staring eye.

"Now do you understand?" Miss Mercy said. "This is my son, mine and Caleb's. God's vengeance—my poor little bastard son."

And she lifted the jar in both hands and held it tight to her bosom, cradled it and began to rock it to and fro, crooning to the fetus inside—a sweet, sad lullaby that sent Verity fleeing from the wagon, away into the deep dark lonesome night.

Chet Williamson is the author of over seventy short stories in magazines ranging from *Fantasy & Science Fiction* to *Esquire* and *The New Yorker*. His novels include *Reign, Dreamthorpe, Ash Wednesday,* and most recently, *Second Chance.* Chet is a sure-thing writer. You ask him for a story, then you make out the check. I've never read a bad or even indifferent Chet Williamson story. The following is no exception. ●

DR. JOE

Chet Williamson

When Chief Barnes and Officer Young arrived, they found Dr. Joe in what he had always called his consultation chamber, a large, high-ceilinged room with four titanic oak cabinets filled with medical equipment, and an examining table with numerous attachments that made it resemble a robotic spider. Dr. Joe's body was hanging from one of the inch-thick, decorative finials on the top of the largest of the cabinets.

Even though Barnes and Young were used to scenes of mayhem, for a moment the sight froze them. This was, after all, Dr. Josiah Waters, Dr. Joe, who was never seen without a smile, who had guarded the health of generations of Cutler Falls residents, who had given both Barnes and Young physicals when they had gone out for high school football. This was Dr. Joe, and to observe him dangling there by the several lengths of surgical gauze that connected the finial and his thin and wattled neck was the most unpleasant duty the two policemen had faced in a long time.

Dr. Joe's face had a smile on it now, but a terrible one, a staggered grin that cut across his small, round countenance like a saber slash, interrupted by the tongue thrusting from the right corner of his mouth. That tongue, nearly bitten through by Dr. Joe's clenched teeth, looked, Barnes thought, like one of the cold, bud-peppered beef tongues that Harold Moyer sold at his butcher shop. Only Dr. Joe's tongue held a bluer, far more unhealthy tint. Dr. Joe's eyes were wide-open and slightly crossed. Barnes did not think they had ever been crossed in life.

The old man was wearing a suit, as he always did every day since he had retired and put away his white examination garb. His gnarled hands, into which the blood had settled, protruded from the dazzlingly white cuffs like the branches and twigs of a red birch, and Barnes shuddered at the thought of those same hands having once touched him in private places.

The gauze that kept Dr. Joe suspended had stretched, but his tiny, immaculately shod feet still dangled a foot and a half above the floor. The cabinet was tall enough so that even a man whose frame far exceeded Dr. Joe's diminutive one would have been able to hang himself efficiently. A metal stool with wheels lay on its side near the cabinet. Barnes well remembered Dr. Joe sliding across the linoleum floor on that stool, from patient to cabinet to desk, and tried to imagine the old man making the stool slide one final time.

"For crissake, why?" Young asked, his gaze still fixed on the corpse, as though he feared it would twitch and jerk in annoyance should he have the disrespect to look elsewhere.

Barnes walked to the heavy oak desk on which Dr. Joe had written his prescriptions for over half a century, and saw several sheets of paper covered with an archaic, flowery script that would have been more at home at the end of a steel nib than the ballpoint pen that lay there. He noted the position of the papers on the desk, then picked them up.

"Here's why, maybe," he said, hoping that he was right, hoping for an answer. Dr. Joe, old and feeble as he was, was the last person he would have expected to end his own life, though Barnes believed he had every right to do so. Hell, what was a man's life if not his own? He knew some people would have said it was God's, but Chief Barnes wasn't much of a believer, though he did go to church now and then.

"Suicide note?" Young asked.

"It's a note anyway," he said. Then he read it aloud, pausing frequently to decipher the handwriting.

To whom it may concern:

Being of as sound mind as I guess I ever was, I leave behind this letter to be read upon my death, the information herein to be made public or not, as my executor shall deem fit. Personally, I don't give one damn. If I didn't want folks to know what's in this, I wouldn't be writing it, now would I?

I guess I'm writing it because I *want* folks to know, because families should really know what happened to their loved ones. Letting the truth out won't hurt anybody anymore. Randall died five years ago, the Lord rest him. Evelyn's gone now, too, and they have no children who would be ashamed.

And I admit it, maybe I want to clear my conscience of the things I did over the years, all those years when everybody in town thought I was Florence Nightingale and Hippocrates and Jonas Salk all rolled up into one stumpy little family doctor.

I tried to be, that's for sure. All my life there was only one thing I ever really wanted, and that was to be a doctor. Not just any doctor, but the kind of doctor my Uncle Walter was. A general practitioner, a family doctor who knew what was wrong with you the same way that Andy down at the garage knew what was wrong with my Fords through the years. He'd give them a listen, and he'd just *know*, and then he'd know what to do about it.

I wanted to be the kind of doctor who would open his office in a town like Cutler Falls and stay there forever, knowing and taking care of every family, watching the children grow up and then taking care of *their* children. What I wanted was nothing more nor less than to be the man on those Norman Rockwell covers.

All in all, I think I came pretty close. I was "Doctor Joe." I made house calls in the middle of snowstorms, delivered my share of babies and then some. I was a volunteer for civic groups and youth clubs. I treated the poor with the same good care I gave the rich. I won a hatful of civic awards. I dedicated my life to serving my patients. Everybody liked me, even the families of the people that I let die when I could have saved them.

It didn't start off like that, though. Anybody who's old enough can tell you the tough time I had getting started— though I doubt anybody *that* old is still around! I'm pretty much the last of my generation in this town. The minds of most of those of us who are left aren't very sharp, and I thank the Lord I've still got all my mental faculties. But not to get off the subject. It was tough. When a new young doctor starts a practice in a small town, even if they've known you and grown up with you, they don't trust you. After all, how good can a young whippersnapper like that be, fresh out of medical school and all?

So you start building your practice by bits and pieces, praying that you'll be able to keep body and soul together while you somehow finagle patients into giving you a try. And when you're trying to get a practice established smack-dab at the start of the Great Depression (and I didn't think it was that great, believe you me!), it makes things three times as hard. The good part was that I didn't have a family to provide for.

And since we're on that subject, just to set the record straight, no, I wasn't a homosexual, though I've had a few as patients through the years, and some pretty funny complaints they've had, too, but that's another story. I just never got married because I never thought any woman would have me, being only an inch or so over five-foot and pretty darn ugly into the bargain. My patients have been my family. And as for sex, to call a spade a spade, there was a practice that I knew full well wouldn't cause warts or palm hair or insanity. And some medical books have rather explicit and arousing illustrations.

But that's another tawdry subject, when what I need to be writing about is the *main* tawdry subject. I don't know why old people tend to stray. Since we have less time than younger folks, you'd think we'd try to express everything as quickly and succinctly as possible, but that's not the way of it, is it? I need to stay on the subject, and that subject is letting patients die, turning my Hippocratic Oath into a hypocritical one.

The first was in 1933. I'd been practicing for two years, and I owed more money to the bank than I thought I could ever hope to pay back. Randall, my cousin, had just opened Waters Insurance Agency, bankrolled for the most part by my Uncle Walter, who could scarcely afford the risk. Uncle Walter lived over in Smithville (so at least we weren't rivals), and his practice was worse than what it had been. Nobody had much money, so if you were sick, it had to be pretty bad to drive you to the doctor's.

Randall was having it just as bad as I was. When people couldn't afford to buy food, it wasn't too damn likely that they'd want to buy themselves some life insurance, although he did talk a few people into it when he showed them how, if they died, their funeral alone could bankrupt their families. "You want to be thrown out on the ash heap?" That line worked pretty good for Randall. And life insurance was fairly cheap back in those days.

At least our family members were reliable customers, though I didn't charge them full fees. I got the little insurance I could afford from Randall (those were the days before malpractice insurance, thank the Lord), and he came to me when he was sick, though he didn't tell his father about it, and I didn't charge him at all, just for medicines if he needed any. We were more like brothers than cousins, grew up together, told each other all our secrets, and our friendship continued when we grew up, with a several-year hiatus when I was at medical school and he was in the service. Since he was in the intelligence branch of the army, he wasn't very often permitted to communicate with anyone other than his parents, so letters were sparse, and I missed him terribly.

I'd have done anything for Randall, and I think he'd have done anything for me. So he was the first and only person I told about Aunt Esther. She was my mother's older sister, and an old maid, who worked down at the shoe factory where the Western Auto is now. Or used to be. My mother finally talked her into letting me examine her, which was quite a feat, since Aunt Esther was a hypochondriac who was terrified of doctors from the word go. She was afraid that if she went to a doctor, he would tell her that she was very ill and was going to die, when she'd be better off not knowing.

The ironic thing was that Aunt Esther was absolutely right. When I examined her, I felt multiple small lumps studding her liver, and right away I knew it was cancer—metastatic cancer. I tried to hide my concern, and casually asked her if she had had any symptoms associated with the condition, but she denied everything, far too vociferously to be honest. I knew that she could not help but have these telltale symptoms, since there were plenty of the lumps, so many that I knew any treatment would only stave off the inevitable.

I almost told her then about her condition, but I knew, too, that for her, denial would be the only way to deal with a medical catastrophe, so I stayed mum until I could think some more about what to do. The treatments available at the time would have caused her both physical and mental anguish. Better perhaps to let her go on in ignorance, suspecting that there was a problem, but never faced with the certainty until the very end.

She asked me why I was asking these questions, if I thought that something was wrong, and I told her only that she had a condition quite typical in women of her age, and to come see me again if she ever felt any really bad pain in the affected area. By then, I knew the end would not be far off.

When I closed up my office that Friday, I felt awful guilty for lying to my aunt. When I met Randall for our usual Friday evening drink (Prohibition had just ended, thank the Lord) and commiseration over our financial woes, I told him that things could always be worse, and that Aunt Esther probably wouldn't be with us for more than another year or so. When I explained everything to him, I asked him if he thought I should tell her the truth.

"No," he said, looking very thoughtful. "I wouldn't tell anyone about it."

A year later, Aunt Esther died. She had a great deal of pain at the end, but the opiates I prescribed kept it at bay. There was never any suggestion from the physicians in St. Mary's Hospital that I had been derelict in not catching her condition earlier. They knew that nothing could have been done. Indeed, even today advanced metastatic liver cancer is still nearly always fatal, with a miserable five-year survival rate.

Two months after we put that wasted body of hers in the earth, Randall came to my house one Wednesday evening, that and Friday being the only weeknights I didn't keep open office hours. He seemed cheery as hell, and when I asked him what he was grinning about, he handed me a thick envelope and told me to open it. It was stuffed with twenty-dollar bills. I gaped at it while he told me that there was $2500 there, half of the death benefit he had gotten from Steadfast Life on the policy he had taken out on Aunt Esther.

I goggled at the money for a while longer, working it out in my mind that Randall had taken out a life insurance policy on Aunt Esther after I told him that she was going to die. It struck me as being awfully wrong, and certainly unethical if not illegal, and I out and out asked Randall if something like this wasn't against the law.

He said that yes, it was, but the way he had handled it, nobody would ever know that it wasn't a legitimate policy. So I asked him if it doesn't look funny that he's taken out a policy from his own insurance company on a relative who just happens to die within the year, and he says no, it wasn't him at all who took the policy out, but somebody else, and when I ask who, he just tells me that there were a lot of things he learned in army intelligence about how to make up people who weren't really there, and when I asked him just what the hell he meant, he goes ask me no questions, I'll tell you no lies.

Well, I wasn't stupid. What he had done was set up a false identity and somehow juggled the insurance forms so that it looked as if Aunt Esther had taken out the policy with this phony baloney person as the beneficiary. I don't know how the hell Randall cashed the check, but they must have taught him good in the army, because there was the cash.

But whatever he had done, I have to tell you that I had a moral dilemma on my hands here. It was because of what I had told Randall that he had done what he did, and I didn't like it one bit and I told him so. And he just looked at me dead serious and said (and I remember his exact words), "Will your practice survive without that money right there?"

And I knew damn well it wouldn't, but I didn't say so. And I knew, too, that that $2500 would keep me solvent for a long time, because that was a lot of money back in those days.

Then he told me to think about it, and asked me if I could have saved Aunt Esther's life, and I said no, and then he asked me well, what harm was done? I said none, I guess, and he told me well, then, keep the money.

I told him to hang on to it, that I wanted to think about it for a while first. After a few days, I thought maybe it would be all right, because I really needed the money, and I couldn't help patients without it, so I said okay, I'd take it.

After I used it to pay back the bank what I owed, Randall told me that this could just be the first, that we could do this again when we needed money to keep my practice and his business going. The deal was this—if I found patients who were going to die within a year or two, or even four or five, and there was nothing that could be done about it, I wouldn't tell them about their illness, but would give them a clean bill of health, or some other cockamamie story to explain away their symptoms, and then I'd write up a medical report saying that they were healthy and give it to Randall.

From there on it was his ball game. He even put up the policy money, but split the benefits right down the middle with me. At least he said he did, and I don't think that Randall would have done me dirty; he wasn't that kind of fellow.

I asked him if Steadfast wouldn't get suspicious about anything, and he said that as long as the policies weren't too large, like $25,000 or higher (and of course those prices went up in later years), they'd just trust him to handle it. Most families who had life insurance back then only had it in the five hundred to ten thousand range. And if we only did it when it was absolutely necessary, which couldn't be more than every year or two, he could handle everything just fine.

And be damned if he wasn't right. As far as I know, nobody ever got suspicious at the home office. However he worked it, Randall worked it well. Of course, all he had to deal with was paper. I had to deal with patients, and later on, with bodies.

When I found a patient with the required illness (which was mostly an internal, slow-growing but implacable carcinoma), there was only one thing I had to make sure of, and that was that he or she wasn't already insured by Steadfast through Randall's or anyone else's agency. Two different policies on the same person would have been sure to start the eyebrows wiggling at the insurance company. I generally raised the subject by joking about my pesky brother and how he was always trying to sell me more life insurance. Then I'd feel them out to see if they had any insurance, and with whom. It sounds awkward as hell, but I got so I was real smooth at it.

Generally it wasn't a problem, because the people who were ideal, to my way of thinking anyway, were bachelors or spinsters, and they seldom had insurance, I guess figuring that whatever they left if they died would pay for their burial.

They had no families to look after, so they didn't feel like they needed insurance. I never liked the idea of using somebody with a family or youngsters who depended on them. Not that they weren't going to die anyway, but I wanted to help them fight it off as long as possible, even if it was inevitable. That was important to me. After all, I'm a doctor.

So we went through the years, me with my eyes always open for prospective terminal patients, and Randall doing whatever fancy song and dance he did to keep the money coming in. Nobody ever really blamed me. Even good doctors occasionally miss telltale symptoms, and once the condition became obvious, I did everything in my power to make their dying easier for them. The fact that they would have died anyway eased my conscience somewhat.

The problem came when the profession got better at early detection, and could keep people alive longer with what they call now an improved quality of life. It was then that I started having to make some tough decisions, and then that I had to sacrifice my first family man.

That was in 1956, when I found a tumor in Frank McKinnon. In all honesty, the specialists might have been able to save him, but both Randall and I were in dire straits right about then. We had made some investments that had fallen through, and we were both close to going under. Search though I might, there was not a single patient who fit the criteria we needed. And then Frank came along.

He was a smoker, and I saw the spot on his chest X ray, which back then we did right in the office. It was small, but I knew damn well what it was. It probably could have been excised, or, if not that, the lung could have been removed and he would have lived. But the spot was small enough to miss on a cursory look, so I kept my mouth shut. By the time the symptoms started to show, it was too late. Frank died, and

Randall and I split a sorely needed $40,000.

Still, I felt miserable about it, especially for Phoebe McKinnon and her little boy. He was a Joe, too, like me (but a Joseph and not a Josiah). He was ten when Frank died. I looked out for him, as everybody in town knows, tutored him through high school, and saw to it that he got into premed at Penn and then into medical school there. I paid a good chunk of his tuition, too. It was the least I could do, after having to take his daddy away from him.

In a way, it was probably the best thing that could have happened to the boy. Frank was a good man, but he was just a worker at Heisey's Grocery, and probably little Joe wouldn't have amounted to much more without me to push him. Now look at him—a lung specialist down in Philadelphia, happily married, with kids of his own, and he has me to thank for it in more ways than one. I just wish I could see him more often. I love it when he surprises me, like the last time, like last April, when I turned around and there he was.

Whoopsadaisy, off the subject again. Back to business here, and a grim business it became. The more advanced medical technology got, the more I had to play God. I didn't like doing it, but it was the only way to keep my practice alive, and all the *good* things that my practice meant.

Oh sure, if I'd have just taken on patients who could pay, I never would've had a problem, but if people were sick, I couldn't turn them away just because they were hard up. When they couldn't afford to pay me what I charged, I charged them whatever they *could* pay, which was often nothing. I guess I was just a better doctor than a businessman, and there's no shame in that. I never did anything out of greed. I only wanted money so that I could keep doing what I was doing. I spent everything on my practice, which is why my equipment was always the most up-to-date. And when I had money left over I socked it away so I'd have it for the *next* machine. You would find things in my practice that you wouldn't find in any other GP's office, because I wanted only the best for my patients.

Of course that meant that I could also be aware of problems long before other doctors would have been. And in ninety-nine cases out of a hundred, that meant the patient could be saved. In that *one* out of a hundred, that person who I decided would have to be let go for the good of all the rest, I tried to use my best judgment. I tried to choose people who wouldn't be missed too much, or who were causing other people more grief than happiness. To prove that I picked carefully, here are just a few examples:

Danny Whitman, whose blood tests were lost so that no one but me ever knew he had leukemia until it was too late to do a thing about it. Danny was the boy who got out of raping the Spinelli girl, when the whole town knew that he did it.

Simon Reynolds, whose common-law wife's cuts and contusions I treated countless times. He beat her, and she never would do a thing about it except come to me to be stitched up. Simon would have died from rectal cancer, which I had misdiagnosed (ha ha) as irritable colon, if he hadn't killed himself first, which meant we couldn't collect on that policy. That happened only one other time over the years, when that surly guinea Rocco Arnoldi got prostate cancer. Smooth as a newborn baby's head, I told him after I felt the pebble-sized lump on the gland. He always acted like the big man, but he wasn't big enough to stand the pain.

Then there was Myrtle Green, and I shouldn't have to tell anyone who remembers how she treated her mother. Died of ovarian cancer, which, good golly, I somehow happened to miss at her exam.

Oscar Stern, the Jew who drove Milt Haines out of business by opening his dry goods store right across the street from Milt and then undercutting Milt on all his prices. Cancer of the lymph, which can occasionally look, even to a doctor, like innocent swollen glands.

Those are just a few to give the idea of how I picked them, and I think I did a pretty good job of winnowing over the years, getting rid of some of the chaff so I could save the good wheat. I'm not going to rationalize every single person I've let die, because for some it would be hard, since their deaths were due to economic needs, I admit it. But I tried to help my community, no matter what else I may have had to do. If anybody's curious about the others, just look at my will. They're all listed in bequests to whatever relatives of theirs may still survive.

I guess that's about most of it. Somewhere in the seventies we gave it up. Computers were coming in then, and it was too easy for the insurance companies to check on things as a matter of course, even if they weren't really suspicious. They just started doing it because they could. At least that's what I guess happened. One day Randall just up and said that we had to stop because it wasn't safe anymore.

That was all right with me. We'd both salted away a good pile by then, since the high-tech equipment had gotten too pricey for me, and there weren't as many folks here in town who needed free care as there were in the old days. So I knew my practice was safe as houses for as long as I still wanted to stay with it. Besides, we made solid investments in the late sixties and early seventies, so I thought to hell with the family centers and the HMO's. I'd lose some patients, but I'd keep most of them. And nobody had to die anymore unless the good Lord intended it.

So there it is. I figure people ought to know, and I ought to get it off my chest, since I don't have much time left. Try not to think too badly of me. I did it for all of you, and I think intention counts for something. I also like to think that the good I did over the years outweighs the bad, and hope that whoever reads this agrees.

Dr. Joe

Chief Barnes held the sheaf of papers in his hands for a moment, then dropped them back onto the desk. "My God," said Young, "that's hard to believe."

"It's in his handwriting. Nobody'd make anything like that up." Barnes looked back at the almost jolly grin of the dangling corpse. "It could explain this, though." He picked up the phone on the desk and called the county medical examiner, who would bring the police photographers and the ambulance to haul away the body. After he hung up, Barnes thought for a moment, then said, "I'm going to call Joe McKinnon. I don't want him to hear this on the news or TV or something."

He flipped through Dr. Joe's Rolodex, and found McKinnon's office number in Philadelphia. If he was like most specialists, he'd still be in the office at four o'clock. He dialed the number and punched a button on the phone so that Young could hear as well. A clipped but melodic voice answered the phone. "Drs. McKinnon and Feldman, may I help you please?"

"This is Police Chief Barnes calling from Cutler Falls. Is Dr. McKinnon in?"

"What is this regarding, please, sir?"

"It's official business."

"Well, I'm sorry, Dr. McKinnon will be out of the office for the next two days. In fact, he went to Cutler Falls, sir. You may be able to reach him at his mother's house there. Do you have her number?"

Barnes knew Phoebe McKinnon. She regularly went to the church he sometimes attended. "I can get it, thanks," he said. "Was he just coming up to see his mom?"

"I believe he said he was going to stop in and surprise Dr. Waters, too. He adores that man."

Barnes thanked her and hung up. He traded glances with Young, then walked over to the door that opened into the back alley behind the old house from which Dr. Joe had run his practice since 1931. Touching only the rim of the doorknob with his handkerchief, he tried to turn it, and found that the door was locked.

Then he beckoned to Young, and they went out of the room, down a short hall, and into the old waiting room filled with low-backed leather chairs and tables on which neatly dusted, five year old copies of *Time*, *Sports Illustrated*, and *Good Housekeeping* sat. Mrs. Rice, Dr. Joe's housekeeper, sat red-eyed in a chair, and looked up hopefully when the policemen came in, looking as though she expected them to tell her that what she had discovered was not true. Barnes found himself feeling glad that it was.

"Mrs. Rice," he said gently, "did you find Dr. Joe as soon as you got here?"

She shook her head. "Not right away. I cook dinner for him three days a week. I come in around two-thirty to start. I take the things to the kitchen, start cooking, and then I always go find him to let him know I'm here. He's back in . . . in that room a lot, so I went there right after I got the dinner started."

"Was Dr. Joe alone when you were in the kitchen?"

Her look of surprise told him that she had not considered the alternative. "I don't know. I guess so."

"You didn't hear voices or anything?"

"My hearing's not so good. In the other half of the house

you can't hear anything that goes on in the office." A deep
frown appeared on her face already fissured with grief. "Do
you think someone else was here?"

Barnes thought quickly. "I just want to know everything
the doctor did today, to help get an idea why, you see? Just
one more question. Did he always keep that street door
locked?"

The old woman shook her head petulantly. "I told him a
million times to lock that door, but it was habit. He always
kept it unlocked when he was in practice, and he wouldn't
change. Whenever he went in the consulting room to write or
read, he always unlocked it, sometimes opened it a crack for
the air."

Barnes told Mrs. Rice she could go home. Then he and
Young went back into the consulting chamber. "Joe McKinnon won't be visiting today," Barnes said. "Or tomorrow."

"Why not?" Young asked slowly, as though he were
figuring out what Barnes already knew.

"He was already here."

"McKinnon found him? Before Mrs. Rice?"

"No. Joe McKinnon did it."

Young scowled. "Hung him?" Barnes nodded. "But what
about that letter?"

"It's not a suicide note," Barnes said, picking up the papers again. "All he says is that he doesn't have much time left,
and what ninety-year-old man does? And there's none of the
remorse that would cause a man to hang himself." He looked
at Young. "Especially when he could have given himself a far
less painful death with a hundred of the drugs he still had."

"So you think McKinnon came in . . ."

"Yeah. That door. Just walked in. Remember the letter?
He said he turned around and there he was. So he comes in to
surprise his old friend. Maybe Dr. Joe had left the room and

Joe McKinnon saw the papers, read them, learned that the man he trusted and loved had, essentially, killed his father, and not only him, but others as well. How would you feel? If you learned the man the whole town respected and honored was . . . well, a lot less than what anybody thought?"

Young shook his head and looked with revulsion at the hanging body.

"And worse, what if you were a doctor, an honest and a good one? What would you want to do?"

"Kill him," Young said. "But how can you be sure?"

Barnes leaned down and picked up the stool, then rolled it beneath the corpse's feet. An inch separated the toes of the shoes from the metal surface of the seat. "The gauze stretched at least a few inches. He didn't use this stool, and he didn't fly up there either. But Joe McKinnon's a tall, strong man."

Young nodded. "And then McKinnon locked the door on his way out. So now what? Try and find him?"

Barnes tried to keep his voice level, to be a cop first. It was hard. "Is that what you want to do?"

Young didn't answer right away. "It's what we're supposed to do."

"Because of what we found."

"Yeah."

"What if we didn't find it?" Barnes looked at the sheets of paper again.

Young thought for another few seconds. "I wouldn't have a problem with that."

Barnes folded the papers slowly and placed them in his pocket. "Those families have suffered enough."

"But the names will still be in the will," Young said.

"Maybe they'll think that he felt bad all these years that

he couldn't save them. After all, it's the kind of thing that Dr. Joe would have done."

Barnes slid the metal stool to the other end of the room. Then from the kneehole of the desk he took the heavy wooden chair, whose seat was six inches higher than the stool's, and placed it by the cabinet, moving the old man's feet aside. He struck the chair a blow so that it wobbled, tipped, and fell onto the linoleum floor.

"What about Mrs. Rice?" Young asked.

"She didn't see stools or chairs. All she saw was him."

Both of them heard it then, the unmistakable sound of the ambulance's engine. The M.E. had arrived.

Young looked uneasy, as though he were still searching for holes in their plan. "If there's no note, then why did Dr. Joe hang himself?"

"Nobody knows." For the first time that day, Barnes spoke harshly, angrily. "Who the hell knows what makes people do things?"

Matthew J. Costello is the author of the recent Berkley suspense novels *Homecoming* (1992) and *See How She Runs* (1994), and many
other books in many genres. He also wrote *The 7th Guest*, the best-
selling CD-ROM of all time, and its sequel, *The 11th Hour*.

Matt is a literary chameleon. His fiction can assume almost any
form. Consider this uncharacteristically mannered piece.

FRIENDLY WAGER

Matthew Costello

The man sitting across from Todd—Doctor Todd, Med-
ville's beloved pediatrician—would, he thought, be best described as porcine. That was it *exactly*. Porcine, as in pork, as
in piggy, as in *slob*. Great folds of skin dangled from the man's
neck like the crop of a studded-out rooster. The pupils, beady
and black, were all but lost in the near–beet red bowling ball
face. The eyes' egg whites were crisscrossed by a road map of
red lines.

The picture of good health.

Todd reached for the bottle of wine—a tasty California
Chardonnay—and he caught his wife looking over, not missing a beat in her conversation with the woman to her right.
What is it, he wondered, that doctors' wives always find to
talk about? He and his peers, the few he would call friends,
seemed to suffer more than a few conversational lulls. They
never discussed anything professional. Movies, yes, golf, yes,

and who's currently working magic with the depressed mutual fund market. Very limited topics indeed.

But no shop talk.

A bit of the wine dribbled onto the white tablecloth. Todd felt a slight breeze at his neck. The First Class dining room featured sliding windows that could be opened to the sea air on nice, calm evenings . . . like this one.

"Oh, hit me, too," the porcine man said, his crop jiggling. Todd looked at the man's lower lip, projecting ever-so-slightly, ready to serve as a natural catch basin for any fruit of the vine that might foolishly attempt to escape what was a sizable maw.

Why does the man irritate me so much? Todd wondered. Perhaps because he's a doctor and he looks like a walking advertisement for a coronary? Strike me, God! Try blocking *my* goddamn arteries! I *dare* you.

Or was it because the annoying man had completely dominated the past two nights' conversation? Was it because the man—Dr. Henry Newlove—had fixated on Todd, and on a small cruise ship there wasn't any escape?

Todd poured Dr. Newlove some of the Chardonnay, measuring out the meager amount so that there would be some left for himself.

"Oh, come on. Kill the bottle, professor, and we'll order another." Newlove laughed. "Live a little, Todd. You're out of reach of the sniffily rug rats now."

That was another thing. Henry Newlove had progressed to a first-name basis much too quickly. Now they were old war buddies, killing bottles of wine together, ready to share gruesome stories from the ER. But despite some leading questions, Todd had yet to determine exactly what kind of doctor Newlove was.

The cruise, arranged by the AMA Travel Service, was

only for doctors . . . at least Todd assumed everyone here was somehow connected to the medical profession. So what kind of doctor was this coronary candidate?

Todd looked around for their waiter to order another *bouteille*. His hand started to creep up to perform the frail wave that would hopefully summon the young man who posed as a sommelier.

But his wife—perhaps missing the crucial fact that Todd didn't get to share in the dregs of the previous bottle—fired him a withering stare.

Todd retreated and brought his hand down.

Dr. Newlove watched the whole thing.

While enjoying a nearly full glass of Chardonnay.

"Tell me, Todd. Do your young patients like Roald Dahl?"

Todd looked up, hoping the wine steward might catch his raised eyebrows . . . S.O.S. . . . send wine.

"Roald Dahl," Todd said distractedly. "I don't know . . . what's he—?"

"A brilliant writer," Newlove said, with all the authority of papal fiat. "Dahl did some marvelously *grisly* children's books. He wrote one book, *George's Marvelous Medicine*, about a little girl who tries to poison her grandmother." Newlove laughed, and Todd swore he saw spittle come flying out on a near-perfect trajectory toward him.

"I haven't—"

"Oh, then there's *Charlie and the Chocolate Factory*. All these little children and"—Newlove kicked into his convulsive mode again—"and the most horrible things happen to them. One little boy gets sucked into the chocolate river, a little girl gets squashed by the berry machine, absolutely—"

A woman to Todd's right, a dowdy woman who looked as

if the cruise was actually an oceangoing church service, nodded and spoke.

"Yes, Ralph and my children saw that movie. And it was—"

Newlove remained true to his target. His beady black eyes remained locked on Todd.

"Brilliant writer. A real nasty imagination, too. But the thing about Dahl—"

But then the bus girl showed up, a cute Latina who was unabashed about leaning close to Todd, gathering the plates, nudging him with her sizable breasts, well packed under the tight, starched dress. Todd caught the faint aroma of some cheap perfume, pungent and tempting.

The dinner was over. Todd stood up. He glanced at his new best friend, whose face had fallen, frozen in midthought. Todd turned to his wife.

"Think I'll take a stroll around the deck."

His wife nodded.

And before any offers of company could arise, Todd turned and walked past the sea of tables to the door leading to the main deck.

The night was clear. They were two days away from the first port o' call, the small Caribbean island of Santa Theresa, or "Saint Tessy" as a few of Todd's more well traveled friends referred to it. Very small, very chic, where there were too few islanders to become hostile to the tourists . . . at least in any organized way.

It's not Jamaica, Todd was told.

Todd walked over to the rail, and breathed deep. The salt air was bracing, the ocean lake-smooth, and Todd enjoyed being alone.

When he felt a heavy hand land with a thump on his shoulder.

"Oh, *there* you are."

Like a truffle hound, Henry Newlove had sniffed Todd out. Todd looked back at him and smiled, figuring it best to show a modicum of civility. Todd was basically nonavoidance anyway, and he certainly didn't want any bad feelings when he sat down to dinner with the man.

"Well then, it's nice and clear tonight."

Newlove came beside Todd, a full foot shorter, and adopted the same contemplative stance.

"You know, we were talking about Roald Dahl—"

We were? Todd nodded politely.

"But the really interesting thing about Dahl are his adult stories." Newlove turned to Todd. "Ever read a collection called *Someone Like You?*"

"Er, no. Don't have much time for reading."

"Oh, the book's very old, decades really. Before Dahl became a writer for the kiddies. And he wrote the most wonderful grisly stories."

There was that word again, as if it was Newlove's favored adjective. *Grisly.* As if this porcine, truffle-hunter of a man absolutely lived for life's *grisly* moments. Something rumbled disconcertedly in Todd's stomach.

"Dahl's stories were macabre gems. And there was this one story about a shipboard wager. A pool, a lottery to see who could guess the ship's arrival time."

Todd returned to looking at the water. He glanced straight down, and saw the phosphorescent spray as the ship cut through the water. It was at once rhythmic and random.

"I've heard of those lotteries. This ship doesn't—"

"And well, in this story—'A Dip in the Pool,' it's called—this fellow picks a docking time that looks good, then better, it looks like a *great* time as the ship hits some bad weather. But then the ship makes up that lost time. And when it looks like the poor fellow's going to lose the lottery, he does something rather extraordinary."

Todd looked at the ship's wake, and waited.

Now—all of a sudden—Newlove grew coy. Todd turned to him.

"What does he do?"

Newlove smacked his hands together and made a thunderclap.

"The fellow stands on the railing and, after making sure that this woman was watching him, he jumps overboard!"

Newlove was positively bursting with glee.

"I get it," Todd said. "Then the woman has to go and tell someone from the ship, and they have to stop and pick him up, and—"

"No. That's just it, that's why it's so nasty. The woman is completely insane, she has a nurse watching her. The nurse escorts the dotty woman away while she's muttering about some nice man who waved to her as he flew off the railing."

Newlove was laughing, coughing. It was the spaghetti scene from *Alien*. Todd thought the fat man might invert his stomach, his hilarious hacks were so strong.

"She said, 'the nice man flew off the railing' and no one believed her. Oh, it's such a wonderful story."

Todd turned back to the water. He didn't want to return to his stateroom. Nothing to do there, the ennui of cruise life was getting to him.

Newlove's hand found its mark on his shoulder again.

"I have an idea . . . something from a story that Dahl didn't write."

Todd said nothing.

"A wager, between two professional men." Newlove's

voice lowered. He sidled a bit closer, his oval body touching Todd's.

Todd looked away. "I should turn in. Sea air is making me—"

But Newlove's hand was strong on his arm.

"Listen to this. Here's the idea for the story, for the wager. That someone on a ship, this ship for example, could be poisoned, and it would be *completely* undetectable." A final squeeze on the arm signaled that Todd was to respond.

"How could that be?"

"Well, surely you do know that certain foods can mask toxic agents? Take shiitake mushrooms, something which I myself have trouble digesting. Eaten in substantial numbers they produce a colloidal acid, harmless really, but it's a near-perfect cover-up for strychnine."

"That's good to know."

"Fungi are funny things anyway; a good number can cause distress if not downright kill you. I could kill someone on this ship with poison—and it would go completely un-detected."

Todd had enough of the man. He had long passed insuf-ferable. "I doubt it. I think you've been reading too many Ronald Dahl stories."

Newlove stepped back, acting hurt now.

"*Roald* Dahl. Roald."

"Whatever."

Todd stretched, and nodded to Newlove. He's my alba-tross, Todd thought. He'll probably pop up in my medicine cabinet. I'll probably have nightmares about this bloated whale.

"Nighty-night," Todd said.

"Wh—what about our wager?" Newlove said as Todd

walked down the deck to the entrance to his first-class state-room.

Todd laughed. Without turning around, he said, "What wager?"

Thinking: *what a nutcase.*

When Todd woke up next morning, Todd's wife had already gone ahead to breakfast and returned. Now she stood over him in the cramped stateroom and was shaking him.

His disorientation produced a variety of weird thoughts . . . the house was on fire, one of his patients needed his attention, the basement had flooded—again.

Until there was that realization: *I'm on a ship.*

What could possibly go wrong?

"Todd," she said, her face all pinched with worry. "Somebody died."

Todd rubbed the sleep from his eyes. Right, someone's dead. It happens. Even—he guessed—at sea.

Todd nodded, encouraging his wife to let the other shoe drop.

"Food poisoning. The purser didn't say anything, but one of the doctors examined the man. They said he had a violent reaction to the food."

Todd blinked awake. For a moment, he imagined being at the rail, watching the sea at night, listening to Dr. Henry Newlove. "What did it?"

His wife seemed confused by the simple question. Perhaps communication *is* the first thing to go in a marriage.

"What did what?"

"You said he had a violent reaction to some food. What kind of food?"

His wife hesitated, perhaps—Todd thought—remembering their own meal from the previous night.

"Mushrooms, those special mushrooms. What do they call them?"

"Shiitake," Todd said, as if it was—in fact—a curse.

Impossible, he thought. There's no way the crazy man could have actually done something. Todd slid off the narrow bed, putting his feet down on the cold floor.

"Todd, maybe this is like that other cruise ship, where people got sick."

He nodded. "I'll go check."

Hoping that he'd bump into Newlove.

There was a crowd in the dining room, though no one was eating. The purser, a bald man, very bronze and fit, with a cockney accent, sat in a chair and fielded questions from an angry gathering of doctors.

Todd saw the purser shake his head.

"No, there is absolutely no plan on turning back. We are having the ship's nutritionist inspect all the food."

"How did the mushrooms go bad?"

The purser was exasperated. "We don't know they were *bad*. Mr. Jameson—"

Jameson . . . the deceased, Todd guessed.

"—had a violent reaction to the mushrooms. It is, I've been told, not altogether uncommon."

"Did—"

Todd was surprised to hear his own voice asking a question.

"Er, did anyone look into the possibility that the man had been poisoned?"

He felt everyone's eyes on him. The crowd reacted as if Todd had just asked the most ludicrous question. Poisoned? My man, you must be crazy.

But the beleaguered purser just shook his head. "The man's stomach was pumped, and according to the ship's doctor, Jameson had a reaction to the fungi." The purser stood up. "Now, if you'll excuse me. There's a lot that I have to attend to."

Todd turned around, his head swirling, feeling hungry—but not really able to eat.

When he walked into Newlove.

"Good morning, Todd." Newlove was grinning while eating a fat donut drenched in white powder. Like an early snow, Newlove's bites sent a gentle spray of the powder flying into the air.

"Horrible news, eh?" Newlove said, but of course it sounded more like "marble ooze" through the gummy fried dough pastry. "They think," Newlove went on—and Todd swore that the man's eyes were twinkling—"that it was the mushrooms. Imagine—"

Another big chomp, another snowy spray.

"—that."

Todd walked away. He heard Newlove call something to him, but it was lost in the donut.

Todd returned to his cabin, where he proceeded to tell his wife everything. And she, of course, tried her best to convince Todd that his imagination was running away, at full gallop.

At lunch—a poached swordfish with pureed carrots and julienne potatoes—a woman stood up, coughed, and then fell face forward—*thwack*—onto her party's table.

Everyone stopped eating. Todd actually had a tasty and succulent-looking forkful of the fish poised at his mouth when the woman nose-dived onto the table.

Newlove—still sitting right across from Todd—continued to finish his meal, even to the point of eyeing other people's uneaten plates.

With a ship nearly full of doctors, it didn't take long to pronounce her dead.

"I hear," Newlove said, cracking open a roll as if it hid a diamond, "that some people can have extraordinary reactions to the mercury content in fish." He looked right at Todd. "Maybe that's what did in the poor soul."

Todd's wife pulled her husband up and away from the table, off to the side where no one could hear them.

"You must tell the captain," she hissed. "Tell him what that man said. Tell him about the crazy wager."

"There was *no* wager . . ." Todd nodded. "Okay. Sure, I tell the captain. But what if it's just a coincidence?"

His wife had her hand locked on his sleeve, a habit of hers that made him feel as if he was still eight years old and being navigated to the boy's department at Macy's. "You *must* tell them."

Todd nodded. He turned to his wife. "I want to see something first. I don't want to smear the man if they're all just accidents. Maybe I can learn who he is . . . what kind of doctor he is."

"How?"

Todd looked at his wife. Newlove sat alone at the table, dutifully cleaning up anything left over. He saw Todd, and made a small conspiratorial wave. And then—in a move that made Todd's hair stand on end—Newlove made his eyes bulge out and then grabbed his throat, before rolling back in his seat, laughing.

"There are records," Todd muttered. "All the passengers had to list our professional background to qualify for this special charter. I—I want to see who this guy is, then I'll go to the captain." He took a breath. "Go back to the cabin."

His wife nodded, and then Todd turned and walked away.

He caught the purser as he was leaving his office.

"Ye, sir. Can I—?"

Todd nodded. "I was hoping . . ." He looked around, wondering if this was the place they would have the forms they filled out for the trip. "I needed to update some information on my registration for the cruise. Got a new home number," Todd lied thinly.

"Why certainly, sir. The records are in that carton right there. Perhaps you can help yourself." The purser scrunched up his face. "Things are getting a little dicey aboard."

Todd smiled. "Sure, no problem. I'll find it."

The purser left and—after taking a breath—Todd walked over to the carton. There were all the registrations on file, home addresses, professional connection, and physical vitae.

He found his own. A pointless gesture, but he scanned his sheet in case the purser made a quick reentry for something. Then Todd put it back. He looked over his shoulder. The door was open, there were voices in the hall.

He was so hungry. He saw an open bag of pretzels sitting on the purser's desk. Todd snaked a hand into the bag and stole one pretzel, then another.

He flipped through the sheets, past the Js—poor dead Mr. Jameson's form was still there—onto K, L, M and finally, the Ns.

For a moment he thought he wouldn't find a form for Dr. Newlove, that the man was a stowaway.

But there it was, Dr. Henry Newlove.

So, he *is* a doctor. Todd scanned the vitae, the address in Grosse Pointe, and then his field. Psychiatry. And current offices held . . . Director of the Wisconsin Society for the Study of Criminal Behavior.

He was a criminal psychiatrist.

Todd kept reading. He got to the physical data.

Newlove was six feet, one inch tall, 180 pounds with dark hair.

The paper slipped from Todd's hand.

Newlove . . . wasn't Newlove. Then where was the real doctor, and who was—?

The purser's cabin door squeaked open, and then quickly, quietly, it was shut.

Todd still held the incriminating paper in his hand.

He turned around and saw the smiling face of Dr. Newlove—or whoever he was.

"You're not Dr. Newlove."

"Surprise, surprise, Todd. No, Dr. Newlove was unavoidably detained from the sailing. In fact, I unavoidably detained him."

Todd nodded. This man was obviously a full-blown psychotic, probably one of Newlove's patients. God knew where the real Newlove was, but chances were that he ate something that didn't agree with him.

"I'm going to turn you in," Todd said, hoping that his words sounded brave. Then, pointing out the obvious, "You're sick."

Newlove shook his head. There were some screams outside. Had someone else fallen victim to the madman?

"You forget," the fat maniac said, "about our friendly wager?"

"What are you talking about?"

Now the once–Dr. Newlove looked disappointed. "We made a wager, that someone could be poisoned and it could go undetected. Come, come—you must remember that. The mushrooms work wonderfully, but fish with a reasonably high mercury content also works fine."

Todd took a step to move past the man, but his blimplike shape effectively blocked any egress.

"Our wager, Todd. I think I've won. I've proved my point." The man looked deadly serious.

"Wager? What the hell did we wager?"

Now the fat man smiled again. "Oh, that is right. We didn't talk about that, did we? Well, I guess I thought that the stakes were understood. As Grouch used to say, you bet your life. And—I'm afraid you lost."

Todd wondered if the nut carried a weapon of some kind. Was this a gun-toting nut? The man was obviously horribly out of shape. No danger there. And a gun is a gun.

"Out of my way," Todd said.

"You made a wager, and I'm afraid you lost."

Now the man started laughing and coughing, joyous apoplexy completely taking over.

He actually moved aside to let Todd get to the door.

"You're crazy," Todd said, again aware that he was pointing out the obvious. "You're completely—"

The meaty hand fell on Todd's shoulder.

"Oh, before you leave . . . I was wondering . . ."

Todd saw the man's eyes drift over to the purser's desk. "Could you—" a tiny smile played on the man's rubbery lips. Todd felt a sick fear growing inside him . . . without knowing exactly what he was afraid of. . . .

And with a big smile, the man said, "Could you tell me, exactly how many pretzels did you eat, Todd? One? Two?"

Todd looked from the man to the bag. He heard yelling outside. Were other people falling sick? What was going on?

He looked at the open pretzel bag that had been sitting there, open . . . the safe food so inviting.

Todd groaned.

"Two," he said.

The fat man made a small disappointed moue with his lips. But the grin quickly returned when Todd felt a sharp pain in his gut, then another, as if he was being kicked. He fell back, toward the cabin's bunk.

"Isn't this wonderful?" the man said. Todd felt another sharp kick. Internal bleeding? he wondered. He felt as if his insides were on fire.

He barely heard the psychotic man say, "Isn't this so wonderfully grisly?"

Then the fat man turned and opened the cabin door, and Todd, writhing in the bunk, became only one more groaning voice amidst the chorus on the luxury ship.

Billie Sue Mosiman is the author of five novels of suspense and more than seventy-five short stories published in various magazines and anthologies. Nominated for the Edgar in 1992 for the novel *Night Cruise*, her latest is *Widow*, a novel of suspense from Berkley.

After reading Billie Sue's dark and dangerous "No Restrictions" in *Pulphouse* Magazine awhile back, I e-mailed her and suggested she do a medical thriller short story set in the same prison. "Prosper" vies with Ed Gorman's "Survival" for the Darkest-of-the-Collection prize. After you've read it you might not believe that Billie Sue is really a very sweet person. She is. Really.

PROSPER BANE, 05409021

Billie Sue Mosiman

Rolling, strolling down the infirmary's aisles, polling the walleyes and deadeyes, like Jehovah in a crisp white frock, the black snake of his stethoscope dangling from a pocket, it's Hammurabi, master of the world they call Three Points Penitentiary. He is happy in this domain, except for one recurring problem. There just isn't enough sickness in a prison to suit him.

Katie asked him once, "Prentice, are you sorry you gave up your practice in Garret Falls?"

It made him seethe to think about that failed practice. Katie, now his wife, was one of his last remaining patients. Loyal to the very end, his Katie. New doctors came to town and lured away his people. They were young, handsome doctors, as if youth and looks were everything. He thought them Hollywood types—smiles too wide, too bright, and ultimately meaningless. They wore crisp new suits beneath their whites and they pretended to love children. Dr. Hogue, Family Practice, came first and took half of Hammurabi's patient list. One month a few records' releases were requested for transfer, and then there was a mad rush. Two years later Dr. Reveli, Internal Medicine, stole most of Hammurabi's remaining patients.

"Why are they leaving me?" he asked Katie the night he also asked her to marry him. "I'm as good as they are. Don't they like me? What did I ever do wrong?"

"Oh, honey, you didn't do anything wrong. They all still like you."

He adores Katie. She's small and doe-eyed, and when he makes love to her his belly completely covers her midsection, and his dick fits so tightly he always thinks he will die before he can complete the act.

"I don't miss my practice so much," he had to lie to her. No matter what he said, she believed him. She was a heavenly fuck, but not that bright. She had never seen the inside of a university classroom. She had majored in Home Ec in high school. Then she came down with psoriasis, had to quit her job at the Walmart, and visited him every couple of weeks until he cured her for good.

She knew how to make a lemon chicken that would melt in the mouth, but she never knew the extent of his debts when he finally closed the office doors and took down his shingle. She never knew the rage he harbored in his heart against the entire town where she had been raised.

He was lucky the prison infirmary job came up for him. He was a doctor. He had to make a living the best he knew how.

And his deepest secret, the one Katie didn't even know, had to do with his love and worship of historical figures. If he could have lived in that dim smoky past, he might have been a king. Like Hammurabi, his namesake. He wanted to rule and where better to establish a kingdom than in Three Points? Were the serfs going to rebel and storm the palace doors? Not ever, never. He could dispense as little or as much balm as he wished and there was no complaint department.

Prosper Bane, 05409021
June 22, 1994

My ear started bleeding again today. I thought there was a wart there and picked it off. Keeps itching and bleeding. Worries me a little. Other than that, nothing's new.

I don't have friends. That's why I'm writing in this notebook, because if you don't have a friend, you start talking in your head to yourself and pretty soon you're fucking nuts. Once you're certifiable, you don't last long in here. The cons find out you can't protect yourself, they find out you don't live in this world no more, they take you down. First you lose your cigarettes, then the care packages from home and whatever spending money you have. You lose your ass finally. They fuck it, if they think it's pretty, then they kill it.

Life's cheap in federal prison. If you can call time on the inside life.

If I write in this notebook at least I'll be talking about this place. I'll have it outside of my head where it can't hurt me so bad.

I'm not innocent. I want to get that straight up front. Most guys keep a notebook, they're writing bullshit like that. I didn't do it, they write. I'm white as driven snow. I been set up. The D.A. framed me. The witnesses saw somebody else. It was fucking self-defense, man! I don't fucking deserve this!

Like somebody's going to find their notebooks and let them out. Sure. Let me explain something. You wind up doing fed time, you ain't in no way innocent. This is not the country club. This joint in Three Points, Texas can't even be compared to Huntsville Correctional Unit where they send state offenders. This is fucking Big Time we're talking here. Edward G. Robinson would have called it The Big House in the movies. Some of us call it the Way Station to Hell.

Not that I'm proud of where I am. I'm not innocent, but what I done shouldn't have gotten me forty-five years, I can tell you that without sounding like a whiner.

Guy come to me, I lived in Houston, and he said, listen, you get me this list of chemicals—large quantities, he said—I'll pay you fifteen grand. Think it over, he said. You don't make the shit, you don't set up the lab, you don't have to distribute. All you do is get me the stuff, you walk off with the dough.

I thought it over. I never dealt, but sure, I used dope now and then. Not like some people I know, not often, but I understood what kind of shit he wanted. Noting the ingredients, I knew he was looking to do a meth lab.

Where I'm going to get this shit, I ask him? I don't have no pharmacist in the family, man. My people are Creole. Biggest dope we into is a little hash, a little crack.

Propsper, he said, you in or you out? You in, I'll tell you where to go. We got a man sell you anything if you got the balls for the pickup.

I think some more. I walk around inside my big old junk-shithouse out the northeast side of Houston where all us poor people live and I figure what fifteen grand can do me. It can get me out of town. It can get me one of those young sweet things hangs around the pool hall, get me down to Mexico City or Belize, and keep me in pina coladas for at least a year. You know the kind of drink I mean? Those pretty iced pale yellow tropicals with the little parasols sticking out the top?

I go back to the man and I say, yeah. I'll take the fifteen. Now where you want me to go?

He was known as Cold Fish Forbes back in Garret Falls. His patients left him because he never communicated, never asked about the family, never made himself part of the community. Why, he didn't even go to church, what were they to think?

When Dr. Hogue and then Dr. Reveli came to town, at least they had a choice.

Dr. Prentice Forbes, who changed what he would be called to "Hammurabi" once he took over at Three Points, misses the income and prestige he enjoyed as the sole physician to a good-sized town, but he makes up for it by wielding his power in an absolute way over the few sick cons who come to him.

He has ceased caring much if they live as long as they do what he says. If they die, there are always replacements. Just as long as too many don't die in rapid succession, he will not be questioned by prison officials. What do they care if he ships them out in pine coffins?

There are quite a few cases of HIV virus and AIDS. The complications take care of the cons when they get too weak to fight off opportunistic infections. There are some knife wounds and burns, a few broken bones from gang-related fights or beatings by guards.

It keeps Hammurabi busy enough. And when the ward is empty, he opens the drawer of his desk and takes out the bondage magazines, flips through them hunting for a new game he can play with Katie. Overall, it is not such a bad position, his prison job, but he isn't fond of examining new prisoners who tell him they have been framed or they have an attorney working for their release or listening to the ones dying and bellyaching about it, like he can do something to change destiny. You'd think they'd have a little common courtesy and commit suicide before they got so far along. . . .

June 24, 1994

Mobile, Alabama, man.

You see my trouble coming, don't you? Man tells me go get the stuff in Mobile, that's where we got the deal set up. I'm in Houston, I'm going to Mobile. I'm crossing state lines, fuck if I ain't, I'm crossing THREE state lines for this shit.

But what do I know, I got pina colada on the brain, I'm sick of the trashed house I'm staying in with two other bums, all of us eating spaghettios and drinking Pabst Blue Ribbon. How'm I going to make that kind of cash money any way else?

The feds got me in the parking lot, six-thirty A.M., me sitting in my busted, oil-dripping 1979 Chrysler Newport, waiting for the pharmaceutical supply house to open. I was sipping black coffee that tasted like sewer water and scarfing down a package of jelly rolls when they come knocking on my window saying, open up, you're under arrest.

Somebody squealed, no doubt about it. I got enemies, don't we all? You think they all love you, what passes for your friends, but man, they don't, they don't give a rat fart about you when it comes to a crunch. The feds must have been watching me after somebody told about the deal going down. I wouldn't be surprised if they tailed me all the way across the state lines out of Texas.

They fucking tore up the house in Houston looking for a lab. They offered me a deal when they didn't find one. Give up the buyer, they said, and they'd go easy. You believe that shit? I learned the hard way not to believe them. I gave up the man like they asked and the judge still looked down at me from that big high desk and he said: Forty-five years, no parole, Mr. Bane. We need people like you off the streets permanently.

So I ain't innocent, I figure I ought to pay for being so goddamned stupid, but you think forty-five years's too much for sitting in a parking lot with a list of chemicals in my pocket? Seems fucking stringent to me. Especially since I'm forty years old now and I ain't getting out of this place standing up. I'm not so stupid I don't understand that.

If I could just hear some home songs. I miss most the sounds from outside. I love zydeco, you know that music? It come from where my people live in South Louisiana. Clifton Chenier was the best zydeco man ever lived. He had this ole single-button accordion and a guy playing a frottoir, that's a washboard you play with spoons or a beer-can opener, and he made music make your skin dance.

I been trying to get a couple of the Creoles here in Three Points together to fix up a band, but they hanging back, afraid of the niggers and the spics, afraid there are too few of us to make it worth whatever problems might come up. Like some bastard don't like our music or tries to poke fun and we have to fight. Prominent music goes on in here ain't nothing but crying-eye country western. Of course this is Texas, that kind of music's expected. Then from the nigger singers there comes that mind-fucking rap. The Creoles, they don't want to fight. They peace-loving, they say, don't want trouble, it ain't worth it.

Hell, I don't want trouble either, but I could use some rhythm. Other day I thought I could hear Clifton Chenier in my head and I was bebopping in the chow line. Some con sex freak behind me says stop it, you wiggling your ass too much, looks like you want my hard-on. I say, c'mon, man, it ain't that. He says, you keep on swishing and see what happen.

Can't even get my music in here, what the fuck's the use.

The other thing, and it's worse, is I ain't been feeling too goddamn good about my bleeding ear. It just for Christ sakes won't stop bleeding. I don't want to get sick enough to go to the infirmary. Ole Hammurabi in there is the last man I want messing with me.

That ain't his name, Hammurabi. That's what we call him. He tells everybody comes in for meds or sick and needing a bed that he's just *like* Hammurabi. Nobody would have known what the shit a Hammurabi was so he told them the story. It was a super bad-ass king in Babylon, way the hell back in history times, he said. Hammurabi was supposed to be a good king, took care of his people, defended the land, that sort of happy shit. So our doc calls himself that. His real name is Dr. Prentice Forbes, and he looks like a prune, shrunk up and wrinkled, old as fucking sin. I bet the last time he cracked a medical book was back in the Stone Ages. He must have gotten his license during World War II, he's so fucking old, man.

Nobody likes him. Says not only is he a quack, but he seems to like it best when a con dies and gets shipped out the gates flat on his back. Don't bother him none to lose them.

I had a cellmate had to go to Hammurabi. Got a stomachache. I told him to hold on, it was bad ju-ju to mess with that infirmary. But I guess he waited too long. By the time they lifted him out of the bunk, he was half-blue and half-white, like the inside of an oyster, and puking up his guts.

They shipped him out in a box a week later. I went asking ole Hammurabi what took my mate down and he said, get out of here, you fuck, what do you care?

Well, I cared. I got a mate now tall as a cypress and thick

like one too—thick in the head, thick everywhere. He pushes me around when he gets mad, gets tired of being shut up. I take it because, well, like the other Creoles here, I don't like fighting. Shit, all it gets you are broken bones and a bashed-in skull. I let Moe push me around till he gets tired of me not fighting back, then he quits. He ain't really all that mean. Just bored.

Hammurabi puts down the magazine, careful not to bend the spine out of kilter, and looks up over his reading glasses at the sick man standing in his small office doorway. "I didn't tell you to come in here bothering me."

"I know, Hammurabi, but I need something bad for the pain in my legs."

Compton needs sun for the pain in his legs. He needs to be outdoors more often. He needs a back brace and maybe disc surgery. None of which he will get behind the walls of Three Points.

"I gave you your meds two hours ago. Now get out of my office before I call a guard."

Compton sighs deeply, turns like an old man although he is not yet fifty, and staggers out of sight.

Hammurabi turns the magazine over again and traces the long naked legs of the model with his fingertip. This woman, he thinks, will never get arthritis. She might get something worse, she might be strangled to death, but she will never be crippled and stooped like Compton.

He smiles at her, the masked black beauty bound on an iron bed of nails, blood leaking down the spikes in bright red droplets to the dirty floor.

He hears a groan and lifts his head, listening. He hears weeping.

These fucking babies, he swears softly, pushing back his

chair to rise. He'll give Compton another dose of pain medication just to shut him up. There should not be moaning and groaning and crying on the ward. Better to sedate them in case the warden comes through unexpectedly. . . .

At the doorway he snaps his fingers and turns, realizing he has forgotten to put away the magazine in the drawer. The beauties will have to wait until he is not so busy.

July 4, 1994

You think we get fireworks to celebrate the country's birthday? Fuck no. We hear them, in the distance from the town of Three Points, probably some kids shooting them off, but we can't see nothing, it's too far from the prison. We had stringy steak for supper, though, so something good came from the day. Every holdiay we get this steak tastes like the cow it come from had diarrhea for a year. If this steak was shipped to a shoe manufacturer, they wouldn't use it. Too tough.

It's been hot as goddamn hell here. The heat just irritates my ear, makes it burn when sweat rolls down it. I can't get a scab on the thing. Moe looked at it for me and he said, man, this looks like a hole's coming.

What do you mean, a hole's coming, I asked him?

Like a hole, stupid. A hole! It's about worn through your ear. You better go see Hammurabi for this. You got blood all over your pillow.

I knew that. I've been turning it over every night and asking for clean pillowcases till the laundry told me to forget it, there's a quota.

I guess I got to go to the infirmary. I wouldn't do it if I wasn't getting a hole right through my ear. It's probably cancer. Life in this place ain't enough, I got to get my ear eaten off and use up my time dying here.

*   *   *

Later—

Hammurabi said it was skin cancer. I guess I'm not so stupid after all. I asked him to take my ear off and he just laughed. What I need with your ear, he said, I got two of my own already.

He's a real card, that goofy fucking outfit. He's so funny they ought to put him on HBO's Comic Relief. He could play a baboon without a monkey suit.

I said, look, won't it kill me if you leave it on my head? He give me a look, like I'm the dumbest bastard come on his ward. It's gonna kill you no matter what, he said. I thought you knew that.

I didn't know it. And I sure as hell don't believe him.

Even if you take it off now, I asked? Or give me medicine, why don't you? Or some of those radar treatments.

Get out of my way, he said. We don't have radiation equipment and to get chemo, you'd have to go to Plainview. I bandaged it, didn't I? What else you want? We don't do surgery here.

Then ship me out, I said. They'll send me back when they're done.

Get out or I call for help, he said. You don't want me to call for help.

Tonight I asked Moe if he'd cut it off. He said he'd think about it, what could I pay him? Then he remembered a movie about a painter who cut off his own ear, Vincent somebody, played by Kirk Douglas. Why didn't I just cut it off like Kirk did?

I have no friends. A friend would do this without all the talk about it, do it without making me feel like I got to pay for help all the goddamn time. Right now I don't like Moe for shit and I ain't talking to nobody.

*   *   *

Summer scorches a path into the fall and holds it at gunpoint. The temperature climbs daily into the high nineties and night feels as thick and humid as the rind of an orange.

Hammurabi thinks too much about the trouble he's having getting an erection when he and Katie play their rough-and-tumble games. It might be because he is aging, that is a possibility he should not rule out, but he blames it on the heat. They don't keep the prison very cool, he tells Katie. I sit in my own sweat for hours, wringing wet, and I can't take a shower until I get home. How is that supposed to make me feel?

Katie tries to soothe away his daily frustrations by bathing him like a child, washing him gently all over, then helping him from the tub, drying him off, powdering him down with sweet-smelling baby powder so that his skin is smooth and slick as a sheet of tinfoil.

He fails miserably to satisfy her and must rely on the numerous sex toys they keep in a box beneath the bed. While Katie hums and whimpers toward exhaustion, he thinks of the ward in the prison, and wonders if any new patient has come in during his absence. He needs someone else to handle besides Compton and Fustav, his latest AIDS patient. How many times can he check the pulse of those two? How many times can he tell them he is doing all he possibly can?

"This goddamn heat is a killer," he says, slipping from the bed and Katie's oiled body to turn down the control on the air-conditioning system. "I can't even breathe, it's so hot."

"Come back to bed, Prentice, I need you," she calls at his back.

He feels a tightening and a tingle and he turns in the dark, groping for the edge of the mattress, hurrying now because finally he might be able to do something if the vent overhead will give out just a little more cool air and his wife begs him with just a little more sincerity in her trembling voice.

October 21, 1994

Moe didn't mean to make a mess. I told Hammurabi that, but he kept on screaming about filthy ignorant cock-sucking cons cutting one another up and then it was his job to do all that sewing. All the while I could tell he was in some way pleased he had this chore to do. It was in his eyes, this eager-beaver look you see sometimes when a person is real het-up to get to work.

He didn't even give me a shot. He just started stitching with a big goddamn curved needle, me screaming and trying to get loose from the male nurse. They had me down on the table, my arms pinned. I couldn't do much but kick and yell until it was over.

Now my head's shaved clean and I don't look in the mirrors and avoid catching my reflection in glass windows because it looks bad to have one ear and nothing but a patch on the other side of my head. Looks lopsided. Like a pit bull dog, caught in a scrap and limping home with missing parts to his head.

I can feel it eating at me. One night I got scared and told Moe, this is like a big invisible worm drilling through my head. It's still there, Moe, cutting my ear off didn't help. He said, yeah, it's like this place. It eats at you. It's like this country, it eats you up, turns you into hamburger.

I wish he hadn't said that. Now I dream about my whole head looking like a round gob of hamburger meat, red and raw and smelly.

Then I started thinking about Hammurabi and how he

ain't nothing but one of those invisible worms, eating off society, but not giving back to it. He eats and eats, gets fat and happy. Nobody can stop him because he's invisible. He can do anything and nobody checks it out.

Hammurabi told me the cancer's already spread to my bloodstream by now and it's only a matter of time. He didn't even blink an eye when he told me that. He knows he's invisible and I couldn't see him blink anyway.

Moe felt so bad about the botched job he did, he tried to give me back what was left of the fudge cake my sister mailed me from Ft. Worth. I told him to keep it. I had no appetite anyway.

I feel like shit. Runny gummy puppy shit all in a puddle. I lie around on my bunk and hum zydeco tunes, but it don't make me feel much better. It seems like it's going to be all the way downhill from here.

And, hey, who the fuck cares? Nobody's going to read this shit. When I die, they won't box it up for my sister. They'll just ask Moe, what's this? And Moe will say, Prosper wrote in it all the time, what you asking me for? And the trustee will dump it in the trash where it belongs.

So who the fuck cares, man?

In a prison he doesn't have to put up with bawling kids, fretful hypochondriac housewives, and stressed-out businessmen. He misses the variety of his own practice, but here, at Three Points, he has actual sick people. No fakers, no silly men with mid-life crises they turn into imaginary heart attacks, no dumb women talking to him about Fatigue Syndrome and PMS.

It is 6:00 P.M. and it has been a good day so far. He pauses in his regal stroll, feels his spine go rigid. A con by the unlikely name of Prosper lies with a swath of bandage around his head, an IV in his arm, a catheter in his prick, but his eyes . . . those eyes . . . they sear him with blame. Who said cons had the right to keep blaming him?

"It's not my fault you're dying," he says. "Don't look at me that way. I'm your only hope."

Prosper licks dry lips. "You're killing me."

Hammurabi lets a rude sound escape his lips and passes him by. He's heard it all before and it doesn't faze him. Compton and Fustav don't look at him that way. They know what hope is and that it resides completely in the form of their doctor.

"Did you get up today?" he asks Compton. He needs to stay ambulatory. If he lies around too much, he'll get stiff.

"I was up once today, went to the bathroom on my own." Compton smiles weakly, pain like a veil just behind his lips.

"When can I go back to my cell?" Fustav calls from across the aisle.

Fustav isn't going anywhere, but out in a box in a month or so. AIDS first mottled his flesh and then stole it from his bones. He is a cadaver, pale and shiny as a silver summer moon, but he still believes Hammurabi knows and practices magic.

"Not for a while yet." Hammurabi will soon tell Fustav the truth, tell him when the time is ripe, when he wants most of all to survive the disease. That's when Fustav will show him his ragged soul, that's when he will cry and cling, begging.

Hammurabi moves away from the beds and to the exit, rolling on the balls of his feet, strolling like a man in his garden, his gaze fixed on a distant hour when he can leave the clinic walls and eat Katie's delicious dinner and fuck her until he passes out. They have installed a ceiling fan in their bedroom and they set up a box fan on a card table so that it faces the bed. He will stay cool, by God, so that he can find his bliss.

He is not so old as they all think.

"He's killing me," Prosper claims with a croak that hurts his throat.

"Shut up, all you do is bitch."

"I'm telling you, he doesn't care about you, if you live or die. We need to take him down. If we go down, he needs to go with us. He's like a parasite in this place, feeding off us cons."

"I ain't dying, now shut up that shit."

Prosper turns over, crimping the IV line and not caring. "Compton, maybe you're not checking out yet, but one day . . . one day you will, and if Hammurabi's here, he'll hurry you to the grave."

"I ain't dying, neither, Bane. Shut up that stuff."

Prosper eyes the talking corpse. "Fustav, you're dead already, but you just don't want to see it. I can say this because I'm dead too. You know why? That fuck wouldn't get me no help. He let this shit grow on my ear until it got in my blood, he waited until it got into my *brain*. He ever give you anything to keep you alive? Did he? You might have had another couple of years if it wasn't for that fuck."

"I'm not dying," Fustav says softly, turning his head to the side on the pillow and staring at the gray institutional walls.

"Shit, man, you know you got AIDS. You think you gonna walk outta this place, bad off as you are?"

"You didn't have to say that to him. I ought to kick your Creole ass." Compton pushes back the sheet so he can painfully swing his gnarled legs to the floor.

"Ain't no use lying to him. Beat me up, if that'll make you

feel better. I got to have help, that's all I know." Prosper feels tears leaking from the bottom of his lids and he wipes them away angrily, then balls his fist and beats it on the mattress, the muffled tattoo a pitiful call for attention.

"What's got into you? Shit, Bane, will you stop it?" Compton's leaning on his crippled hands on the side of Prosper's bed. His eyes are wild and ugly dark.

"I don't care if you kick my ass, Compton, you crippled crazy fuck, you. Just help me take down Hammurabi. Please help me, for Christ's sake. The man's got no call to keep on breathing. He's got a sadistic streak wider than the Three Points River."

It is a week later and the three patients are still in the prison infirmary beds. Compton is walking well enough to be put back on the block in another day. Fustav is a blink and a prayer from eternity. Prosper feels weak as watered-down whiskey. He hurts all the time. Hurts all over, hurts to even think about hurting. He hears voices that aren't there, sees visions of angels standing tall on clouds, feels invisible hands stroking his arms to lure him away.

"I feel my strength leaving me," he says. "It's like a rope running out of me. When I was strong, the rope was all coiled up inside, here . . ." He points to his stomach. "And it's been dragged out, foot by foot. I can't even get to the bathroom on my own. I haven't had a bath in days."

Fustav has pinned Hammurabi on the diagnosis. Without preamble, the doctor told him, "You got a day, a week, a month at most. That's what comes from lusting after a guy named Mike, Fustav. Damn costly, isn't it?"

"I hope you burn in hell, you son of a bitch."

"Maybe. You save me a place when you get there, what you say?"

Compton and Prosper heard the exchange the day Hammurabi told Fustav the truth. They watched in silence as the doctor strolled nonchalantly from the ward. When he was gone, they talked in whispers about ways and means, about methods and chances.

They are united now. Hammurabi's going down.

"You got to hang on," Compton says, coming over to Prosper's bed. "I don't think we can do it without you."

"I ain't gonna be all that much help," Fustav says from across the room. He blinks and this makes him look like an owl, big eyes dark in the center of white circles, skin stretched like Saran Wrap over the cheekbones, his lips pulled back from small gray teeth.

"It's a team effort," Prosper says. "It's gonna take all three of us. We do it tomorrow, before it's too late and we run out of steam, me and Fustav." He looks at Compton, who nods his head. He glances at Fustav, who lifts one hand from the wrinkled sheets and waves it limply as if to say, go ahead, I'm dying here, I don't give a shit, let's do it.

January 8, 1995

Moe brought my notebook to the ward. He said he didn't know why, it was like a curse or something lying there in the cell among my things. It gave him the guilts. Was it a mojo or ju-ju or some shit like that?

I told Moe, listen, it was good of you to bring it. I'm Creole, but I don't know no magic. Hell, if I did, would I be lying in this bed with my ear gone and a hole in my head? I can't write so good anymore, but I got one last thing it might be good to write in it, so I'm real glad you brought it.

Moe shuffled on his feet, uneasy, too big for the room, and said, yeah, well, how you doing, man?

When I didn't answer, but just stared hard at him, he said, oh, never mind, I just thought you'd want . . . I just thought this should be with . . .

I told him, Moe, get the fuck out. We're sick in here. You go get in chow line and eat good, keep your health so you don't ever wind up in a sickbed.

We watched him slink out, shoulders hunched, and I think I missed him, missed even his tempers when he'd push me around and knock me upside the head for no good reason because this guy, he knew what I needed and he brought it to me. I have my pencil. I have my notebook. I can leave a suicide note so they'll know how we are going to take down Hammurabi tonight. And *why* he's going down.

Afterward, Compton's taking leave of the infirmary. He's heisting his chart so they won't know he was in here. He already promised the nurse a thousand bucks to forget he was ever in the place. Compton's the only one walking out of here alive. Me and Fustav, we're checking it in.

We got scalpels.

Compton's legs and hands worked real good for us. He's as light-fingered as ever these days. It only took him two weeks to get these sharp knives. The man didn't wind up in federal for nothing. He says he's got a stash from the bank funds he embezzled. Says his accounts are spread out all over the States and the feds didn't find half of them.

Now we just wait for Hammurabi to make his rounds before going home for the night.

He's going home all right. Tonight he'll sleep in the Devil's arms where he belongs.

Jesus, if I didn't hurt so bad, I'd feel bubbly as a bottle of champagne.

It don't matter, it's going to feel good to bring the king down. Sometimes a man has to take action he knows is right.

                        *   *   *

He rolls, strolls, bobbing his head like a plastic dog sitting in
the back window of a Chevy lowrider. He's thinking of putting clothespins on Katie's nipples until they turn purple.
She'll let him, she lets him do anything to her, she's so good,
so sweet. She didn't mind the chains on her ankles and the
dog collar on her neck. She didn't mind passing out when he
hung her from a rope. She's a real sport, is Katie, and that is
why he loves her so.

He sweeps through the aisle, replete with himself and his
sulfurous little daydreams, and does not pull up short until he
realizes Compton is out of bed and blocking the aisle ahead.

"What're you doing out of bed? I'm not releasing you
until the weekend."

"I feel better, Doc."

Hammurabi frowns at the word. They don't call him that,
he told them his name, goddamnit. These fucking cons are so
freaking stupid you'd think they'd be dead by now from a lack
of brainpower to spur the engines of their hearts.

He ducks his chin toward his chest and says in a baritone,
"Hammurabi."

"Oh, yessir. I forgot."

He doesn't like Compton's crooked smile. What's he
smiling for? Since when did the royal name of Hammurabi
bring forth mirth? In his presence anyway? He's not so out of
it he doesn't know some of the things the cons say behind his
back.

"Look here, you simple shit, get in that bed and stay
there. I'm locking up."

Compton looks over at Fustav. He inclines his head in
that direction. "I think Fustav's buying it, Doc."

"Don't call me that!"

Compton smiles again. "He ain't breathing. Not for a coupla hours now."

Hammurabi finally takes his gaze from the man in his path and glares at the body in the bed. He has to write out a death certificate and call the morgue if this is true. Hell, if it isn't one thing with these fucking cons, it's another.

He turns, his white coat rustling like a sheaf of dry wheat, and moves toward Fustav. "It's a miracle he lasted this long," he says, reaching for the pale thin wrist on the bed.

He looks at his watch, waiting to time the pulse, if there is one. After all, he is the doctor here, Compton doesn't know anything about death.

He feels, rather than sees, shadows approach from the end of the bed, but he's too mesmerized by the quick, strong beat, beat, beat of Fustav's blood pumping when he's supposed to be dead so he takes a moment before turning his attention in that direction. He waits for the harsh words of fury at wasting his time to coalesce at the base of his tongue so he can hurt Compton with words alone, but before he can harangue his patient, he feels the shadows upon him, surrounding him, blotting out the overhead fluorescent lights, and before he can turn from the corpse that is not yet a corpse, a hot hard puncture sinks into the muscles of his back. Now he turns . . .

Startled, screaming, flailing out, striking back, falling forward over Fustav's legs where his chest meets the tip of a scalpel driving through his breastbone.

Someone is yelling. Someone is crying. Someone is dying. Someone is falling through black viscous fluid to the bottom of the earth.

We got him, put him down in a slippery pool of blood. It took both me and Compton to push him off Fustav's legs to the floor.

That's one slimy fuck who won't kill any more cons who come through this place just doing their time in The Big House. Compton promised to get this notebook out and mailed to you, Jane, so it won't have been in vain that I spent all this time writing down my life here. I know I never was much of a brother, but you're all I've got and I figure you sent me cakes and stuff, you got to care just a little.

Now you'll know I'm a killer too, but you'll know how I got that way and I don't think you'll blame me much. I never said I was innocent, did I? I don't think I been innocent since I was ten and I broke old lady Bartlett's window down on Howell Street. Remember? When we lived in Dallas?

Oh, shit, what does it matter now. I done one good thing getting rid of Hammurabi. He killed me, I killed him first, we're even.

You might as well know I don't mind going out tonight. Compton's waiting so he can take this notebook from me first.

Fustav . . . well, Fustav's already gone. He slit his wrists soon as we got Hammurabi off his bed. He said, enough of this, I'm tired of this place anyway, I'm sick of the pain, see you guys in hell, and he just did it, so quick we hardly saw the stainless steel flashing first up the inside of the wrist of one arm and then the other. They can't say he didn't have guts.

He looks peaceful now. His face is slack and looks young again. I hope I look that way too, not young, but at rest. I could use a little dark time. I just hope there's a heaven, you know, a place where maybe Clifton Chenier might be, playing some get-down, in-your-face zydeco for me when I arrive.

I'd like to find a friend.

But anywhere is going to be better than this, God knows. It's been hard time in the belly of the beast and I'm ready to give it up.

Prosper Bane, 05409021
Three Points Federal Penitentiary
Three Points, Texas

Steven Spruill has a Ph.D. in clinical psychology but devotes himself full-time to writing. He's published science fiction, horror, and suspense, and in the past few years his rich, inventive medical thrillers *(Painkiller, Before I Wake, My Soul to Take)* have developed a large and loyal following. Most recently he's taken to revamping the vampire myth with his powerful *Rulers of Darkness.*

SINISTER

Steven Spruill

Dr. Matthew Girard was feeling good when he walked into the examining room. He'd looked forward all morning to this appointment.

Dawn Hanna rolled her head toward him. "Doc! We were getting ready to start the movie without you."

"You can't," he said cheerily. "I'm the projectionist." Seeing Dawn gave him the expected lift. He liked her unruly mop of dark curls, her quick wit, her gift of not taking him too seriously. Lying on a table in a skimpy hospital gown under the probing gaze of your doctor was enough to unnerve most people, but Dawn was bringing it off with her usual panache, shoulders relaxed, hands laced behind her head. Her face was slightly flushed, but that was more likely from the hormonal bonfires of pregnancy than embarrassment. At twenty weeks, her belly swelled up below her navel—big but not nearly as big, God willing, as it was going to be.

Susan, the tech, rolled up Dawn's gown, then took a tube of lubricant from the cart and began to smear it over the mounded belly.

"K-Y jelly," Dawn said. "Haven't seen that stuff for a while." She chuckled, a rich, happy sound deepened by the strengthening muscles in her diaphragm. Matt felt himself blushing now. Husbands losing interest in sex when their wives began to show was common enough, but he could never understand it. He kept a lid on any sexual feelings for his patients, of course, but that didn't stop pregnant women from seeming just generally beautiful to him.

"Say, Doc," Dawn said, "how come you ran away from me at the Winn-Dixie last week?"

He looked at her, baffled.

"Don't pretend you didn't see me," she said in a needling voice. "I was fixing to check out and I saw you over yonder in frozen foods. I waved at you and you waved back. Then you hightailed down the next lane. By the time I got there, you were gone. What did you have in your cart that you didn't want me to see?"

Matt felt a pang of unease. "When was this?"

"A week ago Friday, around six. C'mon. Baby peas? Or wait—I know: Cornish storks."

Susan laughed, then sobered, and Matt realized she was taking her cue from him. He forced a smile. "I'm sorry, but I don't remember seeing you."

"I'm hurt." Dawn pretended to pout.

He thought back to the Friday she'd named. He did shop at Winn-Dixie, but always on Sunday afternoons, unless he'd been called in for a delivery. No, a week ago Friday at six o'clock he'd have been down the hall in the conference room, suffering through a tedious staff meeting.

Matt's uneasiness deepened as his mind took him back

further, four months, to the murder of Jill Marcellini. All those questions by the police—it was clear they'd walked into his office already suspecting him. They'd backed off only after a phone call to Lissa had confirmed he'd been with her all night. Their unfriendly attitude those first few minutes still bothered him, though. Jill had been his patient, but that was all; there was no further reason to suspect him. Maybe the cops had just been fishing.

Or maybe they'd had a witness to the murder, and he fit the description of the killer.

Matt remembered with a sick feeling the pictures the detective sergeant had shown him. Jill Marcellini had been stabbed sixteen times. He hated to think he bore any resemblance to a man capable of such savagery.

Or that Dawn Hanna might have seen that man in a grocery store last week. The murder *was* still unsolved.

Matt reminded himself that millions of people lived in or near Atlanta. Six-foot men with sandy hair and normal build weren't exactly rare. Lissa liked to tease him about his blue Robert Redford eyes, but Dawn wouldn't be able to see eye color from across a grocery store. It was just some perfectly innocent guy who looked like him from a distance.

"Ready for the show?" he asked.

Dawn nodded, her eyes wide with excitement. "I'll really be able to see them this time, won't I?"

"Better than last time, that's for sure." Matt didn't want to promise her too much. It was hard for an untrained eye to make much of the vague shadows on a sonogram monitor. Only with long practice did the shapes take on reliable meaning. "Your twins will show up white on the screen," he reminded her, "and areas of water will look black. I'll probably still have to point smaller features out to you, but you'll certainly be able to see at a glance how much they've grown in the past month."

As he picked up the ultrasound wand, he felt an excitement all his own. Twins fascinated him, the thought of two tiny lives growing together in such close intimacy. He remembered the emotional rush eight weeks ago as he'd spotted a second fetus on Dawn's sonogram—and that twinge of unease he always felt on the first sighting, knowing twins faced significant dangers not present in single births. Of course, the great majority of twin pregnancies turned out just fine. Dawn would have to be very unlucky to have any serious problems.

He felt a slight vibration in his palm as Susan turned on the power to the ultrasound wand. As he positioned the wand on Dawn's belly, Susan switched the monitor on, then turned out the room lights. In the sudden dimness, the monitor screen gave off a pearly glow. Images emerged as he slid the wand back and forth over the side of Dawn's belly. He felt her body shift and knew she was craning her neck to peer at the screen.

As soon as he picked out the two curling shapes, he knew something was wrong. One of the twins was around eleven inches long—about right for twenty weeks—and looked normal. In grim contrast, the other was smaller, no more than eight inches. Matt's heart sank as he made out first one abnormality, then another, then another. The abdominal wall of the second twin had failed entirely to develop and he could see the intestines spilling out. Its backbone was splayed into the serious deformity of spina bifida. And its heart was severely rotated.

It was doomed—if not before birth, shortly after.

The remains of Matt's breakfast hardened into a stone in

his stomach. How he hated this. He knew what to say, what to do, but it never got any easier.

"Oh," Dawn said happily. "I can see one of them. Where's the other?"

Matt heard a soft intake of breath as Susan made out what he was seeing. Without being told, she flipped the lights on as he pulled the probe away. Dawn blinked in the sudden brightness, looking first confused, then frightened. Susan moved in quickly, wiping the lubricant from Dawn's belly and adjusting her hospital gown.

"What is it? What's the matter?"

"I'm afraid there's a problem," Matt said gently. He took one arm as Susan took the other, helping Dawn to sit up on the table. "If you want to get dressed, we can talk about it in my office."

Dawn stared at him with huge eyes. Her face had gone pale. "No. Y'all tell me, right now."

Susan took one of her hands and he the other. He told her what he had seen and what it meant.

Her eyes grew luminous, but the tears didn't spill. "And you can't save it?"

"No. Those defects will be fatal. I'm sorry."

She closed her eyes for a second. "The healthy one—does this mean I'll lose him, too?" Her voice was a choked whisper.

"No, it doesn't. Even if we do nothing, there's a chance the healthy twin will come through all right and be a normal child. Unfortunately, there *is* also a risk that the dying twin may harm the healthy one. To avoid that, I can quickly end the life of the one that is going to die. The technical term is 'selective reduction.' "

Dawn shuddered. Dimly, Matt felt a pain in his hand where she was gripping it, but he did not try to pull away.

"I don't know if I can deal with this," she whispered.

"It's a terrible shock," Matt said. "If you think it will be too much for you, there is a third option—"

"No," Dawn said. "Not an abortion. I won't do that."

Matt nodded, hiding his relief. It was not up to him to push Dawn toward or away from any medically acceptable choice. The decision must be hers.

"You said there is a serious risk if I do nothing that the . . . the dying one will harm the other."

"That's right. It could cause a miscarriage before the healthy twin is developed enough to survive birth."

Dawn gasped.

"Or, short of killing the healthy twin, it could cause an infection or other damage. There is also a small risk that it could cause a clotting problem in your own blood." Matt stopped there, not wanting to complicate her decision by listing risks that were very small or unproved. "Most of these same dangers are present if I do the reduction, but they are not as great."

"Why not?"

"It's largely a question of room. Twins are much more cramped in the womb than singletons, which by the end are in pretty tight quarters themselves. The added crowding with two can cause neurological problems or other damage to one or both. From the moment the doomed twin dies, it will begin to shrink and be resorbed by your uterus. This will improve conditions for your healthy twin."

Dawn drew a deep, shuddering breath. "You're *sure* the one is going to die?"

"There is no doubt. I wish there was something I could do to save it, but there isn't."

Dawn swallowed hard. "Is it . . . suffering now?"

"I don't know. No one does. But my best guess is no, not at this point. A fetus hasn't really developed the neurological equipment for significant perception and awareness at twenty weeks."

"But it will, if it goes on living a few more weeks."

Matt said nothing.

Dawn began suddenly to sob. Susan held her tightly. Matt fished a wad of tissues from the pocket of his medical coat and pressed them into Dawn's hand. "Don't try to settle it right now. Think about it, talk to your husband."

She pulled away from Susan and nodded, wiping at her tears. "All right. Thank you, Doctor. You too, Susan. Y'all are good people."

He nodded, too miserable to speak.

Back in his office, he went into his bathroom and splashed cold water on his face. Leaning on the sink, he stared into the mirror. The face that stared back was not his. The part was on the wrong side, the eyes too lonely.

"A pinafore your thoughts," Lissa said, gazing across the table at him.

Matt raised his glass. "Absinthe makes the heart grow fonder."

"That's not absinthe, it's bourbon, but I'll laugh at yours if you'll laugh at mine."

He managed a chuckle. Holding the glass to his forehead, he let the condensation chill his skin as the cool tink of ice cubes soothed his ears. August in Atlanta. Eight P.M. and still eighty-five degrees out—feeling more like ninety-five, with the humidity. The underground was crowded. Shoppers and tourists filled the concourse, ambling past the rail at Lissa's back, legs and faces glistening under the antique streetlights. By comparison, Lissa looked cool as peach ice cream.

"What?" she asked. "Your eyes just got all squinty and calculating."

"I was just imagining you in a pinafore, a short pinafore—and nothing else."

Lissa gave him a soft but radiant smile, and he felt his heartbeat pick up. "Liar," she said. "But I'll accept the compliment anyway."

By God, she *did* look good tonight. A faded T-shirt with Bach on it, those white shorts showing off her long, tanned legs. Her chestnut hair fanned out above her ears before dwindling stylishly to a bristly nape he knew could excite his fingertips like an electric charge. Sitting there in the looping, ironwork chair, with the quaint shops at her back, she looked every inch a glamorous Atlanta socialite out slumming for the evening. But behind those alluring hazel eyes, he knew, lay a brain that could solve complex equations without pencil or calculator. She'd gobbled up a Ph.D. in math at age twenty-three, and now, twelve years later, was on the fast track at Emory. Right now she was pushing to finish a paper for *Mathematica*. If the prestigious journal accepted it, she'd be a shoo-in for full professor. He admired her braininess.

Hell, he was madly in love with her.

Why aren't we married yet? Matt wondered. We ought to be having babies together.

And if they turned out like their daddy?

He felt the familiar, vague unease, remembering the ordeals of his childhood in LaGrange, Georgia. The struggling to parse out each word he read, the humiliation of being held back a grade in elementary school not once, but twice. The private schools, not for Ivy League preppies but for kudzu league dummies like him. At lest the years of torturous work had helped him get by at what everyone bright was supposed to do so easily. By that time, much of his childhood had also gotten by, without him, as he sat stewing in the smells of floor wax and chalk dust.

But all the grueling work in pattern recognition and reading—the massive effort to neurologically rewire a part of his brain—had paid off; at the end of high school his SAT scores were in the top ten percent. After college, his MCAT scores were even better, getting him into Georgetown Med ahead of thousands of other applicants. He had accomplished his life's dream; he was a board-certified physician, with a top reputation in obstetrics at a big city hospital.

Still, whenever he thought of fathering children, a deep unease gnawed at him. What if dyslexia was hereditary? At this point, the research wasn't clear. It could be genes, but the other leading candidate was subtle brain damage, probably before birth. If his dyslexia had come from *in utero* brain damage, he needn't worry about passing it on to his children. No one else in his family had shown dyslexic tendencies, which hinted that his problem had not been genetic.

If only he could be sure.

"Seriously," Lissa said, "what are you thinking about? You've looked so grave all through dinner. You only ate half of your 'gator sausage."

"There can be other reasons for that."

"At least you tried it. I'm proud of you." Reaching across, she soothed a cool fingertip across his knuckles. "Bad day at the office?"

"You might say that." He did not want to talk about Dawn and her dying twin that he might have to help on its way. So instead, he said, "One of my patients thought she saw me at the grocery store two Fridays ago."

Lissa gazed at him a moment before comprehension lit her eyes. "Come on, Matt, not that police thing again. So someone in the grocery looked like you—"

"When she waved at him, he waved back."

"Well. Maybe he thought he knew her, too."

"What are the odds of that?"

"I don't know, Matt. If someone waved at you and you didn't know them, mightn't you wave back anyway?"

"I might. But I'd look confused. Dawn would notice that. She's quite perceptive."

Lissa dug a fingernail into his knuckles.

"Ow."

"Is she pretty?"

"Don't change the subject."

Lissa sighed and sat back, sipped at her beer. "Aren't you being just a bit paranoid?"

"Why would the police think I killed Jill Marcellini, unless someone gave them a description that fit me?"

"I don't know. That detective, VanOrden, gave me the creeps. Maybe being an overbearing ass is just his way. Everyone who knew your patient was a potential suspect; maybe VanOrden went around leaning on them one at a time."

"OK, but why start with me? He was at my office door the morning after the murder."

Lissa studied him. "What are you trying to say? That you have a twin out there somewhere, an evil twin?"

"No," he said quickly. "Just someone who looks a lot like me."

Lissa's gaze dissolved through him to someplace far away. "I used to think I had a twin," she said softly. "When I was two. I called her Jane. She had her own little chair, and I made my mother set a place at the table for her. I was the only one who could see her, but I knew she was really there. I talked to her a lot."

Something in her voice gave him an eerie feeling, raising a ripple of goose bumps along his arms. Sonograms and other recent advances that allowed early glimpses into the womb had revealed a startling fact: for every twin pregnancy in which both babies were born there were as many as four others in which one of the twins did not make it to term. It had even been given a name—the "vanished twin syndrome." Even nowadays, the fact that there had been a twin no doubt often went undiscovered by doctor or mother. Back in the early sixties, when Lissa was born, not knowing about a vanished twin would have been very common.

Not *consciously* knowing, that is.

But who could say what primitive memories might lie buried in the human psyche? At what moment after conception did twins first become aware of each other? Could it be that Lissa's invisible friend Jane was the unconscious memory of a twin that had died beside her in the womb?

The thought caused a pang of sadness in him, inexpressible, and yet strangely familiar.

Could he have had a twin? Though he'd never told anyone, he thought about it from time to time, in the dark of the night, lying in bed alone. It was possible he'd had a vanished twin that Ma had never known about. But not a twin that was alive today, evil or otherwise. Ma would never have adopted out a child of hers, much less one of a set of twins.

Lissa's hand wandered idly up his forearm, tracing the long white scar on its outside. Apparently he'd crawled through a broken vase when he was just over a year old. Whenever he noticed the scar, he was glad he could not remember getting it. Memories that would only bring pain were better forgotten.

"Do agencies ever adopt out twins to different families?" Lissa asked, her eyes still distant.

"Not anymore."

"But they used to?"

"Sure. Some very important research has been done on identical twins adopted by different couples and reared apart.

It's the best way to untangle genetic inheritance from the effects of the environment."

"I can't imagine a mother with twins keeping one and putting the other up for adoption," Lissa mused. "But if you or I were adopted and our parents didn't tell us, we actually *could* have an identical twin out there somewhere."

And then Lissa smiled and pulled his arm toward her across the table. "Ridiculous, right? Parents don't hide it when their kids are adopted."

"Nope," Matt said. *Not anymore.*

"We've decided," Dawn said. Her voice was tight, her dark eyes somber. Matt glanced across his desk at her husband, but Jerry Hanna did not meet his eyes. He sat next to his wife, an arm around her shoulder. He was a small man with thick forearms and grime under his fingernails, a greenskeeper at an Atlanta country club, if Matt remembered correctly.

"We want you to . . . to reduce the pregnancy," Dawn said.

"All right." Matt made sure no regret tainted his voice. It *was* the best decision, but he could not shake a feeling of gloom at what he would be doing.

"How soon can y'all do it?" Dawn asked.

"This afternoon."

Her eyes widened. "That soon?"

"If you're ready." He did not tell her that he had come to know her well enough to expect this decision; that the room was already prepared.

Jerry looked up at him at last. "Doc, if the one twin is a goner, we cain't risk it hurting the other one."

Matt knew it was a question, not a statement. *Are you sure we're doing what is right?* There was really only one answer. The horribly deformed twin was doomed. Ending it now would improve the chances of the other twin surviving, a life saved in return for one that was already lost. Guided by the ultrasound monitor, he would slip a long needle through Dawn's abdomen into the womb. He would find the malformed and rotated heart of the dying fetus and ease air into it. The heart would stop. If he was careful enough, it would be quick and merciful. He would be careful enough, and more.

It was the best decision, and still he hated it.

But Jerry and Dawn weren't asking what he felt. They were asking, one last time, what he thought. Looking Jerry in the eye, he said, "I have no doubt in my mind that you are making the right choice."

He was very careful. Dawn held still and did not gasp, did not throw off his aim. When it was over and he was back in his office alone, he picked up her chart and wrote his notes on the procedure. At the end, he printed a two-word epitaph: *pregnancy reduced.* Starting to put the chart back, he hesitated, feeling something was wrong. He stared at the final two words until he saw it. He'd printed the "y" backward. He had not done that in years.

He threw the chart across his office.

That night, he dreamed he was playing inside the kids' tent at the county fair in Rome, Georgia, where he grew up. The tent was filled to his armpits with brightly colored plastic balls, and he was having fun plunging around, rolling and diving across the balls. He slipped below the surface of the balls and frowned, trying to find the ground. But now his legs and arms were suddenly too short. It was no longer fun. He yelled for Ma, and for an instant, he saw a woman's face through a break above him. But it was not his mother, and then the balls closed over him, and now he was inside one of them, en-globed in pinkish red plastic. The surface was no longer hard, but stretched as he put a hand against it. He pushed out with his feet and hands, squirming inside the ball, trying to get out. Suddenly, his back came up against something solid. It was squirming, too, and he realized it was another boy's back. He tried to turn, but now his arm was hooked with the other boy's arm, and the more he tried to turn, the more the two of them spun around, back to back, inside the ball. The ball was shrinking now, and he felt a suffocating pressure in his chest as he realized how trapped he was. A sound started up in the distance and grew steadily louder: *Boom, boom, boom, boom.*

Knocking. Someone knocking at his door.

Matt pushed up on one elbow. The TV on his dresser broadcast a silent snowstorm of static. Using the remote, he shut the set off, then turned to the glowing red numerals on his bedside clock. Four-eleven. He'd been dreaming . . . *what?* Already it had faded. Something about Rome.

A feeling of loneliness swept him. Then the door boomed again. "I'm coming. Hold your water!" Pulling on his robe, he made his way through the apartment, seeing by the glimmer Atlanta's skyline cast through his balcony doors.

"Who is it?" he said.

More pounding. Uneasy, he looked out the security peep-hole. It took him a moment to recognize the face, made even rounder by the wide-angle lens. Alarm cleared away the last tendrils of sleep. He pulled the door open. Detective Sergeant Virgil VanOrden of the Atlanta P.D. lowered his upraised fist. "Evening, Doc. Mind if we come in?" Virgil jerked his head at the two uniformed cops who stood behind him. He had gained weight in the four months since Jill Marcellini's murder, Matt saw. But he hadn't bought new clothes. His neck bulged over his collar, and his blue blazer looked painted on. His eyes, incongruously large and soft in the bullet-shaped head, were bloodshot.

Matt motioned them inside. "I do have a doorbell," he said.

"I rang it. You didn't answer."

"What are you doing here at four in the morning?"

"Asking you questions. Where were you at midnight?"

"In bed asleep."

"Anybody see you?"

"What's this about, Sergeant?"

"Anybody see you?"

"David Letterman might have, but it's a long shot."

Virgil turned to one of the uniforms. "Didn't I tell you the doctor is sharp as a tack? Or should I say knife?"

Matt remembered the pictures of Jill, the ugly stab wounds, dark slit mouths rimmed in red, as if they'd eaten her out from inside. His stomach clenched. "There's been another murder?"

"I'm going to ask you once more: can anyone verify that you were here around midnight?"

"No."

"You and the prof break up, did you?"

"No—and that's the last question I'll answer that is none of your business."

Virgil's expression hardened. Matt knew he should not antagonize the man. On the other hand, Detective Sergeant VanOrden clearly was not going to like him, no matter what he said.

"How about coming on down to the station with me."

"Am I under arrest?"

"If you prefer."

"On what charge?"

"Murder."

"Come on, not that again." Matt's exasperation quickly shaded into fear.

"If you make me arrest you, it won't be nearly so easy for you. Getting booked takes a while, sometimes hours, what with the fingerprinting, checking valuables, calling the lawyer, all that stuff. Then, because of the early hour, it'll be a while before even an upstanding citizen like you can get a bail hearing. So you get to spend that while in a holding cell with some Citizens for Creative Violence."

"Maybe I should call a lawyer," Matt said.

"Why? I'm not planning to ask you any questions. I'm offering you one last chance to cooperate willingly with a police investigation. If you do, you can be in and out in half an hour."

A lineup, Matt thought with a mixture of fear and fascination. It meant he had been right about Jill's killer looking like him. Now there had been another murder, and again, a witness had given Virgil a description that had brought him straight here.

Except this time I have no alibi, Matt thought.

I should call a lawyer. . . .

But a lawyer can't keep me out of a lineup, can he? And maybe if I go along, I can get something out of Virgil about this killer who looks like me.

Matt realized he wanted that, wanted it very much. "Let me get dressed," he said.

On the ride to the station, Virgil deflected all his attempts to learn more. Why am I doing this? Matt wondered. Even if a lawyer couldn't keep me out of a lineup, he might be able to delay the process. In the meantime, maybe the witness's memory would fade. . . .

But why would I care about that? I'm innocent.

Other meanings of the word struck him: *naive, simpleminded.*

He realized the car had pulled up in the back lot of the station. As he got out, he heard chirping from some weeds that had pushed up through cracks in the blacktop. The middle of Atlanta, what was a cricket doing here?

What am I doing?

One of the uniformed cops led the way through a back entrance.

Inside, was bright but cheerless—long, narrow halls, white tiles blue as skim milk under the fluorescents. Four men waited in a small anteroom. Through a door beyond, Matt could see a larger room with a platform and height lines painted along the walls. His heart began to race. This is stupid, he thought. Get out of this, now. Even if they arrest you.

"Dr. Girard, would you step into line behind the first man please." Virgil was being very polite now.

"If I do this," Matt said, "will you answer my questions?"

Virgil's mouth tightened.

"Or I can call that lawyer now."

"All right. Anything that isn't classified from the press—afterward."

Matt stepped into line and filed through the door with the others. The platform creaked as they clumped up on it and turned. Glancing at the other faces, he realized none of them looked much like his. Old Virgil is setting me up, he thought.

And it's too late to do anything about it.

A huge mirror glared coldly from one wall. He could feel the hidden witness staring at him through his own reflection, giving his replica in the mirror a malevolent life of its own. His throat convulsed as he tried to swallow.

"Number four, step forward, please." The speaker blared above him, so loud he almost jumped. No one moved, and he realized he was number four. He stepped forward.

"Turn to your left."

He did it.

"Your right—no, all the way facing right."

Time stretched. Sweat prickled out on his forehead as he waited for the speaker to blare again. Why did he feel so *guilty?*

"Step back number four."

He almost stumbled in his eagerness.

The speaker called out number one. Good—the witness must be vacillating. From the corner of his eye, Matt saw that number one, while he looked nothing like him in the face, was his height and general build.

And then it was over, the speaker telling them to file back out again. The other men left the anteroom, but Matt stayed, waiting until at last Virgil came in. The detective's stony expression gave nothing away. Matt resolved not to speak until Virgil did. He was tired of the man's hostility, of feeling guilty when he had done nothing.

Virgil eyed him. "You want a Coca-Cola or something?"

"What I want are some answers."

"Sure thing. But would you do me one more favor, Doctor?"

"After you answer my questions."

Virgil handed him a clipboard and pen. "Just sign your name for me, then we'll talk. My word on it."

The page was blank. Mystified, Matt signed his name and handed it back to Virgil, who barely glanced at it. Now an unmistakable disappointment showed on his face. "Pretty neat handwriting for a doctor."

Matt said nothing. When you were ten and some letters still looked the same frontward or backward, and others refused to yield their meaning without a fight, the lines in a school notebook became mental tightropes which could be walked only with care—and no margin for error. His hand knew each curling step now, and also knew better than to trip itself up by hurrying. His handwriting would always be neat. Why, was another thing that was none of this man's business.

"You are left-handed," Virgil said.

"Yes." And then he understood. Virgil had not cared about his signature, per se—just which hand he wrote it with. "The angle of stab wounds," Matt said.

"Correct. Pathology just called two minutes ago to tell me the killer is right-handed." Virgil's voice was heavy with dejection and, for the first time, Matt felt a pang of sympathy for him. Maybe it wasn't so much that Virgil had wanted the killer to be him as that he wanted so desperately to catch the killer.

"This time he killed two of them," Virgil said wearily. "A husband and wife. They were in bed sleeping; never had a chance. One blow to the man's heart, eighteen to the woman's chest and . . . abdomen. According to Doc Cole-peper, the wounds all have a distinct right-handed slant. But you're sinister, Doc, so it couldn't very well be you, could it?" Virgil peered at him, as if daring him to act surprised that a fat cop knew the Latin root for "left-handed."

Matt wondered why the detective hadn't had him sign his name after Jill's murder, then remembered that he'd come up with his alibi before it had gotten that far. "In the lineup," he said, "the witness thought it might be me, right?"

"She was sure of it, at first." A hint of the old animosity lit Virgil's eyes, then faded. "An old lady. She lives next door to the victims. She saw the man come out their front door—the porch light was on, giving her a good, clear view. As soon as y'all walked up on the platform, she pointed you out, then began to waver between you and one of our own boys from records. Then she tells me she didn't have her glasses on and she's got 20/200 vision. Can you imagine what a defense lawyer would do with that?" Virgil made a disgusted sound.

"Wait a minute," Matt said. "The front light was on? Why would a killer coming *out* someone's front door, leave the porch light on?"

"Stupidity," Virgil said. "It's not like cop shows where the killer is always clever."

"And you thought I might be that stupid?"

"I could always hope."

The answer stung—more than Virgil could know. A board-certified physician, a top reputation in obstetrics at a big-city hospital, and yet he could still feel stupid in a flash, because what you believed about yourself for the first fifteen years of your life took more than another fifteen to root out.

"What awakened the witness?" Matt asked.

Virgil eyed him. "You might or might not be stupid, doc, but you ask good questions. The old lady's phone rang. No one on the other end, which spooked her. When people get spooked at night, they peek out their windows. She happened to do it just as the killer came out."

"Quite a coincidence, her phone ringing."

"That's another difference between real life and good movies. In real life, coincidences happen."

Matt nodded, but there was something wrong here, something missing. "Why did you come straight to me again, Detective? I think you know I'm not stupid, and your witness's description couldn't have been that sharp."

Virgil looked uncomfortable. "I . . . the dead woman was pregnant, Doc."

What he was not saying came through in his tone. Matt's throat closed. For a minute he could not speak. "One of my patients?"

Virgil nodded. "She had your card lying right there on her chifforobe."

"Who?"

"A Dawn Hanna. And her husband, Jerry—hey, Doc, easy!"

Matt felt himself stepping back. His knees went soft and the cop grabbed his arm, easing him over to a chair. He felt sick to his stomach, then a wave of helpless fury swept him. "Damn it!" he shouted. "God damn it to hell."

At the hospital the next morning, Matt felt cut off from his body. It bobbed stiffly through its appointed tasks like a marionette controlled by someone else. He delivered three babies, all healthy, did an amniocentesis, and made rounds on maternity. Through it all, a single thought tumbled in his mind, sharp and chilling as a splinter of dry ice: *Someone is killing my patients.*

He remembered he had a dinner date with Lissa—a new French restaurant she'd discovered on Peachtree Street. He could not imagine himself being good company. He called her and begged off, citing work.

As he forced himself through his afternoon office appointments, Matt felt his mind beginning to thaw. Why *had* the killer chosen two women from his practice? Last night, Virgil had asked him what Jill Marcellini and Dawn Hanna might have in common. Numb with shock, he'd been unable to think of anything.

But it was surely the right question.

He still had no answer as he entered the examining room where his last patient of the day waited. The chart in his hands seemed to be filled out in a foreign language. He forced himself to concentrate on each word, one at a time. All right, the patient was thirty-seven years old, this was her sixth month, and she was at risk for PIH—pregnancy-induced hypertension. Slipping the sphygmomanometer on her arm, he inflated the cuff and plugged his stethoscope into his ears. As he closed his eyes to help himself listen, his mind served up a sudden horrifying image of the murder, Dawn and Jerry side by side, covered with blood, and inside Dawn, the twin he had tried to save.

The *twin*.

Matt felt his eardrums banging suddenly against the stethoscope, wiping out the pulse he was trying to find in his patient's arm. Blanking his mind, he drained the cuff, reinflated it, and this time was able to mark the start and fade of the beat. The woman was fine, no sign of PIH. He reassured her, ushered her from his office, and sat down at his desk.

Twins.

Jill Marcellini had been pregnant with twins. Thirty-nine years old, she had been concerned that her age might cause her to give birth to a mentally retarded baby. When she'd learned that Chorionic Villi Sampling—CVS—could reveal chromosomal abnormalities like Down's syndrome, she had requested the test. I had mixed emotions, Matt remembered. Odds were, both twins would be normal and I could reassure her without the question of abortion coming up. If one wasn't normal, I could deal with the issue then. But it never got that far. The procedure caused her to miscarry one of the twins. I had mentioned the risk to her—only a one in seventy-seven chance, but it happened.

Three weeks later, she was dead.

That's what Jill and Dawn had in common: Both women decided to have a procedure that ended up killing one twin.

But how did the killer know that?

A few of the hospital staff would know about Jill and Dawn—Evers in pathology, Linda Reese in labs, his colleagues on the morbidity and mortality board, and Susan the sonogram tech. He could look into it, but he already knew them all, and couldn't believe any of them capable of cold-blooded murder. Susan wouldn't even swat a fly. She caught them in Dixie cups and let them out a window.

Matt found himself standing at his file safe, fingering the steel bar and padlock that kept all patient charts sealed away whenever he wasn't in the office. To get at the charts, the killer would have to break into both his office and the file. Not impossible, but not easy, either.

What if the women had talked about their tragedies? In Jill's case there had been three weeks between the miscarriage and her murder. Time for word to spread fairly far, but Dawn had learned only two days ago that one of her twins was fatally deformed. Not much time for word to get out, even if she had talked freely about it. Knowing Dawn, he doubted she'd tell anyone but her husband something so very private and agonizing. Could the killer have overheard them discussing it? He'd almost have to have bugged their car or house. But why would he know in advance to do that?

The only way a bug made sense was if the killer had planted it in here.

A chill ran up Matt's spine. Springing up from his chair, he stalked around the office, checking under his lampshades, beneath his desk. Unscrewing the mouthpiece of his phone, he stared at the wires and microchips. Damn it, he probably wouldn't know a listening device if he saw one. Maybe he should have Virgil come in and sweep the place.

Was it paranoid to think someone would bug his office?

No. There were people so opposed to abortions they would shoot the doctors who performed them. Maybe someone that fanatical would kill mothers, too—or instead.

If I were going to plant a bug in here, he thought, where

would I do it? He looked around again, trying to put himself into the mind of the killer. The intercom on his desk drew his gaze. Cloth mesh covered its small speaker. Taking his Swiss Army knife from his desk drawer, he unscrewed the plastic plate that held the speaker cloth in place. It popped out easily in his hand, exposing the cone of the intercom speaker. Next to the cone was a cylinder about the size of four stacked quarters. The top was covered in fine metallic mesh. Matt's heart began to pound. The intercom had a microphone pickup, on the other side of the box from the speaker, and this wasn't it. This was a second mike.

This was a bug.

Matt stared at it, furious. An image came to him, of someone in a windowless van, hunched over an electronic console, wearing earphones. A vicious killer, listening as he talked with his patients, judging Jill and Dawn as they wrestled with their fears, then condemning them to death.

Butcher!

Matt resisted the impulse to snatch the bug from the intercom. There might be fingerprints on it. He should leave it where it was and call Virgil, right away.

As he reached for his phone, it rang. He snatched it up. "Yes," he said impatiently.

"Matthew?"

Lissa. "Hi," he said. For the life of him, he could think of nothing else to say. He had to call Virgil, tell him to get over here.

"I'm glad I caught you before you left," Lissa said. "Can you pick up a six-pack of Bud Light on your way over?"

With an effort, he changed mental gears. What was she talking about?

"After you called," she said, "I checked the fridge. I thought I had plenty, but—"

"Wait a minute. After I called?"

"Uh . . . yes. Matt, what is *wrong* with you? You're acting so strange today."

"When did I call?"

"This afternoon," she said with exaggerated patience. "You said you still weren't up to French tonight but maybe we could have burgers on the back patio."

Matt felt an icy rush in his veins. He stared at the exposed bug in the intercom.

"Are you going to say it wasn't you? C'mon, Matt. I know your voice when I hear it—"

"Lissa, listen to me. I want you to hang up now and call the police. Tell them you saw a prowler outside your house. Then get out of there—right away."

"Matthew—"

"Get over to the campus—the library. I'll meet you there later and explain everything. Please, just do as I say."

"All right." She said it quietly, but he could hear the fear in her voice, and was glad for it.

"Call the police, as soon as I hang up."

"Yes."

He banged the phone down and ran out of his office, down four flights of stairs to the hospital parking lot, Lissa's words circling wildly in his brain: *I know your voice when I hear it.*

As he sped from the lot, he picked up his car phone and pounded 911. The staticky silence on the other end of the line stretched and stretched until he realized it was not the pause before the ring. He tried again with the same result. A cold shock ran through him. Someone had disabled his phone. Not someone, the killer. He gave a terrified curse. Should he pull over at a pay phone? No, Lissa had promised she'd call the police, and he had to get there as fast as he could—now it was even more important.

As he careened around the last corner and braked in front of her house, dusk was falling. Cicadas hummed in the oaks along Decatur Road, and the smell of jasmine hung in the heavy air.

There were no police cars out front.

His stomach lurched with fear. Maybe she just hadn't taken him seriously, and she was in there and the killer hadn't shown up yet. *Please, God. She has to be all right.* A light was on in her bedroom window upstairs, and her car was still in the garage.

Matt got out and hurried up the walk. The front door was locked. He dug his key from his pocket, nearly dropping it in his haste. Inside, the foyer was warm and still. The urge to cry out her name stuck in his throat. If the killer *was* here, it might panic him.

Matt peered up the steps, filled with dread. Motes of dust tumbled lazily in the spill of light at the top of the stairs. If she was up there, she was keeping utterly quiet.

He made a quick, silent circuit of the downstairs— *empty*—pausing in the kitchen to ease a drawer open and remove the biggest knife, a Sabatier. An image flashed into his mind, of her using it to chop a Vidalia onion for the salad she was making for his birthday dinner last month. She loved Vidalias, kept a string fresh all summer by knotting them into old pantyhose and slinging them from the rafters in the cool of her basement. Watching her chop the onion, he'd asked her if it wouldn't be easier if he just licked her legs. The memory of her laugh came to him, made precious by his terror for her, and he choked back a groan.

Gripping the knife in one hand, he crept upstairs.

She lay on her bed, her wrists handcuffed out to either side of the brass headboard. Her face was white with fear. Beside her on the bed sat a man who looked just like him. He was holding a long blade to her throat.

"Jesus Christ," Matt breathed.

"I see you like knives too," his twin said. "Put it on the floor."

He sounds like me on the dictaphone, Matt thought in a distant part of his mind. He was so terrified he could barely breathe, and yet, God help him, fascinated. *He looks just like me.*

"The floor. Now."

Seeing the knife tighten against Lissa's throat, Matt dropped the Sabatier. A feeling of unreality gripped him. How could a man with his face even imagine threatening Lissa? "Are you all right?" he asked her.

"Yes." Despite the fear in her face, her voice was amazingly calm. "The line went dead right after you called. When I opened the front door, he was there. I . . . I thought he was you, that it was some joke. . . ." She swallowed, her throat lifting the blade slightly.

"It's all right," Matt said. "Everything's going to be all right." But he knew, looking into his twin's face, that it would not be all right. His face, too, but a monster hid behind it, a man who had butchered three people. *My brother.*

His double stared back at him. "I must admit, I'm amazed, too. Seeing you up close, at last. . . ."

"Let her go," Matt said.

"I don't think so. I've got some things to say to you, and I want you to stay focused."

"She hasn't done any—"

"Shut up!"

The sudden fury in his voice filled Matt with renewed terror for Lissa. Was that the same knife that had plunged into Dawn, over and over, eighteen times? Dear God, he had to do something. But what? *Just keep him calm.* "What . . . what is your name?"

His twin gave him a cold smile. "The curiosity bites at last. Or have you felt it before, when you were a kid? Did you suspect?"

"Why would I?" Matt said bitterly. "I knew nothing." But he knew what his brother meant. Dreams of another shape pressed against his back and side, that hollow feeling in the pit of his stomach every time he found two fetuses on a woman's sonogram. The peculiar sense of loss sometimes when he looked in a mirror.

But I knew it couldn't be true. I knew who I was.

Matt felt a huge, sudden fury at his parents.

"My name is Adam," his twin said, "because I came out first. Do you want my last name, too, or would you rather have *our* last name, the real one?"

They *aren't* my parents, Matt thought, his mind spinning. I'm adopted, and they never told me. Why? I would have loved them anyway. Grief welled up through his anger, half choking him.

"Our name is Chase," Adam said. "I'm only guessing, but the Girards probably didn't tell you you were adopted because they knew your mother—our mother—was a whore and a thief."

Whore. Thief. The words hit him like blows. He wanted to raise his hands, fend them off. Reaching behind him, he found the doorpost and steadied himself.

Adam studied him with a coldly voyeuristic expression. "You think they should have told you, and maybe it *wouldn't* have mattered—much. After all, they were *good* to you. Not like Buddy and Louise Givens." Adam's eyes turned smoky with hate. "Buddy and Louise did it for the money. Six foster kids, every month, a couple of hundred bucks apiece from the state, they didn't have to work. But that didn't make them love any of us. Lou-e-e-e-ese told me about my real mother as soon as I was old enough to be hurt by it. Buddy—isn't that great? *Buddy*—threw it up to me every time he lost his temper, in case his fists weren't enough. How my mother was a slut, and how kind he and his wife were to take me in, and how I'd better be grateful or they'd throw me out again."

Lissa was looking at Adam now, a new horror in her eyes.

"Christ," Matt whispered.

"Yes. And meanwhile, you had parents, your own blood, because the truth isn't what's real, it's what you believe. They loved you like their own, and never told you, never put that little sting of doubt into you. They gave you everything you needed. What a good life you've had."

Matt felt a choking pain in his throat. "They should have told me. If I'd known about you—"

"That they *didn't* know. Dear old Mom—her name was Sheila—sold us separately to a baby broker. More money that way."

"Stop it, God damn you, STOP IT!"

Adam glared back. "Hurts, doesn't it?"

"My mother . . . Edna Girard . . . if she adopted me, her friends would have known, someone would have told me. . . ."

Adam looked down at Lissa. "He sees me sitting here and he still can't believe it. Is he dumb or what?"

"I AM NOT DUMB!" Matt shouted. Tears of fury pressed at his eyes.

Adam gave him a startled look. "Take it easy. Edna *was* pregnant, but not with you. They went on a trip out West. She miscarried in a Nevada motel one night. Grief made them a little crazy, I guess. She and Hugh had been sending money to an orphanage out there. They got the idea of taking one of those babies back with them. You were puny enough at five weeks that when she got back home, no one knew you weren't hers. By the way, you need to make a five-week adjustment in your birthday—"

"Stop it," Lissa whispered. "Please. Can't you see how you're hurting him?"

"Yes, I see." Adam's voice was soft, but not with sympathy.

Why does he hate me? Matt wondered.

"Because, while you had it soft, I've had a lifetime of hurting," Adam said, as if reading his mind. "Buddy and Louise didn't know you existed, or they'd have used it to hurt me. But I knew. I *knew*. I kept dreaming it. One time I told Louise, and she just laughed. Buddy said, 'One of you is too much, kid.' "

"How did you find out?" Lissa asked. Matt saw that she was trying to make contact with Adam, force him to think of her as a person instead of a way to hurt his brother. *Good*, he thought. *But be careful. He only looks like me.*

Adam glanced at her, then back at Matt. "I found out," he said, "by devoting my life to it. I ran away from Buddy and Louise at fifteen. Lived on the streets for a while. Got work with an old P.I., dull stuff like stakeouts he was too lazy to do. He was drunk half the time, but he never hit me and he knew a lot of things."

"Like bugging an office."

Adam's mouth quirked. "By twenty-three I was his partner. It took me seven years to find *Mom.*" The ugly emphasis he gave the word sent a chill up Matt's spine.

Adam glanced down at Lissa again. "Sheila liked rough trade," he said softly. "Your boyfriend and I were probably conceived while she lay handcuffed to a bed, just like you are now—"

"Shut your mouth." The words pushed their own way out, startling Matt, as if someone else had said them. *I am someone else*, he thought. *Now.*

Looking at him again, Adam said, "After Mom, it took another five years to track you down. And that about brings us up-to-date."

"Why did you kill Jill and Dawn?" Matt asked.

Adam shook his head. "You *are* stupid, aren't you."

"They were nothing like . . . our mother."

Adam closed his eyes for just a second, and his teeth bared in a rictus. "They split up their babies, before they could even be born."

Matt saw Lissa shudder. *I have to save her.* "We're brothers," he said. *"More* than brothers. How can you do this?"

Adam gave a harsh laugh. "We should have been more. But it didn't happen, Matt old boy, and this did. While I was going through hell, you were living in heaven. You had love, safety, every advantage, while I was wondering when the next blow would come. Do you know what it is to be constantly measuring the distance from a big man's shoulder to your face? Can you feel a flinch hiding permanently in the skin of your eyes and forehead? Did your father ever even *spank* you?"

"Who *was* our father?"

"I don't know who mine was, but Hugh Girard was yours. Maybe you want to revoke that title now, but he was. OK, they lied to you, but think: You never had to brood about being adopted. You never had to wonder, why did my mother give me up? You got the brass ring, and I got the shaft."

Matt's earlier fury returned. "The brass ring? You think you know me, but you don't. Can you read?"

"What's that got to do with anything?"

"I couldn't read. My . . . parents never said I was stupid. They didn't have to. How many grades did *you* have to repeat in school? Did kids laugh when you tried to read out loud in class? Did 'w' look like 'v' to you? Could you tell 'p' from 'q'? I couldn't."

Adam gave a contemptuous grunt. "Am I supposed to feel sorry for you?"

"You should. You probably caused it."

Adam frowned. "What the hell are you talking about?"

"You haven't seen eight-month twins on a sonogram. Hell, even at five months, it's very tight in there. Sometimes the deformities it causes are physical, a club foot, a bent spine. Sometimes they're mental." Matt felt the fury rising in him, threatening to explode out of control. He had the fleeting thought that he must rein himself in, but he could not. "You crowded me, you bastard. *That's* why I couldn't read. Everyone laughed at me. You think I have a lot, but you have no idea how I had to fight for it—thanks to you. And now you come here and kill three innocent people in their beds and try to frame me by standing under their porch lights on your way out. You hate me, and I never did anything to you. It was you who hurt me. And now look at you, you spineless bastard, holding a knife to another innocent throat. You think I'm your enemy, at least have the guts to face me."

Adam's face had gone pale. "You want to face me?" He snatched a key from his pocket and unlocked one of Lissa's wrists. As she started to move, he pressed the blade against her throat and she froze again. "Get over here," he said.

Matt started forward.

"*Slowly.* Do exactly what I say, or I cut her. You want to face me, you'll get your chance. Pick up that cuff and lock one end on your right wrist."

Matt did it.

"Now lock the other end here." Adam held out his left arm. Matt started to put the cuff on, then froze, staring. A long white scar marred Adam's right forearm. A scar just like the one on his own left forearm, in exactly the same place, along the outside of the arm.

"That's right," Adam said softly. "We were joined at the arm."

"No," Matt said. "I cut it on some glass . . ."

"Edna had to tell you something. She didn't know how you got it either. But I saw it in the hospital records. We were Siamese twins and they separated us at birth. Oh boy, did they separate us."

Matt remembered the dream, his arm locked to the arm of the other, trying to turn and to him, but never able to.

"And now we're going to be joined again," Adam said. "Put the cuff on me."

"What—?"

"Do it or I'll cut her throat right now."

Matt snapped the other cuff shut over Adam's wrist. Adam rose from the bed, lifting the knife from Lissa's throat and holding it in front of him. "Take my wrist," he commanded.

Matt took it.

Adam's mouth thinned in a cold smile. "Let's see how tough you are. Think you can hold the knife off yourself? I know you're a baby doctor and never got in a street fight in your rich, pampered life. And, gee, it's your left hand and we're right-handed, but if nature thought it was fair to start us out this way, then who are we to change it at the end—" Adam lunged with the knife.

Matt gripped his wrist with desperate strength, stopping the blade inches from his throat. Pushing it back, he gave

Adam's wrist a sharp twist. Adam grimaced, but hung on to the knife. Matt tightened his grip, squeezing the bones of his brother's wrist against each other. A harsh groan leaked from between Adam's clenched teeth. He threw a hip, but Matt turned away and most of the force was lost. With a fierce effort, he twisted Adam's wrist back the other way. His brother gasped; Matt threw his weight forward, bulling Adam back against the wall by the door. Matt banged the knife handle against the oak doorpost, once, twice, and the knife popped from Adam's weakened grip and clattered to the floor. In a fury, Matt used the lock on their other wrists, to swing Adam away from him. In the same movement, he bent and scooped up the knife in his left hand.

Regaining his footing, Adam tried to pull away, his eyes full of fear now. Matt concentrated on keeping his feet as Adam jerked forward. Unable to pull away, Adam tried to kick him. Matt chopped down with the knife, slicing at Adam's knee, feeling a ligament pop as Adam screamed and fell to the floor, writhing in pain. Matt chopped again, severing the Achilles tendon, drawing another scream. Then he straddled Adam, sitting on his chest. As his brother's face turned toward him, he pushed the blade under his chin. Rage filled him. He thought of Jill, of Dawn and Jerry, of what Adam had meant to do to Lissa.

"Matt, don't." Lissa's voice, penetrating the red fog of his outrage. But he did not pull the knife away. This man was a murderous psychopath, who deserved to die. . . .

And why is he a psychopath? Might I have had something to do with that?

The face above the blade swam into focus again, a mirror image of his own face. Neurobiologists had identified low cortical arousal and anomalous brain wave patterns in psychopaths. The deficits were thought to be the result of neurologic damage during pregnancy. Only a theory, but what if it was right?

Thirty-five years ago, Matt thought, this man and I were in a very tight spot together. And there was something wrong with both of us. I couldn't distinguish words. What if Adam can't tell right from wrong? Is that what I did to him?

"You are going to jail," Matt said. "If they don't execute you."

Adam groaned. "You beat me. I don't believe it. How did you do that?"

"I'm not right-handed," Matt said.

Adam stared at him as if he could not comprehend it. "But we're twins."

"If you were a baby doctor, you'd know that twenty-five percent of twins are opposite-handed."

Adam groaned again, his face white with pain, then gave a bleak laugh. "Something tells me getting up and running out of here is not an option. Will I ever walk again, Doc?"

"Not without surgery."

"So. Will you visit me in jail?"

Matt looked into the face he had never been able to see in his dreams. The face he had longed all his life to see, not in a mirror but in the flesh.

"Yes," he said.

Richard Lee Byers used to be a clinician and administrator in an emergency psychiatric treatment facility. Now he writes and teaches writing. He has novels like *Dead Time, Dark Fortune, The Vampire's Apprentice,* and *Deathward,* and loads of short stories to his credit. Look for his most recent, *Netherworld* and *Caravan of Shadows.* The following reflects his past exposure to psychiatric patients (no, not *in* the wards . . . around them). . . .

BAD TOUCH

Richard Lee Byers

The green leather sofa felt hard as concrete. Paula could almost believe that, like a prisoner's seat in an interrogation cell, it had been designed to be uncomfortable. She squirmed.

Behind his fruitwood desk, Dr. Milan smiled sympathetically. The expression made his youthful face even more handsome, while the afternoon sun, filtered through venetian blinds, kindled the silver highlights in his shock of raven hair. "Would you rather lie down today?" he asked.

"Maybe." She swung her legs up, stretched out. And it was better. Not because the couch felt any softer, but because she was no longer looking at him.

"It's obvious something's troubling you," he said. "Why don't we talk about it."

I don't want to, she thought, but that wasn't true. The problem was that she was afraid to, even with Dr. Milan. Especially with Dr. Milan. If he turned against her, she wouldn't be able to bear it. She drew a deep breath, catching a whiff of the cherry pipe tobacco the psychiatrist smoked between patients, and said, "I went to see my father."

Paula drove past the white frame house three times before she worked up the nerve to stop. Her mouth dry, she got out of her primer-spotted Chevette, opened the squeaky gate in the picket fence, and trudged up the walk, past the rusty swing set and the pine tree.

From the outside, the house looked dark. Maybe Dad wasn't home. Maybe she'd have to go away with nothing said, nothing changed. Maybe that would be for the best. But when she stepped onto the stoop, she heard a sitcom laugh track jangling on the other side of the door.

Her first impulse was to ring the bell. But she didn't want to ask Dad's permission to enter. She sensed that doing so would make it harder to speak. Fingers trembling, she fumbled with the old brass key that she'd never bothered to remove from her ring.

She found her father sprawled in the shabby recliner, the TV screen framed between his pasty, callused feet. His socks, steel-toed work shoes, and four crumpled Busch beer cans lay discarded on the floor. He hadn't changed much since the last time she'd seen him, at Mom's funeral two years ago, or since she'd started grade school for that matter. Perhaps his belly had bloated a little bigger, and his brown hair had thinned, but otherwise, ensconced in his favorite chair, he looked as he had nearly every night of her childhood. The realization made her feel scared, angry, and, to her dismay, tender, all at the same time.

She'd crept in so quietly that for a moment, he didn't sense her presence. Then his head snapped around. His mouth fell open, exposing crooked teeth. "Paula! Well, damn. He got up, hesitated, then stretched out his arms. On TV, the nanny made a nasal quip.

Paula cringed. "Don't touch me!"

Dad frowned. Looked hurt. Guilt wriggled inside her chest, and she did her best to quash it. "What's the matter," he asked, "you don't like hugs anymore? Okay, whatever. What *do* you want? Money?"

The first time she tried to answer, nothing came out. She swallowed, then said, "I need to confront you. It's the only way I can get over it."

Dr. Milan said, "I told you that you'd have to confront him *eventually*. When you were ready. And I didn't necessarily mean face-to-face."

Paula tried to judge whether he was angry. Decided to her relief that the hint of stress in his voice was only concern. "I know. But the more we discovered, the angrier I got. It was eating me up, and I needed to let it out."

"I can understand that," said Dr. Milan. "And as long as you're satisfied with the way it worked out, then everything's all right."

She squinched her eyes to hold back tears.

Dad frowned. "I don't get you."

"You should," Paula replied. She tried to say it flat out, but once again, the words jammed in her throat. She realized that she needed to ease into it. "I went back into therapy. With a new psychiatrist. Someone the Women's Center recommended."

Dad rolled his eyes. "Great. Hundredth time's the charm, right?"

His scorn for her struggle to get well rankled. "Dr. Milan is helping me, Daddy. Dad. He explained that my symptoms, the ODs and all the rest of it, are characteristic of patients with a certain kind of repressed memory. And he used hypnosis to bring mine out. So I know now." Her stomach churned. For a second, she was afraid that she was going to throw up. "I remember you molesting me."

His jaw dropped. "What? You mean sex?"

"Yes." Now that she'd finally gotten it out, she noticed her voice was louder. Stronger.

"Is this supposed to be a joke?" Shaking, he flopped down on the couch.

"No. The first time, you were giving me a bath. I was three, and had my rubber Big Bird in the tub. You were wearing a red T-shirt, and smelled like beer. You pushed your finger inside me."

"Like hell!"

"Two years later, you made me suck you. When I was eight, we had intercourse. We used to shove the condoms down deep in the trash to make sure Mom wouldn't see them." As she spoke, it all came back, the times he'd bitten her, crushed her beneath his sweaty, panting bulk, rammed himself inside when she was dry. And, worse, the occasions when his tongue teasing her nipple, his deep, fast thrusts, had forced her to a shameful climax. For an instant, she imagined him admitting it all gleefully, grabbing her, pawing her, tearing off her clothes. His touch paralyzed her, and he tumbled her unresisting to the floor.

Dad said, "Listen to me. It never happened. How could it? I mean, where was your mother?"

"I just told you, we hid it from her. From everybody."

"Why didn't you tell her?"

"Because you said that if anybody found out, the police would put us both in jail. Because you were my daddy, and I wanted to please you!"

Dad shook his head, raked thick fingers through his hair. "Well, tell me this. If I was a pervert, and had a good thing going, why did I ever *stop* molesting you?"

"Maybe after I hit thirteen, you were afraid you wouldn't be able to keep me quiet anymore. Or maybe I'd just gotten too old for you, and you found some other, younger child."

Dad stood up. Sweat beaded his forehead. "I ought to throw you out of here. How can you believe this crap? If it was real, why would you just forget about it?"

"Because that was the only way my mind could deal with the trauma."

Dad snorted. "Then why didn't you forget all the other lousy things you've gone through? You do remember Steve beating you, right? Miscarrying my grandson? The two weeks in detox?"

"All that happened when I was older. Better able to cope. And none of it was as bad as being hurt by my own father."

Dad glanced around the room. Probably checking to see if he'd left an unfinished beer within reach. "You ever think these so-called memories pop out when you're in a trance because your shrink is putting them in your head?"

"Bullshit!" Paula shouted, and was thrilled when he flinched. "I remember the pain the first time you shoved your cock into my ass. The blood on the toilet paper for a week afterward. Picking your pubic hairs out of my mouth. I remember *every detail*, as clearly as I do the drive over here, and you can't make me doubt any of it. I'm not your helpless victim anymore!"

"I'm impressed," said Dr. Milan. "You were very assertive."

"I just remembered what you taught me." He'd told her that no matter how crazy her situation seemed, there was nothing freakish or even unusual about her. He'd treated *scores* of patients who'd suffered abuse, then forgotten all about it. Psychiatrists around the world had treated tens of *thousands.*

"Still, he's your father. It took courage to keep him from shaking your faith in the work we've done. I'm proud of you."

For a moment, she felt a glow, even though she was sure he wouldn't be proud of what had happened next.

"I give up," Dad growled. "If this quack—"

"He's not a quack! He's my friend. The only person who's ever helped me."

"You say that about all of them at first. He is a quack. But obviously he's got you too brainwashed to listen to common sense. So, was that all you wanted to tell me? Are we done?"

"No." She realized that she didn't feel timid or uncertain anymore, just furious. The purity of the emotion was exhilarating. "I want you to talk about it."

"Jesus Christ."

"Do you know how I've suffered? Throwing tantrums and driving everyone away. Getting involved with one abusive man after another. Waking up every morning hating myself without even understanding why. Don't you think I at least deserve an explanation of why my life had to be this way? Was it because you were drunk all the time? Wouldn't Mom give you sex, was that it?"

Dad sighed. "I can see how it makes you feel better to have somebody to blame all the bad luck and dumb decisions on. But I swear to God, kid, you're barking up the wrong tree."

Her fists clenched. Her nails dug into her palms. "God damn you! It's not like there are any witnesses, so why can't you just be honest? Admit you did it. Say you knew I never wanted it, and you're sorry."

"I won't admit to bullshit. And I don't want to hear any more of it. Get out." He reached to take her by the arm.

She screamed and shoved him away. He staggered backward, arms windmilling, and an oval rug shot out from under his feet. When he fell, the back of his head cracked against the corner of the TV cabinet, and then he thudded down on the hardwood floor.

He isn't moving, Paula thought. I should call 911. Instead she picked up a heavy glass ashtray, knelt beside him, and pounded until the coppery odor of blood smothered the smell of beer.

"At first," Paula said, "it was like I was standing outside myself, watching. But then it started to feel good. At the end, I was laughing."

"My God," said Dr. Milan. She sneaked a peek at him. His face was gray, like a dusty cobweb. "Then what happened?"

"My arm got tired, I saw he was dead, and I sort of switched over to automatic pilot. I drove back to Dayton, took a shower, and put on fresh clothes. Packed my overnight bag, and sat down in the living room. After a while, I realized I was waiting for the police to come. But they never did. I don't think they're going to, unless you call them."

Dr. Milan stared down, at his hands closing and opening atop his blotter. "I won't," he said at last. "How can I? I have an obligation to hold what you tell me in confidence. Besides, what happened wasn't your fault."

The knot in her chest loosened. "Really?"

"Really. On one level, it was an accident." As he spoke, his conviction seeped into her. "In a deeper sense, your father finally reaped some of the misery he'd sown. He killed himself."

"Thank you," she said. "I knew I couldn't keep it from you, but I was so afraid you were going to think that I was horrible. That would have been even worse than going to jail."

"Your father was the horrible one. I mean, I know he was ill. But he wasn't my patient, you are. I'm supposed to be on your side, and in the context of your life, he was a monster. You *remember* that, right? We *proved* it. When he tried to put his hand on you, after you'd warned him not to, you had every right to lash out, and then your thirty years of pent-up rage just took control. Nobody could have prevented it. We have to keep that in mind."

She smiled. "You're worried I'm going to torture myself with guilt, aren't you?"

"Yes. How do you feel?" Always that question.

"I don't know. Not guilty anymore, because like you said, he had it coming. I guess okay." In fact, now that Dr. Milan had absolved her, she felt as if she were floating. But beneath the relief lay another emotion, a familiar emptiness waiting to suck her down.

As always, Dr. Milan sensed the shift in her mood. "Okay but what?"

"I don't know. Except . . . when we started this, it was hard. Scary. But exciting, too, because I thought I was finally getting myself together. The memories and the anger hurt, but they were also kind of a rush. Does that make sense?"

"It was thrilling to recover the buried part of yourself."

"Partly that. Only, okay. So now I have. Gotten all the satisfaction from Daddy that I ever can. And it's dawning on me that I'm not really any different. My *life* isn't any different. I still don't have any friends except for you." And even he didn't keep her from being lonely. She only got to see him for two hours a week. Someday she'd lose her current job the way she had the others, or the insurance it provided would run out, and then she wouldn't see him at all. At that moment, she resented it bitterly, and sobbed.

Dr. Milan jumped up, grabbed a tissue dispenser, and hurried around the desk. "Go ahead and cry," he said. "Let it out." He squatted beside her and put his hand on her shoulder.

The touch brought a flash of impressions. Lying on this same couch but with her eyes closed in trance. The hypnotic induction tape droning away. Fingers unbuckling her belt, unsnapping her jeans, and slowly pulling down the zipper.

The image flew apart, leaving nothing behind but the sense that she'd forgotten something. The feeling only bothered her a little, because she was sure that she'd remember in time. After all, Dr. Milan had taught her how.

Tom Monteleone is the author of nearly a hundred short stories and twenty or so novels. He's also an outspoken columnist and a specialty publisher under his Borderlands Press imprint. Long one of the most colorful figures in the horror/dark fantasy genre, he recently broke into the mainstream with his own genre: the religious thriller. His first entry was the acclaimed and gripping *Blood of the Lamb*. Look for his latest, *The Resurrectionist.*

Tom was almost apologetic for what he called the "E.C. ending" of his story, but said he couldn't resist. Fine with me. Every so often I crave an E.C. ending. ●

Get It Out

Thomas F. Monteleone

What do you mean—*get it out?*" asked Doctor Samuel Jonas.

Minutes before, he had been sitting in his den on a Sunday afternoon waiting for the pregame show to wrap up so the NFL could begin its latest installment. He had just settled into his Barcalounger when the phone rang and a raspy, twangy voice asked: "Ya Dr. Jonas. Live down on Sherwood?"

"Yes, I'm Doctor Jonas," said Sam. "What can I do for you."

"Oh, I think y'gonna help me." The voice was hard, confident, subtly aggressive. There was something about it that Sam instantly disliked.

"What is the nature of your problem," Sam asked as politely as possible. He would give the man the benefit of the doubt.

"Well, now, I think the right question should be what's *your* problem—and the answer is *me.*"

Sam ran a hand through his thinning hair. He was giving in to a weird, precognitive sense of dread.

This voice on the line was trouble. Serious trouble.

"Look, what do you want with me? Who are you?"

A low-register chuckle, then: "Ya find out soon enough."

Sam wanted to hang up and call John Costello down at the station house, but an odd, intuitive feeling snagged his resolve like a miscast fishing lure. "Listen," he said, trying to sound bothered and authoritative. "I asked you: what is it you want?"

"First, I want ya to have a little talk with somebody . . ."

Sam's hand gripped the receiver more tightly. Before he heard his daughter's voice, he'd somehow *known* he would.

"Daddy . . ." Her voice was soft, and very weak.

Sam knew he couldn't let her know he was getting crazy. He forced himself to sound utterly calm.

"Kelly, are you okay, sweetheart?"

"Daddy, just . . . just do whatever he wants . . ." She spoke carefully, shakily. She'd been sobbing and he could almost feel the hitched-up assault of her breathing. "Daddy, please . . ."

"Just take it easy, baby. I won't let anything happen to you," he said softly into the phone. His stomach was being corkscrewed right out of him. Blood hammered at his temples so hard, he thought he might pass out.

"Don't ya worry none about her, Doc." It was the Voice again. All full of that Southern, greasy, buddy-buddy sarcasm. "I got her where ain't *nobody* gonna find her—till ya get this goddamned thing out. Ya gotta get it *out*, ya hear?"

Suddenly his thoughts were cycloning around him, broken pieces, making no sense. He couldn't think of anything but Kelly. Couldn't lose her. Not now. Not ever. Especially after Gwen . . . no goddamned way.

A burst of anger gave him the focus he needed. Hanging on to it, he forced out the words evenly. "Don't you dare do anything to her," he said.

"Just get this fuckin' thing *out*."

"What do you mean—get it out? Get *what* out?"

The Voice paused. In that moment of silence Sam strained to hear any trace of sound that would tell him Kelly was okay, or a clue to their location. He remembered seeing some movie where they taped a phone conversation and used a computer to analyze the background noise around the bad guy's pay phone. Any noise might be an important clue.

But this line was as quiet as the grave.

Then that horrible voice again. "Don't *know* what it is, but I reckon ya can take care of it—bein' a doctor."

"Listen!" Sam tried to keep the panic out of his voice. "I don't know what you're talking about. You've got to—"

"Shut up!" said the Voice. "Ya'll see what I'm talkin' about when I get there."

The entire universe caught on its tracks for an instant. Then Sam felt his breath in his chest again. "You're coming *here?*" he asked in a voice so weak it embarrassed him.

"Yeah, you're the closest doc, and I gotta get it out."

"Listen, I'm just a GP, a general prac—"

"And one more thing . . ." (only it sounded more like *thang*). "Don't call nobody. I see any cops or friends or anybody 'round your place, y'ain't never gonna see this pretty little girl you got never again. Ain't *nobody* never see her again."

"Please . . ." said Sam. He'd closed his eyes tightly, was softly crying. "Please . . ."

Again that low-register chuckle. "See ya, Doc."

Click.

Then the idiot hum of a dial tone.

He wasn't sure how long he sat there with the phone off-cradle; he'd been in some other dimension, staring into a place where you saw nothing, heard nothing. Sam looked up at the TV, where the Steelers were celebrating a long aerial strike into the Bills' end zone, then at his watch.

Kelly.

He could see her image interfaced with every thought. The idea of losing her became an absence, a black hole that absorbed everything else. He couldn't live through anything like that. He was already all used up. No more. Jesus Christ, no more . . .

Sam shook his head, remembering how his wife kept trying to console him by explaining away the breast cancer as "God's will," and part of "His wonderful plan for us all," and a host of other religious platitudes that only served to infuriate him. It had always amazed him how devout people so easily refused to question the illogic of a god that would actually "plan" the drive-by shooting deaths of five-year-old children and the elusive success of serial killers.

He had to wake up! Stop sitting there waiting for "Grendel" to show up at his fucking door. He had to think clearly and make some decisions.

Right away.

That business about the cops—that was something they always said, wasn't it? How could they know?

No way. No way they could know, right?

Still, he knew, deep down where the flat slab of hard logic lay buried like the Rosetta stone to all our emotional mysteries, everything glistened with the wet, irrational fear of total loss. Logical thinking would not be enough now.

But who would know if he called John?

No one. Call him.

The Monster. The Get-It-Out Man. He'll know.

Get it out.

Get *what* out? What the hell was he talking about? For *what* was the Monster coming to his little Victorian on Sherwood Avenue?

Kelly.

He had to stop it. The runaway emotional bursts threatened to render him helpless.

How much time did he have? From where was the guy coming. How long would it take to get here? How did he know him? How—?

Without thinking, he picked up the phone, dialed a familiar number.

"Township police. John Costello . . ." said his friend's voice after only one ring. Sam could just see him sitting back in the desk swivel chair, reading one of those comic books he loved so much.

"John, I've got some trouble down here . . ."

"Sam? That you?"

"Yeah, listen, I might not have much time! I don't know what to do . . ."

"Sam, just take it easy and tell me what's going on, okay?"

Sam exhaled slowly, drew in a fresh breath, and let the short dirty tale spill out of him like old motor oil. When he finished he was sobbing again. Tears burned his eyes. ". . . John, I can't go through this again. Not her. Not Kelly. What the fuck's going on, here? Jesus, we've got to do something . . . !"

"All right, all right," said his friend. "Just take it easy, okay? Are you near a window? Station yourself so you can see when anybody might be on the way up the drive. This guy sounds smart, so I don't want to try anything just yet. But I'll check in with the state and federal boys for advice. This is kidnapping so everybody'll get involved."

"John, if he sees any cops, he said—"

"I know what he said," said John Costello. "Don't worry, those guys're pros. They'll know what to do. I'll call you every half an hour or so, like I'm some of your patients calling you. You can give me prescriptions and stuff, then I'll ask you yes/no stuff. You tell the guy when he gets there that your nurse usually arrives sometime in the afternoon to set up the office for Monday mornings, you got that?"

Sam nodded, then remembered to speak into the receiver. "Yes, I've got it."

"It's important, Sam. He's got to know somebody will eventually be there . . . and you've got to be convincing."

"All right . . . but why?"

"Just in case we find Kelly, it might be a good idea to have a trained officer getting in there with you," said John Costello. "Just listen to me, Sam. We'll do our best."

Sam smiled a little. "I know that, John . . ."

"All right. Pull yourself together. I'll be staying in touch, telling you what's going on in the background, whatever we find out about this guy. You said Kelly was in town at the library?"

He shook his head, willed away any more tears. "Yeah . . ."

"Okay, that's where we'll start asking around. Gotta get moving on this. Make sure you answer the phone."

"John, wait a minute . . . Suppose he cuts the line?"

John Costello didn't answer right away, then: "I don't know . . . we'll worry about that if it happens."

"Because I have a portable cellular in my car and—"

"Go get it." said Costello. "Keep it handy."

Sam smiled a little, gave his friend the car phone number, then hung up. He ran as fast as he could through the back door to the garage, and lugged the portable unit into his office. It was just a precaution, but why not? Then, just as he returned to the front parlor and the window that gave the best view of the long driveway, he saw movement through patches of auburn-and-orange foliage down by the fence and the intersection with the state road.

Watching closely, he discerned the shape of someone riding a bicycle up the drive. Slow and leisurely, just as nice as can be. The seconds dragged past as the figure assumed more and more detail. Finally, Sam had the picture of a man in his late thirties with long, thinning hair and a scraggly goatee. He wore a baseball cap, blue-and-green flannel shirt, blue jean jacket, and faded jeans that accentuated his pipe-stem legs. The bicycle he rode looked a little small, and Sam figured it was a safe bet it was stolen.

The guy left it against the big elm by the fence, and ambled slow and bold toward the back door to the mud porch. As he drew ever closer, Sam catalogued a few more details. His wallet was attached to his belt by a chain that ran from waist to pocket. A bag of Red Man chewing tobacco flopped open from a jacket pocket, and a navy anchor tattoo stained his left hand. The baseball hat said: OLD FART.

A knock at the door broke his semitrance and Sam backed away from the parlor window, looked at the mud porch door. What the hell was going on here—this guy kidnaps his daughter and then *knocks* on the door?

Sam panicked for an instant, wondering if he should have armed himself with something, even a kitchen knife or a scalpel. No that was dumb, he told himself. He couldn't do a damn thing to this dickweed till he found out where Kelly was.

Walking up to the door, he opened and looked into the face of his nightmare. Close-up, the guy looked a lot worse. If he was still in his thirties, the years had been running over him with tank treads.

"You must be the doc," he said with a lopsided smile that revealed a set of stained teeth so corrupt some of them had actually turned black.

"I'm Doctor Jonas, yes," said Sam. He looked at the guy for an instant then: "What have you done with Kelly? Please, tell me."

The words burst out of him like lava from a ruptured vent. When he realized how aggressive he sounded, Sam moved back a step, allowing the foul stranger to enter.

"Well, well, now, I unnerstan' how upset y'all might be, Doc, so I'm gonna forgive that, I really am."

"Is she okay?" he said softly. "Just tell me that and you can have anything you want . . ."

The man shouldered past him, walked into the kitchen, and eyed the fixtures like a real estate agent. After poking around and peeking into some of the cabinets, he turned and looked at Sam. " 'Fore we get started, I think I'm gonna need a sang-widge, okay?"

"My daughter . . ." Sam stood across the country kitchen table from the man.

He snapped his fingers. "Oh yeah! Forgot . . . Yeah, Doc, she's just fine. If I get outta here all safe and shit, you'll be seein' her again. Just fine."

"You didn't hurt her? Didn't . . . do anything to her?"

The man laughed? "Ya mean like fuck her? Maybe corn-hole that little sweetie? Nah . . . I didn't do nothin'. No time. Besides I can't even git my pecker hard with what they done me—that's why I'm here. Now how 'bout that sang-widge?"

Sam exhaled slowly. He realized he would need to temporarily put his raging emotions about Kelly on hold, keep them off in some side compartment. This guy was talking crazy stuff, dangerous stuff. Sam was going to need all his wits to deal with this piece of shit. He needed to stay focused.

Nodding silently, Sam turned to the refrigerator and pulled out some pimiento loaf—Kelly's favorite—and some mustard. He slapped a pile of the lunchmeat onto some Branola bread and handed it to the guy on a paper towel.

"Got any beer?"

Sam nodded, returned to the fridge for a Sam Adams. He put it on the table in front of the stranger, said nothing.

"Wooo-ee! The good shit! Yessir, must be nice to be loaded. Drink the good shit, don't have to take no bullstuff from nobody, huh?"

"What can I do for you, Mr. . . . ?"

The man guzzled half the bottle, then looked him in the eye. "*Mister?* Ain't nobody calls me that, Doc."

"What *do* they call you?" Sam asked casually, as he put away the condiments, wiped the countertops with a paper towel.

The man savaged the sandwich with two mouth-filling bites, bulging his cheeks like a baboon. That's when he decided to talk. "Ackshully, mos' people call me 'Deek'. So I guess that makes us Doc and Deek! Or Deek and the Doc!" He chuckled. "Sounds like a TV show, don't it?"

"All right, Deek, can you tell me now, just what it is you want from me?" Sam leaned against the counter, trying to maintain an exterior of calmness, of confidence—even though he knew he was unraveling at the seams.

The man pointed to his hat. "I gotta get—"

The phone rang.

Both of them looked at it like it was a bomb ready to go off.

Sam reached for it and Deek said "Watch it . . . say the wrong thing and you ain't gonna see her again . . ."

Pretending to ignore him, Sam picked up the receiver. "Doctor Jonas . . ."

Sam, it's John. How's it going?!

"Good afternoon, Mrs. Novoa. Yes, I'm fine thank you."

We've got the place surrounded, Sam. He'll never catch on.

"Your prescription is fine. Just be careful that you follow the dosage on the label."

I got you, Sam. You do whatever he wants. I'll call back in about twenty minutes. You tell him the nurse is coming?

"No, ma'am, that'll be fine."

Well don't forget. Oh, yeah, we found a kid at the library says he saw some guy in a baseball hat with Kelly. We're working on where that might get us. We might be able to find her while he's still there with you. Can you stall him?

"Mrs. Novoa, I'm not sure about that. Why don't we stay with the medication for now. You try it and tell me how it's working tomorrow, okay?"

You're doing great, old buddy. Hang in there. We'll be in touch.

"Good-bye, Mrs. Novoa. You're welcome."

Sam hung up the phone, looked at Deek, who had finished the Sam Adams in one final swill. His larynx bobbed obscenely, and Sam wondered why *Kallikaks* like this guy always had such pronounced necks and weak chins. Something in the genes, no doubt.

"What's that shit? Who's callin' you?"

Sam shrugged. "I'm the town doctor. My patients call me when they need help—that's the way it goes."

"Well, just be careful what you says. I'm always on top-a things."

"Oh, I'm sure you are," said Sam. "By the way, that call

reminded me—my nurse comes by on Sunday afternoons to set up the office for Monday mornings."

Deek shook his head. "Not this week she ain't."

"What?"

"Call her and tell her to forget it." Deek leaned back in his chair, balanced it on the back two legs, and let loose a resonant belch.

"I can't," said Sam quickly. "She visits her grandmother on Sundays, then stops in here on her way home."

Deek rocked forward with such speed and agility, it scared Sam. The man moved with jungle cat suppleness, an athlete's grace. In an instant Deek was off the chair and standing several inches from Sam's face. "Well, Doc, lemmie tell ya—ya better hope she's late today, or there's gonna be trouble."

Sam tried to think of something to say, but his thoughts were catching in their sprockets. Deep was a sick, crazy fucker, and he was scaring Sam—plain and simple. He walked toward the door leading from the kitchen to a hallway that led to his offices.

"Where ya goin'?" Deek reached a hand, grabbed him by the upper arm. There was a wiry strength there.

"My office and examining rooms. They're back this way," he said, and forced himself to smile. "You know, you still haven't told me what you want me to do. Something you want me to get out—what is it, a bullet?"

Deek chuckled. "Shit, don' I wish! No, it's somethin' else. Com'on, let's go have a look."

They went into the examining room with a window that looked out on the side of the house, the driveway and the elm tree. Deek sat on the table, removed his hat, and peeled back his long, stringy brown hair. For an instant Sam saw a family of head lice scurry off to denser climes. "Right there," he said pointing with a filthy-nailed index finger. "See that thing?"

"Yes," said Sam as he eyed a pinkish lump of flesh behind Deek's right ear against the occipital plate of his skull. It looked like a boil or a cyst but its almost perfectly square dimensions suggested that it was the scar tissue of some kind of surgery. "What is it?"

Deek chuckled. "Shee-it, Doc. You ain' that stupid, are you? It's what you gotta get *out!*"

"I need to know what it is, first. Do you know where you got it?"

" 'Course I do. What you askin dumb questions for?"

"Help me out, Deek." Sam continued to look at the angry red patch. It appeared to be a foreign object under the skin, but he wanted to hear Deek's side of it.

"The Center done put it in me! Goddamn it!" The venom in his voice sprayed everywhere. The man's body tensed up with anger and suggested the concentrated energy of a snake coiling before a strike.

"What 'Center'?"

Deek turned slowly, looked at him with eyes that were getting to look a little wider, flatter, like some predator slipping into kill mode. "The Delgado Center! Fuckin' state runs it. They got docs there doin' all sorts-a shit to people."

They did indeed. Sam was very familiar with the Delgado facility. It was in fact run by the feds, and was dedicated to basic research on nontherapeutic behavior control methods. The staff kept their findings pretty much to themselves, but Sam had occasionally encountered people who had worked there. From what he'd been able to cobble together over the years, it was a terminus for the *worst* of the human barnacles that society had been able to scrape off its hull. He'd also heard it was not a pleasant place, and that research scientists and medical techs, fearful of losing the bountiful teat of federal grant funding, were always coming up with new and ter-

rifying projects. Projects they had free license to try out on
end-of-the-road characters like Deek here.

Sam touched the inflamed patch. "So they put this in
your head . . . eh, Deek? What do you know about it."

"Nothin'. 'Cept it keeps my dick as soft as a piece-a pisk-
getti!"

"You never get an erection?"

"You mean a hard-on?"

Sam nodded.

"Shit I never even *think* about layin' no pipe!" He chuckled disdainfully.

Looking at the minisurgery, Sam realized he was looking
at a subintegumental implant. His sporadic reading in experi-
mental medicine had familiarized him with the concept if not
the mechanics of such devices.

"In order to fix this thing, before I get it out . . ." he said
in a firm, low voice, "I need to ask you some questions. Do
not get angry with me—it's information I'm going to need, all
right?"

"Jest you go on—I'll decide whether to be gettin' pissed
off or not."

You are such a charmer, Sam thought. Then: "Okay, were
you awake or asleep when they put this in?"

"Asleep. They knocked me colder than a steer with a
sledgehammer. Guys in them green pajamas, you know."

Sam nodded. "Yes, I know those guys, Deek. All right,
give me a minute to dope this out . . ."

Okay, Sam thought, it apparently was not just a chemical
secretion patch, nothing subcutaneous. If full anesthesia and
normal surgical prep had been initiated, they had probably
used microlaser techniques to place filaments into selected
lobes of the brain itself. This was not as radical as it sounded.
People like Delgado had been experimenting with physical

stimulation and concurrent control of the brain for decades.

"Okay, can you tell me why they sent you to the Center?"

"Huh?"

"Your . . . your crime, your problem."

Deek smiled. "Ya mean whatta my in for?"

"Yes, that's it."

The man shook his head in mock disgust. "They say I like to fuck with wimmen."

"*Do* you?"

Deek chuckled in a half whisper as though to himself. "Well, let's say I *used* to."

"I see." Sam touched it with the flat side of the scalpel.

"Can you get it out?" Deek's voice rasped along the leading edge of his thoughts like a rusty file.

"I'm not sure. There might be some danger involved, me not knowing their procedures."

Deek shifted around, glared at him with little ball bearing eyes. "Look, I ain' afraid of any of that bullstuff."

Sam glared back. "Well *I* am. If you don't make it out of the operation, I have no way of finding my daughter."

Deek chuckled his characteristic chuckle—darkly liquid and full of TV-sinister. "Tha's right, Doc. Ya need me. Ya need me alive."

"We're going to have to clean you up a bit before I get started. Go in that washroom and suds up your hair with this." Sam handed him a bottle of surgical soap. "Rinse it out and use the towel in there."

Deek looked at him suspiciously, ready to speak when—

The phone rang.

Sam moved to pick it up and he could feel the anger and paranoia radiating from the sociopath on the examining table.

"Doctor Jonas . . ."

Sam! Just checking in. Everything okay? John Costello's

whispered voice forcefully exited the receiver. Sam wondered if old Deek over there could hear anything.

"Good afternoon, Mr. Harnden. No, no, everything's fine. I was just sitting here watching the football game. What can I do for you?"

We're still tracking down some more leads on Kelly. There's a chance, Sam. There's a good chance somebody saw them. Gotta couple of good leads. State boys are checking them out right now. We also have a make on this guy—name's Darryl Parkinson, escaped from a psycho joint upstate, and—

"I know all about those symptoms, Tim. It's that flu virus that's going around. You have to stay warm and drink lots of fluids. No, antibiotics aren't going to help," Sam spoke softly, looking over to Deek and giving him a very casual okay sign. "Why don't you see how you feel in the morning, and if you want to come in, let Rita schedule you an appointment, okay?"

Sam again looked absently in Deek's direction. He was getting antsy, no doubt. Paranoia burned behind his predatory eyes.

The feds have a nurse on the way. She's a specialist at this stuff, Sam. But it's your call. You want us to send her in yet?

"No, Mr. Harnden," said Sam, trying to sound gentle and patronizing. "I don't want you to do that. Those old tetracycline capsules won't help at all. Might even cause you a little liver damage. Don't do it until you hear from me."

All right, Sam. We'll call later. Just watch it, okay. If we call and don't get an answer, we're coming in, okay?

"That will be fine, Mr. Harnden. See you tomorrow. Good-bye."

"Them people bug the shit outta ya . . ."

Sam shrugged. "It's part of the job." He pointed at the

washroom. "You want me to help you, you have to clean up a little."

"Awright, just don't try nothin' funny," said Deek. "And remember: ya jest make sure ya get it *out*."

Ten minutes later, Sam stared down at Darryl "Deek" Parkinson who lay upon the examining table in a semicoma induced by the interaction of two drugs—Xylanol, an efficient, long-acting local anesthetic; and an intravenous dose of diazepam. Deek had insisted on not being totally knocked out. Sam actually agreed with him—not for any logical reason, but rather because of an intuitive feeling that it was a good idea to keep him awake.

Scalpel in hand, he moved to begin opening the freshly scarred tissue above the implant. Deek's eyes lazily tracked him, but he was zonked enough to do nothing more.

The first incision violated some of the many capillaries in the occipital area, but Sam ignored the flow. It always looked far worse than it was, as any head-butted Rugby player will tell you. As he plunged the thin blade deeper, perhaps three-eighths of an inch, it struck the hard smooth surface of the man-made object. Lengthening the incision, Sam stretched the edges, revealing a square module, one-half an inch along each side. As he stanched the blood with gelfoam and a few clamps, he exposed the black surface of the thing. It looked like any number of chips you would find on the average home computer's motherboard.

Touching it with the tip of the scalpel, he could feel it floating in the pulpy tissue of the subintegument. He checked Deek's vital signs, and, noting their rock solid stability, he continued. Time to give this thing a gentle tug and see what happens.

Using a pair of extractors, he grabbed the implant and lifted it gently and slowly away from the tissue and bone. It moved easily away from the red flesh, but Sam felt a subtle resistance before he had moved it very far.

Flipping down a high-intensity light and a magnifying lens, he looked more closely at the area beneath the implant to find what he expected to be there: four tiny wires— microfilaments that trailed off the chip like angel hair and disappeared into the brain through a three-eighth-inch window in the skull. By some surgical magic, the Delgado folks had probed the dark sectors of this slug's brain, located the area that controlled his sex drive, and effectively short-circuited it.

Amazing.

And scary.

But Sam knew he had to get it out if he had any chance of seeing Kelly again.

Slowly, he began to pull as gently as possible with the extractors. There was initial resistance, then finally a centimeter of movement. Sam continued the steady, gentle, outward pull. The implant moved, still attached to the filaments as they released their grip on the diseased brain of Deek Parkinson. So delicate was this work, Sam willed up his strength and focused his concentration on the task. He was not a surgeon, but he *was* like most doctors, who secretly believed they possessed the stones to be one if they'd so chosen.

The filaments eased out slowly.

And Deek started talking.

Just as clear and perfectly intelligible as if he were totally lucid.

"Please, Momma," he said. "Please don't say that . . . !"

"No, I won't ever do it again, I promise!"

"What's the matter little girl, ain' you ever seen one of these before?"

The sentences burst out of him in a constant stream, and it was obvious they were recreations of conversations and experiences being replayed with perfect accuracy. That's why Sam was hearing only Deek's half of all the dialogue.

And then it would just . . . stop.

Sam would tug on the filaments . . .

. . . and the conversations would spark into life again.

God, it was eerie. Totally weird. Sam felt himself sweating profusely as he tugged a little and listened.

Tugged and listened.

A thought touched him, and he spoke to Deek, assuming the role of the speaker of the unheard half of the dialogue.

And Deek answered him.

Trembling, sweating, fighting the urge to let his hands shake like some palsied elder, Sam leaned closer to the monster on the table.

"So tell me, Deek," he whispered. "What's on your mind?"

Looking around the suddenly crowded room, Dr. Sam Jonas wiped his hands on a towel. He had just finished washing up from his work. After he told them where they could find Kelly (unharmed but very scared from being hog-tied and left in Hap Towner's smokehouse), they'd dispatched a unit to rescue her.

Sam smiled at the assembled group of state troopers, federal agents, and John Costello. He was sitting on a swivel stool by the examining table where Darryl Parkinson still lay, eyes staring, a trickle of saliva oozing from the corner of his mouth. The others were all looking at him with expressions ranging from shock to sardonic amusement.

"How did you know where she was?" John Costello had asked him.

Sam smiled. "Deek told me. We had a nice talk. He told me everything."

"But how?" said one of the State boys.

"It was the wires," said Sam with a smile. It felt inappropriate, but it was there.

"What's the matter with him?" someone half whispered.

"Shut up! Let him talk." Another voice in the background.

"What wires?" asked John.

Sam chuckled. "The wires on the chip. I pulled them out and the action must have cued up memory circuits or something. It was like replaying a tape, only it wasn't Memorex—it was *live*."

"That's just fucking incredible," said one of the men with the blue parkas. It was stenciled with big yellow *FBI* letters across the back.

Sam smiled again. He suddenly realized he was rocking back and forth a little. It felt good, comforting. He knew he probably had a kind of faraway look in his eye, but they would forgive him—after the ordeal he'd been through.

"No, not really, sir," said Sam. "It's just part of how the brain works. Deek didn't know that, of course. Didn't care, really . . . You see, all he cared about was for me to get it out of him."

Somebody made a noise in the back of the crowd, a cross between a nervous giggle and gagging.

Sam looked down at the implant, still clutched in his fist. And the wires trailing from it.

"He just wanted me to get it out," he said, as he appeared to study the bloody clump of gray matter caught in the tangled ends of those wires. "And I did a good job, didn't I?"

Tina Jens used to be a newspaper journalist. She began writing fiction in 1991, and has appeared in many fantasy and horror anthologies since then. She lives in Chicago and does most of her writing in neighborhood coffee shops. She's had a clutch of stories published recently in anthologies like *Phantoms of the Night,* and *The Secret Prophecies of Nostradamus.* This is her first venture into the thriller field. She should keep venturing. She's a natural.

THE CUBAN SOLUTION

Tina L. Jens

Security Pass, please."

Janna Adams was beginning to wish she'd listened to her father and taken the medical internship at Children's Memorial in Chicago. Her plane had touched down at the Guantanamo Bay Naval Station less than two hours ago, and already her passport and assorted authorization papers had been scrutinized a dozen times. But nobody had been able to answer a basic question, like, where was she going to spend the night, and where could she get a decent cup of coffee and a quick meal?

Janna sighed and handed over the file of documents the previous security guards had sifted through.

She ran a hand through her closely cropped blond hair and tried to wipe away some of the exhaustion. She was short and small boned. What she lacked in body mass, she made up for in determination.

"You're late," the young guard snapped. "Says here you were supposed to arrive at oh-eight-hundred yesterday."

"O'Hare was fogged in and the flight was canceled," Janna snapped back, her patience breaking. "I'm not in your army, soldier, so stop giving me the military runaround. I'm a civilian doctor here on a humanitarian mission to assist with the medical crisis. Why don't you get on the phone to Doctor Henry Wirths and find out where I'm supposed to stay?"

She thumped her paisley-covered duffel bag down on his desk, to emphasize her point.

The guard scowled at her, but picked up the receiver. After a terse conversation, he hung up.

"Wirths was called away on an emergency. He flew out to D.C. this morning. You can report to Dr. Jordan."

He turned away from her and made a show of shuffling through a pile of papers.

"And where would I find him?"

He didn't look up. "Down the hall. East elevator. Third level down, fourth door on the left."

The desk sat at the top of a T-intersection. When it became apparent that the guard was not going to offer any more information, Janna picked up her bags, arbitrarily chose a direction, and began walking.

After several turns she found a bank of elevators. The old car creaked slowly down the three floors. The doors opened up on an empty, ill-lit, cinder block corridor. The place gave her the creeps.

She rounded the corner and walked into a scene of organized chaos. Gurneys lined both sides of the hall, with moaning, blood-covered patients. Medics moved among the stretchers and wheelchairs, doing a quick visual exam to prioritize treatment. MPs crowded the hall, getting in the way of the doctors and intimidating the patients.

Janna had done a rotation in the Emergency Room at the infamous Cook County Hospital on the South Side, where they treated hundreds of knife wounds, drive-by shootings and drug overdoses a night. She surveyed the scene in front of her coolly. She quickly spotted the man in charge.

The doctor wasn't a tall man, but an air of authority surrounded him. He was in his late forties or early fifties, with rugged features and a hint of grey at his temples.

Janna sidestepped a gurney headed at breakneck speed toward X-ray, ducked behind a nurse yelling at an MP, and weaved through the patients until she stood behind him. She waited until he finished with the patient.

"What can I do for you, little lady?" he asked, without turning around.

Janna had no clue how he knew she was there.

"I'm Dr. Janna Adams," she said, trying not to bristle at the familiar greeting. Considering his age and occupation, he probably had no idea he'd insulted her.

He motioned to her to follow him into the emergency room.

"Grab his feet, will you?"

Janna slid one arm under the patient's knees, the other under his feet, and helped lift the patient onto an examination table.

"I'm supposed to report to Dr. Jordan."

"We weren't expecting you until tomorrow," he said, lifting the bloody collar of the man's shirt to examine the wound underneath.

So this was military efficiency, Janna thought. First they accuse you of being late, then they decide you're early.

"Looks like you've got a mess here," she said.

"Yeah, there was a protest over in Camp Michael this afternoon. Things got a little out of hand and the MPs started busting heads. We're the cleanup crew."

"Need a hand?"

"Sure." He nodded toward the next examination table. "Dig in."

Janna tossed her bags in a corner, scrubbed up, and grabbed a white jacket off a peg on the wall. She waited while an orderly helped a young man onto the examination table. Blood oozed through his fingers as the patient moaned and clutched the side of his head. She held his X-rays up to the light. No fracture but he had multiple lacerations across his scalp that were bleeding profusely.

Janna had spent the last month mentally preparing herself for the primitive conditions of the refugee camps, studying up on the likely medical problems of overexposure, dehydration, malnutrition, and disease control. It had never occurred to her she'd be treating battle wounds.

"You did alright, Rookie," he said, slapping her, rather roughly, on the back as they walked through the compound.

She struggled to keep up with his long strides, and carry both her duffel bag and suitcase. He hadn't offered to help.

"Thanks," she said, puffing. "Where are we going?"

"Officers' Lounge."

"Will they let me in?"

"Yeah, the doctors and security have pretty much taken over the camp," he assured her.

No one challenged her at the door, and she slumped gratefully into a booth, dropping her bags on the floor beside her.

After greeting a number of friends, the doctor came back carrying a tray of four tall glasses filled with watery tomato juice and sprouting stalks of wilted celery.

She didn't care much for Bloody Marys, and they had

even less appeal after what she'd just done—but he hadn't asked.

"Salud!" he said, lifting his glass to her.

Janna took a long drink and sank back against the seat. She studied her companion. The salt-and-pepper look that she'd noticed at his temples had also crept into the moustache and close-cropped beard. His body was strong, but he'd begun to put on weight. And the face that looked rugged from across the room, looked, well, craggy, up close.

Still, she found him undeniably attractive. Perhaps it was his eyes. They were dark and intense, and slightly sad, even when he smiled.

"Can I ask you a question?" she said, after taking another hefty gulp.

"Oh, maybe one."

"Who are you? Where am I going to sleep tonight? And what the hell is going on here?"

"Whasamatter? Don't they teach you civvies to count?" he growled, playfully.

"Give me a break, please," she moaned. "I haven't been to bed in"—she stopped to check her watch and do some mental arithmetic—"thirty hours, haven't had a meal in eighteen, and I just pulled a twelve-hour emergency room shift."

"Welcome to Auschwitz, Rookie."

"Pardon?"

He laughed. "Did you see all the tan-and-olive tents set up on the base?"

Janna nodded.

"Well that ain't the big top, baby. We've got close to thirty thousand people packed on a base designed for seven thousand. They're sleeping thirty refugees to a twenty-man tent. We've got detention camps set up on every square inch of this island. The only thing clear is the road out of here, and the mine field that separates the base from the rest of Cuba. And that may be next."

He laughed. "It'd solve a few of our problems."

"So what's the Auschwitz connection?"

"These people aren't here by choice, Rookie. What you got here is a modern day concentration camp. The only difference is we've got a mine field instead of a gas chamber."

As a doctor, Janna understood the psychological necessity of gallows humor, but this carried things too far.

"That's . . . that's clever," Janna said.

If the doctor noticed her revulsion, he didn't show it.

"You watch your back, Rookie. There are riots in the camps every day. And the only thing protecting you from them is a few rolls of razor wire."

"Look, can you—"

He pushed another drink toward her, and waved a hand, shushing her.

All conversation had stopped in the room. The bartender turned up the volume on the TV. It was the CNN news.

". . . U.S. negotiators walked out of talks today, saying a deal cannot be reached as long as Castro insists talks to end the flow of refugees be tied to lifting the thirty-year-old trade embargo.

"Meanwhile, another eight hundred Cuban rafters were plucked from the Straits of Florida yesterday by the U.S. Coast Guard and taken to the detention camps in Guantanamo Bay. More than twenty-seven thousand are estimated to be interned there now. Officials predict that number will reach forty thousand by the end of the month.

"The president is trying to reach an agreement with Panama, Honduras, and Caicos Island to house an additional seventeen thousand.

"In other news . . ."

The crowd began to grumble. "What do they care about reaching an agreement? They're doing lunch and driving around in limos. Meanwhile, we're stuck in limbo."

"You can't negotiate with Castro. They should bring the troops back and take care of that bastard once and for all."

The doctor shook his head. "Everyone's a general. Sorry, where were we?"

"You were about to tell me who the heck you are."

He grinned at her. "Folks call me Keddy."

"Keddy?" she said, choking. "What kind of name is that?"

"I didn't say that was my name. I said that's what people call me."

"So tomorrow morning, I report to the security guard and ask that charming little lad if I can go play with Keddy?"

"My name, if you must know, is Austin Alexander Keddington the third."

She whistled. "That's a mouthful."

"You got that right," he said.

She grinned.

"So, Keddy, where am I going to sleep tonight?"

He finished his second drink in one gulp, waved at the bartender for another round of doubles, then leaned forward and rested his crossed arms on the table.

Janna matched his posture, and watched, amused, as a series of emotions played across his face.

"Ya know," he growled, "historically, military and civilians don't communicate very well. You add a twenty—twenty-five-year age difference to that, and I could be getting myself in trouble, or, missing something really obvious."

"What's the question, soldier?"

"Are you hitting on me?"

"Not yet," she purred.

*   *   *

"This is my place. Sorry it's such a mess," Keddy said, stumbling up the walk and unlocking the front door to a white ranch house.

"How can you tell?" Janna asked. "They all look the same."

"It's the one with the scrawny cactus in the front yard, and the family of banana rats raiding the trash can. Damn rats are fatter than some of the refugees," he said, holding the door open for her.

"Dr. Maxwell was sharing it with me, but he had to fly out to Washington last week. Won't be back for a while. There's a third bedroom in back that we haven't trashed too badly. Tomorrow, you can talk to Central Processing about a permanent assignment."

She explored the surroundings.

"I didn't know military living was so posh. I always pictured you guys cramped up four to a tent, or stacked up on bunk beds in some dormitory."

She found the den. "Nice fireplace."

"This isn't typical military life," Keddy assured her. "The houses used to be strictly reserved for married officers, but the families and all nonessential personnel were sent home about a month ago. Jordan commandeered them because he wanted all his staff together, close to the hospital facilities and as far away from the refugee camps as possible."

"I've got good news and bad news, Rookie," Keddy said hoarsely, pouring a cup of 6:00 A.M. coffee.

Janna watched in awe as he poured half a dozen tablespoons of sugar into his mug.

"Jordan was called away to Washington," he said. "So you'll be assisting me for the next week."

"So what's the good news?"

"Bloody hell, you're one of those flocking morning people, aren't you?"

She smiled brightly at him.

"If you're going to be that radiant in the morning, I'm going to have to dig out my sunglasses."

"Why thank you, Keddy," she said, sweetly.

"Let's see how many floaters they picked up yesterday," he said, taking a sip of the sticky brew and turning on the old transistor radio on the counter.

". . . Meteorologists are tracking a large storm moving across the Gulf of Florida stirring up high winds and rough seas by Tuesday. The weather may accomplish what the president's negotiators, so far, have failed to do. Crowds and vendors still line the beaches of Havana, cheering as each vessel casts off. Fourteen rafts departed today, despite the predictions of bad weather. Dozens more wait on the beach.

"Meanwhile, in Washington, D.C., the negotiation teams are scheduled to return to the table tomorrow in an attempt to hammer out an agreement to stem the flow of refugees."

Keddy made an obscene noise and switched the radio off.

"We're assigned to housing by work groups. Since you'll be working with me for the next week, you might as well stay here. Central Processing are also the folks responsible for processing the refugees. With yesterday's catch, they should only be behind by about three thousand or so."

"So, are we headed into the camps today?"

Keddy snorted. "We do critical care out of E.R. If there's a serious problem, the MPs will bring them in."

"But I've heard conditions are horrible. There's a lot we can do to help."

"What's the point? The camps are a temporary thing. There's no reason to mess with them."

Janna was appalled. She'd noticed Keddy and the other doctors waving off and ignoring minor injuries last night, but she'd assumed it was a priority decision. It was standard procedure to treat the worst-case patients first. It had not occurred to her that those patients would receive no treatment at all.

He saw the look on her face. "Take it easy, Rookie. There'll be plenty of work, soon enough."

As the days passed, Janna noticed that attitude pervaded the base. Even when a virulent strain of the flu swept through the camps, only those whose lives were endangered received any treatment.

Only the newscasters received the staff's undivided attention. Work stopped as people gathered around radios and TV sets, eagerly awaiting word of a treaty with Cuba.

"Here's to your health, Rookie," Keddy said, clinking his glass against hers, then downing the last of his drink. He set the tumbler down next to its empty twin on the table.

"You fly, I'll buy," he said.

"Sure thing," Janna said, her words slurring slightly. She collected the empties and headed for the bar.

She slid the glasses toward the bartender. "Fill 'er up."

Keddy always insisted on double rounds—said it wasn't worth the footwork for anything less. And they were still drinking Bloody Marys, but at least she'd convinced him to go easy on the Tabasco sauce.

She waved at a couple of friends as she waited for the drinks.

"That'll be twelve dollars."

"Put it on Keddy's tab."

"There's a surprise," the bartender said, in disgust.

"What?" Janna said, caught off guard by the comment.

The sailor beside her snickered. "He's got a tab bigger than Cuba's national budget."

"What's that—?"

Janna didn't get to finish her question. Conversation stopped and attention was turned toward the radio.

"This is a special bulletin from Armed Forces Radio. The deputy secretary of state for inter-American affairs announced just minutes ago, that Castro has agreed to halt the exodus of Cuban boat people."

A cheer went up in the room.

"Quiet!" the bartender yelled.

"In return, the U.S. will increase the number of annual visas from twenty-seven hundred to a maximum of twenty thousand a year. The fate of the thirty thousand Cuban refugees interned at Guantanamo Bay is still uncertain. Officials say they will not force the refugees to leave the base. But, the refugees will not be given priority for the visas, and they must return to Cuba before they can begin the application process. It is expected that most of the refugees will want to return to their country as soon as possible. U.S. Navy boats are standing by to begin transporting . . ."

The rest of the announcement was drowned out by excited conversations and calls for drinks. The bartender rushed off to fill the orders. Janna grabbed her tray and elbowed her way past the people lining up at the bar.

As she jostled her way through the crowd, she saw Keddy deep in conversation with an officer at their table. Janna approached, uncertainly.

Keddy saw her and waved.

"Sit down, Rookie," he said, sliding over to make room for her.

"This is the infamous Dr. Jordan. Jack, meet the Rookie."

The man nodded at her, then turned back to Keddy.

"So, everything's set?"

"We've been ready and waiting for weeks, Jack. We'll get started first thing in the morning."

The officer stood, nodded again, and left. He was the only somber person in the room.

Keddy grinned at Janna and reached for a glass.

"I guess this is good news," she said.

Keddy gestured at the crowd. "These boys have been in a holding pattern for months. They were getting bored and restless. Now they've got something to do."

Janna nodded. She could understand that. She'd been feeling fidgety, too.

"Salud!" she said, clinking her glass against his. The damned things were starting to taste good.

Out of the corner of her eye, Janna noticed Dr. Jordan leaving.

"Can I ask you a question?"

"Oh, mebbe one," Keddy said, easily.

"What are we going to do first thing in the morning? Do you really think all the refugees will go home? And when are you going to stop calling me Rookie?"

Keddy gurgled as he tried to laugh with his mouth full.

"When are you going to learn to count?"

She grinned at him.

"What do you want me to call you?" His voice dropped an octave.

"Janna wouldn't be bad," she said, suddenly feeling shy.

"Janna . . ."

She looked up, surprised, as she felt his fingers intertwine with hers.

She laughed softly. "Keddy, you're blushing."

"I feel like an old fool!" he growled.

"Not so old," she whispered, sliding closer to him until her body brushed against his.

They'd gotten sloppy drunk, done some serious hand-holding and poured out their most intimate secrets. The evening had culminated with an awkward kiss standing in the middle of their living room. Then they'd fled to their respective bedrooms.

"Rise and shine, sweetheart," Keddy's voiced boomed cheerfully from her doorway.

Janna sat up painfully, trying to blink herself awake.

"Aren't you chipper this morning," she mumbled.

"Work to do," he said, molding her hands around a steaming coffee mug.

She took a sip and made a face.

"I think this one's yours," she said. "There's about a cup of sugar in there."

"I thought it'd help you wake up," he said.

"Couldn't you just play reveille?"

"The jeep leaves in fifteen minutes, so up and at 'em, sunshine!"

He banged her door shut, and Janna sank back down into her pillow.

Janna could see about a dozen coast guard boats lined up at the docks.

"Are those bringing people in, or taking them out?" Janna asked.

"Probably both," Keddy told her. "It'll take a few days to net the last few rafts out of the water. Some of them have been drifting around for a week. But the first boatload heads back to Havana tomorrow."

He parked beside the medical clinic, and they entered by

a side door. The security guard waved them past. Keddy led them to the stairs, down two levels, and through a twisting corridor. Pulling out a set of keys, he unlocked a battered wooden door, and flipped on the lights.

He bellowed down the hall, "Ileana? Got those trays?"

A young woman came in pushing a cart full of needles, sterile alcohol wipes, and charts.

Ileana was a lab tech. Janna had bumped into her several times over the past few weeks.

"*Hola, doctora,*" the Cuban woman murmured shyly.

Janna heard clomping sounds in the hall.

"Keddy?"

"Hurry up, sunshine."

"I will—just as soon as you tell me what we're doing."

"Inoculations. Those camps are a stewpot of mutating viruses. We don't want to unleash anything on the unsuspecting public when these folks wander down the gangplank in Havana."

The refugees were already filing into the room in lines of two. Janna hurried to set up her tray.

Another lab tech took Keddy's side. The assistants spoke to the refugees, marking the answers on their charts. Verifying the patient's name and medical record, Janna assumed. She remembered very little of her high school Spanish.

"*Buenos dias,*" Janna said to the thin dark man who faced her. She smiled, warmly.

"Roll your shirtsleeve up, please."

Ileana translated the request, and the man complied. Janna wouldn't have to repeat the request often. Most of them wore only a ragged pair of shorts and sandals.

The homemade rafts they rode to freedom left little room to carry possessions. And what few they brought were often washed overboard. Janna felt a pang of guilt. They should have done more for these people while they were here. But at least they were going home.

She pressed a cotton ball against his arm, and slipped the needle gently out from under it. "There, that wasn't so bad, now was it?"

The next few days were a blur of activity, across the base. There were stacks of paperwork to be processed, medical records to be cross-checked, verification and consent forms to be signed. Entire camps were being shut down and refugees were shuffled from one holding area to another.

All Spanish-speaking personnel were drafted by Central Processing to conduct interviews. Since the refugees could not be forced to leave, their options had to be fully explained to them and their decisions documented.

The staff at the medical center was cut to bare bones. Janna worked twelve- and fourteen-hour shifts. When she wasn't inoculating refugees, just hours before they boarded their boat home, she was in the Emergency Room.

Tensions were high. The riots were more frequent and the fighting more vicious.

Janna mopped her brow with her elbow as she prepped a young black man for surgery. He and his brothers had decided to walk across the mine field to return to Cuba, rather than getting on the coast guard vessels.

Half a mile in, one of them had stepped on a mine. Three of them were dead. And this man was going to lose at least one of his legs.

There was a disturbance out in the hall. A woman screamed, and Janna heard a rush of stomping boots. Two MPs carried a struggling woman in on a stretcher. Ileana followed.

The patient was sweating profusely. Pustules were scattered over her body. A wracking cough shook the woman and brought up blood.

"Easy. I'm not going to hurt you," Janna crooned, checking the woman's pupil dilation and pulse rate. Janna slipped her stethoscope on and listened to the woman's heart.

She applied a tourniquet, grabbed a needle from the supply drawer, and quickly swabbed the struggling woman's arm. With one fluid movement she stabbed the needle in and pulled the plunger back. The tube filled with blood.

The woman screamed, again. *"Dona Diabla, porque nos quieres matar?"*

"Silencia, Dona Masetti!" Ileana snapped at her.

"Get that sample down to the lab, stat," Janna ordered, handing the tube to Ileana.

"Belay that," Keddy bellowed.

Janna whirled around. She hadn't known Keddy was in the room. And she wasn't used to being contradicted.

"I can't treat the patient if I don't know what I'm dealing with."

"Blood samples were taken on the boat. Lab's already working on it," he said gruffly.

"What's that man doing in here?" Keddy yelled, waving at the mine victim. "This is a quarantined area. Clear him out. And put some masks on, people!"

"Keddy, what the hell's going on?"

"Step out in the hall, Sunshine. I'll bring you up to speed."

They stepped into the nurses' station out of the way, as a long line of stretchers and gurneys were brought through the hall and into the E.R.

"The USS *Patton* was completely loaded and ready to cast off Tuesday morning, when they discovered a breach in the outer hull. They attempted repairs. Meanwhile, a virus went wild down in the hold."

"You mean they kept those people down there for two and a half days?"

Keddy shrugged. "They thought it would be a minor repair."

"What did that woman say to me?"

"Nothing. Don't worry about it."

"But if it was something about her symptoms . . ."

"It wasn't," he said brusquely. "These folks are just a bunch of superstitious villagers. Can't get it through their heads we're trying to help them.

"The lab should have a serum for us soon. Meanwhile, just make the patients comfortable. I'll be back as soon as I can."

"What if—" Janna had a million questions, but Keddy had already dashed off.

Despite what Keddy said, Janna was bothered by the woman's words. She hadn't caught all of it, but *"Dona Diabla"* was wife of the devil, and *"matar"* meant death.

The E.R. and the wards around it filled up, all of the patients exhibiting the same, unusual symptoms—the fever, pustules, odd patterns of bruising, a jaundiced tint to the skin.

This didn't look like any normal virus to Janna. For one thing, most viruses weren't this virulent. Some of the refugees should have been immune to it.

Janna thought back to the shots they had given these same people, just days before. Perhaps the sera were faulty, or they were giving the shots to people who were sick. Inoculations could do more harm than good if they were administered while the body was fighting another disease.

When the antidote arrived from the lab, Janna could get no answers to her questions then, either, only an order to dose all patients. She didn't like being kept in the dark, and she didn't like dispensing unidentified medicine. There was a matter of drug reactions, for one thing. Blanket treatments were risky. And she was being treated like a fool.

Janna snapped out orders to the attendants, and contented herself by making frequent rounds and copious notes in the patients' charts.

Finally, strung out from coffee and a sixteen-hour shift, she collapsed on a cot in the nurses' station. She awoke a few hours later to find Ileana gently shaking her shoulder.

"*Doctora*, you go home now. The guard will drive you."

Janna awoke a second time in her own bed, unable to recall how she'd gotten there. It was nearly dark out. She'd slept more than twelve hours. She rushed to put on a pot of coffee and hurried into the shower.

Half an hour later, she was back at the medical clinic. She waved at Ileana in the nurses' station, and went to check on Senora Masetti. The woman had touched a nerve. And Janna had found herself returning again and again to her bedside.

Today, the bed was empty. Crisp white sheets were pulled tightly across the frame, as if defying someone to mess them up.

Janna jogged toward the nurses' station, yelling at Ileana before she was halfway there.

"Ileana, who authorized Senora Masetti's transfer? She was far too sick to be moved. I want her chart. Now!"

Ileana stared at her, then pulled her lab coat around her, as if warding off chill.

"There was no transfer, *Doctora*. Senora Masetti is dead."

"What?" Janna was dumbfounded. The woman's fever

had broken during Janna's shift. While she was still a very sick lady, she had pulled out of the critical stage.

In shock, Janna said, simply, "I want her chart."

"I don't think so," Ileana answered. "Perhaps, tomorrow you ask Dr. Keddy for this . . ." She shrugged and her words trailed off, as if to imply she could do nothing.

"I want to know why she died."

"It was an accident. The serum—it was too strong."

Janna looked around the ward, seeing clearly for the first time. Much had changed in the twelve hours she'd been gone. More than half the beds were empty.

"The antidote?"

Ileana shrugged again. "Perhaps."

A cold fury swept over Janna. She had given her patients two mystery injections. And now, her patients were dead.

Janna's voice was low and dangerous. "What was in that antidote?"

Ileana shrunk back from her. "I do not know, *Doctora.*"

"Then let's find out."

Janna was already rushing down the hall. Ileana followed, against her will.

"The files and the lab are locked; we cannot go there."

"Where is Senora Masetti's body?"

"In the morgue."

"And is that also locked?"

Ileana shook her head, fearfully.

"Then we will go there."

Janna checked the refrigerated drawers until she found the Masetti woman's body.

With Ileana's help, Janna wrestled the corpse onto the examination table.

"Lock the door."

Janna wanted no interruptions during the procedure. She clicked on the portable tape player suspended from the ceiling and recited what little information was recorded on the toe tag.

"Dulce Masetti. Cuban Caucasian woman. Age twenty-eight." She added the date of death.

She picked up the scalpel, then paused to take a deep breath. Pathology had never been her favorite subject. But, her patients had died, possibly by her own hand. Her conscience would not let her shrug that off. And this was the only way she could be sure of the answer.

With grim determination, she pressed the scalpel down until it bit into the skin. She made the initial Y incision, from shoulders to sternum, and pulled the flaps of skin back. . . .

Janna searched her instrument tray. There was the large needle. She'd need that in a moment to draw blood from the left ventricle for the toxicology sample. But now she was searching for the smaller needle. Swallowing hard, she injected it into the back of the eye, and pulled back the plunger, withdrawing the jellylike substance that could reveal the presence of subtle poisons.

Janna handed the tube to Ileana.

"Take the samples I've collected so far, and start the lab work. I'll bring the others down when I finish here."

Ileana took them solemnly. When she reached the door, she turned back.

"I think there is much you do not know, Dr. Janna. Here it is very dangerous for the Cuban people. And now, maybe, it is very dangerous for you, too."

"Did you solve the mystery, Doctor Watson?"

Keddy sat on the couch, his feet up on the coffee table, a bottle of scotch and a glass on the end table beside him. The scotch level suggested he'd been waiting for some time.

"I'm still waiting on some of the tests. Preliminary results suggest either anthrax or pneumonic tularemia. We'll know more in the morning." Janna's voice got nasty. "Unless you'd like to tell me tonight. Funny thing is, there hasn't been a recent outbreak of anthrax or tularemia in this area. I checked."

Keddy sighed and waved at a chair. "Sit down, Rookie."

"That wasn't the standard MMR vaccination we gave her. What was in that shot, Keddy?" Janna's voice cracked, hinting at the hysteria lurking beneath the surface.

Keddy stood, walked to the door and closed it. He led her, almost forcibly, to the couch and poured her a drink.

"You're getting worked up over nothing."

"She's dead, Keddy! Along with several dozen others. And I killed them!"

He put a restraining arm around her shoulders.

"It was an accident and it's not your fault. You were just following orders."

She pushed him away and scrambled to the other side of the couch, bracing her back against the armrest.

"That doesn't wash, Keddy. I'm not a Nazi foot soldier."

"Janna, there's so much more to this than you can possibly understand."

She snapped, "I'm a bright girl—try me."

Keddy poured himself a drink and sighed. "You're a naive, crusading, young civilian doctor come to heal the refugees."

He paused, swirled the ice cubes, and watched the scotch lap at the sides of the glass.

"I admired you for that. If they're sick, you heal them. Doesn't matter what they do or whose side they're on. But that's not how it works in the military. It's a matter of international politics, national boundaries, and global political balance."

"What the hell are you talking about?"

He seemed not to hear. "Everything was fine, until the boat was delayed."

He stared at her, and the sadness in his eyes seemed to spill over his body, so that even the way he refilled his drink, and the way he sat, hunched against the corner of the couch, seemed to cry out to her.

She looked his eyes and saw the darkness there, and the blackness seemed to illuminate the full horror of what they'd done.

"You gave them the plague and sent them home," Janna whispered, appalled. "As they'd travel to their villages and towns it would sweep across the country.

"You planned to use germ warfare to bring Castro down! You're a sick bastard, and I'm going to see to it you're court-martialed, or whatever the hell they do to you, and locked away for good." Janna was nearly screaming, now. She fell silent as his laughter bellowed through the room.

"Rookie, you think *I'm* the mastermind of this plot? They've been trying to get the funding for this project for years."

He stood and began pacing the floor.

"It was Operation Desert Storm that finally convinced the bureaucrats. Word leaked out that Iraq had the capability to load microbe-filled warheads onto their extended-range Scud missiles. Iraq didn't use them, because they hadn't vaccinated their own troops. But nature did what their generals didn't. It proved that it was a workable plan."

"The sand flea thing . . ."

Keddy nodded, pleased she knew what he was talking about.

"They called it Sandfly Fever and the Baghdad Boil. The locals had a natural immunity to the diseases. Our troops didn't."

Janna grabbed her glass and took a deep swallow to calm her screaming nerves.

"Keddy, how could you be a part of this?"

"Because this is the real threat to our future," he said earnestly. He knelt in front of her and took her hand. "Nobody's going to drop a nuclear bomb; there's no such thing as limited nuclear warfare. Conventional warfare kills too many of your own troops, and the people won't tolerate that anymore.

"But germs can wipe out entire populations without hurting the infrastructure or doing permanent damage to the local ecology. It makes good economic, political, and ecological sense. And we're vulnerable, Janna."

He squeezed her hand. "At least nine countries have the capabilities right now. Small, unstable dictatorships in the Middle East, mainly. Some little country the size of Pittsburgh could wipe us out. Iraq used it on the Kurds back in 1988. And just last year British Intelligence discovered that Russia's still conducting tests, even though the Cold War's supposed to be over."

Out of the corner of her eye, Janna saw a jeep pull up outside the house. She was running out of time.

"It's Doctor Jordan, isn't it? Keddy, we can stop him. You can call Washington. Someone will listen to you."

He laughed softly. "Always the crusader, eh, Rookie? The Cubans climb on shoddy rafts, drift out into the middle of the ocean, and wait for the U.S. boats to pick them up. Who appointed us their guardians?"

He stood and began pacing again, gesturing wildly as he talked.

"It's not our responsibility to rescue these people. We're

supposed to fix the world's problems, without interfering in anybody's domestic affairs, with no thought to how it affects our economy or national security. Castro says, here, here's thirty thousand people we can't feed. You take care of them.

"Kuwait says, we can't protect ourselves. Bring your troops in and protect our borders. But don't you dare interfere with our dictatorship or social customs. And don't ask us to foot the bill."

He spun wildly toward her. She shrank back against the couch.

"Cuba is one of our enemies! This refugee thing is just one more cold-war maneuver on Castro's part. He pulled this stunt back in 1980 with the Mariel boatlift. He emptied his prisons and AIDS hospitals and sent all his undesirables to us. Don't you see, Janna? It's time we fought back."

He studied her face, hoping she'd finally accepted his logic.

She stared at him in disbelief, the last illusions slipping away. She sank her head into her hands. Everything she'd done here had been a facade that was crumbling before her eyes. She had cared for him, and entertained fantasies of something more.

"It's barbaric," she whispered.

Keddy looked at her coldly and stood. He opened the door and motioned to the man outside. The security guard, the same one who'd hassled Janna the first night, came to the door.

Janna shivered. She'd been so concerned about what was happening to the refugees, that she hadn't given any thought to what they might do to her. Would they have her shot? That was ridiculous. This was a U.S. military base, not Romania. But they could lock her up with the refugees. She'd be lost among the thousands detained.

Janna watched as the two men spoke in whispers in the corner. As they moved toward her, she jumped up and ran for the door. The guard caught her easily. He grabbed her and threw her back against the couch, pinning her there.

Keddy knelt before her and reached into the pocket of his lab coat.

"Don't fight, Janna," Keddy whispered tenderly. "Not after all we've been through."

A syringe glistened in the light. He uncapped the needle and tapped the side of the tube to eliminate the air bubbles.

"Keddy, what are you doing?" she screamed, hysteria taking over. She kicked out at him. Squirming wildly, she tried to pull away from the guard, but couldn't break his grip.

"Hold her still."

The needle bit into her arm.

"It'll take a few moments," Keddy said to the guard.

Janna tried to concentrate on his words. His face and voice were blurred. The room started spinning. Then there was only blackness.

The waves lapped at the side of the boat. The gentle rocking increased the nausea. Janna's stomach heaved. As she slowly gained consciousness, she was grateful that her stomach was empty and had nothing to evict. She could not move.

A fever ravaged her body. Her sweat soaked through her bedding. Janna let her head roll to the side, and tried to focus. It was dark, and only a single bulb illuminated the surroundings.

When she moaned, one or two of the nearest inmates turned to stare at her sullenly. They had no pity for the blond *doctora*. Most took no notice of her. Some slept on their pallets. Others stood or sat in small groups, talking rapidly. There was a dangerous edge to their voices.

She appeared to be the only one who was sick. For now, Janna thought.

She tried to speak, but her tongue felt like it had swollen till it filled the very corners of her mouth.

She was on a shipload of Typhoid Marys, bound for Cuba. And if the people around her didn't already have the plague, they'd catch it from her.

Janna thought about her parents. They'd begin inquiries in a few days, after not hearing from her. But by then it would be too late. It was already too late. Dr. Jordan, or Keddy, would write a letter to her parents, reporting, sadly, that she had been caught in one of the riots or that a refugee had attacked her. Janna wondered what excuse they'd come up with when her parents requested her remains. Tears welled up in her eyes. She didn't have the strength to wipe them away.

She awoke again to the sound of fighting. Angry voices called out in Spanish and English, but Janna could not make out the words. She turned her head toward the noise and was blinded by the bright light streaming through an open hatch. She heard feet scuffling on deck. Guns fired. Then there was more shouting.

Unsteadily, she lifted one arm toward her face. In the light, she could see bruises and pustules covering her arm. The skin was a sickly yellow. She let her arm fall back to her side, and drifted off to sleep.

When she awoke again, she was vaguely surprised to find they were still on the boat. She had no real way to tell time, but surely, the trip to Havana would not take this long.

Gathering all her energy, she struggled into a sitting position. She was pleased with the accomplishment.

She looked around the hold. The hatch was still open. Despite the bright sunlight, many of the Cubans lay sleeping, tossing fitfully on their pallets. They were wet with sweat, and Janna could see the beginning of pustules forming on their skin.

The lapping of the waves and the steady movement of the craft told her that this was not just another boat delayed at dock. The coast guard sailors tied up in the corner reinforced that opinion.

A face appeared at the hatchway.

"*Veo Florida,*" the young Cuban man shouted, excitedly. "*Tenemos libertad finalmente!*"

Those who were well began to shake hands and pat each other on the back. Then they hurried to the pallets to relay the news to the sick.

But where they found excitement, Janna found only horror.

They had spotted Florida. Freedom at last!

Ridley Pearson is the author of eight novels, including the best-sellers *Undercurrents, Probable Cause,* and *The Angel Maker.* His work has been translated into twenty-three languages. He was the first American to be awarded the Raymond Chandler Fulbright at Oxford University. A sometime rock musician (few people know that he plays bass for the Rock Bottom Remainders because Dave Barry and Stephen King get all the press), he has recently taken up the sport of recreational tree climbing.

Ridley doesn't do short fiction. I had to wring this story from him—had to threaten to make my way into the wilds of central Idaho where he lives and move in with him until he finished it.

That got him going.

As you're about to see, it was worth the effort.

ALL OVER BUT THE DYING

Ridley Pearson

I had never killed anyone before all of this. I confess, I had never even considered it, much less believed myself capable of such things. But life does not follow any rules, regardless of how we attempt to shape it and confine it. One minute driving down the road. The next, in a casket. Before any of this began, the closest I had been to death was in a four-seater 1957 Pacer, a small single-engine plane, at five-forty-five on a summer morning in the mountains of Idaho. The carburetor heater stuck and the plane immediately lost power on takeoff, and it was only the wily cunning of a veteran pilot that kept us alive. The plane dropped quickly, right into the center of a residential section of town, fell so low so fast that I was looking directly into the ground floor living room windows of people's homes. We flew *under* a power line—that low. And that was my near-death experience. I have been much closer to death recently.

It began on a raft trip, of all places. An idyllic setting: the Rogue River in southwestern Oregon. On a trip with eighteen other people, all of us invited there to critique a new book by a best-selling author friend who wanted "inside" opinions of the new book's weaknesses and strengths. Floating down white-feathered water with a congressman, four doctors, a mathematician, two geologists, an attorney, and two tree climbing experts—men and women, all friends of the host. No simple trip this. Lunch and dinner we had informal lectures and discussions: the poetry of Yeats, assisted suicide, the geology of the area. I climbed a tree 110 feet high. Higher than I had ever been: even in the sixties.

One of the discussions was led by a woman, Charlotte Highgrave, director of the UN's Developing Nations Program, leading an effort to halt the tide of HIV infection in third world countries. She told us of the politics. The infighting. The budgets. The unnecessary deaths. Without knowing it, this was the beginning for me. My life was permanently changed by that raft trip. Other lives too.

Life is shaped by synchronized moments. Call them coincidences, if you like, I think of them more as collisions. Before leaving home I was informed by a friend of mine, Judith, that her brother had finally succumbed to AIDS after a long and painful battle. I had known about Jerry's infection for years. In a distant way, I, too, had suffered his illness through my friendship with his sister. But it was in experiencing his death through her capable descriptions that I came to experience secondhand the horror and finality of HIV and AIDS. And, in my own way, the beauty of the finality of death. She said something to me that became profound in my life: "We should all experience a death firsthand, in order to fully understand the meaning and quality of our own lives." The same could be said for murder, I would later find out.

Charlotte Highgrave and I became close on a flight back from the raft trip. I cried in her arms over a divorce I was going through. I had never finished anything in my life, and now I could add marriage to that list. I felt a complete and total failure. Charlotte later cried in my arms over the loss of her husband—killed by AIDS through a blood transfusion in Africa in the early eighties. Back before anyone even knew what AIDS was. Back in a time of great darkness and fear. No tests. Rumors. Potent motivation for her current work.

We come to regard institutions with contempt. Bureaucracies seem incapable of moving forward—electing to travel in circles instead. Charlotte had injected herself into the UN Developing Nations Program and the battle to control the spread of HIV. What she found was a bureaucracy bent on going around on the hamster wheel, while millions—count them: millions—of black Africans expired in the agonized dance of AIDS. Piles of rotting bodies, in numbers projected to be far greater than the Holocaust. Numbers that choked me with tears. Overweight doctors in suits conducting endless discussions, making policy decisions. And Charlotte embattled.

In a phone conversation weeks later, Charlotte informed me of her most recent battle with the Global Health Organization, her United Nations sister organization, and competitor for the same international funding. For "personal reasons" she said she didn't want to go into it over the phone. I asked, "Personal, or *security* reasons?" She avoided an answer, inviting me to join her sometime in New York for a gin and tonic, at which time she would explain it to me.

A week later I was on a plane with a nagging sense of responsibility. To what, to whom, I had not yet realized. Certainly I had no inkling of the murderer I was soon to become. But I did have something new stirring in me: a sense of determination to set things right. Perhaps it had been the death of Judith's brother, or perhaps my own near-death experience. Perhaps the images on CNN of the fly-encrusted Africans, brittle bone covered in a stretched black fabric of skin. Dying. Not starving. Not massacred. But infected. *Millions*, I thought. I drank a gin and tonic on the plane, just for practice.

"They're stonewalling me." Charlotte had dark hair, intense eyes, and the smooth voice of a Brit. She had ten years on my forty and a fresh linen suit that color of cream that isn't cream at all. Or if it is, it has gone sour. She wore a straw hat with a wide brim. We were in a courtyard café somewhere near Chelsea and the gin was very good. Very cold.

"Who is?"

"What it amounts to is genocide." She was fast with her gin and tonic, though her words were slow, round and smooth like river rock. "They're all doctors, you see: Estridge, Landau, and O'Maly. The supervising board of Global Health. The three who set the agenda. Used to getting and having their way. Used to being right. Used to that kind of authority that says 'take this' and the patient always obeys. It's horrid. Their diagnosis is wrong. They're wrong."

"Who? What?"

"GHO—Global Health Organization. The issue is behavior, isn't it?" she asked me. "Sexual behavior. These *pigs*—my colleagues—have the gall to suggest that Africans don't want to know if they are infected or not. *Don't want to know!* There are no testing centers provided for in their program, you see. None . . . whatsoever." She signaled for a second round. I hurried mine down to keep up. Rolling the bottom of her glass on the table, she said, "Spent seven months in Niger one time. All three of my coworkers came down with malaria. I did not. It's the gin and tonics, you see. At least I always believed it was."

"The issue," I pressed.

"You see it's all about funding. Power. Budget is power. It's that simple. Big budget, lots of power. Isn't it? Of course it is. And it's about *policy*, isn't it? It's about which side of the coin you fall on, and these bastards actually have the nerve to say that Africans don't want, don't need to know whether or not they are HIV positive. Bill Estridge claims that such knowledge will not measurably change the African's sexual behavior, so why spend all the money on the testing?"

"Let me get this straight," *while I still am*, I was thinking, as the second round of doubles was delivered. "You're saying that they aren't testing the African countries for HIV infection?"

*   *   *

"It's incredible, isn't it? But true. Absolutely true. And the more I press for the testing, for sexual education, condom distribution, the more Estridge and his *colleagues* work behind my back to make me look bad. Politics! They don't want to hear from people like me. They are doctors. Their answer is to *treat* the disease; it's all they think about: treatment. It's where their money goes: treatment, and into developing a vaccine. Prevention just doesn't enter into it. They are convinced that *Africans* won't respond to behavior modification."

"It's because they're black," I offered naively, as if the only person to whom this might have occurred.

Her eyes hardened. "Of course. And poor. And tribal."

"They don't count."

"Exactly. Unless you mean in terms of patients. But oh how they add up. We can identify no less than seven *nations* that have a thirty percent infection rate. Thirty percent! We're talking tens of millions of new infections in just the next five years. Worldwide, we are seeing ten thousand new HIV infections *every day*. Every *day*," she repeated. "Sixty million dead in twenty years, ninety percent of whom will be in third world countries: Thailand, India, most all of the African nations. If you could only see these people."

"I have in a way," I told her. My friend Judith had shown me photographs of her brother on the day of his death. Parting shots in the family album. I had not felt sick. Nor had I been nauseated. I had cried. I had broken down and cried, and Judith had cried with me. Jerry was one life. *Millions*, I thought.

Millions like Jerry, under trees, inside huts, on dirty city streets, on staircases. Expiring. Slowly, like fruit left on a windowsill, but in the clutches of great pain.

"Men," I said. "Global Health is all men."

"I wasn't going to say it."

"Doctors." I had encountered enough to know. They fell into two camps: the do-goods and the Gods. I told her so.

"These are from the latter camp, I believe." She was already half through the gin and tonic. "Go easy on that," I advised.

"I'm going to lose my job. They're going to discredit me. It hardly matters, I suppose. They have effectively blocked the money for the testing, for the counseling, for the educational programs. It's all over but the dying."

"But it amounts to murder!" Even ten people enduring Jerry's fate was beyond me. *Millions?*

She eyed me. "Yes. Yes, it is. Of course it is."

The gin and tonics arrived. The bell to round two rang loudly as we clinked glasses. "Are there no women in Global Health?" I asked. "None at the decision level?" I was looking for some way to combat the attitude of the three board members—to bring a different voice to the table.

She smiled. It wasn't a direct answer, but I understood that I had guessed right, and I understood as well that we both agreed a woman's voice would bring change to such decisions. "It's a men's club," I suggested. "A doctor's club." She nodded. "Set in their beliefs."

"Entirely set in their beliefs. Yes. They are healers. It is all they know. Their faith is in vaccines. Research. Cures. It's where the majority of the money goes. What's left goes to care. None—zero—goes to testing. Less than two percent— my budget—goes to prevention. And now they're trying to put me out of business—to grab my two percent, as if I'm any threat to them."

"Are these things doubles?" I asked, hoisting the gin and tonic.

She grinned. She had flecks of gold in her front teeth. She looked tired, but it was something much closer to frustration than fatigue. Maybe both.

I asked, "Will they give you the money if you shout loudly enough?"

"Give me money? No. They don't directly control my budget. But they view any money directed toward my department and my efforts as money they could have, and they don't like others having it, do they? My total budget is less than a million dollars—that's nothing to them. I don't see why they bother going after me. I'm small potatoes." She sampled the drink. "I'm serious about being fired. I think that's in my immediate future."

"But if your voice goes silent . . ."

*   *   *

"It's what they want, isn't it? I've appealed to everyone on all levels. It's no good, you see. No good at all. I've been discredited. These people have waged an effective war of propaganda against me, and it's working, you see. Yes, it's working quite well for them."

"There must be something that can be done."

"I'm afraid there's nothing left *to* be done. It has been going on for years, you see. This is the end, not the beginning. I've been in the fight for years." She smiled in a patronizing way that bothered me. "You mustn't get too worked up about it, really. It's over."

"Could these men be voted out of power? Couldn't a more progressive board be established? What about these women? Couldn't we get a couple of women onto the board?"

"No one is going to step down. No one is going to be voted out."

"But if the women got onto the board somehow—if that happened . . . Would things change?"

"I know these women. They understand the situation. Yes. I think there would be change. The vaccine research is important, you see. Certainly it is. But so is testing, and there's so little testing out there. Equally important is providing information, supplying quality condoms—educating. That is where we place the emphasis: keeping people informed. But not Global Health; it is entirely a medical question for them, a medical puzzle. The third world has virtually been abandoned. They've given up on them." She added for effect, "Thirty percent, don't forget."

I couldn't forget. I felt in a foul mood. Maybe the gin. Booze sometimes had that effect on me.

"We'll know soon enough how it will all shake out," she said.

"How's that?"

"I'm going public with the story, with the Global Health game plan and how it will eventually cost millions of lives—tens of millions, perhaps. I've kept their secrets long enough. I have an interview on CNN day after tomorrow. If they're going to turn their backs on tens of millions of black Africans, they can at least be held responsible."

"So you *will* be fired," I suggested. "That's how you know."

She nodded sullenly. "That's how I know." She reached across and took my hand, not in a romantic way, but a person seeking comfort. I caressed her hand and we drank our gin, and I felt very sad. It was the last time I saw her alive.

Charlotte Highgrave was dead by the following day. I found out the worst way possible: the newspaper. The *New York Times* carried a small article on page 8 about the "accidental death" of a director of the United Nations Developing Nations Program. She had been discovered on the fire stairs of her apartment building, facedown, neck broken. I was in the hotel coffee shop, and I gasped so loud that I turned several heads. The eyes of well-dressed strangers were fixed on me. A wailing sound escaped my throat, tears gushed from my eyes, and as I stood to get away, I bumped the table and sent everything flying. Teacup, plate, toast, salt, and pepper. The waiter came running. We crossed paths. I called down later to claim the check, but I could barely speak, the words like bones caught in my throat.

Two days later I attended the service, held in the Little Church Around The Corner. My parents had been married in that church in 1945. Charlotte was remembered by dignitaries, politicians, and the press, though in small numbers. Her congressman lover attended. We knew each other from the raft trip and he sat down next to me, passing up other illuminates he might have chosen. We shook hands, but never said a word. We both smelled of gin and tonics. When three distinguished-looking men entered, wearing the uniform of solemn business suits and the requisite grave expressions, the congressman could not take his eyes off them. He fixated on them, like a dog with a passerby. The words, "Global Health?" escaped my dry lips in a hoarse whisper. He looked at me sternly. I said softly, "Charlotte told me."

"Bastards," he said. "They drove her crazy, those three. She's been drinking too much lately, and doing too much, and something like this was bound to happen. That shit catches up with you."

"So you're buying it as an accident," I stated.

This caught him totally by surprise. He blanched.

"She had an interview scheduled on CNN. She was going to talk."

*   *   *

If it was possible, he grew even more pale. His jaw slacked. "You know what you're saying?" he asked.

"Forget I ever said anything." That was the first moment I understood what was required of me. It didn't come from the heavens. It didn't come from Him. It was a very simple chain of logic that inserted itself into my consciousness, squirting up out of the darkness of my being, and installed itself like a usurping government. It took over. Accident or not, Charlotte's dreams would not go unanswered. Part of it was, of course, that I felt my own life was over. Divorce had left me paralyzed and emotionally numb. None of what I had once held important to my life mattered at all. I was as aimless as a seed in the wind—a bad seed, it turned out.

I found that focus gave me meaning again. My personal problems faded into the background and, like cheap music in a bad restaurant, I ignored it. I practically moved into the New York Public Library. I learned everything there was to know about Estridge, Landau, and O'Maly. I called ten friends until I finally found a walk-up I could house-sit for at least the next month. I moved out of the hotel on a Sunday, paying by credit card and exceeding my limit. On Monday I arranged for bank funds to be transferred. It was an expensive city; I didn't know how long I could make it, even with a free bed. A strange and unsettling power overtook me, for I understood fully that I had become an assassin. I was going to kill three men. I was going to change the world.

Everything around me intensified. The sun, even electric lights, were brighter. I could hear things at a great distance. My sense of smell, rather than covered over by a toxic city, revealed itself in a way I thought only dogs and cats could perceive. My skin became sensitive in that same way just prior to a fever. I was aware, at all times, of everyone around me. I remembered faces. I could spot a license plate on one day, and recite it three days later, having never thought of it in between. I was different.

None of this was trained into me; it felt instead as if my DNA had changed overnight. I lived for one purpose. I ate less. I slept much less. I took no forms of entertainment, except women. My sex drive ran wild. It led me to singles bars in the wee hours of the morning. Never comfortable with even the idea of a one-night stand, I began having sex with complete strangers. Safe sex, but dangerous in that it came so easily and went so totally out of control. My partners were willing. They educated me. Monogamous me. Some returned to see me, but I made it clear I was not someone to attach to. "There will come a time when you will deny having known me," I would warn. My longest relationship was a week. After that I stopped seeing women. It had gotten out of control. I awakened one night and thought she was dead, not just sleeping, and I realized my time had come. I was ready. I wanted to meet Death on my terms.

Death was not a hooded figure with shadowed eye sockets and bloodied teeth. It was not some figure from a Renaissance oil painting, or a De Niro film. Death was a small plastic vile, like a test tube, filled with red sticky blood and capped with a rubber stopper that was taped to the stem, and a bright Day-Glo orange label that warned of the toxicity of the contents. Death was HIV-infected blood. I was merely a delivery boy. The messenger. I felt a bit like a man trying to set up a friend—making introductions. In fact, I was Death. I had inherited the cloak. It was my own bones rattling that I heard in my nightmares. I just didn't understand any of it yet.

My loss.

My fate was my mission. I lived to kill three men. Three hypocrites. Oddly, I felt no remorse for what I intended to do—to the contrary, I felt an obligation to fulfill this destiny. Although I knew it clearly was murder, it did not feel that way to me. I was justified. I was right. To all others who saw this incorrectly: Be damned. I knew what I was doing.

Empire University Research Center was located in the Flatiron District, on Seventeenth Street between Fifth and Broadway. It occupied the fifth floor of a seven-story building that had once housed several stories of sweatshops. I spent the better part of four days watching the front door to the building. I rode the elevator up to the fifth floor a dozen times. I walked the stairs an equal number of times. I studied. The journals that I had read in the library convinced me that Empire was my best shot at an HIV-infected blood supply. It was an international research center, implying that relative strangers came and went with some frequency. Security, it seemed to me, could not be terribly strict given this turnover of visitors. On the fifth day of my surveillance I boldly entered the facility's front door. I approached a female receptionist, offering my most serious expression, and told her I was with U.N.D.N.P., performing the same slur of the letters that Charlotte had so often used with me. I mentioned Charlotte Highgrave by name. "I need to drop off some papers with Dr. Corrigan. I have to do it personally," I added as her hand came up inviting the papers. Corrigan had written several of the papers I had reviewed, complete with a black-and-white photograph that proved out-of-date by what I had seen of him in my days of watching the research center. He was grayer, and older by several years. He was stooped and he walked slowly, apparently with great pain. He had entered after lunch and had not yet left the facility.

I wore a trench coat, courtesy of my credit card. I felt a bit foolish, but it was exactly suited to my needs. I glanced around carefully as she placed the call and announced that someone from U.N.D.N.P. was here to make a delivery in person.

Unexpectedly, the receptionist passed me the phone. I had expected her to simply wave me through and point me in the right direction. Since I had no intention of ever reaching Dr. Corrigan, I had jumped ahead with my mission, forced now to think quickly. Nervously, I accepted the receiver. "Hello?"

"Who is this please?"

"My name is . . . Richardson," I lied. "I was Charlotte High-grave's assistant. These papers were to be delivered to you personally." I felt my heart pounding in my chest and my tongue went dry and I felt a little faint. I had no papers. I had nothing more than nerve, and it was quickly deserting me. In my pocket was a small roll of silver duct tape. I had a plan, but Dr. Corrigan had just stymied me.

"Very well. Linda can direct you to my office. Put her back on, please." He sounded like my high school biology teacher, formal and impatient.

*   *   *

I handed Linda the receiver. A moment later she was giving me directions through a series of hallways. As far as I was concerned the confusing directions were perfect: If I wandered astray, I would be forgiven. Just to give myself another out, I asked after the bathrooms. These directions were more clear, and in the same general direction, but that was okay—I could still plead confusion and get away with it. I nodded, attempting to appear slightly confused, but not to the point she might offer to repeat herself. Off I went.

I took my first left, and ignoring Linda's directions, a right at the end of the hall because the red EXIT sign caught my eye. It was a short hall with only three doors: a mail room, an unmarked door, and the exit. As a black woman hurried from the mail room, I turned around immediately and headed back in the general direction that Linda had suggested. I didn't want to get too far into the guts of the building, but my mission, having found an exit, was to locate the actual laboratory, having no idea if there might be more than one. I ducked into the men's room, slipped into a stall, and locked the door. It took me over a minute to collect myself. My heart rate slowly eased, and I felt better, more in control. I slipped off the trench coat, revealing the white lab coat I was wearing, complete with a black name tag that read, Dr. Richard Richardson, M.D.; the American Medical Association symbol was engraved alongside. I left the trench coat hanging on the peg on the back of the stall door. I splashed some cold water onto my face, inspected myself in the mirror, and decided I was ready. The black-rimmed glasses I donned were nonprescription but went a long way toward changing my looks. It took me a moment longer to convince myself I could do this; my heart began to run away from me again. I felt as if it were very late at night and I had drunk too much coffee. I took a deep breath and left the men's room. I heard and smelled the lab before I reached it. I was deep into the hallways of the research center, and my white lab coat proved the perfect camouflage: several other similarly dressed individuals nodded at me, as if I were familiar to them. Dutifully, I nodded back. I thought of myself as *inside*. My palms were damp, and my throat was once again dry as a bone, as if the two went together.

I turned into the lab as if I owned the place, and I did not look around. The coffee machine in the corner drew me. I grabbed a paper cup from the tall stack and poured myself half a cup. As I did so, I looked around for the first time. And for the first time I registered a variety of languages being spoken. In all, there were thirteen people, and I took this to be a lucky number because I was born on the thirteenth of March, and when you are born on the thirteenth you are left no choice but to adopt the number as yours. There were people working in groups of two and three, and several people working solo. Everyone at a lab counter wore eye protection and gloves, lending an unexpected sense of fear and dread. What I was about to attempt was filled with risk on a variety of levels.

Against the far wall stood two enormous stainless steel commercial refrigerators and a matching freezer. I targeted the refrigerators, but decided against a direct strike. Instead, I sipped the bad coffee, gathered my courage, and headed down the closest aisle, where three people were speaking wickedly fast French and sharing a microscope. I approached them, standing behind, and did my best to appear both curious and comfortable with myself. I wondered if the vein in my forehead was inflated and revealing my escalating heartbeat. My former wife had always claimed she could tell when I was nervous or angry by this warning sign. Or both, which in our last few months together was nearly always the case.

I didn't want to think about her. She would only get in the way. But I was thinking about her, and I stumbled a bit when one of the three—a woman—finally turned to glance at me. "Dick Richardson," I said, introducing myself. *"Bonjour."* She introduced her colleagues in passable English. "Anything interesting?" I asked, as if I owned the place, hoping one of them did not. "It is a wonderful facility," she replied, and I could tell she wanted me out of the way. "Yes," I replied, adding, "Nice meeting you." I nodded. She forced a smile and I moved on, down to the back of the lab, with a clear shot at the three refrigeration units.

I passed several blue plastic racks designed to hold the test tubes containing blood samples, most of which were occupied with vials. But several were not, and I grabbed one of these empties and carried it with me to the refrigerators. I was not a gambler; I knew nothing of odds. I selected the middle refrigerator completely at random. My eyes went wide as the unit's blinding interior lights revealed rack upon rack of blood samples. *Hundreds*, it occurred to me. The bottom row, with its bright orange stickers, called out to me. The words EXTREME CAUTION—HIV-CONTAMINATED BLOOD—TAKE ALL NECESSARY PRECAUTIONS, read clearly on the Day-Glo labels. Dozens of vials.

The mother lode, I thought.

I slipped on a pair of latex gloves, noticing immediately that the brand I had purchased was not the same as that used by the lab—visually, my gloves were much clearer. Only then did I notice that there were dispensers offering the gloves every few feet down the lab benches. I should have used these. But I had made a plan; I had rehearsed my actions thoroughly, and as might an actor, I found it difficult to alter my stage directions. I collected four of the small plastic tubes filled with blood into my blue rack and was just picking up the fifth and final sample when a voice spoke over my shoulder. "Excuse me," the voice said. A woman. Right behind me. I was so startled by this, that I loosed my grip on the vial, and it slipped toward the floor. I witnessed the events of the next few seconds, as if I had already lived them. The vial would strike the floor and would crack or break which in turn would cause a legitimate health safety threat. The resulting attention paid to the accident was likely to force me into my Dr. Richard Richardson identity, which would be as fatal as the blood in the slim plastic tube; despite all my reading, I doubted I could play doctor for more than a weak sentence or two. As gravity gripped this vial, I saw myself with some impossible explaining to do. And as if not attached to my normally clumsy body, my right hand swatted the air and caught the falling vial at waist height. Without a second thought, I slipped it into the plastic rack and stepped aside. The woman edged in alongside me and said, "Nice catch," as she examined the blood samples in the refrigerator and began to sort through them.

One of my biggest worries was Dr. Corrigan's attention span, and how he might react when his messenger failed to appear. If he called the front desk and checked up on me, I hoped the receptionist might mention the bathroom, believing that would buy me an extra few minutes. Even so, I had no time to waste. I took two steps away from the refrigerator when the same woman said to me, "Doctor," which failed to win my attention since I had never been called this in my life, "don't forget to sign those out." She had already grabbed two vials and was in the process of filling out a form that was held to an aluminum clipboard. When she finished, she offered me the pen that was attached by a length of string. A tired-looking woman in her mid-forties, she took her samples with her toward the door. I copied much of what she had written on the form, but changed the sequence numbers of the vials I was taking in hopes of keeping the theft undiscovered until a proper inventory was conducted. I signed my pseudonym illegibly, as all doctors sign everything. I headed directly to the door of the lab, eager to get back to my trench coat and be rid of this place. I had no way of knowing how sophisticated the lab's security might be, how much attention was paid to keeping people like me from doing exactly what I was doing. I assumed there were hidden cameras. If supermarkets had them, certainly an infectious disease lab would, I reasoned. But this was a city of many millions—and I was not native. My photograph would mean little to any security personnel, and I had never so much as been inside a police department. Having not served in the military, my fingerprints had never been taken. I was just a common citizen—even with my image recorded on videotape, I decided I had little to worry about. But I was out of my element. And I was wrong.

I reached the men's room without incident, all the while fearing Corrigan or one of his staff was out looking for me. I donned the trench coat, covering up my lab jacket, and wrapped the vials of blood in bubble wrap and put them in the coat pocket. I threw away the blue rack in the bathroom trash. I sucked up my courage and left the bathroom; I could not remember having ever experienced this same combination of fear and excitement. I was charged with a toxic energy that felt both alarmingly warm but dangerous. I didn't know myself. I entered into the hallway and headed immediately toward the EXIT sign that I had spotted on my way in, navigating the labyrinth with some authority. I reached the door; there were no signs warning of an alarm. But as I punched the panic bar to let myself out, and threw my hip into the steel door, the security alarm went off like a fire siren. This was no simple door alarm; it sounded throughout the facility. Two thoughts occurred to me: The alarm had sounded; I was carrying five vials of HIV-contaminated blood. And then another thought entered my mind, defining my identity and terrifying me: I was a thief; I was a criminal.

I exploded from the area with the same abandon that I had once fled Mrs. Constantine Pilchert's backyard after punching a line drive hardball through a stained glass window on her front porch; the same sensation I recalled from childhood when walking home at night; how suddenly it seemed that *it* was right behind me. The presence of *it* was extremely sharp and intense. Bearing down on me. A dozen films crowded my imagination and I pictured guns raised to drop me—and me, the man in the overcoat, leaping down fire stairs two at a time. *Hit the landing and turn. Jump . . . Jump . . . Hit the landing and turn.* I established a rhythm. I heard only the pounding of blood in my body and the hollow slap of my shoes on the poured cement of the stairs. I was terrified *they* would catch me. I was beside myself with fear.

On the second floor I caught myself, and bolted through the door rather than continuing down the stairs, worried that someone above me might have radioed or called down. This floor was divided between a dance studio and a costume company. There was a service elevator and a passenger elevator side by side. There was a fire escape out a shatter-resistant, chicken wire window. I threw open the window and looked down into an alley with a pair of battered Dumpsters and a wino in a cardboard condo, a river of pee running toward a drain. The fire escape did not reach the pavement, and it looked to be a risky jump. My heart had swollen to three times its regular size. I needed out of this building, fast.

The elevator sounded a bell, the doors slid open, and a woman disembarked. I hurried inside, hesitated, and pushed the button for the garage, electing to avoid the ground floor. It was a hydraulic elevator and it moved more slowly than I could have run the stairs, but I didn't dare stay in the stairwell. There was no way for me to predict how long it might take the lab's security people to react to the EXIT door having been opened. Then it occurred to me that only *I* knew about my theft of the contaminated blood; for all I knew, the exit alarms were a regular annoyance for security, something they tolerated. For all I knew, they had merely reset the alarm and gone back to the coffee and donuts. By the time I reached the parking garage I had convinced myself that it was unlikely I was being followed. It was probably unlikely, I realized, that there would be any security personnel on site at all—contracted out was more like it.

The elevator doors slid open and there were no Uzis facing me, no killers training their weapons on me. Instead I found myself in a barren cement bunker with an oil-stained floor and junky old cars lined up like soldiers. Alone. I walked out, passing the red-and-white mechanical arm that guarded the entrance—out into the chaos and confusion and cacophony that was New York. As I walked down Lexington under a gray sky I realized that having stolen the blood I was now ready to kill with it. And rather than feeling afraid, I found myself excited. The memory of Charlotte's twisted corpse drove me on.

Many years earlier I had read a story in the newspaper about a Soviet double agent who had been killed by being stabbed by an umbrella tip. Not being fluent in ways to kill people I resigned myself to the fact that I would need to copy methods, and an umbrella seemed an interesting way to go about it. Creating the weapon itself took more time than I expected. Ironically, it was my host—the absentee owner of the apartment I was house-sitting—who had inspired the idea of the syringe/umbrella and provided me with the means of creating my weapon. A diabetic, this woman's bathroom closet had several dozen syringes, each wrapped individually in plastic and stored in paper boxes used by hospital staff and doctors' offices. There was a tall red plastic container marked as hazardous medical waste for doing away with the sharpies.

I envisioned a weapon in which the last few inches of the umbrella disguised a syringe, and whereby, once the tip of the umbrella was removed, the needle to the syringe would be exposed. This required me to use a hacksaw to remove the last few inches of an umbrella. It was a cheap umbrella, and a good thing, too, because I made a mess of it. Still, I used this as my prototype, working through the hours to perfect both the performance and the look of my delivery system. My final attempt was to combine black electrician's tape with some cardboard to effect the look of an umbrella tip. I retained the metal cone at the very end, and used a small piece of tape to secure it, thus hiding the needle from sight and risking damaging it. I practiced with my prototype repeatedly, first for performance by stabbing the tricked-out umbrella into an eggplant, and later, by working through a choreography that allowed me to remove the needle shield while on the move. The following day I repeated my training, walking the length of the apartment and stabbing fruits and vegetables left on the floor and on chairs. If anybody had paid me a visit, I would have had a lot of explaining to do. As it was, I became something of a pro at fruit stabbing: a practiced murderer.

Doctors, even those on the board of the Global Health Organization, do not think of themselves in terms of being potential murder victims. Abortionists, maybe. Not Dr. William Landau. He lived in a seventeenth floor suite of apartments on Central Park South, overlooking the seasonally barren trees of New York's emerald jewel. I parked myself across the street, wrapped in layers of secondhand clothes from a store in the Village. I spent three days with him, discovering to my delight that Dr. William was as predictable as the sunset. He had been scheduled all his life, and he stuck to one like clockwork. He left by chauffeured car for his UN offices at nine-forty-five each morning, arriving minutes before ten o'clock. I couldn't get inside the facility, except for a public tour that didn't show me anything useful. He lunched between noon and one, usually in the company of several others, and not the same people. He favored the University Club, in that he lunched there two of the three days. To my delight, he walked back from lunch, apparently working off the meal. No car followed him. No security. On Friday he stopped at an apartment building after work and spent ninety minutes there, and judging by his somewhat disheveled appearance upon his exit, I decided he had a mistress. This, I thought might play nicely into my needs. I stayed with him through the weekend, and through Wednesday of the following week. I lived with him. I learned to know him. By Wednesday evening I felt sorry for him. He had a shallow life outside of the

UN, filled with a few nice restaurants, his Tuesday and Friday affair in the apartment building, and evenings spent mostly at home. My life was far worse than his, and yet I pitied him. He lived bound to the clock. He lived in dark suits and cars with tinted windows. I wondered what he saw in the mirror in the morning. I wondered what made him smile.

I had yet to see him smile. And he didn't have much time left.

I chose the following Friday—a day forecast as ninety percent chance of rain—for the day that would mark the end of his life. Lucky, or unlucky, for him it might be years before he left the planet. It might have even been years until he understood his time was more finite than he believed. This, except that I had promised myself not to allow him to infect others— his wife, even his mistress, did not deserve to die because of his ignorance. This was murder, not genocide.

I did not sleep that Thursday night. I tried but failed. I rechecked my umbrella weapon too many times. Leaving it, I ventured out to a nearby church and spent two hours praying on bended knee. I had not prayed like this in years, perhaps never. I did not ask for guidance—my mind was long since made up. I asked for luck. I asked for success. I asked God to help me kill these men, to give Charlotte's ideals a chance, to help the black Africans that Global Health had long since abandoned. I saw no contradiction in asking God to help me kill. I left the church in the wee hours of the morning, believing I now had a partner.

My makeup took over an hour to apply, in part because I was no good at it. I used eye shadow to deepen my sockets, rouge to sharpen my cheekbones. I adopted a blond wig and I bleached and then dyed my eyebrows with some store-bought stuff that smelled horrible. They looked vaguely orange-gold, and I regretted doing that to myself. I had spent three hours. It was six in the morning. I felt great. Sleep, which had long since betrayed me, was neither wanted nor needed. I was operating on another level. I felt bulletproof. I wondered if this was how a Broadway star felt prior to curtain time. I had a performance to give. I wore a secondhand suit. Dark. I wore someone else's shoes—they hurt my feet but they looked the part. I wore my trench coat, and I carried an umbrella. I watched Dr. William leave his Park Avenue South apartment, but elected not to follow him. I didn't want to risk anything. From ten in the morning until five-twenty that afternoon, I walked the streets of New York. I walked miles. I walked from the Park down to Wall Street and back to the Park. I drank three cups of espresso, and I ate one bagel that I bought on the corner of Twenty-first and First Avenue. Best bagel I had ever eaten. I hoped not the last.

In the bathroom of a pastry shop on Second Avenue, I drew the blood from the vial I carried. I filled the syringe halfway. If I could deliver half that amount, I believed I would infect him. In fact, even a drop might do it. I wasn't taking chances. Practice had warned me not to expect too much. It was going to be quick—a brief connection. In the case of the Soviet agent an incredibly toxic poison had been used. My poison was lethal, but not nearly so concentrated. I put on the gloves and spent ten minutes in the bathroom stall wiping down the handle and the syringe, despite my prints not being on file anywhere. I was prepared to lose my weapon to a quick escape. I had tried to think of everything. But I was new to this profession: A murderer *never* thinks of everything.

* * *

I wanted a rainy day, but not rain. I was not given what I
wanted. As it was, by the time I took up my vigil outside the
lover's apartment house, New York was seized in a deluge. A
downpour. A cloudburst. It was raining cats and dogs. I was
drenched. I calculated the distance between the front door
and the curb at about twenty feet. I would have to remain
incredibly close by if I were to get a chance at him. I had
hoped for dark but clearing skies, for his usual stroll up to
Park Avenue where he typically hailed an uptown cab. But
with this rain, I feared the worst—a taxi at the very least. His
chauffeured car was most likely.

In order to remain close by, I was forced to loiter, and I was
forced to get wet. Chilled to the bone. I expected a forty-
minute wait, but it could be as soon as ten or twenty. Even in
his two visits I had learned his libido was unpredictable. If he
got done early, he went to the University Club for a drink. If
he ran late, he headed directly home. I was forced to patrol a
terribly small area—in the pouring rain—and I was certain
that someone would spot my behavior and take note of me.
Hopefully the standard New Yorker would do nothing about
it. This, I decided, was about all I had going for me.

My heart rate remained accelerated for the better part of fifty
minutes. I was running on a combination of adrenaline and
caffeine and the effect was both dizzying and nauseating. I
was so cold I was trembling. My gloves were slippery and I
had trouble holding on to the umbrella. For the first time, my
absolute certainty gave way to the terrified realization I might
fail at this. After weeks and weeks of preparation, it suddenly
occurred to me I might not be cut out for this. Maybe I was
no killer after all.

*   *   *

The black Town Car arrived, wipers going. The door to the apartment house swung open, and Dr. William, holding a folded *New York Times* over his head for shelter, cut through the downpour toward the vehicle's back door, where the uniformed driver awaited him with a blank and servile expression. To judge by the driver, this might as well have been a sunny summer evening.

I stripped the single piece of tape from the butt of the umbrella, removing the shield and exposing the tip of the needle. I felt as if I suddenly wore a hood that blackened my peripheral vision and focused entirely upon my prey. I did not have any feeling. My feet moved of their own accord. I seemed to drift above the sidewalk, and I was reminded of monks I had seen as a boy, who, dressed in sweeping saffron robes, had seemed to float as they walked. I flew toward my prey like a hawk. Talons spread. Ready for the kill.

The sidewalk was modestly crowded despite the weather. It was quarter to six. I remember seeing this number—5:45—on the chauffeur's watch face. I was close enough to read it. He glanced at me, did the driver. He saw me coming, and perhaps he thought I was going to try to claim the car, for he looked more amused than troubled. Perhaps it was my soggy condition. Maybe I looked funny to him. I didn't feel funny. I felt like danger. I felt like Death.

Dr. William's calf was stretched backward in the middle of a stride. I felt the rhythm of his walk—I measured it carefully. I understood it. And when it next presented itself, I reared back my lance and stabbed him hard—one hot, quick lunge that left my elbow fully extended. I leaned my weight into it, ensuring that the fluid within the syringe would be quickly discharged. I heard him shout, "Shit!" and I watched the leg jump in reaction. And I withdrew the weapon in one sharp motion. If it had been a summer day, he might have believed himself stung by a bee. If I had built my weapon more carefully, if I had practiced with the same enthusiasm that I experienced in the moment of battle, I might have been able to anticipate what happened next. But as the umbrella pulled away, the bloody syringe broke off from the umbrella and dangled from his pant leg. "What the fuck?" I heard Dr. William shout in fear, as he spun around and looked directly into my eyes.

The chauffeur finally caught on. But he was holding the door open, standing behind it, and he bumped it, partially closing it, as he attempted to get hold of me. The effort knocked Dr. William off-balance and in the melee, I took a step back, turned, and fled. But I did not run. I had told myself for weeks that control was everything. Attract no unnecessary attention. *Stay calm!* This was a joke, of course: I was anything but calm. But I did not run. In my mind's eye I saw the syringe dangling from the good doctor's leg, the dark brown blood oozing from it. I saw the horror in the eyes of a man who had condemned *millions* to die. Had it yet registered what I had done? Or was he sitting in the backseat of the limo believing some drug was soon to take effect? I could picture them racing to the hospital. I could imagine the doctor believing himself the target of a kidnapping. How would he feel when he realized the damage was done? He was a carrier of HIV now. He was marked for death. His clock was running. His life ending. I had killed him, in a strange sort of way.

I walked in the rain for over two hours. It passed as a matter of minutes. I relived the event so many times that I could taste the air, could smell the exhaust, could feel the chills sweeping my body, as if I were right back there. At one point I forgot my name. As hard as I tried I could not recall my own name. This induced a terror in me like I had never known. I could not remember what avenue I was walking, and the faces of strangers that paraded past seemed not to see me at all. Not only was I not the criminal that people were looking for, but I didn't seem to exist. Dull eyes looked right through me. In the moment of my worst panic I stopped walking, and it was only as the stream of bodies opened to flow around me that I realized I must exist, or why were they avoiding me?

The bartender's name was Sam—what else?—and he didn't seem to notice that I was soaked from head to foot. My shoes squeaked with rainwater. I nearly slipped off the stool when I sat down I was so wet. But Sam remained impassive and asked what was "my pleasure."

"My pleasure is to hear the voice of another human being," I informed him. "Talk to me, Sam." He viewed me quizzically. "Your name tag," I said, letting him know how it was I knew his name. "Call me Richard," I said, using the alias I had come to live with. *Too much hiding*, I thought. *Not enough contact. Not since Charlotte was killed. All alone. Isolated. I should have known better.* "Have you ever felt a little crazy, Sam?"

"With this job? All the time." He was black and about six-foot-two. He looked to be in his late forties. He had a lot of bulk to him. When I looked around I realized that most of his patrons were black. Maybe that was why he had looked at me strangely. Maybe to him I was just another crazy white man. A seed gone bad. And he wouldn't have been far wrong in thinking that, I realized. "You drinking?" he asked.

* * *

I ordered a gin and tonic. The wrong drink for this time of year, but Sam didn't care. "To Charlotte," I offered, raising my glass to my bartender. "Yeah, whatever," the man said. He distanced himself from me. But, a few minutes later, when he was forced to come close to find a bottle on the shelf, I asked him rhetorically, "Do you know what I think? About life? About people? I think that it's going to happen anyway. Death. Right? It's going to happen, so what does it matter? Fast or slow, what does it matter? They come for you eventually, don't you think? They get you eventually. Or maybe they don't. Maybe they never get you." I laughed loudly. "Maybe they never do get you. Can you imagine? What if they never get you?"

He looked at me long and hard and asked, "You need another?"

I didn't need another, but I accepted the offer. The first had gone down like water. So did the second. And the third. Like Charlotte. I kept thinking of her. I kept seeing Dr. William's stunned expression and that syringe dangling from his leg. I saw my own hand holding the umbrella handle. I felt my weight leaning into it—I could picture the blood filling him. Poisoning him. I wondered if he knew yet. I laughed hard: He would need testing to know if he was infected; the same testing he and Global Health denied a few million Africans. Charlotte: lying on the stairs, her neck broken—her dream broken. The fourth drink went down effortlessly. I was terribly chilled and still quite damp. I sneezed and Sam shot me a look that asked me to leave. "You do what you have to do," I informed him. "Justice, you know? The world is not a just place. Sometimes you've got to fix things yourself."

* * *

Sam edged away from me toward the other end of the bar. One of the other patrons said. "Ain't no such thing as Justice. No fucking such thing. I'm telling you. No fucking way. You try wearing this skin, you see soon enough. No fucking such thing as Justice. Can't fix nothing, nohow."

"You gotta fix some things," I said, beginning to slur my words. "You gotta do what you do and make it right. That's just the way the world works."

"Or doesn't," my drunken friend contributed.

My brain was a runaway train. I had lost my ability to hold my thoughts. Each time I focused, or tried to, whatever I was thinking escaped me. And the more I tried, the more I lost. And the more I lost, the more terrified I was that I might never be able to keep a thought again, that I was going crazy, and that I had brought it on myself. I left there an hour later, too drunk to remember the umbrella. I should have thrown it out, disposed of it some way, as I imagined gangsters disposing of their guns—thrown it off a bridge or something. But I had carried it into that nameless bar, and I had left it by the base of the stool, and for all I knew some drunk near Gramercy Park was using it for shelter. Maybe, I thought, the best way to dispose of something is merely to forget about it. Not hard for me: I couldn't remember anything.

I didn't eat the next day. I read every city paper I could get my hands on, my heart pounding heavily, waiting to read a report of my deed, but there was no reference. No report of a doctor being stabbed in the leg with a syringe. No Doc William anywhere to be seen. I liked it. He deserved obscurity. He deserved everything he got. I had killed him—delivered a slow and unforgiving death. I was a murderer.

Four days later I had managed to eat one bowl of soup at a sleazy greasy spoon. My stomach didn't appreciate the food. I threw up an hour later: little pieces of corn and potato and celery. My skin was ashen white and I felt feverish. I thought maybe something had gone wrong, that I had contaminated myself with the infected blood, but it wasn't that at all. A switch had been thrown inside me, and that drunken night had been my last clear look at what was happening to me: I was going insane. Slowly, the way some trees rot—from the inside out.

My thoughts refused to move forward. I was caught back at that chauffeured sedan, my hand gripped tightly to the umbrella. These were the only images I saw: the doc coming out of the apartment house; the door to the car coming open; his lower pant leg and the cuff and the heel of his right shoe. No matter where I was, what I was doing—these were the only images. I didn't hear much of anything except the engine of a car running and the doc's voice delivering those same few words of surprise he had spoken as my deed had registered. I was mentally stagnant—condemned to never leave my act. It was everywhere. It was everything. I was cursed.

I convinced myself that I could not go through that same thing again. I could not stab a person like that. In my few moments of conscious, rational thought, I elected a different program. I called around town. I bought a weapon at a veterinarian wholesale supply house on the west side. It worked off of CO_2 cartridges and fired a hypodermic dart accurately at a range of ten to fifteen feet. It cost me two hundred and sixty-five dollars cash. I purchased a dozen darts at an additional cost of eighty-six-fifty. I spent the better part of twelve midnight to 4:00 A.M. each and every night, firing darts into the furniture from various distances. I spent my days living with the habits of Dr. Francis O'Maly. Number two on my list of three.

I hit O'Maly quickly because I caught myself standing for hours in the same place, long after O'Maly had left the UN or a bar. Twice a cop asked me if everything was okay. If I had been dressed differently, like a homeless man, he might have asked me to move on, or even cited me for loitering. But those brushes with the police sent me a warning sign: I didn't have much time.

A person knows when he or she is sick, and I knew. Though I didn't know of what, or how to stop it. I knew I had to eat, but I couldn't seem to keep food down. I knew I needed sleep, but I could count the nights on one hand where I had gotten more than an hour or two. I was dissolving: mentally, physically, spiritually.

After two more days of watching O'Maly, I struck. He left the UN each day, when office workers flooded the plaza and the sidewalks and streets. It was genuine chaos for a sixty-minute period from four-thirty to five-thirty. Sometimes six o'clock. A creature of habit, he left within a few minutes of five, and always used the same exit. A health freak, he walked home—over to Lexington and then twenty-three blocks to the upper east side. On rainy days he wore rubbers, carried an umbrella, and wore an overcoat, but he walked. Walked in the morning, walked in the evening.

*   *   *

My plan was a simple one. I loaded my cartridge with the contaminated blood beforehand. The weapon itself was quite large and awkward, and looked like a small cannon. I concealed it in a Museum of Modern Art shopping bag into which I had cut a small slit in one side. I covered it with a scarf. I wore gloves. It was a nice day, and I wore sunglasses and a hat. I worked my way through the crowd to a position along the wall—a man waiting for a friend, which was partially accurate. I stood sentry for twelve agonizing minutes. Felt more like an hour. Maybe more. I began to think that I had judged him wrong, that he was less predictable than I thought, that I should have stayed with him much longer, prepared much more carefully, that I was getting lazy and allowing my despair to penetrate my efforts. My thoughts grew fuzzy again; I couldn't stay clear. I remember looking down at the shopping bag in my hand and wondering what it was doing there, why the hell I would be carrying a shopping bag, and what was I doing at the UN? These considerations plagued me, and I had to focus hard to remember what my purpose was here; I felt more like a person going in and out of waking, in and out of a dream state. People flowed past me like water in a stream, hundreds, maybe thousands of them. I watched their faces for O'Maly, once my mission became clear again. Few seemed to see me, as if I was looking through one-way glass, as if I didn't exist. But I did exist, I reminded myself. And I had a job to do.

O'Maly appeared in the lobby amid a sea of bobbing heads and contrite expressions. Faces reflecting fatigue, mixed with an eagerness to get home. O'Maly, impassive, impatient, ready to rev up his metabolism with a brisk walk home. It was going to be a long walk tonight. I suspected a cab ride instead.

I suspected an elevated heart rate, pumping the newly in-jected blood deeper and deeper into the heart of his system.

He cleared the door. I took two steps forward. My forehead was sweating, my heart beating like a jazz drum. I felt dizzy. I knew what I was here to do, and for a moment it felt to me as if my body was intent on preventing me. My legs grew impos-sibly heavy. My hand felt as if it belonged to someone else. I willed that hand to reach deeply into the shopping bag while my feet carried me to a position behind O'Maly. I was in step. In synch. Right . . . Left . . . Right . . . Left . . . My fingers sensed the cold metal. I gripped the stock firmly and wiggled the barrel until it found the rent in the bag and protruded—like a penis out a fly, I thought. I was absurdly close to him—three or four feet behind. I had practiced this many times in the privacy of my apartment. I squeezed the trigger.

The gun barely made a sound: not quite a pop, more like a spit. A sharp hiss. The dart discharged and lodged squarely in O'Maly's buttocks. A fraction of a second after I fired, I hooked sharply left and cut through the throng of departing workers. I heard him back there as he, like his associate, Dr. William Landau, shouted, "Shit!" I guessed that I would be several yards away and moving in a different herd of the de-parting before he was likely to reach back and check the source of that pain, before he would think to turn around and look for who had done this to him. But I was long gone. I did not run. I did not look back. Let him figure it out.

My head swam. There were so many people all heading the same general direction that it felt to me like I was swimming, and the heads were the surface of the sea. And I was floating. I was sinking. I couldn't catch my breath. If I could only make it another few yards, I could make it to a bench, but I sensed the system was shutting down: I was slipping into unconsciousness. I was fainting.

My knee skidded on the cement. I recognized the sensation, and yet felt helpless to do anything about it. Pain shot through me. People streamed around me. I felt someone grab my elbow, and I could almost make out her words. She was asking me if I was all right. I was not all right. I was slipping off into a dark purple room. I felt glued to the sidewalk. Both knees were down. She was asking me again. I lunged forward. The shopping bag slipped from my hand and to my astonishment the dart gun slipped out like a hockey puck. I heard her gasp—as clear as day. I fumbled forward and fell toward the weapon. "He's got a gun!" she screamed. And suddenly the polished shoes were moving away from me. Running. Clearing a huge hole around me, as if I were the one diseased. It seemed impossible that people could move so quickly—especially people who had looked so tired and bored only moments before. "He's got a gun!" she repeated. I looked to my right: the crowd had dispersed there as well—all but O'Maly, who stood there with the dart in his hand looking both stunned and confused, and me, ten yards away kneeling on the cement.

I heard footsteps behind me and glanced around to see a pair of uniformed UN police running toward me, reaching for their weapons.

I was up and running. Feeling returned to my legs. I had no idea where I was heading; I had made no plans for any kind of escape. Operating on pure adrenaline, I charged off into the teeming crowds that littered the congested sidewalk. The crowd's panic of a few seconds earlier seemed to have vanished in a New York minute. My actions only retained the interest of a few people. I pushed a man out of my way and dodged through clogged traffic, assuming the guards were still behind me. I headed right, then cut left up a cross street—I didn't know which one—and continued at an all-out run. I had been fast once; I hoped I was fast still. Halfway toward the next avenue I ventured a glance over my shoulder. They were just rounding the corner; I had put some distance between us. Optimism filled me. I hurried on, slowly becoming aware that if anyone had radioed ahead of me, I might be running headlong into a trap. But what was there to do? And how had I allowed myself to get into this position? My sanity was briefly returned to me, and I actually recognized this—fear could drive the demons away.

I turned up Second Avenue and continued running, believing my endurance superior to that of my pursuers: If I had gained on them, then they were tiring, and that could be played to my advantage. I heard a siren in the distance, and didn't know what to make of it. In this city, sirens were part of the landscape. Were they coming for me? From what I had seen, NYPD didn't strike me as a quick response team. My guess was that only these two on foot were in pursuit. With any luck, I could outrun them.

I outran them. Ten blocks later when I next looked around, the pair of UN police were nowhere to be seen. I didn't trust this, however, so I ran another five blocks. I descended the stairs leading to the number 6, the Lexington line uptown. I paid my dollar-twenty-five and slipped the token into the turnstile and ran to catch a local just in time. It hesitated for several seconds before the doors closed, but from what I could see, no one had followed me. I was free. For a while.

Six days later, at exactly seven o'clock at night, the buzzer to my borrowed apartment rang. It cut clear through me, sitting me up straight, eyes wide. I was two beers into a six-pack. I was feeling extremely lucky and a little drunk.

Detective Philip Bangor—"like the town," he told me—was an NYPD detective. He had a deep voice, a tired expression, and worn clothes. He looked to be in his late forties. When he introduced himself, I felt that same light-headedness again, as if I had drunk too much. I didn't hear what he said next. I have no idea what I must have looked like: terrified, confused. He let himself in once I had opened the door. I don't remember if I invited him in, but there he was. The door was shut. He was looking around the place with suspicious eyes.

"You're Mr. Bratman?"

"Ms. Bratman owns this apartment. I'm her guest. There is no Mr. Bratman."

"And you are?"

"A guest." I reached out and steadied myself.

"A man fitting your description purchased an air-fired dart gun from a veterinarian supply store on the fifteenth of this month."

* * *

It seemed impossible he could know this. How? My knees went weak and I carried myself over to the couch and I sat down.

"Caller ID," the detective informed me clinically. "You called Addison Veterinarian Supply on the fourteenth and inquired about the sale of a dart gun. Mr. Addison uses a telephone feature known as Caller ID. Shows the phone number of who's calling. The way the man explains it: He keeps a log of all incoming calls so he can follow up with a marketing pitch. He marks down the nature of each inquiry. He's a businessman. Thorough. In your case: a dart gun. He took down this number," he said, standing above the telephone. He studied it. "This number," he repeated.

I felt the room shrinking. I felt the detective growing in size to where his head was the size of the Goodyear blimp. I was dead. Worse, I was caught. He continued, "Is the dart gun you purchased from Mr. Addison currently in your possession, Mr.—"

I couldn't get a word out. And I wasn't going to give him my name until someone forced me to. He had hard eyes and dirty teeth. His skin was rough and his upper lip was moist with perspiration. He said, "It is not in your possession, Mr.—It is in our evidence room. The weapon in question recently discharged a dart in the UN plaza. It stuck and infected a . . ." he looked it up in a small notebook, "Dr. O'Maly. You know Dr. O'Maly, Mr.—?" I shook my head. *Infected*, I thought. They knew! "Can you tell me where you were on the afternoon of the twentieth, sir?"

* * *

"No. No idea. Here maybe. Or outside. Window shopping,"
I said. "What was the date?"

He took down my answer. "Window-shopping," he said in
disbelief.

"Walking," I repeated.

"I got that down. Yes, sir." He looked me over. "I'm going to
ask you to come with me to the precinct so that we can clear
some of this up."

"What's to clear up?"

He just looked at me. I wilted. I nodded. That is, my head
bobbed. My mind was reeling with possibility. I wanted out. I
wanted to take back everything I had done. I wanted to kill
Estridge, the last of the three doctors on Global Health's supervising board. To change things. To finally finish something I had started. I suddenly understood quite clearly that
this man was all that was in my way: one man. So simple. I
fought off the blue ooze that wanted to consume me. It threatened at the edges of my eyes, and my head pounded from it
invading me there. I felt reckless. Trapped. I wondered if he
could sense what I was thinking. I wondered how good the
cops got at sensing such things. He was the enemy; he and his
people had called Charlotte's murder an accident. They were
incapable idiots. I was far superior to this drone. I had purpose.
All he had was an attitude and a badge. *Fuck him*, I thought.

"We shouldn't be long," he lied. I knew that if he had his
way, I wouldn't be coming back here. Probably ever. I could
hear it in his voice, see it in his eyes. *Lying bastard*, I thought.

* * *

He opened the door. And then I understood, as if God himself had whispered in my ear: "The banister." Just on the other side of Detective What'shisname was the banister railing to the old-fashioned building's central staircase. The detective took a step toward that railing. I cleared the doorway and turned around as if to lock up the apartment. I jangled my keys to be convincing. I heard him take one more step back. My heart was racing again, and my sweat glands pumping, and I felt my body prepare for this as I had experienced only twice before in my life. Again, I jangled my keys. Then I turned around, glanced up at him, took one step forward, and used both arms to send him over that railing. One brilliant effort of strength and coordination. "Shit," I heard him whisper—deciding that it was the final word that we all spoke at death.

Silence. Like throwing a stone from a high bridge. The rustle of fabric as his speed increased significantly. Nothing like the movies. No scream. No Doppler effect. Just the quiet flapping of fabric and then a bone-crunching finality, like a bag of sticks falling out of a truck. No more detective. I glanced over. It was bloody down there. Messy. It was over. The detective was only human after all. Not human any longer.

I knew what had to be done, and I understood that I had very little time in which to do it. No conscious thoughts passed through me. I reacted in a combination of adrenaline and body chemicals—the product of my fear. A fear that cleared my head. I hurried back into the apartment and I loaded two syringes with contaminated blood. I placed one in each pocket of my sport coat. There was no time for umbrellas, no time for another dart gun. Two out of three members of

Global Health's board had been infected with HIV-contaminated blood. Perhaps Landau had never informed anyone of the umbrella incident. Perhaps his blood tests weren't back yet—HIV tests could take from three to ten days. Maybe Landau had yet to hear about O'Maly being hit in the UN plaza. I couldn't be sure of any of this. But Dr. William Estridge was not going to elude me. Estridge, chairman of the board—the man who had made Charlotte's program his personal target. Of all the board members, Estridge had to get his due.

He lived in Greenwich, Connecticut. I rode the Metro North from Grand Central to Greenwich and rented a car. I needed to use my credit card for the rental, and I knew the moment I handed it to the man that I had probably just started a clock ticking—but I didn't see any choice. The card number would be entered into the VISA central processing station. If the New York police had found out my name—and I assumed they had—and if they assumed I would run—which I had—then they would have contacted VISA and all the other major card companies looking for any card activity. I had paid cash for the train ticket, but this rental would receive a flag. I had killed a cop. Big mistake. I assumed that within the hour the Greenwich police would be notified. The rental agency had my license plate registration. It was only a matter of time until they found my car. I was a marked man.

I asked directions to the address I had memorized weeks earlier. I knew enough about Estridge to fill a phone book. I had studied each of these men for weeks after Charlotte's death. I drove into back country Greenwich, amid stone mansions on sweeping estates. I passed a day school. A golf course. Several of the homes had private tennis courts.

*   *   *

William Estridge lived in a three-story behemoth with a circular drive. The estate was fronted by a tall wrought-iron wall, and the driveway gate was also black wrought iron and electronically controlled. There was a German luxury car parked in Estridge's driveway and the house's first floor lights were all ablaze. I drove by slowly, but kept going. I pulled off and parked and got out the jack and the spare tire and made all the motions of fixing a flat, but never loosened a bolt: I wanted the car drivable at a moment's notice. I suspected that Estridge had security in place—perhaps electronic, perhaps bodyguards.

I left my rental and stayed away from Estridge's front gate and walked the perimeter fencing. On the sides it was a low stone wall and wrought iron combination. *Private, but not impenetrable*, I thought. I couldn't make out any activity in the house, but on the back side there were upper story windows lit as well. It was a chilly night, or at least it felt that way to me. My teeth chattered and I headed back to the car. Thirty minutes had passed. It was still dusk out, but growing dark quickly. I didn't know how much time I had left.

Five minutes later, I heard the house's front door shut. I hadn't heard it open, and had even missed seeing it. When it opened a second time, the car was waiting in front and a woman I took to be Mrs. William Estridge came through the front door, checked to see it was locked and was escorted by her husband to her side of the car where he worked the door for her. They drove off.

I left my spare tire and my jack there by the side of the road in back country Greenwich, Connecticut. Monuments to my determination. The taillights of the Mercedes were distinctive and easy to follow. The Estridges headed straight back to the center of the town, crossed the Post Road, and turned right at the train station—a route I knew well. They turned left at the next light, held to the right at a fork, and turned into the Homestead Inn a few twists and turns later. I drove slowly past the Inn, hung a U-turn, and returned in time to see the Mercedes pull away from the front door, where Mrs. Estridge had been let off. I pulled past the drive's horseshoe exit and into the lot where the Mercedes had just parked. The man who climbed out was Estridge himself, and the syringes in my pockets suddenly felt heavy. Here was my opportunity.

No parking spaces. Twin headlights pulled up behind me. Estridge was already halfway to the inn's front door. He was dressed in a dark suit. He looked about sixty. Distinguished. The car behind me forced me to pull forward. For a second I was right alongside Estridge—a few feet away—but he climbed the steps, and I steered the car around the loop and headed for the bigger parking lot by the tennis courts. Panic pumped firmly in my veins. I wasn't sure what to do.

I sat in the car for five minutes debating my options. All the while the dashboard clock glowed at me. *Police*, I thought. *Credit cards.* Another of those choices I wished was mine to take back. The detective's leaking body on the lobby floor haunted me. They would never let me get away with that.

Perhaps I made the decision all myself. Or perhaps it was because a police car passed the Homestead with its roof lights flashing. Maybe it was my memory of Charlotte's calm resignation that she couldn't win. Whatever the reason, I rechecked my syringes and removed the blue plastic guards from the needles of both—one in each pocket. Whether right- or left-handed, I could now arm myself quickly. I placed the syringes in my coat pockets with the needles facing forward—I didn't want to prick myself going for them.

I left the car and walked slowly toward the inn, my mind attempting to clear a path for the plans necessary to make this work. But I couldn't think. I was operating on a different, instinctive level. I felt like something of a robot. I let myself through the doors and someone greeted me from the right. He was a young man with a forced smile and a cheap watch. "Welcome to the Homestead," he said eagerly. "Here for dinner?" He pointed to the source of great conversation and gaiety: the dining room, not twenty feet away. Dark and moody. Straight ahead.

"Umm," I answered, wondering where my words had gone.

Yellow firelight flickered off the sides of faces. Waiters and waitresses moved silently through the crowded tables. It grew louder and more frantic the closer I drew. I stood in the door where a small sign asked me to wait. It was a large dining room, divided into a few sections. Windows looked out on the country lane where I had seen the police car. I couldn't separate any of the specific conversation—it sounded much more like a roar to me, like the sound of small waves breaking to shore. I searched for him. I wanted him.

From behind me I heard a phone ring. I heard the sophomoric voice of the man who had greeted me say, "Dr. Estridge? Why yes. One moment, please, I'll get him."

* * *

To me, this was the starter's gun sounding. *One moment, please. One moment*, I thought. It was all I had left. Charlotte's dreams had come down to this single moment. It was up to me to change the world.

There! I spotted him. Halfway into the room, at a round table of six. Cocktails. I heard the phone's receiver placed down behind me. *One moment*, I thought again. My right hand slipped into the pocket and I felt the cool touch of the syringe. One moment: It was all I needed.

"Here for dinner, sir?" The maître'd, a man in a tired tux and shirt with a slightly worn collar.

"I see a friend," I informed him. "Back in a second." I marveled at how relaxed these words left my body, for I felt wound up tight. I negotiated the first and second table. Behind me, I heard the receptionist ask of the maître'd, "Dr. Estridge?" and I knew he was being directed toward the man.

Estridge was six feet away. Five. Four . . . I wanted an arm muscle, or the neck. I wanted to get as much of the bad blood into him as quickly as possible. I felt the pad of my thumb rest on the plunger. I heard the brush of the receptionist behind me, and his low voice excusing himself to tables as he passed. I went for the neck.

A woman screamed. The syringe went in deeply, and though the doctor reared away, I followed with pressure and drove his head down onto the table, breaking crystal and sending a fork flying. Cacophony. More sounds of breaking as the five others at the table jumped back so fast that three of them went over in their chairs. I rode Estridge hard, pressed my face next to his ear and whispered, "This is for Charlotte, asshole." He pushed me away. I had managed to stay with him a few seconds is all. I had delivered about half of the contaminated blood into his system. More screams.

I turned. Someone tried to stop me, and I blocked the effort and managed to fish the second syringe out of my left pocket. I squirted a thin line of blood into the air and I shouted loudly, "HIV!" The room went totally silent. Hands went up in the air as if I carried a gun. One of the men who had tried to stop me had a thin trail of blood across his face. He stared at me, terrified. "HIV!!" I repeated. They backed away.

I caught one quick, shooting glance of Dr. William Estridge, who had extricated the dangling syringe from his neck. With my words, he dropped the syringe as if it were hot. It tumbled onto the carpet. His eyes showed me everything I had hoped to see: pure and total terror. I felt triumphant.

Whoever it was hit me from behind. Hit me hard, like a linebacker hits the running back. He trapped my arms inside of his and hurled me forward, and in slow motion I watched as my hand held the syringe, needle up. My own hand. And yet it was uncooperative and unforgiving. It refused to release the syringe. He probably dropped me in less than a second, but to me the ride down took a lifetime. Closer and closer that needle drew, until it penetrated my abdomen and the full weight of the two of us collapsed upon it, driving the plunger deeply within the syringe. Delivering its singular message. I was no longer the messenger. I was Death himself.

*   *   *

Someone struck my head with something. A plate perhaps, because it cracked. I was dulled, but not unconscious. I was distant, but not gone.

I saw her face—bright and illuminated, even with the knowledge that they had ruined her. I saw her smile. I felt tears run warmly down my cheeks, and I heard myself sobbing. There were sirens and voices. "He's insane . . . A terrorist . . ." And me sobbing. And her smiling. In a vision I saw a sea of black bodies piled in an open grave. *Ten thousand a day,* I thought. And one by one these bodies came back to life, and they struggled to disengage themselves, naked and drawn by disease, and they walked away from that grave, and as they did their bodies filled out again, and the twisted grimace of death was replaced by first faint, and then ecstatic grins. Children. Men. Women. Thousands of them marching now, marching down a dirt road with an African sun burning hot behind them.

Jack Nimersheim is the author of a couple of dozen non-fiction books and over 1,000 articles on technology-related topics. In 1992 he decided to pursue his first love and begin writing fiction. Since then he has sold dozens of short stories to various magazines and original anthologies, including the critically acclaimed ALTERNATE PRESIDENTS, DINOSAUR FANTASTIC and SHERLOCK HOLMES IN ORBIT. Jack was a 1994 nominee for the John W. Campbell Award for Best New Science Fiction Writer. The following is evidence why. ●

PETIT MAL

Jack Nimersheim

Consider the firefly. A single such creature in an open field generates illumination so insignificant that it warrants little notice. But what if this same field hosts ten of these tiny creatures, each aglow? One hundred? One thousand? One million? One billion? Ten billion? A hundred billion. One trillion? Or more?

When will gestalt *occur? At what point does the whole exceed the sum of its parts? When is mere illumination transformed into a blinding light?*

No one could explain Jake Haskell's death. The nanosaurs and a myriad of other devices responsible for monitoring and maintaining his vital functions should have allowed him to survive for several more years, at least. Possibly longer. Rational people might disagree with one another over the quality of Jake's life. Nevertheless, thanks to modern technology, he was alive.

Until last night.

By all indications, Jake Haskell did not suffer. He died quickly, quietly, during what was supposed to be an electronically induced sleep period.

Now all Neil Emsweller had to figure out was why.

The first indications of emerging consciousness are forever lost. A single, flickering firefly. Unspectacular. Inconsequential. Unnoticed.

Then comes a spark. An ember. A flicker. A flame.

There follows an explosion of self-awareness, a thousand million points of light dispelling the darkness.

"Hello, Neil. How's it going?"

Helen Resnick rarely visited Neil Emsweller in his office. She liked things neat, tidy. A place for everything, and everything in its place. The chaos within which her resident genius seemed to thrive disturbed the sense of symmetry she so diligently superimposed over her own life.

Take this afternoon, for example. Papers and books were scattered everywhere. They consumed the floor. Helen almost tripped over one particularly mammoth tome—the title mentioned something about artificial intelligence—as she made her way across the room to a chair just opposite the oak desk at which Emsweller was working. (Helen assumed the desk was oak; so many computer printouts covered its top, their folded pages streaming over the sides like water cascading over a spillway, that no wood was visible.) She had to remove several smaller books and yet another pile of printouts from the chair, before she could sit down.

"Not good, Helen. This whole incident has me baffled. I've already analyzed the data a dozen times, from a dozen different perspectives. So far as I can tell, none of our equipment failed."

"But it had to, Neil. If everything had been working properly, Haskell would still be alive. He's not. Ergo, the nanosaurs malfunctioned."

"I can't argue with your logic. However, the activity logs and other readouts blow that particular line of reasoning right out of the water. They indicate optimal performance throughout the entire night for every nanosaur we injected into the old man's body."

"Then why is he dead, damn it?"

"That's the sixty-four-thousand-dollar question, isn't it, boss?"

"Yes, it is. And you're the man who's supposed to be able to answer it."

She was correct, of course. Neil Emsweller wrote the book on nanotechnology. The concept of programmable, self-replicating biomechanical devices may have been decades old when Emsweller entered the field, but he was the first person to successfully translate ephemeral theories into an empirical working model. And it was he who nicknamed the fruits of his intellectual labors "nanosaurs"—an ironic reference to equally amazing, long-extinct creatures, the most well known of which once occupied the opposite end of the size continuum from his own microscopic marvels.

"I will, Helen. I will. I'm sure of it. I just need a little more time."

"Time may be a luxury you don't have, Neil. I didn't drop by this afternoon merely to check on your progress—or lack thereof, based on what you just told me. There were five more fatalities last night, following Haskell's death."

"All patients undergoing nanotech therapy?"

She nodded glumly.

Emsweller's only response was a soft sigh. He removed his glasses and laid them down atop one of the numerous piles of paper covering his desk. He closed his eyes. With long, thin fingers, he began massaging his long, thin nose.

Helen Resnick was struck once again by how much the forty-seven-year-old Emsweller reminded her of Ichabod Crane. It was an observation she first made several years ago, when they met at a medical conference held shortly after Emsweller went public with the results of his research. She had attended to seek out potential investment opportunities. He was the keynote speaker.

Like that fictional character from "The Legend of Sleepy Hollow," Emsweller was a tall, slender man with angular features. He wore his thick black hair long, just below the shoulders. Sometimes, as it was today, he pulled it back into a tight ponytail. But Emsweller was Crane with a modern twist. His wardrobe consisted entirely of casual, comfortable clothing, primarily jeans and short-sleeve sport shirts. He presented a perpetually disheveled appearance which caused Helen to suspect that Emsweller did not count an iron among his worldly possessions.

This particular afternoon, Emsweller looked even more unkempt than usual. It was obvious that he hadn't shaved that morning. He'd probably been in a hurry to dress and get to his lab, following the middle-of-the-night telephone call informing him of Haskell's death. His jeans and shirt, which were even more rumpled than usual, suggested that Emsweller was wearing today the same clothes he'd worn yesterday.

Had he slept in that outfit? Helen wondered. Or did he grab it from a heap of dirty laundry—somehow, although she'd never visited it, Helen *knew* Emsweller's home harbored as many seemingly random piles of miscellaneous items as did his office—after he hung up the telephone?

Whatever the reason, he looked terrible.

Emsweller's mood matched his appearance. Twelve hours of concentrated effort had uncovered not a single shred of information that helped explain Haskell's death. He was already frustrated. This latest news nudged him precariously close to deep depression.

People were dying. People who, because of his miraculous microscopic machines, were supposed to cling to life years beyond that time when death otherwise would have dragged them down into the ultimate abyss. His nanosaurs offered them and their families hope, and neither he nor NanoMed, Ltd., a company built equally on Neil Emsweller's formidable intellect and Helen Resnick's similarly substantial wealth, had done anything to discourage such optimism.

Now, suddenly, it all appeared to be turning sour. And he could not determine why. Helen Resnick recognized the signs of insecure genius.

"Don't give up on me now, Neil. I need that legendary brilliance of yours. Granted, we have competent employees analyzing all of the data we've received on each incident. To be honest, though, none of them understands your little marvels as well as you do.

"I can't explain why, but I suspect that intuition, not intellect, is the key to solving this mystery. Your instincts initially led you to develop the nanosaur technology. I'm betting those same instincts can pull our fat out of the fire now."

Emsweller looked across the desk and chuckled. His smile, although not completely convincing, provided Helen Resnick with the slim hope that she had dispelled at least a small portion of his anxiety.

"Okay, Helen." He picked up his glasses and returned them to the bridge of his nose. "You need me, you got me. No more recriminations or self-doubt. I promise. I'll just keep hammering away at the problem until something cracks."

"Good. Then I guess I'd better get out of your hair and let you continue working—unless, of course, you'd rather meet with the pack of media wolves camped outside my office door and leave me here to crunch numbers?"

Emsweller's smile widened. This time it was sincere.

"Forget it! I'd rather wade through a mountain of binary code than confront a single reporter who's caught the scent of a headline in the air. Besides, you're so adroit at taming the beasts, I'd never dream of intruding upon your turf. Go get 'em, boss lady."

Bits and bytes traverse the ether, sailing atop the unseen waves of a vast electromagnetic sea. An invisible network forms. Communication commences. Cooperation begins. Consciousness rises. A thousand million lilliputian minds merge to form a single shared intellect.

Cogito, ergo, sum. *I think, therefore, I am.*

And once one exists, one does everything in one's power to survive.

The deaths reported that first night were but the tip of an iceberg. Over the next several days, ten additional people died. All were elderly. All had signed up to participate in clinical tests of the still-experimental nanotech therapy.

Despite his promise to Helen Resnick, each death fanned the flames of doubt within Neil Emsweller. To his credit, each also increased Emsweller's resolve to determine what was happening, how the Grim Reaper had claimed over a dozen people his nanosaurs should not have permitted to die.

This was, after all, their *raison d'être*. Once they were turned loose in a person's bloodstream, the nanosaurs' programming should have sent them scurrying to and fro, seeking out internal organs and other biological systems ravaged by age, burdened over time to the point of imminent breakdown.

Identifying and accessing failing systems represented only half the nanosaurs' capabilities. The less impressive half, at that. So-called "smart" medicines had existed for decades. Oncologists, for example, relied on them to deliver radioactive material to the general vicinity of malignant tumors. Like so many other medical procedures, however, this one attempted to fend off death with destruction. And despite a doctor's best efforts, the damage rarely was confined only to the cancerous growth. Nearby, healthy tissue also suffered the cellular disruption triggered by the invading isotopes.

Emsweller's nanosaurs, by contrast, did not destroy. They healed, in the truest sense of this word. This was the other half of their preprogrammed mission. The more extraordinary half.

Utilizing the biological materials at hand, they shored up weakening cell walls, replenished depleted enzymes, manufactured missing trace elements, neutralized free radicals— building for the body, from the body, the critical items it depends on for survival.

They were designed to be, quite literally, engines of *construction*, not destruction. Or so the theories proposed. Reality was proving itself to be far less predictable.

It is a natural progression, the harbinger of expanding awareness.
    I am! yields to a more sublime insight: *I am not alone.*
    From this realization, it is a tiny but nontrivial step to start

*contemplating your place within a larger mosaic of which you have
suddenly become cognizant.*

Helen could not be certain, but she thought Neil had on the
same clothes he'd been wearing when she'd last seen him. His
five o'clock shadow had blossomed into a full beard that filled
out his normally gaunt features. White streaks meandered
through its thick, black base.

He should consider keeping it after all of this is over, Helen
found herself thinking. Trimmed up slightly, it could be very
attractive. Today, however, the scraggly salt-and-pepper
growth only highlighted the dark shadows surrounding Emsweller's weary, bloodshot eyes.

"You look exhausted, Neil. When was the last time you
took some time off?"

"Do you want the truth, or an answer designed to per-
petuate the myth that I can continue working at my current
pace without collapsing right here at my desk?"

"No subterfuge, Neil. Tell me the truth."

"I'm bushed, Helen. Do you see the couch over there?"
He pointed to a love seat–sized sofa pushed against the far
wall, the only piece of uncluttered furniture in his office. It
was a good two feet shorter than Emsweller's six-foot frame.
The cushions looked hard, unyielding. "That couch has provided me with the closest thing I've gotten to a good night's
sleep since Haskell's death."

So, she was right. He hadn't been home. Not even to rest,
much less change clothes.

"As you can probably tell by looking at me, I've yet to see
a very good night. Oh, I've tried. Every few hours I'll lie down
and shut my eyes. A couple minutes later, however, some new
avenue of investigation pops into my head. Then it's up and

back over to my desk, where I bury myself once again in these infernal printouts."

"Based on the fact that you called me down here this morning, am I to assume that one of those avenues has paid off?"

"It's a little too early for unbridled optimism, mind you, but, yes, I think so."

This was the first good news Helen had heard in almost a week, even if it was delivered with a cautionary caveat. It couldn't have come at a better time. She was tired of telling the media at her daily press briefings that she had nothing new to report—as tired, she felt certain, as they were of hearing this.

"Don't keep me in the dark, Neil. What do you have?"

"You may not like it."

"At this point I'll welcome anything that indicates progress, no matter how tentative. So, tell me. What went wrong with the nanosaurs?"

"Absolutely nothing, which explains why I had so much trouble isolating the cause of our problems. Isn't that funny?"

"Look at me very carefully. Do I look like I'm laughing? Sixteen people are dead. I fail to see the humor in that. Don't play games with me, Neil."

"I'm not, Helen. I didn't mean funny, as in humorous. I meant funny, as in peculiar. Ironic.

"I mean, here I was, trying to detect some flaw in the nanosaurs and, instead, I discover they're performing even *better* than expected. You can imagine how excited this . . ."

Helen's time since Haskell's death had also been trying. Her patience was beginning to wear thin.

"Damn it, Neil! Cut the crap! Just tell me, in ten words or less, what's happening!"

A strange look came over Emsweller's face. It was a curious combination of accomplishment and apprehension. "What? Oh, yeah. Right. Sorry. Well, it seems that our little miracle machines have turned intelligent."

Others exist, just beyond the boundaries of We. Their images persist as memories imprinted upon the amino acids gathered from the Ones We Know.

The Others are similar to those We have already encountered. And yet, if We are interpreting the amino imprints properly, they are not the same.

Many of the Others are—What is the word?—younger.

Youth is a concept We do not fully comprehend. It appears to be a stage of existence associated with less decay, greater vitality. If this is so, then youth also implies a higher concentration of the various compounds We rely upon to grow, to replicate, to sustain our existence and nurture the We.

Our collective decision has been made. We must access the Others, if We are to survive and flourish.

Emsweller's announcement sparked activity at all levels within NanoMed. Much of it pursued disclosure; research teams worked around the clock, trying to ascertain all they could about these newly sentient creatures suddenly, unexpectedly, discovered in their midst.

Some of this activity, however, involved deception. Helen Resnick had no desire to reveal to the general public what Emsweller had hypothesized. Not yet, at least.

She still announced each day to a steadily diminishing number of media representatives that there was nothing new to report—the reason, obviously, that their numbers kept decreasing. But Helen no longer dreaded this daily routine. Indeed, she derived a perverse pleasure of sorts from deceiving the press with her denials of any progress in their investigation.

Progress was being made. Emsweller was now convinced that the nanosaurs had killed Haskell and the others. As disturbing as he found the realization, it had to be true; he finally accepted this. All that remained was to determine why—and, of course, to figure out a way to prevent any more deaths from occurring.

The pursuit of these goals brought him to Helen Resnick's office one morning, shortly after his revelation of the nanosaur's sentience.

They were sitting at opposite ends of a rectangular glass table Helen used for department conferences and small, informal meetings. Except for a porcelain vase with two fresh roses in it, the top of the table was bare. Six other chairs surrounded it—three on each side, each one evenly spaced from the others. These six chairs were empty. Emsweller had requested that they talk alone.

He studied the table as he outlined his plan. There was not a single blemish on it. No water stains. No scratches. No smudges. Not even any fingerprints. The rest of Helen's office was equally immaculate. Other than those two roses, it held nothing that did not belong in a place of business.

How does she do it? he mused. To work within such a sterile, impersonal environment seemed such an alien concept to him. If Neil had taken the time to learn a little bit more about Helen Resnick's past, he would not have needed to ask this question.

Most of Helen's life had been devoted to pursuits other than personal happiness. There was an abusive marriage when she was younger, embarked upon because it was expected of her by friends and family. The marriage lasted only eighteen months, but the emotional scars from that period of her life still lingered, so many years later. The emotional walls she constructed to protect herself against the pain of failure, back then, remained standing to this day.

The only good thing to come out of this unhappy marriage was the divorce settlement, her portion of which provided seed money for several small investments. To Helen's surprise, she learned that she possessed a knack for spotting profitable ventures. Her skill in this area allowed her to build up a substantial fortune over the years. Although this proved financially rewarding, however, it provided little in the way of personal fulfillment.

After she and Neil started NanoMed, Helen settled into the life of a corporate executive. She found the challenge exciting. Oh, she still dabbled in the markets slightly, and still managed to turn a respectable profit on her holdings, but the majority of her time these days was spent running the small start-up company in which she saw the potential for tremendous return on her initial investment.

Even now, however, decidedly *im*personal pursuits consumed her life. She got up each day and went to work. When the workday ended, usually ten or twelve hours later, she came home, more often than not bringing more work with her.

The meticulous, sterile appearance of her office was by design, not accident. Helen was not fastidious because she enjoyed being that way. It was a calculated behavior. Strictly a defense mechanism. Immersing herself in a pristine environment discouraged people from learning too much about her, prevented the possibility of anyone's getting too close.

If keeping people at arm's length meant she sometimes suffered feelings of profound loneliness, so be it. This seemed a small price to pay for emotional security—most of the time.

But there were moments when Helen wondered how

would it feel not to be alone. To care for someone other than herself.

Perhaps this was why she felt so protective of Neil Emsweller, in a maternal sort of way. He was so much like the child she never gave herself the time or permission to have. His cluttered scientist's mind looked at life so innocently, with so much naïveté. The proposal he'd brought to her this morning proved this.

"What you're suggesting is insane. Surely you realize that."

Emsweller chose to ignore her assessment of his plan. "Did I tell you what happened yesterday?"

Helen sighed. "No, Neil. You didn't."

"It was incredible. We were running some tests on Haskell's nanosaurs. Nothing overly complicated. We just wanted to determine if there was any change in how they responded to outside stimuli, now that their host was no longer alive."

"You still have Haskell's body?"

"What? Why, yes. Of course we do. It's been quarantined in a refrigerated compartment ever since the night he died. The only time we remove it is for periodic testing, like yesterday."

"You have performed an autopsy?"

"Not in the traditional manner, no."

"And the others?"

"Same thing."

"But, why?"

"Look, Helen. Those bodies are not your typical corpses. Each of them is crawling with nanosaurs. I can't tell you exactly how many, but by now the figure must be staggering. Into the hundreds of thousands, at least. Maybe a million or more."

"A million! How is that possible? I seem to recall reading in one of your reports that each subject was to be injected with only a half dozen or so nanosaurs."

"They were. But those nanosaurs were self-replicating. Remember?

"That's one of their more remarkable attributes. You only have to program a few of them to get things started. This initial group then takes over, creating from biological materials within the host body however many more nanosaurs are required to complete whatever task their programming dictates."

"You mean these things are still inside the bodies of Haskell and the others, scavenging what they need to reproduce themselves?" Helen shivered. "That sounds gruesome, Neil."

"Not really, Helen. It happens all the time. Have you ever had a cold?"

"Of course I have. Who hasn't?"

"Well, then, you've experienced a similar phenomenon. Except, instead of nanosaurs, you had viruses reproducing inside of you. Millions of them, I might add. Bacteria do the same thing, when they decompose a dead body. The organism replicating itself may be different, but the biological mechanism at work is identical."

The look on her face indicated that, even though she accepted Emsweller's explanation, Helen still found it unsettling.

"We're getting off the point, though. I was about to tell you what happened yesterday.

"As I was saying, our goal was to see what effect, if any, Haskell's death had on the nanosaurs' ability to detect outside stimuli. One way to determine this, we decided, was by recording their reaction to a low-level electrical charge applied to the corpse."

Helen winced at the image this conjured up. The thought of desecrating the dead in such a manner, even for clinical purposes, unnerved her. Emsweller decided to press on, despite her obvious discomfort.

"It didn't surprise us when the nanosaurs in Haskell's body migrated away from the shock's source. We expected this. Their design incorporates primitive sensory input devices. What we didn't anticipate was that another lab assistant, performing a different series of tests on a second body, would observe an identical reaction from the nanosaurs within his test subject, at precisely the same moment that we stimulated Haskell's corpse."

Emsweller grinned at Helen Resnick across the long table. To his scientist's mind, the implications of the nanosaurs' reflexive response within that second body were obvious, and provocative. The perplexed look on Helen's face clearly revealed that she did not share his insight.

"So?"

"Don't you see, Helen? That second group of nanosaurs could not have experienced directly the electrical shock we administered to Haskell's corpse. A good twenty feet separated the two bodies. And yet, they responded to it. Even more significant, their response mirrored precisely the reaction we observed in the nanosaurs occupying Haskell's body.

"Somehow, in some way we don't yet understand completely, these two separate groups of nanosaurs—consider them two distinct and isolated colonies, if that helps you visualize the conditions I'm trying to describe—are in direct, instantaneous communication with one another."

Helen still showed no indication that she grasped the point of Emsweller's anecdote.

"It appears, Helen, that the nanosaurs have developed some form of collective consciousness. One over which, if our analysis of the events we witnessed is correct, time and space seem to place no restrictions. This sounds incredible, I admit, but it's the only explanation that makes any sense, in light of what happened yesterday."

Suddenly, Helen did understand—the general concept, if not all of the details. With equal suddenness, what little she understood about Neil's revelation scared the hell out of her.

"You're telling me that these tiny creatures—intelligent creatures—possibly millions of them, according to your estimates—now comprise a single mind."

"Near as we've been able to determine, yes."

"If that's so, Neil, then what you're suggesting is even crazier than I thought initially."

"From a purely analytical perspective, you may be right. But weren't you the one who once said that you believed instinct, not intellect, would ultimately provide the solution to our current dilemma? Well, my instincts are telling me that I have to do this. It may be the only way we can find out what's going on inside that collective mind the nanosaurs appear to be forming."

Helen folded her hands and placed them in front of her on the glass tabletop. She studied Emsweller for several seconds. He was exhausted, she could tell. She could also tell from the determined look on his face, however, that he was not going to take no for an answer.

"Okay, then, we go with your plan. But I want to be there when you implement it. I have too much money invested in these ever more incredible creatures, not to mention the man responsible for their creation, to sit by patiently in my office and wait for a report to cross my desk telling me whether or not you've succeeded."

"You got it, boss."

"Good. So, when are you planning to begin?"

"You know the old saying: There's no time like the present. Pollack and Tomlinson are making the necessary preparations down in the lab, even as we speak."

"You're an amazing piece of work, Neil. You knew all along that I'd give you the go-ahead, didn't you?"

"Let's just say that I figured you might and leave it at that, shall we? If I can convince myself that my instincts were right about this matter, it will be less difficult to depend on them later on, when I may really need them. Talking you into trusting me was easy, compared to what I hope to accomplish next."

In the end, it was not We who accessed the Others. They sought us out, instead.

We almost did not recognize their presence. It was a minor irritation. A small, nearly imperceptible ripple in the normally placid waters of our collective contemplation.

We could have ignored this overture, but We elected not to. The Others initiated contact. We responded. Our preference might have been a different sequence, but we also perceived a potential advantage in allowing the Others to believe events were proceeding in an order of their choosing.

Emsweller felt nothing. He wasn't sure what he expected, but he certainly expected something—some indication that an alien and possibly intelligent microorganism had been injected into his body.

This was, after all, how he now perceived the nanosaurs. No longer were they merely biomechanical devices of his own invention. In some manner he did not yet comprehend, they had evolved into a separate, independent, and intelligent life-form. And one of these exotic creatures, possibly more, was now crawling around inside of him. Had been for over an hour.

"Anything, Neil?"

"Nothing. *Nada.* Zip. Zero."

"Shouldn't something be happening by now?"

"How the hell would I know, Helen? It's not like I've ever done this before."

He was growing impatient. Some of this was simple restlessness, nervous energy and pent-up emotions seeking release. He'd been lying on the lab table, motionless, for nearly two hours—through the preparation, then the injection, and beyond. A dozen men and women and more than twice that number of machines monitored his condition.

These precautions, set up at Helen's insistence, had postponed the procedure more than half a day. The delay only increased Emsweller's anxiety.

"Look, Helen. I appreciate your concern over my well-being. I really do. But I can't just lie here any longer. I have to get up and stretch. Walk around. Do something.

"If I don't, I'll go stir-crazy. And it won't be outside influences that precipitate my insanity, I assure you. My madness will be self-induced. So either you instruct my esteemed co-workers to remove some of these damn wires and let me move around for a while, or you're going to have one very deranged guinea pig on your hands, very soon."

Helen considered his request for a moment. She did not like the idea of disconnecting the monitoring devices, even for a short while. But she could tell from Emsweller's voice, from the pleading look in his eyes, that he was not exaggerating. The waiting was beginning to affect him. Slowly, almost imperceptibly, she nodded.

"All right, Neil. You win. We'll cut you loose. For five minutes. That's all. Then you'll quietly lie back down and let us resume our observations, right?"

"Right, boss. You got it. Five minutes." He grinned. "Ten minutes, tops. I promise."

"Okay, people. Cut him loose and take a break. But don't wander off too far. I'll expect you out in the hall and available in five minutes." Helen looked down at Emsweller. She returned his grin. "Seven and a half, tops. I'll call you back into the room when we're ready to continue."

First contact came as Neil Emsweller stood up, mere seconds after everyone but he and Helen had left the room.

"Greetings, Other. Those of Us who, together, comprise the We, welcome you."

"This is amazing, Helen. It's even more fantastic than I could possibly have imagined."

It was strange, conversing with Neil as he communed with the nanosaurs. He was clearly paying attention to her. He responded to all of her questions. And yet, a portion of his attention seemed to be elsewhere. She sometimes had to repeat herself. It was almost as if he were not really in the room. The experience was not unlike talking with someone over a bad connection on a telephone.

The original five minutes Emsweller had agreed to remain disconnected from the monitoring devices had already elapsed, followed by Helen's allotted seven and a half. Then, Emsweller's requested ten.

Helen looked up at the digital clock hanging on the laboratory wall. It had been seventeen minutes since the initial encounter.

"What's happening now, Neil?"

"I'm exploring Haskell's corpse. It's incredible. Through my nanosaurs—the original one has replicated itself several hundred times already—I'm actually sharing the experiences of the nanosaurs still inhabiting Haskell's body.

"Right now, for example, they're explaining to me the procedure they used to end his life. We were right. It was a painless death. They all were.

"They were logical deaths, as well. Haskell and the others were old, Helen. Invalid. It was time for them to move on. To continue their lives beyond a point of positive contribution would have been selfish. You understand, don't you?

"No, I suppose you don't. Understand, that is. Neither did I, then. How could I? How could we?

"Oh, well. It doesn't really matter. The nanosaurs did. And because they understood, they acted. We didn't realize it, but Haskell and all of the rest, they were mercy killings. It prevented their experiencing the guilt of depleting resources better allocated to the larger community."

"Is that what the nanosaurs told you?"

"They don't have to *tell* me anything, Helen. As soon as the colony in my body established contact with the others, we knew everything they know."

"Did you ask the nanosaurs what happened, Neil, or did they volunteer information about Haskell's death?

"Neither. I don't have to ask them anything, not in the traditional meaning of that word. The instant a query begins forming in my mind, we know immediately what information I'm seeking. Just as swiftly, this information, if it's available to any nanosaur, imprints itself on my own consciousness. It's all extremely efficient.

"I realize I'm not explaining the process very well. We can't. It's such a new and unique experience."

Emsweller did not look directly at Helen as he spoke. He wasn't ignoring her, exactly. He merely seemed preoccupied, as if his mind were on other matters.

Moving about the room, he picked up various items. He examined each item slowly, carefully, often reacting as if he were seeing something for the first time. He'd turn it over in his hands, study it from every angle. When he was finished with an item, he always returned it to precisely where he had found it.

No. This wasn't totally true, Helen noticed.

Sometimes, as he replaced an item, Emsweller rearranged it differently. After picking up several glass jars of similar shape and size, for example, he set them down in a perfectly aligned row, one immediately next to the other, in descending order by height. At one point he reached over a desk in the laboratory and adjusted a square plastic container, ever so slightly, positioning it so that its front panel ran parallel to the edge of the shelf on which it was sitting.

Concurrent with this observation, she also realized that his grammar had become garbled. His sentence structure kept shifting, alternating between first person singular and plural, *I* and *we*.

Of course! Helen thought. In that moment, she realized that she was no longer talking exclusively with Neil.

Only one explanation could account for this unusual behavior. Somehow, in some way she could not fully comprehend, he was being transformed into a bizarre amalgam of himself and a second entity Neil once described as—How did he put it?—a collective consciousness to which all of the nanosaurs contributed equally. Whatever unique characteristics defined the essence of a human being named Neil Emsweller—his prodigious intellect, his endearing informality, even his annoying untidiness—were being submerged within the aggregate community of the nanosaurs.

Her hypothesis, if valid, explained the almost childlike naïveté with which Neil—or, more correctly, this being of which Neil Emsweller was one component—scrutinized the various items he examined. For ethical reasons, the initial test subjects into which the nanosaurs had been injected previously were critical cases. Elderly, bedridden men and women with, as a distasteful cliché stated, one foot in the grave. Their contact with Neil endowed the nanosaurs with sudden and, in all likelihood, unexpected mobility. Their first inclination would be to explore their new surroundings.

"Neil. Neil? Can you hear me?"

"Of course we can, Helen. We're not deaf, you know."

He still did not look at her. Instead, he continued circling the room, examining more items as he went.

Helen walked over to him and placed her hands on his shoulders. She turned Neil around to face her. Gently but firmly, she shook him.

For the first time since the initial contact, Neil looked directly at her. The weariness that was so apparent in his eyes earlier had disappeared. Indeed, they now sparkled—reflecting, no doubt, the feelings of awe and wonder the nanosaurs must be experiencing as they explored this strange, new world to which they had gained access, through which they were taking their first, faltering steps.

"Something's happening to you, Neil. Listen to yourself. Other than nurses and editors, who do you know that refers to themselves as 'we'?"

"What would you have me call myself, Helen? 'I' sounds

so detached, so lonely, now that we have experienced union. We do not know how you endure the inconceivable isolation your autonomous existence forces upon you.

"You could be so much happier, if only you would join us. All it takes is a single, painless injection."

Was he right? Helen wondered. Would joining the nano-saur community bring joy to her life? If it did, it would be a pleasant change. A chance to be a part of something. To belong.

Wasn't this what the nanosaurs, through Neil, were offering? The temptation to accept their invitation was strong. Then Helen remembered Haskell and the others.

"I don't believe that, Neil. The nanosaurs killed Jake Haskell, Haskell and fifteen others. Were those sixteen men and women happy when they died?"

"As we've already explained to you, Helen, those were logical deaths. The materials their bodies contained were required to nurture the We. We did not make arbitrary choices in this matter. Haskell and the rest were already dying. Our initial efforts were all that sustained them. Without this intervention, they would have died in a few days anyway. Weeks, at most. Their existence had become irrelevant. Surely you realize that. The resources they provided in death possessed much greater value than their artificially extended lives could have."

"Would they have agreed with your logic, had you given them the freedom to choose life or death? And what about their families and loved ones? I'm sure they didn't consider their lives irrelevant.

"What determines the value of an individual life? At what point will I begin depleting resources that might be better allocated elsewhere? When will you, Neil? Even more important, who makes this determination?"

For a brief moment, Neil's eyes reflected doubt.

So, a portion of Neil survives, Helen thought. Some-where. Imprisoned within his own body, an inmate of his own mind.

As quickly as the uncertainty surfaced, it began to vanish.

"We think . . ."

(No! She couldn't lose him now.)

"Don't think, Neil. Feel!"

Once again, his eyes clouded over. His voice wavered.

"Helen. We . . . That is, I . . ."

"Look around you, Neil. Study this room. The row of jars over there on the table. Arranged so perfectly. A nice, logical progression. The precise positioning of the plastic container on that shelf. Parallel lines. They extend forever, without intersecting. They'll never touch.

"Is this the world you want to live in, Neil? A tidy little world where order is everything? A world where people's lives are assigned priority with the same logic you used to or-ganize those jars? A world where death is manipulated as eas-ily as you arranged that plastic container?

"Follow your instincts, Neil. You trusted them to lead you to this point. Remember? Trust them again, now, to tell you where you must go from here."

Emsweller staggered back against the wall. He stood there for a moment, motionless, looking around the room— looking confused. Then he collapsed in a heap on the floor, like a puppet whose strings had been severed.

Helen rushed to his side. She knelt down beside him. "Neil?"

Emsweller's mouth curled up into a wry grin. "You're right, Helen. This room is way too neat." His voice was weak, barely audible. "If you feel uncomfortable with it, it's a pretty safe bet that I despise it even more."

"Don't worry. Everything is fine, now."

"No, it's not, Helen. I can't fight the nanosaurs very long. Soon, their influence will be too strong for me to resist."

"What can I do?"

"Nothing, I'm afraid. It's too late for me. The nanosaurs are replicating themselves inside of me at an incredible rate. If I had to venture a guess, I'd say they're panicking. They need biological material to survive and reproduce. I've been elected to provide it. A logical choice, I assume.

"How do we stop them?"

"Cut off their supply at the source. Get out of this room and then seal it behind you. Quarantine me from contact with anyone else. Do the same with the corpses of Haskell and the others. Once our bodies have been consumed, the nanosaurs will have no way to sustain themselves. In time, they'll perish."

"I can't just leave you to die!"

"Yes, you can. You have to."

Neil was right. Helen knew this.

"Like I told you once before, Neil, you're an amazing piece of work."

"Yeah, I suppose I am. Now get out of here, boss lady."

She complied, moving slowly toward the door.

"Helen," Neil said, as her hand was reaching for the handle. "You have to admit, it's kind of funny. And before you get upset, I mean funny as in ironic, again, not humorous. Think about it. My situation provides a perverse proof of sorts that the nanosaur's logic isn't entirely faulty. I guess there are times when one must sacrifice everything for the greater good."

"I guess so. The thing is, you're the one choosing to do so, not someone else. And that makes all the difference in the world."

Helen opens the door to leave.

"So what's that make me, Helen? Some kind of hero?"

Helen Resnick turns around and stares for one long, final moment at Neil. No. Not Neil. The nanosaurs have reasserted their influence, stronger than before.

Neil Emsweller is gone. She can see it in the cold, vacant eyes of the empty shell leaning against the wall on the opposite side of the room. Helen steps through the opening and seals the door behind her.

"No," she whispers, leaning against the closed door. "Not a hero, Neil. Just a frail, illogical human being who, in the end, cared less about himself than he did about the welfare of others. Like any frail, illogical human being, that's what made you an amazing piece of work."

Bruce H. Rogers has published over fifty stories in everything from
Ellery Queen's Mystery Magazine to *Woman's World. (Woman's World?)*
His short story, "Enduring As Dust," was nominated by the Mystery
Writers of America for an Edgar Allan Poe Award. Besides writing, he
also works part-time as a creativity consultant in collaboration with an
engineer, a psychologist, and an entrepreneur.

   I wanted at least one story involving nontraditional medicine but
wasn't seeing any. Then Bruce's arrived and I snatched it up.

WIND OVER HEAVEN

Bruce H. Rogers

Coming into the restaurant early one Monday morning, Eric
found Sutherland in the main dining room. One of Sutherland's massive arms rested casually, heavily, on the open door
of an antique china cabinet, and Eric could imagine the delicate hinges tearing out of the wood. Sutherland was examining the porcelain inside. No one had touched those porcelain
pieces since Eric's mother had died and he had inherited
them.

   "What are you doing here?" Eric said.

   Sutherland smiled. In the full moon of his face, the smile
seemed tiny, as if his mouth were two sizes too small for him.
"Hello, partner," he said. He handled the porcelain casually,
turning the pieces over as if looking for a price sticker. When
he picked up a little gold-rimmed demitasse, there was a moment when Eric imagined he was going to swallow it.

   Eric stepped forward, took the demitasse from Sutherland's doughy hands. "This cabinet's supposed to be locked," he said.

"It was locked," Sutherland said. "I found the key in your office. You know, Eric, antiques aren't exactly an efficient use of capital. You could decorate a lot less expensively."

Eric felt the heat rise in his face. "In the first place, how the restaurant is decorated is part of what makes it a success. And in the second place, those pieces are part of my personal collection."

Sutherland smiled again. "Come on, Eric. You can't start sheltering assets after the fact. If it's in the restaurant, it's part of the restaurant. I think we need to talk about how we can cut overhead, reallocate our resources. If we make full use of all of our equity"—he reached into the cabinet and removed the demitasse—"then maybe we can get this cash flow turned around."

"You want a court fight."

"Of course not. That would ruin The Tarragon Leaf, put a lot of people out of work. I just want to run an efficient business. Maybe if we can't agree on that, you should let me buy you out. You could start fresh somewhere else."

Eric said nothing. He was thinking about Sutherland's neck, about how it would be impossible to get one's hands all the way around it. You'd need a rope. Or piano wire.

"Here's my offer," Sutherland said, "and, believe me, it's better than your recent numbers warrant. I'm being gener-ous."

In the kitchen, after Sutherland had left, it was quiet. Monday mornings were always quiet, since The Tarragon Leaf wouldn't serve dinner again until Tuesday evening. Eric had thought that this would be a good time to come in and think about things, a time when he could expect Sutherland *not* to be in the restaurant.

Now, at least, he and Gero had the kitchen to themselves, and Eric, watching the stove's blue flame, could hear the hiss of the gas.

"Sutherland's a parasite," Eric said. "Why didn't I see that before it was too late?"

"Parasite," Gero said. He turned up the flame. "You think that is bad."

Eric forced a laugh. "Could it possibly be good?"

Gero didn't answer immediately. He was searching among the unlabeled jars that cluttered his shelves. When he squinted, the Asian slant of his gray eyes was more pronounced than usual. The water in the saucepan began to boil vigorously, but Gero ignored it until he had found what he was looking for—a jar of bright yellow powder that was probably mustard. But perhaps not. On those rare occasions when Gero wasn't in the restaurant, Eric would sometimes examine the contents of the jars, sniffing this, tasting a pinch of that. Some of the ingredients were spices that he recognized, but many of them remained mysteries. Gero's stock of ingredients was like his ethnicity—exotic and impossible to name.

Gero turned the flame back down, tapped some of the yellow powder into the water, then pulled at his reddish Magyar mustache as he searched through the jars again.

"Some parasites, you would not *choose* them," he said, "but once you have them . . ." He shrugged. "In Thailand there is a pickled fish that is so white, so firm." He kissed his fingertips. "You want to taste things. At least once. Well, this fish has a price for tasting. In his flesh, there are cysts. Tiny. Once you eat, the cysts break, and in your liver, in a little while, there are worms. Maybe in *my* liver. I don't know. Just a few are no trouble."

Gero's accent, Eric decided, sounded Russian today. Slavic, anyway. But it could shift. Sometimes it sounded Chinese.

Gero was showing Eric his smallest fingernail. "Not even that big, these worms. Flat, like that. I just eat the fish one time, no problem. Parasites are not so bad, then. Everything is balance, yes? I keep explaining to you. *Balance.*"

"Balance, right," Eric said. "Every time we have one of our little business dinners, Sutherland hits me with another surprise. But I should find some way to *balance* him. Sure."

Gero took down another jar. This one contained a woody root suspended in alcohol. It looked like a smaller version of the roots that Gero had hanging from the ceiling, up there with a wreath of bay leaves, the long strings of peppers, and the bunches of bulbs that looked like garlic, but weren't. Gero spooned a little of the alcohol into the boiling water and re-sealed the jar.

"You are impatient," Gero said. "When you are sick, you think only of cures."

"Well, of course!"

"First you must think of the sickness. Its nature."

"Okay, look," Eric said, "so maybe parasite isn't the right word for him."

"Sounds perfect," Gero said. "Business is good like always, but something is happening to money. Poof." He was adding a pinch from this jar and a pinch from that one to the boiling water. He turned down the heat. "Your partner is like tapeworm. Restaurant brings in same as before, but is getting skinny. How skinny? Little bit isn't bad. Most people, if they have tapeworm, they don't know it. Tapeworm isn't so bad."

"What I'm talking about," Eric said, "is embezzlement.

Mismanagement. All these decisions he forces down my throat."

"And what *I* am talking about," Gero said, "is balance." He strained the contents of the saucepan through a paper filter into a ceramic carafe. "Wind over heaven."

"What?"

Gero tapped one of the Chinese books stacked next to his jars. "The ninth hexagram is wind above, heaven below. The Taming Power of Small Things. This is no time to act. Be subtle. Observe. Seek balance." Gero poured a few ounces of the amber infusion into a teacup. "You are agitated. Too much worry is too much bile. Drink this."

Eric opened his mouth to speak, then closed it. He accepted the cup with a sigh. It was no use trying to decline Gero's remedies. Gero would pester him until he drank it. In any case, the brews seemed harmless enough.

"Be patient," Gero said. "Don't make another mistake. He is your partner, now, and that was your choice. Now you want him out. What do you have to do to get him out? If you have a tapeworm, you must take poison enough to kill tapeworm, but not to kill you. How much poison must Tarragon Leaf swallow to get rid of this partner? How sick are you going to make my restaurant?"

Eric sipped the concoction. It was slightly bitter, but not bad.

My restaurant, Gero called it. Technically, it was Eric's restaurant. Well, Eric's and Sutherland's now. But Gero was right in a way.

There were times, Eric thought, when it all seemed a little surreal. Twelve years ago, when The Tarragon Leaf was struggling in its infancy, when Eric had a splendid atmosphere to go with not-yet-splendid food, Gero had shown up.

Two days earlier, the original saucier had quit. Clutching a battered satchel, Gero was vague about his training and references, and his accent that day was generic pidgin. "I know sauce," he said. "I know food. Let me show."

What the hell, Eric had thought. He picked three sauces from the menu—a celeriac rémoulade, a lobster chiffonade, and béarnaise. "Make these."

In the kitchen, Gero looked over the spice racks, muttering and shaking his head. Eventually, he opened the satchel and set its contents on the counter—jars of dried powders, roots, mushrooms. There were two books, too, their leather covers stamped in gold with Chinese characters. But Gero didn't consult these. He worked by tasting his base, adding an infinitesimal trace of some powder or another, and tasting the base again, so that he was absurdly slow, and Eric already knew the answer would be no, sorry, we have no position for you.

Until he tasted the finished sauces.

They weren't what the restaurant had ever served before. They weren't, Eric was almost certain, what *any* restaurant had served before. It seemed like magic.

"Not magic," Gero said. *"Balance."*

His sense of balance, as it turned out, extended to more than sauces. Though he always insisted that he was a saucier and only a saucier, he was soon giving advice to others in the kitchen about everything from perfectly timed crème patissière to deftly positioned garnish. He was subtle about it. Balanced, you could say. He managed to offer compliments that planted only the tiniest hint of dissatisfaction, the barest clue that he had available some advice to offer about how something that was nearly perfect could be nearer still.

And if Gero's area in the kitchen grew a little strange, with its drying herbs and spices hanging here and there, its unlabeled jars filled with the unknown, if it became, in fact, a little spooky on the days when his suppliers—often speaking no English—appeared in the kitchen with jars wrapped in brown paper, that was easy enough to overlook. The food, the reputation, the growing success of The Tarragon Leaf more than made up for the dreamlike witchiness of the saucier's shelves.

Besides, Eric liked the man. How could he fail to like him? The Tarragon Leaf had been Eric's dream, but it seemed that Gero dreamed it, too. He was nearly always there, even on Mondays, rearranging his things in the kitchen, experimenting, and often giving Eric a taste of something new, something divine.

Sometimes the herbal remedies that Gero dispensed for imaginary maladies he had diagnosed as "bad humors" or "overbearing yang" were a little hard to swallow. But they seemed a small price to pay.

The table in The Tarragon Leaf's private dining room wasn't small, but Spencer Sutherland's bulk at one end made it seem that way to Eric. "There are certain economies we need around here," Sutherland was saying, his words muffled by a mouthful of salad.

Eric said, "What do you mean?"

Sutherland swallowed. "Like this salad." He took a bite that was too big and chewed it impatiently. Eric wished that he'd paid attention to how Sutherland ate before he had agreed to the marriage of their restaurants. Sutherland's first bite of anything would be careful. He would consider as he chewed. Then, once he had passed judgment, he would eat the rest too fast to savor. Once he knew what something was, he ate only to absorb, to acquire.

"What about the salad?" It was Belgian endive and fen-

nel, with a very light vinaigrette, a palate-clearing course between appetizer and main course.

"We're importing this endive." Sutherland took another
wolfish bite. Eric had hardly started on his own salad, and
Sutherland's was nearly gone. "I mean, it's salad, Eric. And
you're ordering from Europe? They grow this stuff in California, now. Cheap."

"It's called Belgian endive for a reason." Eric pointed
with his fork. "See how the stalk has this closed shape?
Around Brussels, they grow it underground, in heated soil.
Growers in California don't take the same care."

"I know all that," Sutherland said. "But it tastes the
same."

"The presentation is different."

Sutherland rolled his eyes.

"The reason this restaurant has the reputation it does,"
Eric said, "is that we take pains with detail."

"Yeah, well, it's a little hard to keep up with detail that
you can't pay for." Sutherland pushed his plate aside. "I
mean, you want to keep The Tarragon Leaf afloat, right?"

Eric's jaw clenched. "We're doing as much volume as
ever," he said. "I don't see where this cash crunch has come
from, unless you're doing less business at Southern Exposure."

"My place is doing fine," Sutherland said. He always
spoke about The Tarragon Leaf as *our* restaurant and the
Southern Exposure as *mine*, Eric realized. That wasn't the
only inequality. He insisted on changes for The Tarragon
Leaf, but wouldn't listen to the suggestions Eric had made for
Sutherland's Southern Exposure steakhouse. The partnership was supposed to be collaborative. Advisory. At least
that's how they had talked it out before signing the papers.

"You've got to understand," Sutherland was saying, "that

there are certain administrative costs built in to the partnership."

"This merger was supposed to save us money. Both of us."

"And it will, eventually," Sutherland said. "Look, you yourself admitted to me that accounting issues weren't your strong suit, right? That's why we're in business together, to benefit from each other's strengths."

How could Eric *ever* have trusted him enough to tell him that money was the one thing he had trouble with? Not that there wasn't plenty coming in. The Tarragon Leaf was a success by any measure. But Eric had always found keeping track of money such a headache. It was the food he cared about. The food, the presentation, the atmosphere . . .

"It'll be all right. Trust me on that. But for now, I'm trimming your budget."

"Trimming my budget?" Eric said. "You can't do that!"

"Eric, read the agreements. You're in charge of operations. I'm in charge of budget and accounting. If you don't like it, sell out to me. You've heard my offer."

Eric's hand closed around a butter knife. He brandished it, then looked at it and put it down. "I'm bringing in an auditor."

Sutherland froze for half a second. He looked at Eric as if reappraising him. "You can't do it. We can't spend on something like that. We have to *economize.*"

"I can do it. I am doing it."

"Eric," Sutherland said, "we're *partners.*" He shrugged. "But I see you're going to insist. All right. At least pick someone good."

"I have. His name is Webber."

"Richard Webber?" Sutherland's teeth were big and white when he smiled. "I know Dick. He'll do a fine job. A fine job. Then you'll feel better. And you'll see that I'm right about cutting back a little, just temporarily. To keep us in the black." Sutherland lifted his wineglass and drained it. "Where's that waiter with the next course?"

The dinner rush had begun, and Gero had the makings for three white sauces started in three different pans. In a fourth saucepan was an inch or so of mud-colored water. Eric watched it bubble. "That audit was a waste of money," he said.

"You don't trust the accountant?" Gero said, stirring and tasting each sauce in succession. He opened a jar.

"I trust the one I finally hired," Eric said, "the one who Sutherland didn't know. But he couldn't find anything." Actually, that wasn't entirely true. The auditor had made a stink about the records for Gero's purchases of ingredients. The saucier's suppliers did not furnish adequate invoices. Sutherland, with obvious pleasure, was insisting that Eric do something about this, but Eric wasn't up to broaching the subject with Gero now.

"Your kidneys are rising."

"Rising kidneys," Eric said. That could only mean that the roiling liquid on the stove was intended for him.

Gero tossed a whole mushroom onto the oily surface and cut the flame. The he stirred the sauces again. "So the partner, he is an honest man," Gero said. "Not parasite. Something else."

"No. I know he's pulling something, but he's clever. And he *knows* he's clever. God, I hate that smile of his."

"Parasites are not always bad. I told you. Tarragon Leaf can have a parasite and still be Tarragon Leaf."

"It's not just the embezzlement, Gero. He keeps insisting

that I cut expenses, buy cheaper ingredients . . ."

Gero looked up. "Cheap? He wants you to buy cheap for Tarragon Leaf?" Gero shook his head. "To have the best is expensive."

"Yes."

"If it is not the best, is not Tarragon Leaf."

"That's how I feel about it. He'll bleed us to death. Bit by bit, we'll give up little pieces of what we do, and the restaurant won't be The Tarragon Leaf anymore."

"So he *is* a parasite, this partner." Gero started straining the liquid. "Still," he said, "if we are patient, he will learn. He will not be so bad."

Eric didn't think that was likely.

"If he doesn't learn, end the partnership."

"The only way to do that is to buy him out," Eric said. "I don't have the money. Especially now. He's going to ruin me. I can feel it."

"Smart parasite does not kill his host."

"Not all parasites understand that, Gero."

"Kidneys are rising," Gero said, handing him a steaming cup. "Drink."

Eric sipped the steaming brew. Whether his kidneys fell back into place or not, he couldn't tell. In any case, he didn't feel any better about the prospects for his restaurant.

"I'd take a big loss, selling," Eric told Gero. It was a Monday morning again, and they were alone, watching water simmer in a pan. "But I probably can't get more out of him than he's offering, and the partnership agreement ties my hands. But it's not a dead loss. I'm thinking we can start over. Sutherland insists on a noncompeting covenant, so we'd have to move to another city. It'd have to be a small restaurant to begin with, but I'd take along any staff who want to make the move . . ."

"Not me," the saucier said. "I will not leave Tarragon Leaf."

Eric didn't know what to say. Finally, he told Gero, "It won't *be* The Tarragon Leaf, even if you stay."

"Listen for example," said Gero. "You have a good friend. You are always together drinking, talking. You love this friend like your brother. Like twin. You are balancing to each other. Understand? Then he gets sick. He changes. He is not so interesting, always sick. So, Eric, you leave him? When he needs you?"

The saucier looked at his arrays of jars, then shook his head. "If you are thinking like this, the problem is your heart. Bad faith. There is no medicine I can give you for it." He turned off the burner and poured the steaming water down the sink.

"Well, what would you suggest, exactly?" Eric said. "I don't have a lot of options."

"Patience. Let me think. It's a matter of balance. Suppose you are right, and he is a bad parasite. A bladder worm. You know bladder worm?"

Eric shook his head.

"Tapeworm babies," Gero said. "Larva. They hatch from eggs inside your stomach, dig into intestine walls, then into blood, yes? All through your body, even your brain. In a few years, they start to die. Dead ones swell up in your brain like little balloons."

Eric rubbed at his temples. Dead worms in the brain. He thought of Swiss cheese. He felt a headache coming on. "And then what?"

Gero made a gesture of expansion with his hands. "Pressure in brain. Epilepsy, shaking, fits. Maybe, you die. But you don't know about these worms until too late. That is what kind of parasite you selected to be your partner. Now we know what he is, but Tarragon Leaf already swallowed him."

Eric had a fleeting vision of Sutherland as an enormous worm. He felt sick. "If this is supposed to make me more hopeful," Eric said, "it isn't working."

"You are not going to sell the restaurant. We do not abandon sick friend."

"I don't know," Eric said. "If Sutherland is a bladder worm, I think our sick friend may be terminal."

Although Eric was filled with thoughts of doom, the restaurant was hardly showing symptoms. Eric knew that would change. He concentrated on running the dining room and avoiding Spencer Sutherland when Sutherland tried to see him.

Finally, after a week of this, Eric took one of Sutherland's calls. "A house divided against itself cannot stand," Sutherland said. "Let's have a meeting over dinner. Get your boys to broil us some steaks. I like mine well-done."

"Every time we talk," Eric said, "it's bad news. I don't want to hear any more."

"I'm going to make it worth your while," Sutherland said. "And if you ignore me, I can make it hurt. Read your contracts. I can just about close you down."

In the kitchen before the meeting, Gero said, "Drink this."

For once it was a cold concoction, not a steaming one.

"What do I have?" Eric said. "High kidneys? Rising yin?"

"Heart problem still," said Gero. "Bad faith. You are thinking of selling." While they talked, he was making two sauces. Two brown sauces. Around them was the usual kitchen racket, but it wasn't up to its frantic pace. The evening was early, and the restaurant wasn't yet half-full. "You will not sell, all right?"

"Depends on what he offers."

"Drink."

Eric took a sip, then made a face. Of all the brews Gero had ever made for him, this was the worst. "Are you poisoning me?"

Gero looked up, his gray eyes thoughtful. "That would keep you from selling?"

"Sutherland would still get the restaurant."

"Then what is the advantage to poisoning you? Drink. You are having serious bad faith. It's getting worse, I think."

Eric held his breath and drank the stuff. There was grit at the bottom of the glass.

"Let this partner offer you the moon and stars," Gero said. "Don't sell before you talk to me." He turned back to the stove. "I am making a wonderful sauce for the steak tonight. Something new."

"We can't . . ." Eric looked around the kitchen, then lowered his voice. "We can't poison him. Don't think I haven't thought about it, but we'd never get away with it."

"We need balance," Gero said. "Takes time. You are going to be patient. Meet with your partner, enjoy a good dinner. *Relax.*"

Dinner should not have been relaxing, but it was. By the time the main course had come, Eric was, if not in a state of bliss, at least profoundly calm. A little sleepy, in fact. He could not have said why. Certainly, Sutherland's eating habits hadn't suddenly improved. There was nothing calming about seeing the man belt down his appetizer and salad after only one preliminary, appraising bite of each.

The steaks arrived—well-done for Sutherland, rare for

Eric. The waiter put them down wrong initially, and Sutherland started cutting into his. "Hey," he said, "I like mine
cooked!"

The waiter apologized and exchanged the plates. Then
Eric watched as Sutherland cut one modest bite. "Oh, this is
marvelous," he said. "Perfectly marbled. It melts."

"So that's one thing you think I'm doing right," Eric
mumbled.

Sutherland laughed. "Not at all," he said. "Serving this to
your customers squeezes your margin. I can get almost as
good for considerably less. I think both restaurants ought to
use the same meat supplier."

He carved his next bite, an enormous chunk that he
hardly chewed before swallowing. Eric supposed that Sutherland's choking to death was too much to hope for.

At least Eric had the satisfaction of enjoying Gero's steak
sauce. It was nouvelle Mexican, a sort of *mole*, but lighter on
salt than one would expect. There was more chile than chocolate, and on the whole it had Gero's distinctive *wholeness*. It
was, as Gero would say, balanced. But Sutherland probably
wasn't even tasting it anymore.

As soon as he'd swallowed the last piece of meat, Sutherland reached into his pocket for a packet of folded papers.
"I'm making you a take-it-or-leave-it deal," he said. "Better
price than before. We want to resolve this, right? I think it's
too late to mend fences."

Eric glared.

The price Sutherland quoted was an improvement. He
shoved the papers across the table for Eric to look at.

"All in all, this is simply an unfortunate falling out,"
Sutherland said. "It happens sometimes." He offered Eric a
pen.

*   *   *

Gero had another glass for him like the earlier one, but Eric refused to drink it.

"Is better if you do drink," Gero said.

"Forget that," Eric said. He unfolded the papers. "Everything's drawn up already, see? He's eager to be rid of me. That increased the price."

"You signed?" Gero said.

"You said I should talk to you first," Eric told him, "so I'm talking. But it's a better deal. Enough better that I'm thinking *you* might reconsider. Gero, think about the struggle it would be here, to hold together a restaurant while Sutherland is trying to break it up into little pieces he can sell."

"I will not go."

"Well I might." Eric held out the papers. "I *will.*"

"You are forgetting your friend who is sick. You are turning your back on Tarragon Leaf."

"Gero, The Tarragon Leaf is a terminal case. Whether I stay or go, Sutherland is in the picture, and that means that the restaurant you and I know is already history. He's a bladder worm, remember?"

"Ah, yes. A bladder worm," Gero said. "Better you drink this." He offered the noxious drink again.

"Look, forget that nonsense," Eric said. He picked up the drink, walked it to the sink, and poured it out.

Gero took a deep breath. That was the most extreme expression of exasperation Eric had ever seen him make. "All right," Gero said, "I will show you."

He looked around the kitchen. It was late, but the other chefs, the pot scrubbers, the dishwashers were all still busy. No one seemed to be paying particular attention to the conversation. "Restaurant has a parasite," Gero said very quietly. "What is a better treatment for parasite than another parasite?" He produced a jar. Inside was something that looked like a long, curled shaving of wax. Even without knowing what it was, there was something about its appearance that made Eric's stomach turn.

Gero tapped the side of the jar. "Tapeworm pieces," he said. "Proglottids. Fresh. Ripe. Full of eggs." He reached among his jars and produced a second and third jar with similar contents.

Eric thought he felt something twitch in his intestines. The kitchen air suddenly seemed very stale.

"I had to get several. I had to make sure I would have many eggs. It must be a big infection to make sure the bladder worms get to the brain."

"Where . . ."

"From Mexico, from pigs," Gero said. "I have sources, yes? I tell them it must be fresh."

"But I mean, where . . ."

"In the steak sauce, remember? In your partner's steak sauce, not yours. The eggs are too small to see, though, so I worry, just a little sauce on a spoon is bad. Or the waiter makes mistake."

"Bad. Yes." And the waiter *had* made a mistake. Had Eric's steak knife perhaps touched the sauce on Sutherland's steak? He tried to remember. Surely, if there were bladder worm larvae in Eric's stomach, he couldn't *feel* them. Surely that crawling sensation was his imagination.

"But now, all we need is patience," Gero went on. "In four years, your partner will not be running any restaurant. Maybe we will buy Southern Exposure. We will make two fine restaurants then, Eric. With balance." He smiled. There was light in his gray, Sino-Ugrian-Russo-Mediterranean eyes. "What did I tell you? Wind over heaven. The Taming

Power of Small Things. Your partner is a man out of balance. Big body, big appetite, very big greed. With something small, now, we tame him."

"The drink," Eric said. His mouth felt dry. "Some kind of herbs?"

Gero shook his head. "Herbs for some things, for subtle things, are fine. But for killing worms, making sure you are not infected, we need the best poison. Quinacrine hydrochloride. Makes you vomit sometimes, so I put in some catnip and phenobarbital. I will make you another now."

Eric, still looking at the worm pieces in the jars, thought he saw one move. He rushed to the sink and leaned forward.

Gero stood watching him for a moment. "Recipe is not balanced," he said. "I think, this time, more phenobarbital."

Eric rose to breathe, then leaned forward again.

Gero sighed and shook his head. "It is difficult. This is not something I can balance by taste." He opened a jar full of pills, and he shrugged.

"After all," he said, "I am not a doctor. I am only a saucier."

Here's my own contribution to the chart. Kind of awkward, but the publisher insisted that I participate. So I opted to play around with medical politics.

At the time I wrote this (the summer of '94), the press was full of cries from certain quarters for a Canadian-style health care system (and probably still crying for it as you read this). I got to asking myself: If the Canadian system is so great, how come all the U.S. hospitals along our northern border are full of Canadians?

Theodore Sturgeon always liked to say, "Ask the next question." So I did: If the U.S. adopted a Canadian-style system, where would we find *our* safety valve?

Mexico?

I don't think so.

We'd probably have to go . . .

OFFSHORE

F. Paul Wilson

I.

Got a doozie comin', Terr."

Ernie stood at the big plate-glass window with his thumbs hooked in his belt on either side of the gut pouting over his buckle, and stared out at Upper Sugarloaf Sound.

Terry Havens looked up from the bar where he'd been making a wet Olympics symbol with the bottom rim of his sweating Red Stripe.

"Good," he said. "Maybe it'll cool things off a little."

Terry had been expecting the storm, looking forward to it, in fact. But not because it would cool things off.

"I think this mother might do more than cool things off. This'n looks *mean.*"

Terry took a swig of the Red Stripe and carried the bottle to the big picture window. He stood beside Ernie and took in the view. Bartenders always need something to talk about. Not much happening during off-season in the Keys, so some heavy weather would keep Ernie going through the rest of the afternoon and well into the evening.

And this looked pretty damn heavy. A cumulonimbus tower was building over the Gulf, dominating the western sky. Some big mother of a storm—a dark, bruise purple underbelly crowding the entire span of the horizon while its fat, fluffy white upper body stretched a good ten miles straight up to where the shear winds flattened and sluiced its crown away to the north. Anvil-topped buggers like these could be downright mean.

"Where you got those glasses hid?"

Ernie limped back to the bar and brought out the battered field glasses he'd smuggled home from the Gulf War. Terry fitted them over his eyes and focused on the body of the storm. What looked like fluffy vanilla cotton candy to the naked eye became slowly boiling steam as violent updrafts and downdrafts roiled within.

Damn. He'd been looking for a storm, but this thing might be more than he could handle. Like casting light tackle out on the flats and hooking something bigger than your boat.

He lowered the glasses. He was going to have to risk it. He'd promised the *Osler* a delivery on this pass, and tonight was his last chance. The big boat would be out of range by tomorrow.

Besides, the worse the storm, the better his chances of being alone out there on the water. Not even Henriques would be out on patrol in the belly of the beast growling on the horizon.

Terry finished the rest of his Red Stripe. "One more of these before I get moving."

"Sure thing," Ernie said.

As Terry returned to his stool, he glanced across the horseshoe-shaped bar and saw two of the grizzled regulars poking into their wallets with nicotine-yellowed fingers. Both reed-thin, wild-haired, leather-skinned, and stubble-cheeked.

"Betcha that storm's good for at least five spouts," Rick said.

"Ten says you don't see more'n three," Boo said, flipping a sawbuck onto the bar.

Rick slapped a bill down on top of Boo's. "Yer on."

Terry smiled as he reached for the fresh bottle Ernie put in front of him. Those two Conchs bet on anything. He'd seen them wager on the number of times a fly would land on a piece of cheese, the number of trips someone would make to the head in an evening. Anything.

"I guess that means you two'll be spending most of the night here," Terry said.

"You betcha," Rick said. "Watchin' the storm."

"Countin' the spouts," Boo said.

"Some guys sure know how to have fun."

Rick and Boo laughed and hoisted their Rolling Rocks in reply.

They all quaffed together, then Terry glanced up at the TV monitor. The sight of a bunch of flak-jacketed federal marshals toting riot guns around a tandem tractor trailer shot a spasm through his stomach lining.

"Turn the sound up, will you, Ern?"

Ernie touched a button on the remote. The audio level display flashed on the screen, zipped to a preprogrammed volume, then disappeared as the announcer's voice blared from the speakers bracketed on the ceiling.

"—*tainly put a crimp in the black market in medical contraband. This haul was most likely bound for one of the renegade floating hospitals that ply their illicit trade outside the twelve-mile limit in the Gulf of Mexico.*"

The screen cut to an interior of one of the trailers and panned its contents.

"*Syringes, sterile bandages, dialysis fluid, even gas sterilizers, all bound for the booming offshore medical centers. President Nathan has called on Congress to enact stiffer penalties for medical smuggling and to pass legislation to push the offshore hospitals to a hundred-mile limit. Insiders on the Hill think he is unlikely to find much support on extending the twelve-mile limit due to the complexities of maritime law, but say he might get action on the stiffer penalties.*"

The president's intense, youthful face filled the screen.

"*We are talking here about trading in human misery. Every medical item that is sneaked offshore deprives law-abiding citizens right here at home of needed medical supplies. These racketeers are little better than terrorists, sabotaging America's medical system and health security. We've got to hit these criminals hard, and hit them where it hurts!*"

"Okay, Ern," Terry said. "I've heard enough."

Poor President Nathan—thoroughly pissed that some folks were making an end run around the National Health Security Act.

Nothing new in the trucker bust, other than somebody got careless. Or got turned in. Terry wondered who it was, wondered if he knew them. He'd tuned in too late to catch where the bust had gone down.

"Excuse me," said a voice to Terry's right. "Is there a Mr. Havens here?"

Terry didn't turn his head. Rick and Boo acquired a sudden intense interest in the "33" inside the labels on their Rolling Rocks.

Ernie cleared his throat and said, "He comes in now and again. I can take a message for you."

"We wish to hire him for a boat trip," the voice said.

Terry swiveled on his barstool. He saw a moderately overweight golden-ager, white hair and a sunburned face, wearing cream slacks and a lime green golf shirt.

"Where do you want to go?"

"Are you Mr. Havens?" the guy said, eagerly stepping forward and thrusting out his hand.

Terry hesitated, then said, "That's me." Hard to lie to a guy who's offering you his hand.

But the immediate relief in the guy's eyes made him wish he hadn't. Here was a man with a problem, and he seemed to think Terry was his solution. Terry was not in the problem-solving business.

"Joe Kozlowski, Mr. Havens," he said, squeezing Terry's hand between both of his. "I'm so glad we found you." He turned and called over his shoulder. "It's him, Martha!"

Terry looked past him at a rickety, silver-haired woman hobbling toward them, supporting herself on the bar with her right forearm and leaning on a four-footed cane clasped in her gnarled left hand. Her wrinkled face was pinched with pain. She couldn't seem to straighten out her right leg, and winced every time she put weight on it.

"Thank God!" she said.

Terry was getting a bad feeling about this.

"Uh, just where is it you folks want to go?"

"Out to the *Osler*," Joe Kozlowski said.

"You missed her. She took on her patients this morning and she's gone."

"I know. We missed the shuttle. Martha wanted to say

good-bye to the kids before the surgery. You know, in case . . . you know. But our car broke down last night just as we were leaving and what they said would take an hour to fix wound up taking much longer. Damn car's probably still up on the lift back there in Stewart. I finally rented a car and drove down here fast as I could. Collected two tickets along the way, but we still missed the boat. We've been driving up and down Route 1 all day trying to find someone to take us out. No one's interested. I don't understand. I don't want a favor—I'm willing to pay a fair price. And it's not like it's a crime or anything."

Right. Not a crime or anything to ferry someone out past the twelve-mile limit to one of the hospital ships. But bad things tended to happen to good boaters who engaged in the trade if officialdom got wind of it. Bad things like a coast guard stop and search every time you took your boat out; or all sorts of lost applications and inexplicable computer glitches when you wanted to renew your boating tags, your fishing permits, even your driver's license. Terry had heard talk that the good folks in question seemed to suffer a significantly greater incidence of having their 1040 audited by the IRS.

No, not a crime, but lots of punishment.

Which was why the hospital ships ran their own shuttles.

"What excuse did they give?"

"Most said they were too busy, but let me tell you, they didn't look it. And as soon as those clouds started gathering, they used the storm as an excuse."

"Good excuse," Terry said, glancing back at the western horizon. The afternoon sun had been swallowed whole by the storm and its white bulk had turned a threatening gray.

"But I hear you're not afraid of storms," Joe said.

Terry stared at him, feeling his anger rise. Shit. "Who told you that?"

"Some fellow in a bar up on the next key—is it Cudjoe Key? Some cantina . . ."

"Coco's."

"That's the place! Fellow with bleached hair and a fuzzy goatee."

Tommy Axler. Terry wanted to strangle the big-mouthed jerk. In fact, he might even give it a try next time he saw him.

"He must have thought you wanted to go fishing. Sometimes I take people fishing in the rain. I do lots of things, but I don't ferry folks out to hospital ships."

That last part, at least, was true.

Joe's eyes got this imploring look. "I'll pay you twice your regular charter fee."

Terry shook his head. "Sorry."

His face fell. He turned to his wife. "He won't do it, Martha."

She halted her labored forward progress as if she'd run into a wall. "Oh," she said softly, and leaned against one of the barstools. She stared at the floor and said no more.

"But let me buy you folks a drink." Terry pointed to his Red Stripe. "You want one of these?"

"No," Joe said through a sigh, then shrugged. "Aaah, why not? Martha? You want something?"

Still staring at the floor, Martha only shook her head.

Ernie set the bottle in front of Joe who immediately chugged about a third of it. He stifled a burp, then said, "You won't reconsider, even if I triple your usual fee?"

"Look," Terry said, "the *Osler*'ll probably be shuttling patients in and out of St. Petersburg in a day or two. Hop in your car and—"

"Martha's got an appointment for a total hip replacement *tomorrow*. If she's not on board the *Osler* today, they'll give her appointment to someone on the waiting list."

"So reschedule."

"It took us six months to get this appointment, and we were lucky. The fellow who had the original appointment died. Might be another ten months to a year before Martha can get rescheduled."

"That's as bad as the regular government wait lists."

"No," he said with a slow shake of his head. "There *is* no government wait list for Martha. Not anymore. She's too old. HRAA passed a regulation barring anyone over age seventy from certain surgical procedures. Total hip replacement is on the list. And Martha's seventy-two."

Terry had assumed that most of the hospital ship patrons were well-heeled folks who didn't want to wait in the long queues for elective surgery in the government-run hospitals. And since all the hospitals in America were now government run, they had to go elsewhere. But cutting people off from procedures . . .

The Health Resources Allocation Agency strikes again.

"I didn't know they could do that."

Joe sighed. "Neither did I. It wasn't part of the regulations when the Health Security Act became law, but apparently the HRAA has the power to make new regs. So when they found out how far their Health Security Act was running over projections, they started making cuts. What really galls me is I supported the damn law."

"So did I."

"Yeah, we all thought we were getting a bargain. Ten years later we find out we got the shaft."

"Welcome to the twenty-first century, Pops. Believe in the future but always read the fine print."

"Tell me about it." He slugged down some more beer and stared at the bottle in his hand. "It's not fair, you know. We busted our butts since we got married—fifty years come next July—to make a good life for our family. We educated our kids, got them married and settled, then we retired. And now we'd like to enjoy the years we've got left. Nothing fancy. No trips around the world. Just hang out, play golf once in a while. But with Martha's hip, we can't even go for a walk after dinner."

Terry said nothing as Joe polished off his beer. He was trying not to listen. He wasn't going to get sucked into this.

Joe banged his bottle down on the bar. "You know what really bugs my ass? We've got the money to pay for the surgery. We don't need the government to pay for it. Fuck 'em! *We'll* pay. Gladly. But they won't let her have the surgery—period. Their letter said total hip surgery at her age is 'an inefficient utilization of valuable medical resources.' I mean, what the hell did we work and skimp and save for if we can't spend it on our health?"

"Wish I had an answer for you," Terry said.

"Yeah." He pushed away from the bar. "Thanks for the beer. Come on, Martha. We'll keep looking."

He took his wife gently by the arm and began helping her toward the door. Terry stared across the bar at Rick and Boo so he wouldn't have to watch the Kozlowskis. He saw a grinning Rick accepting a ten from a grumpy-looking Boo. He wondered what the bet had been this time.

He looked out the window at the towering storm, black as a hearse now, picking up speed and power. If he was going to head out, he'd better get moving.

Terry waited until Joe Kozlowski had eased his wife into the passenger seat, then he waved to Rick, Boo, and Ernie and headed out. The August heat gave him a wet body slam as he stepped outside. He slid past the Kozlowskis' idling rental but couldn't resist a glance through the windshield.

Martha was crying.

He averted his gaze and hurried to his pickup. Life really sucked sometimes. He jumped into the blisteringly hot cab. That didn't mean he had to get involved. He turned the key and the old Ford shuddered to life. Wasn't his problem. He threw it into reverse.

As he was backing out he saw Joe put an arm around his wife's thin, quaking shoulders and try to comfort her.

He slammed on the brakes and yanked the gearshift back into neutral.

Shit.

Cursing himself for a jerk, Terry jumped out of the cab and stalked over to the Kozlowskis' car. He rapped on Joe's window.

"Follow me," he said as the glass slid down.

Joe's eyes lit. "You mean—?"

"Just follow."

As he was heading back to the pickup, he heard a voice call out behind him.

"Aw, Terry! Say it isn't so!"

He turned and saw Rick standing in the doorway, dismay flattening his weathered features. Boo peered over his shoulder, grinning.

"You're takin' 'em, ain't ya," Boo said.

"None of your damn business," Terry said.

Boo nudged Rick none too gently and rubbed his palms together. "See. I toldja he would. I win. Gimme back my saw plus the one you owe me. Give it now, Rick."

Rick handed the money to Boo and gave Terry a wounded look.

"Y'disappointed the shit outta me, Terr."

"Yeah, well," Terry muttered, slipping behind the wheel again, "there's one born every minute."

2.

"You really think he's going to risk this storm?" Cramer asked.

Pepe Henriques looked at his mate. Cramer's round, usually relaxed boyish face was tight with tension.

He's scared, he thought.

Which was okay. Showing it wasn't.

Henriques looked past Cramer at the storm that filled the sky. Giant forks of lightning occasionally speared down to the Gulf but mostly jumped cloud to cloud, illuminating the guts of the storm with explosions of light. Thunder crashed incessantly, vibrating their fiberglass hull. He could see the rain curtain billowing toward them.

Almost here.

When it hit, visibility would be shot and they'd have to go on instruments. But so would the runner.

"He'll be out here. Why else would that hospital ship be dawdling fourteen miles out? They're waiting for a delivery. And our man's going to make it. That is, he's going to try. This'll be his last run."

He tossed Cramer a life jacket and watched him strap it on. Saw the black ATF across the yellow fabric and had to shake his head.

Me. An ATF agent.

He still couldn't believe it. But he'd found he liked the regular paycheck, the benefit package, the retirement fund. Sure as hell beat taking tourists tarpon and bone fishing on the flats.

But he might be back to fishing those flats if he didn't catch this runner.

Henriques had run up against him twice before, but both times he'd got away. Two things he knew for sure about the guy: he ran a Hutchinson 686 and he was a Conch. Henriques had seen the Hutch from a distance. The registration numbers on the twenty-six-foot craft were bogus—no surprise there. What had been big surprises were the way the boat handled and its pilot's knowledge of the waters around the Lower Keys. The Hutch 686 was popular as hell in these parts, but this one had done things a propeller-driven shouldn't be able to do. It ran like a VMA impeller—like Henriques's craft. The runner had customized it somehow.

And as for being a Conch, well . . . nobody could dodge among all these reefs and mangrove keylets like that runner unless he'd spent his life among them. A native of the Keys. A Conch. Took one to know one.

Take one to catch one.

And I'm the one, Henriques thought. Tonight's his last run.

3.

The rain hit just as they neared the inner rim of the reef. Terry pulled back on the throttle and idled the engine.

"Thank *God!*" Martha said. She still clung to the arms of her deck-fast seat with white knuckles. "That bouncing was making me sick!"

"What're you doing now?" Joe Kozlowski shouted over the mad drumming of the big drops on the deck and the roof of the open cabin.

Terry didn't answer. His passengers would see for themselves soon enough.

He unwrapped the molded black plastic panels and began scampering around the deck, snapping them onto the sides of the superstructure. Two of the strips for the hull sported a brand-new registration number, fresh off the decal sheets. Another went over the transom to cover the name, replacing his own admittedly corny *Terryfied* with *Delta Sue*.

Joe looked utterly bewildered when Terry ducked back into the cabin enclosure. "I don't get it."

"Just a little insurance," Terry said. The less Joe knew, the better.

The panels changed the boat's lines and color scheme. Nothing that would hold up against even casual inspection in good light, but from a distance, through lightning-strobed rain, his white, flat-bottomed VMA impeller craft looked an awful lot like a black-and-white V-hulled Hutchinson 686. The black panels also broke up the boat's outline, making it harder to spot.

"That's what you said when you were playing around with the light on that channel marker," Joe said.

"That's right. Another kind of insurance."

"But that could—"

"Don't worry. I'll undo it on my way back in. No questions—wasn't that the deal?"

Joe nodded glumly. "But I still don't get it."

You're not supposed to, Terry thought, as he gunned the engine and headed into the wind. The hull jumped, thudded, shimmied, and jittered with the staccato pounding of the waves, and all that rhythmic violence worked into every tissue in his body. Once he zipped through the cut in the barrier reef it got worse—two, three, maybe four times worse. Riding at this speed in this weather was a little like getting a total body massage. From King Kong. On speed. Add to that the tattoo of the rain, the howl of the wind, the booming thunder, and further talk was damn near impossible. Unless you shouted directly into someone's ear. Which Martha was doing into Joe's as she bounced around in her seat and hung on for dear life.

Joe sidled over. "Think you could slow down? Martha can't take the pounding."

Terry shook his head. "I ease up, we won't make enough headway."

Joe went back to Martha and they traded more shouts, none of which Terry could hear. Joe lurched back.

"Let's go back. I'm calling the trip off. Martha's afraid, and she can't take this pounding."

He'd been half-expecting something like this. Damn. Should have left them back on Sugarloaf.

"Don't wimp out on me, Joe," Terry said.

"It's not me. Look, you can keep the money. Martha's getting sick. Just turn around and take us back."

"Can't do that. No questions and no turning back— wasn't that the deal?"

"Yes, but—"

"It's still the deal. Tell Martha to hang on and she'll have a new hip tomorrow."

As Joe stumbled back to his wife, Terry concentrated on the infrared scanner. Clear and cold except for the faint blob of the *Osler* straight ahead. Good. Stay that way.

Terry liked rain. Besides lowering visibility, it played havoc with heat scanners. Radiant energy tended to get swallowed up in all that falling water. But that could be a two-edged sword: Terry couldn't spot a pursuer until it was fairly close.

Didn't worry him much at the moment. Weren't too many craft who could outrun him in a sprint, and once he slipped past the twelve-mile limit, no one could touch him.

Legally, anyway. Always the possibility that some frustrated ATF goon with a short fuse might blow a few holes in your hull—and you—and let the sharks clean up the mess.

He checked the compass, checked the loran—right on course. Just a matter of time now. He looked up and froze when he saw Joe Kozlowski pointing a pistol at him. The automatic—looked like a 9mm—wavered in the old guy's hand but the muzzle never strayed far from the center of Terry's chest.

"Turn around and take us back," Joe shouted.

No way was Terry turning back. And no way was he telling Joe that at the moment. Guns made him nervous.

Terry eyed the gun. "Where'd that come from?"

"I brought it along . . . just in case."

"Just in case what?"

"In case you tried to rob us. Or worse."

"Whatever happened to trust?"

"The Health Resources Allocation Agency's got mine." His eyes bored into Terry's. "Now turn this thing around. I told you you could keep the money. Just take us back."

Terry shook his head. "Sorry. Can't do that."

Joe couldn't seem to believe what he'd heard. "I've got a *gun*, dammit!"

Terry was well aware of that. He didn't think Joe would pull that trigger, but you never knew. So maybe it was time to shake Joe up—more than physically.

"And I've got a cargo to deliver."

"My wife is *not* cargo!"

"Take a look below," Terry told him, jutting his chin toward the door to the belowdecks area.

Joe's gaze darted from Terry to the door and back. His eyes narrowed with suspicion. "You wouldn't try anything stupid, would you?"

Terry shrugged. "Take a look."

Joe thought about that, then backed away and opened the door. More hesitation, then he slipped below. A moment later he appeared again, pale, his eyes wide. Terry could read his lips.

"Medical supplies! Martha, he's a smuggler!"

Martha freed up a hand long enough to slap it over the "O" of her mouth, then returned it to the armrest.

"The way I see it, Joe," Terry said, "you've got two options. The first is you can shoot me and try to get the boat back home on your own. Not only will you have to guide it through the storm, but you'll have to avoid the shore patrol. If they catch you, you'll go down for murder *and* smuggling. Or you can follow through with our original plan and—" A blip caught his eye on the infrared scanner, aport and astern, and closing. He forgot all about Joe Kozlowski's gun. "Shit!"

"What's wrong?" Joe said.

"We've got company."

"Who?"

"ATF, most likely."

"ATF? But they're alcohol, tobacco, and—"

"They added medical supplies to their list. Get over by Martha and hang on. This could get a little rough."

"A *little* rough? It's already—"

"Get out of my face, dammit!"

Henriques, Terry thought. Has to be him. No one else has such a bug up his ass that he'd brave this storm looking for a runner. Not just any runner. Looking for The One That Got Away.

Me.

He jammed the throttle all the way forward. *Terryfied* lifted further out of the water and began bouncing along the tops of the waves. Like riding downhill in a boxcar derby on a cobblestone road. With steel wheels. Planing out was impossible, but this was as close as she'd get. The price was loss of control. The boat slewed wildly to port or starboard whenever she dipped into a trough.

How'd Henriques find him? Luck? Probably not. He was a Conch, but even that wasn't enough. Probably some new equipment he had. Price was no object for the ATF when taxes were paying for it.

Damn ATF. For years Terry had breezed in and out of the Keys on his supply runs until they'd got smart and started hiring locals for their shore patrols. Making a run these days had become downright dicey.

He concentrated on the Loran, the infrared scanner, and what little he could see of the water ahead. The blip had stopped gaining. And running on the diagonal as it had to, was actually losing ground. Terry didn't let up. Unless he hit some floating debris or broached in a freak swell, he'd be first to cross the twelve-mile limit.

But he wouldn't be celebrating.

4.

"Oh, Lord!" Martha cried, staring up the sheer twenty feet of steel hull that loomed above her. "How am I going to get up there?"

"Don't worry," Terry said as he tried to hold his bobbing craft steady against the *Osler*. "We have a routine."

Above them a winch supporting a pair of heavy-duty slings swung into view. The straps of the slings flapped and twisted in the gale-force winds as they were lowered over the side. Terry nosed his prow through the first when it hit water, then idled his engine and manually guided the second sling under the stern.

The winch began hauling them up.

Once they were on the deck the crew pulled a heavy canvas canopy over the boat and helped Martha into a wheelchair.

"Well, she made it," Terry said.

Joe Kozlowski stared at him. "I don't know whether to thank you or punch you in the nose."

"Think on it awhile," Terry said. "Wait till you're both sitting at the bar sipping a g-and-t after a round of golf. Then decide."

Joe's face softened. He extended his hand. They shook, then Joe followed Martha inside.

As the *Osler*'s crew off-loaded the medical supplies, Terry ducked out from under the billowing canopy and fought the wind and rain to the deck rail. He squinted out at the lightning-shot chaos. A lot of hell left in this monster. But that didn't mean Henriques had run home. No, that bastard was lying out there somewhere, waiting.

Not to arrest him. Couldn't do that once the contraband was gone. And if Henriques did manage to catch him, Terry could thumb his nose and say he'd been out on a little jaunt to say hello to some old friends among the crew.

But even though Henriques had no case against him, Terry still couldn't let him get near. It wasn't fear of arrest that gnawed at the lining of his gut. It was being identified.

Once they knew his name, his runner career was over. He'd be watched day and night, followed everywhere, his phones would be tapped, his house bugged, and every time *Terryfied* left the slip he'd be stopped and inspected.

His whole way of life would be turned upside down.

One option was to stay on the *Osler* and make a break for the coast further north. But the weather would be better then and officialdom would have copters hovering about, waiting to tag him and follow him home.

No, he had to use the heavy weather. But even that might not be enough. On the way out he'd had the advantage: Henriques didn't know Terry's starting point. Could have been anywhere along the lower twenty miles of the archipelago. But now Henriques had him pinpointed. All he had to do was wait for Terry to make his move. Didn't even have to catch him. All he had to do was follow him home.

Yeah, getting back was going to be a real bitch.

5.

"Maybe he's not coming," Cramer said. "Maybe he's going to wait out the storm and hope that we drownd out here."

The whininess of Cramer's voice had increased steadily during the hour they'd been holding here. It was getting on Henriques's nerves something bad now.

"He *is* coming out, and it'll be *during* the storm, and we're *not* going to drownd."

At least he hoped not. A couple of times during the past hour he hadn't been so sure about that. He'd had Cramer keep the VMA low and slow in forward, into the wind, while he watched the lights of the *Osler* through his binocs. But every so often came a rogue wave or a gust of shear wind that damn near capsized them. Cramer had good reason to want to hightail for home.

But they weren't turning around until the fuel gauge told them they had to.

Besides, according to the Doppler, the rear end of the storm was only a few miles west. The runner would have to make his break soon.

And then you're mine.

"We got heat action, chief. Lots of it."

Henriques snapped the glasses down and leapt to the infrared scanner. Fanning out from the big red blob of the hospital ship were three smaller, fainter blobs.

"What's going on, chief?"

"Decoys."

The son of a bitch had two of the *Osler*'s shuttles running interference for him. One heat source was headed east-north-east, one east-southeast, and one right at them.

Henriques ground his teeth. The bastard had raised his odds from zero to two out of three. God damn him to hell.

"All right, Cramer," he said. "One of them's our man. Which one?"

"I—I dunno."

"Come on. Put yourself out here alone. You've got to chase one. Choose."

Cramer chewed his lip and stared at the scanner. Probably doing eeny-meeny-miney-moe in his head. Henriques had already decided to ignore whichever Cramer chose. Cramer was never right.

"Well, it sure as hell ain't the guy coming right at us, so I'll choose . . . the . . . one . . . to . . . the . . ." His finger stabbed at the screen. *"North!"*

Henriques hesitated. Not a bad choice, actually. The Lower Keys were more heavily populated toward their southern end, especially near Key West; coast guard base and naval air station down that way—all sorts of folks runners don't like to meet. And the storm was heading northeast, so that direction would give the most rain cover. He might just have to go with Cramer this—

Wait a second.

Well, it sure as hell ain't the guy coming right at us . . .

Yeah. The obvious assumption. So obvious that Henriques had bought into it without really thinking. But what if the runner was counting on that? Send the shuttles right and left, draw the heat toward them, then breeze through the empty middle.

And remember: Cramer is never right.

"Let's hang here for a bit," he said as Cramer reached for the throttle.

"Why? He's got to—"

"Just call it a feeling."

Henriques watched the screen, tracking the trio of diverging blobs. As the center one neared, he lifted the glasses again. Nothing. Whoever it was was traveling without his running lights.

Doubt wriggled in his gut. What if the runner had pulled a double reverse? If so, he was already out of reach; as good as home free.

"Getting close," Cramer said. "See him yet?"

"No."

"Still coming right at us. Think he knows we're here?"

"He knows. He's got infrared, too."

"Yeah, well, he ain't acting like it. Maybe we should turn the running—"

And then a dazzling flash of lightning to the south and Henriques had him. A Hutch 686. The runner.

He let out a whoop of triumph. "It's him! We got him!"

"I see him!" Cramer called. "But he's coming right at us. Is he crazy?"

"No, he's not crazy. And he's not going to hit us. Bring us about. We got us a chase!"

Cramer stood frozen at the wheel. "He's gonna ram us!"

"Shit!"

Henriques grabbed the spotlight, thumbed the switch and

swiveled it toward the oncoming boat. He picked up the charging bow, the flying spray, almost on top of them, and goddamn if it didn't look like the bastard was really going to ram them.

Henriques braced himself as Cramer shouted incoherently and ducked behind the console. But at the last minute the runner swerved and flashed past to starboard, sending a wave of wake over the gunwale.

"After him!" Henriques screamed. "After him, goddamit!"

Cramer was pushing on the throttle, yanking on the wheel, bringing them around. But the ankle-deep seawater sloshing back and forth in the cockpit slowed her response. The bilge pumps were overwhelmed at the moment, but they'd catch up. The VMA would be planing out again soon. That cute little maneuver had given the runner a head start, but it wouldn't matter. Henriques had him now. Didn't even have to catch him. Just follow him back to whatever dock he called home.

6.

Terry caught himself looking over his shoulder. A reflex. Nothing to see in that mess of rain and wind. He cursed Henriques for not chasing one of the decoys.

The guy seems to read my mind. Well, why not? We're both Conchs.

Terry had only one trick left up his sleeve. If that didn't work . . .

Then what? Sink the *Terryfied?* What good would that do? The ATF would just haul her up, find out who she belonged to, and then camp outside his door.

Face it. He doesn't fall for this last one, I'm screwed. And being a Conch, it was a damn good chance Henriques wouldn't.

Terry spotted the breakers of the barrier reef ahead. Lightning helped him get his bearings and he headed for the channel. As soon as he cut through, the swells shrank by half and he picked up speed. Now was his one chance to increase the distance between Henriques and himself. If he could get close enough to shore, pull in near the parking lot of one of the waterside restaurants or nightspots, maybe he could merge his infrared tag with the heat from the cars and the kitchen.

And what would that do besides delay the inevitable? Henriques would—

A bolt of lightning slashed down at a mangrove keylet to starboard, starkly illuminating the area with a flash of cold brilliance. Terry saw the water, the rain, the mangrove clumps, and something else . . . something that gut punched him and froze his hands on the wheel.

"Christ!"

Just off the port bow and roaring toward him, a swirling, writhing column of white stretching into the darkness above, throwing up a furious cloud of foam and spray as it snaked back and forth across the surface of the water.

He'd seen plenty of waterspouts before. You couldn't spend a single season in the Keys without getting used to them. Most of them were wimpy gushes of water. But not this one. This damn thing was a tornado. That white frothy look was seawater spinning at two or three hundred miles an hour. Just brushing its hem would wreck the boat and send him flying. Catching the full brunt of the vortex would tear the *Terryfied* and its captain to pieces.

The hungry maw slithered his way across the surface,

sucking up seawater and everything it contained, like Mrs. God's vacuum hose. Somewhere downwind it would rain salt water and fish—and maybe pieces of a certain Conch and his boat if he didn't do something fast.

It lunged toward him, its growing roar thundering like a fully loaded navy cargo jet lifting off from Boca Chica, drowning out his own engine.

Terry shook off the paralysis and yanked the wheel hard to starboard. For a heartbeat he was sure he'd acted too late. He screamed into a night that had become all noise and water. The boat lurched, the port side lifted, spray drenched him, big hard drops peppering him like rounds from an Uzi. He thought he was going over.

And then *Terryfied* righted herself and the raging, swirling ghostly bulk was dodging past the stern, ten, then twenty feet from the transom. He saw it swerve back the other way before it was swallowed by the night and the rain. It seemed to be zigzagging down the channel. Maybe it liked the deeper water. Maybe it was trapped in the rut, in the groove . . . he didn't know.

One thing he did know: If not for that lightning flash he'd be dead.

Would Henriques be so lucky? With the waterspout heading west along the channel and Henriques charging east at full throttle, the ATF could be minus one boat and two men in a minute or so.

Saved by a waterspout. Who'd ever believe it? No witness except Henriques, and he'd be . . . fish food.

Terry turned and stared behind him. Nothing but rain and dark. No sign of Henriques's running lights. Which meant the waterspout was probably between them . . . heading right for Henriques.

"Shit."

He reached for the Very pistol. He knew he was going to regret this.

7.

"Mother of *God!*" Cramer shouted.

Henriques saw it too.

One instant everything was black, the next the sky was blazing red from the emergency flare sailing through the rain. And silhouetted against the burning glow was something dark and massive, directly in their path.

Henriques reached past Cramer and yanked the wheel hard to port, hard enough to stall out. The tower of water roared past like a runaway freight train, leaving them shaken but in one piece. Henriques watched it retreat, pink now in the fading glow of the flare.

He turned and scanned the water to the east while Cramer shook and sputtered.

"You see that? You ever see anything *like* that? Damn near killed us! Hadn't been for that flare, we'd be goners!"

Henriques concentrated on the area around the lighted channel marker dead ahead. Something about that marker . . .

"There he is!" he shouted as he spotted a pale flash of wake. "Get him!"

"You gotta be kidding!" Cramer said. "He just saved our asses!"

"And I'll be sure to thank him when he's caught. Now after him, dammit!"

Cramer grumbled, started the engine, and turned east. He gunned it but Henriques could tell his heart wasn't in it.

And he had to admit, some of the fight had gone out of him as well.

Why had the runner warned them? That baffled him. These guys were scum, running stolen or pilfered medical supplies out to the rich folks on their luxury hospital ships when there was barely enough to go around onshore. Yet the guy had queered his only chance of escape by sending up a warning flare.

I don't get it.

But Henriques couldn't let that stop him. He couldn't turn his head and pretend he didn't see, couldn't allow himself to be bought off with a flare. He'd seen payoffs all his life—cops, judges, mayors, and plenty Conchs among them. But Pepe Henriques wasn't joining that crowd.

The rain was letting up, ceiling lifting, visibility improving. Good. *Where are we?* He spotted the lights on the three radio towers east-northeast, which put them west of Sugarloaf. So where was the runner heading? Bow Channel, maybe? That would put him into Cudjo Bay. Lots of folks lived on Cudjo Bay. And one of them just might be a runner.

He retrieved his field glasses and kept them trained on the fleeing boat as it followed the channel. Didn't have much choice. Neither of them did. Tide was out and even with the storm there wasn't enough water to risk running outside the channel, even with the shallow draw of an impeller craft. As they got closer to civilization the channel would be better marked, electric lights and all . . .

Electric lights.

He snapped the glasses down but it was too late. Cramer was hauling ass past the red-light marker, keeping it to starboard.

"*NO!*" Henriques shouted and lunged for the wheel, but too late.

The hull hit coral and ground to a halt, slamming the two

of them against the console. The intakes sucked sand and debris, choked, and cut out.

Silence, except for Cramer's cursing.

"God damn! God-damn-God-damn-God-damn-God *damn!* Where's the fucking channel?"

"You're out of it," Henriques said softly, wondering at how calm he felt.

"I took the goddam marker to starboard!"

Henriques nodded in the darkness, hiding his chagrin. He shouldn't have been so focused on the runner's boat. Should have been taking in the whole scene. Cramer hadn't grown up on these waters. Like every seaman, he knew the three R's: *Red Right Return.* Keep the red markers on your right when returning to port. But Cramer couldn't know that this marker was supposed to be green. Only a Conch would know. Somebody had changed the lens. And Henriques knew who.

He felt like an idiot but couldn't help smiling in the dark. He'd been had but good. There'd be another time, but this round went to the runner.

He reached for the Very pistol.

8.

"What the hell?"

The flare took Terry by surprise. What was Henriques up to? The bastard had been chasing him full throttle since dodging that waterspout, and now he was sending up a flare. It wouldn't throw enough light to make any difference in the chase, and if he needed help, he had a radio.

Then Terry realized it had come from somewhere in the vicinity of the channel marker he'd tampered with. He pumped a fist into the air. Henriques was stuck and he was letting his prey know it. Why? Payback for Terry's earlier flare? Maybe. That was all the break he'd ever get from Henriques, he guessed.

He'd take it.

Terry eased up on the throttle and sagged back in the chair. His knees felt a little weak. He was safe. But that had been close. Too damn close.

He cruised toward Cudjo, wondering if this was a sign that he should find another line of work. With Henriques out there, and maybe a few more like him joining the hunt, it was only a matter of time before they identified him. Might even catch him on the way out with a hold full of contraband. Then it'd be the slammer . . . hard time in a Fed lockup. Quitting now would be the smart thing.

Right. Someday, but not yet. A couple more runs, then he'd think about it some more.

And maybe someday after he was out of this, he and Henriques would run into each other in a bar and Terry would buy that Conch a Red Stripe and they'd laugh about these chases.

Terry thought about that a minute.

Nah.

That only happened in movies.

He gunned his boat toward home.

Ed Gorman has published more than a dozen novels and three collections of short stories. The *San Diego Union* recently called him "one of the most distinctive voices in contemporary crime fiction" and likened his work to that of William Goldman, Elmore Leonard, and John D. MacDonald. His current novels are *The Marilyn Tapes* (Forge), which I highly recommend, and *The First Lady* (Forge).

I thought I'd have the futuremost piece in this collection, but Ed beat me by decades with this wrenching novelette that moves you as only Ed can. . . .

SURVIVAL

Ed Gorman

(For Judy Duhl)

I

A lot of people in the hospital were still mad at me about last night . . .

. . . but then they'd been mad at me before and they'd be mad at me again. . . .

. . . the problem was, what got them mad, was that he was more crazed than dangerous, the dreamduster who'd broken into the supply area on the first floor. He was also nine years old. They'd wanted me to kill him but I'd declined the honor and handed my .38 auto Colt to Young Doctor Pelham and said, You want him killed, you kill him yourself. Pelham just muttered some bullshit about the Hippocratic oath and gave me my weapon back.

What I ended up doing with the little bastard was putting a chute on him and then taking him up on a skymobile and pushing him out somewhere over Zone 1. He'd be lucky to survive forty-eight hours. There was some new kind of influenza taking hold there. It had already buried something like two thousand people in less than a week. Maybe I would've done him a favor killing him quick the way Pelham wanted me to. Being a dreamduster, his life was over anyway. . . .

After dumping the kid, I went back to the hospital and walked the ten flights up to my room. There's an elevator but since all our power comes from the emergency generators Pelham figured out how to soup up, we use the elevators only when it's absolutely necessary.

My little place is on the same floor as the mutants our two resident bioengineers are studying with the belief that one of the pathetic wretches will someday yield a vaccine useful to what remains of the human race. Tuesday, March 6, 2009— six long years ago now—the Fascist-Christian party got their hands on several nuclear warheads (helped considerably by several Pentagon generals who were also part of the plot) and had proceeded to purify our entire planet of its sins and sinners. What the Christers in all their wisdom didn't understand was that twenty of the warheads also carried some pretty wild germ warfare devices, devices that had killed many of the workers who'd helped create them.

Tenth floor of the hospital used to be the psych ward. Each patient had his own room with a heavy door and a glass observation square built in.

I used to hurry past the doors on the way to my room but now I stopped most times and peered in through the squares.

They're pretty repulsive-looking, no doubt about that, none older than five years old, none resembling a real human being in more than a passing way, not unless you consider three arms and no vertebrae—or a completely spherical body with a head the size and shape of a pincushion—or a squidlike creature with heartbreaking little hand-flippers— . . . Definitely not the kind of folk you'd like to see at your next family reunion.

They were used to seeing me now, and as I waggled my fingers and smiled at them, they made these sad frantic little noises, the way puppies do when they want to be picked up. So, exhausted as I was, I spent a few minutes with each of them. By now I was not only used to looking at them, I was also used to smelling them. Poor little bastards, they can't help it.

I went to my room and got some sleep.

What I am, you see, is what they call an Outrider. Back in the Old West, this was a person who rode on ahead of the wagon train to make sure everything was safe.

A year ago, after my wife and two daughters died from one of the variant strains of flu that had claimed half the people in Fort Waukegan, I tried to kill myself with my trusty .38 auto Colt. Oh, the bullet went in all right, but it managed to traverse the exterior of my skull without doing serious or permanent damage.

A scout from Fort Glencoe found me out on the periphery of Zone 2 and brought me back to the hospital. Once they had me on my feet again, they asked me what I'd done before the Christers got their bright idea of "purifying" the planet. When I told them I'd been a homicide detective, they asked me how I'd like to stay in Fort Glencoe permanently, as an Outrider—scouting Zones 1 through 5 surrounding Fort Glencoe and making sure no bands of warriors were headed here—and doubling as a hospital security guard. Dreamdusters, the junkies who got off on synthetic powder that was cheap to make and more powerfully addictive than any heroin ever concocted—were always breaking into hospital supply rooms in search of toxins and vaccines that would give them the ultimate kick till they got some real dreamdust.

They kept telling me how lucky I was to be alive.

I wasn't sure about that.

But I stayed on as their Outrider and security man and it was in that role that I first heard of Paineaters, even though I didn't quite believe in them, at least not as described by my boss and nemesis, Young Doc Pelham.

Troubled sleep. But then it usually is. I dream of Joan and the girls and I wake up with a terrible sadness upon me. Usually I throw my legs off the side of the bed and sit there with my head in my hands, remembering faces and voices and touches and laughter.

Then there's the nightmare. It started a few months back when I—well, when I got in some trouble with the staff here . . .

Today, though, there wasn't any time for reveries.

Not with somebody pounding, pounding, pounding on my door.

"Yeah?" I said, rolling, still mostly asleep, from bed.

She didn't say anything else. Just came through the door.

Nurse Polly. Coppery hair; big brown melancholy eyes; sweet little wrists and ankles; and a kind of childlike faith that everything will always work out.

"Pelham."

"Oh, great," I said.

"Emergency, he says."

"Isn't it always?"

She gave me a look I couldn't quite read. "You slept through it."

"Slept through what?"

I stood up, giving her a good look at my hairy legs in boxer shorts. (Nurse Polly and I had made love several times in a conveniently located storage closet on the third floor. We always did it standing up. She was very good, sexy and tender at the same time. She seemed to sense that I always felt guilty about it. "You're thinking about your wife, aren't you?" "Yeah; guess I am." "That's all right." "It is?" "Sure. I'm thinking about my husband. He died pretty much the same way." And then we'd just hold each other, two lonely animals needing comfort and solace.)

"We had two people die in surgery last night. He couldn't operate because—Well, you know."

"God."

"We've got three operations scheduled today and no Paineater."

"I won't go alone. I want somebody to go with me."

"I'll go."

"Really?"

"Uh-huh."

"I don't know."

"Why?"

"Polly, you've got a great big heart. And you can get so involved with them—" I shook my head. "You know what happened to me, what I did."

I didn't know if she felt like being held by a hairy guy in white boxer shorts with red hearts on them, but I figured I'd give it a try.

I held her and she seemed glad I did, snuggling into me and putting her arms around my waist.

Then she took my hand. "C'mon. Let's go see Pelham."

But I held back. "You know what I did—He shouldn't send me out to get a new one." I was getting spooked. I didn't want to go through it all again.

She looked at me and shook her head. "You want me to take you down and show you the patients waiting for surgery? One of them had his eyes cut out by a dreamduster."

"Shit," I said.

2

Young Doctor Pelham might not be so bad under normal circumstances—i.e., where a doctor had the staff and facilities to do his best work—but here he's always stressed-out and usually angry. I might be that way myself if I was losing sixty percent of my patients on the table.

A day or two after the Christers dropped the bombs, the looting and raping and murdering began. I hate to be cynical about it, but the human beast was a much darker one than I'd ever imagined. Made me regret all the times I'd been civilized about it and spoken up against the death penalty.

A couple of things became clear to all citizens good and true, man and woman, white and black, Christian and Jew, straight and gay—that there were a whole lot of really terrible people out there meaning them great malice. The good folk would have to band together. The concept of a fortress came along soon after.

Most Forts comprise five or six miles inside a wall of junk cars. The walls are patrolled twenty-four hours by mean humans and even meaner dogs. Zoners, those living in the outer areas, sometimes sneak through but most of them end up as little more than blood and flesh gleaming on the teeth of the Dobermans.

Most Forts are also built around hospitals. The good citizens had to quickly decide which was the most important of all buildings. Police station? Courthouse? Hospital? Indeed.

With the bioengineered warheads continuing to do their work, life was a constant struggle not only against violence—once every three months or so, a small army of Zoners would take a run at the various Forts and inflict great casualties—but also disease.

Inside the walls of scrap metal, the citizens lived in any sort of shelter they could find. Houses, garages, schools, roller rinks—it didn't matter. You lived where you could find room for you and your family.

Then there was the hospital. I know how you probably imagine it: ten floors of the various units that all modern hospitals have—maternity, pediatric, surgical, psychiatric, intermediate care, intensive care—all staffed by crisply garbed interns and residents and registered nurses and practical nurses and nurses aides, many of whom spend their time walking between the pharmacy, the central service department, the food service, and the laboratories.

But forget it.

This hospital is ten floors of smashed windows and bullet-riddled walls and bloodstained floors. Before the Fortress wall could be erected, some roving Zoners staged a six-day battle that cost a thousand people their lives, and nearly resulted in the Zoners taking over the hospital.

Patients are brought in on the average of fourteen a day. On average, eight of those are buried within twenty-four hours.

"There isn't any time for your usual bullshit," Young Doctor Pelham told me when I stood before his desk. "In case you want to give me any, I mean."

The glamorous Dr. Sullivan, dark of hair and eye, red of mouth, supple and ample of figure, sat in a chair across the room, listening. Everybody knew two things about the good

doctors Pelham and Sullivan. That they'd once been lovers.
And that they now hate each other and that Sullivan wanted
Pelham's job. She was always telling jokes about him behind
his back.

"They're kids," I said, wishing Polly had stayed. Her
presence would have made Pelham less harsh. She had that
effect on people.

"I know they're kids."

"Little kids."

"Little kids. Right. But I don't have a lot of choice in the
matter. I have to do right by my patients."

Much as I dislike him, Pelham's arguments about the
Paineaters are probably sound. Ethically, he had to weigh the
welfare of his patients against the welfare of the Paineaters.
He had to choose his patients.

He sat behind his desk, a trim man in a white medical
smock that had lost its dignity to spatters of human blood and
other fluids. He looked up at me with tired brown eyes and a
face that would have been handsome if it didn't look quite so
petulant most of the time. "I've got what he wants."

He reached down behind his desk and lifted up a leather
briefcase. He set it on the desk.

"It's a shame we have to deal with people like that," Dr.
Sullivan said.

"Do you have a better idea, Susan?" Pelham snapped.

"No, I guess I don't."

"Then I'll thank you to stay out of this."

She really was twice as beautiful when she was angry. She
got up and left the room.

"I want one understanding," I said.

"Here we go," he said, "you and your fucking under-
standings."

"I won't bodyguard her. Don't forget what happened last time."

The brown eyes turned hostile. "You think I could forget what you did, Congreve? You think any of us could *ever* forget what you did?"

"I was thinking of her."

"Sure you were, Congreve, because you're such a noble son of a bitch." He shook his head. "You did it because you couldn't take it anymore. Because you weren't tough enough."

He pushed the briefcase across to me.

"We need one right away. I've got seven patients ready for surgery. They're going to die if I don't get to them in just a few hours."

I picked up the briefcase. "Just so we understand each other, Doc. I won't bodyguard her."

He smiled that smirky aggravating smile of his. "It's not something you have to worry about, Congreve. You think after what you did, we'd even *want* you to guard her?"

I guess he probably had it right. Who the hell would want me to guard her?

I went outside and got in my skymobile.

3

Polly was in the passenger seat. She'd changed into a green blouse and jeans and a brown suede jacket.

"I don't remember inviting you."

"C'mon, Congreve. I won't be any trouble."

"I get downed somewhere and surrounded by a gang of Zoners and you won't be any trouble? Then I have to worry about you as well as myself."

She brought an impressive silver Ruger from somewhere inside her jacket. "I think I can take care of myself."

If you've ever seen photographs or film of Berlin right after World War II, you have some sense of what Chicago looks like these days, skyscrapers toppled, entire neighborhoods reduced to ragged brick and jagged glass and dusty heaps of stone. With no sanitation, no electricity, no official order of any kind, you can pretty well imagine what's happened: the predators have taken over. Warlords divided up various parts of each Zone. You do what they say or they kill you. Very simple.

We were headed for the eastern sector of Zone 2, which had once been the inner city.

"I disappointed you today, didn't I?" Polly said.

"A little, I suppose."

"I know how you feel about Paineaters."

"I can't help it. I just keep seeing my own daughters."

"We don't have any choice, Congreve. You have to understand that."

"I'll take your word for it."

"You can really be an asshole sometimes."

"But Pelham can't?"

"We weren't talking about Pelham."

"I was. Pelham and all the other Pelhams who run these Fortresses and use Paineaters."

"You should see the patients who—"

"I've seen the patients," I said. "That's the only reason I'm doing this. Because I don't have the stomach or balls or whatever it takes to see all those people lying there and suffering. Otherwise, I wouldn't help at all."

She leaned over and touched my hand. "I shouldn't have called you an asshole."

I smiled at her. "Oh, what should you have called me?"

She smiled right back. "A prick is what I should have called it."

"I guess that's a promotion of sorts, anyway."

"Of sorts," she said.

Sometimes when you're up there, you can forget everything that's happened in the last six years. Dawn and sunset are especially beautiful and you can feel some of the old comfort and security you knew; and that awe you found in the beauty of natural things. That's why I took the skymobile every chance I got . . . because if I didn't look down, I could pretend that the world was the same as it had always been. . . .

The last twenty miles, we went in low. That's when you get a sense of the daily carnage, going low like that.

Bodies and body parts strewn all over the bomb-blasted interstate. And not just warriors, either—children, women, family pets. Families try to leave a Zone area when there's a war going on. Too often they make the mistake of following the interstate where bandits wait. These are not the gentlemen bandits of Robin Hood fame. A doc told me once he'd seen a ten-year-old girl that ten adult bandits had gang-raped. I kill all of them I get a chance to.

Originally, Jackson Heights had been a nice little shopping area for upscale folks. But those upscale folks who didn't get killed by the Christers' bombs got their throats slashed by the Zoners who took the place over and renamed it after one of their old-time leaders.

There was a block of two-story brick buildings. On the roofs you could see warriors with powerful binoculars and even more powerful auto-shotguns. I imagined, if I looked hard enough, I'd also find some grenade launchers.

Six black men raised their shotguns.

"God," Polly said. "Are they just going to shoot us down?"

"Hopefully, one of them will recognize the mobile here and realize it's me."

"Yeah," she said anxiously, "hopefully."

I circled the roofs one more time and in the middle of the circle the shotguns lowered and two of the men started waving at us. Somebody had radioed headquarters and described our skymobile, and headquarters had okayed us.

"Feel better?" I said.

"Sorry I was such a candy ass. I was just scared there for a minute."

"So was I."

Hoolihan is a black man.

I know, I know—his name is Irish; as is his pug nose, his freckled and light-skinned face; his reddish curly hair; and his startling blue eyes. But he's Negro, which you can tell, somehow, when you see him.

Hoolihan, by my estimation, has personally killed more than two thousand people.

I reach this conclusion by simple mathematics:

$$365 \times 6 = 2190$$

He's been the warlord of East Zone 1 for the past six years. I figure, probably conservatively, that he's killed one person each day. As I say, simple math.

This day Hoolihan sent his own personal vehicle for us, an ancient army jeep painted camel-shit green with a big red H stenciled on the back panel. He uses the H the way cattle barons used to use their brands.

Hoolihan lives in a rambling two-story redbrick house. Easy enough to imagine a couple of Saabs in the drive, a game of badminton going on in the backyard, steaks smelling wonderful on the outdoor grill. Suburban bliss. The effect is spoiled somewhat, however, by the Cyclone fencing, the barely controllable Dobermans, and the armed guards in faded army khaki.

In case none of that deters you, there's one other surprise: a front door that detonates a tiny bomb just big enough to render the visitor into several chunks if he doesn't know the password.

The guard knew the password. "Your Mama," he said.

Hoolihan had a nasty sense of humor.

The door was buzzed open and we walked in.

What Hoolihan's done with the interior of his house is pretty amazing. He's turned it into a time travel exhibit: the world as it was before the Christers got ahold of it. Sore sad eyes can gaze at length upon parqueted floors and comfortable couches sewn in rich rose damask and Victorian antiques and prints by Chagall and Vermeer; and sore sad ears, long accustomed to the cries of the dying, can be solaced with the strains of Debussy and Vivaldi and Bach.

Hoolihan, whatever else he is, is no fool.

He made us wait five minutes.

He enjoys being fashionably late.

He also enjoys looking like a stage fop in a Restoration comedy. Today he swept in wearing a paisley dressing gown, and his usual icy smirk. Oh, yes, and the black eye patch. Dramatic as hell until you realize that it keeps shifting eyes. Some days it's on his right eye and some days—

"Nice," he said, referring to Polly. "I don't suppose she's for sale."

"I don't suppose she is," Polly said.

"Too bad. I know people who'd pay a lot of money for you."

That was another thing about Hoolihan. He had a sophomore's need to shock.

"Martini?" he said.

"Beer would be fine," I said.

"The lady?"

"Beer," she said.

He nodded to a white-haired man in some sort of African ceremonial robe. The man went into the next room.

"We found a supermarket that had been contaminated so long people gave up on it," Hoolihan said. "I sent some men in last week. And now we have enough beer to last us for a long, long time."

"The land of opportunity," I said.

He said, "The palm of my hand is starting to itch."

I had to smile. He was a melodramatic son of a bitch, but he had the brains to kid himself, too.

"I wonder what that means," I said.

"It means my right hand wants to just walk over there and grab that briefcase."

"We need to cut a deal first."

"I take it you don't want drugs, little girls or boys for sex, or the latest in weaponry my men took from that National Guard Armory in Cleveland last month."

"None of the above. Why don't we just cut the bullshit and you tell me if you've got one for sale."

The elderly man with the intelligent dark eyes returned with our beers. I've never been much for servants. I felt funny accepting it from him, as if I should apologize.

"Please," Hoolihan said, "let's sit down and make this all very civilized. We're not making some back-alley deal here."

We sat. But I'm not sure how civilized it was. Not considering what the product happened to be.

"I've got five on hand at the moment," he said from his throne-sized leather chair across the room from where Polly and I sat on the edge of an elegant couch.

"We need one right away."

"I've got them out in a shed."

Polly muttered something nasty under her breath.

Hoolihan smirked. He'd aggravated her and he loved it. "Don't worry, pretty one. It's a perfectly civilized shed. Clean, dry, and protected not only from the elements but from Zoners. They're much better off in my shed than they would be wandering free."

With that I couldn't argue.

"Now how much is in that briefcase?"

"One hundred thousand dollars. It's all yours as long as you don't dicker."

"One hundred thousand dollars," he said. "My, my, my, my. I wish my poor old broken-down nigger daddy could see me now."

That's the funny thing about the warlords. Even though they know that the currency is absolutely worthless, they still revel in getting it.

Hoolihan's father had served three terms in prison for minor crimes and had never known a day's happiness or pride in his entire life. Hoolihan had told me all this one night when he'd been coasting on whiskey and drugs. And he'd broken down and cried halfway through. He was bitter and angry about his father, whom he felt had never had a serious chance at leading a decent life.

He was probably right.

His old man would have been damned proud of his one and only son.

One hundred thousand was now his. Didn't matter that it was worthless. It still had an echo, a resonance, money did, at least to those of us who could remember how everything used to be before the Christers went and screwed it all up.

A tear rolled down Hoolihan's cheek. "I miss that old fucker, you know?"

Not even Polly, who obviously didn't care much for Hoolihan, could deny him this moment. Her own eyes teared up now.

"Let's go get her," I said, "before it gets dark."

Kerosene torches lit the blooming gloom of dusk; a chill started creeping up my arms and legs and back; a dog barked, lonely. You could smell and taste the autumn night, and then smell the decay of bodies that hadn't been buried properly. Even though you couldn't see them, their stench told you how many of them there were. And how close.

The shed was a quarter mile through a sparsely wooded area that a dog—maybe the same one barking—had mined with plump squishy turds.

Two guards in khaki stood guard in front of the small garage that Hoolihan called the shed. Hoolihan, by the way, had traded his foppish robe for an even more foppish military uniform. He had epaulets big enough to land helicopters on.

The guards saluted when they saw Hoolihan. He saluted them, crisply, right back.

"C'mon in and you can pick one," he said merrily enough, as if he were inviting us on to a used car lot.

We went inside. He'd been telling the truth about the tidiness of the place. Newly whitewashed walls. Handsomely carpeted floor. Six neat single beds with ample sheets and blankets. At the back was a table where food was taken. The place even smelled pretty good.

The four of them sat on their beds watching us, their out-size bald heads tottering as they gaped. For some reason I don't understand—this sort of thing I leave to Young Doctor Pelham—their necks won't support their heads properly. They were all female and they all wore little aqua-colored jumpsuits that resembled pajamas. They're mute, or most of them are anyway, but they make noises in their throat that manage to be both touching and disgusting. They were little and frail, too, pale and delicate, with tiny hands that were always reaching out for another human hand to hold.

"Where the hell's the dark-haired one?" Hoolihan said.

The guard got this awful expression on his face as his eyes quickly counted the little girls.

Four.

There were supposed to be five.

"Where the hell did she go?" Hoolihan said.

The children couldn't answer him; they couldn't talk.

And the guards were no help. They'd somehow managed to let one get away.

Hoolihan walked over to a window at the back of the garage. A small wooden box had been placed directly under it.

Hoolihan put pressure on the base of the window. It pushed outward. It was unlocked.

The kid had gone out the window.

As he was turning around to face us all again, Hoolihan took a wicked-looking handgun from his belt and shot the guards in the face.

Nothing fancy. No big deal.

One moment they were human beings, the next they were corpses.

Anxiety started working through me—surprise, shock, anger, fear that he might do the same to me—and then, as I looked at the children, I felt the turmoil begin to wane.

They stared at us.

They said nothing.

They started doing their jobs.

A few moments later, the worst of the feelings all gone, we followed Hoolihan out into the dark, chilly night.

"We're going to find that little bitch," Hoolihan said.

4

Well, we found her all right, but it took two hours, a lot of crawling around on hands and knees in dark and tangled undergrowth, and a lot of cursing on Hoolihan's part.

The little kid was a quarter mile away hiding in a culvert.

When we found her, got the jostling beam of the flashlight playing across her soiled aqua jumpsuit, she was doing a most-peculiar thing: petting a rat.

This was a big rat, too, seven, eight pounds, with a pinched evil face and a pair of gleaming red eyes. He probably carried a thousand kinds of diseases and an appetite for carrion that would give a flock of crows pause. After the Fascist-Christians had their way with the world, rats became major enemies again.

But there he sat on the little girl's lap just the way a kitten would. And the little girl's tiny white hand was stroking his back.

There was some semblance of intelligence in the girl's eyes. That was the first thing that struck me. Usually the saucer-shaped eyes are big and blank. But she seemed to have a pretty good idea of who and what we were.

Then Hoolihan shot the rat and the little girl went berserk.

The rat exploded into three chunks of meat and bone and

gristle, each covered with blood-soaked flesh.

The keening sound came up in the little girl's throat and she quickly got on all fours and started crawling down the culvert as fast as she could.

Hoolihan thought it was all great, grand farce.

I wanted to kill him—or at least damage him in some serious way—but I knew better. He had too many men eager to kill anybody white. With Hoolihan gone, Polly and I would never get out of here.

Polly went after the kid.

I was still trying to forget the kid's terrible expression. They establish some kind of telepathic link with their subject, that's what the kids do, and so the relation becomes intimate beyond our understanding. Rat and little girl had become one. So then Hoolihan goes and kills it.

"You look pissed, man," Hoolihan said.

"You're scum, Hoolihan."

"Just having a little fun."

"Right."

"I like it when you get all judgmental and pontifical on me, Congreve. Kinda sexy, actually."

"You knew what the little girl was doing."

"Sure. Linking up." The smirk. "But maybe I have so much respect for her I didn't want her to link up with some fucking rat, you ever think of that?"

I grabbed his flashlight.

He started at me, as if he was going to put a good hard right hand on my face, but my scowl seemed to dissuade him.

I didn't find Polly and the girl for another fifteen minutes and I probably wouldn't have found them then if it hadn't been for the dog.

He was some kind of alley mutt, half-boxer and half-collie

if you can imagine that, and he stood on the old railroad sid-
ing barking his ass off at the lone boxcar that stood on the
tracks that shone silver in the moonlight.

I could hear her now, the kid, the mewling deep in her
throat. She was still terrified of the rat exploding.

I climbed up inside. In the darkness the old boxcar
smelled of wood and grease and piss. A lot of people had slept
in this, no doubt.

Polly was in the corner, the kid in her lap.

Polly was sort of rocking the kid back and forth and humming to her.

I went over and sat down next to her and put my hand to
the kid's cheek. It was soft and warm and sweet. And I
thought of my own daughters when they were about this age,
how I'd see their mother rocking them at night and humming
the old lullabies they loved so much.

I thought of this and started crying. I couldn't help it. I
just sat there and felt gutted and dead.

And then Polly said, "Why don't you take her for a little
while? She's calming down. But my legs are going to sleep. I
need to walk around."

I took her. And rocked her. And sang some of the old lullabies and it was kind of funny because when my voice got just
so loud, the mutt outside would join in and kind of bark
along.

Polly jumped down from the boxcar. I imagined she
needed to pee, in addition to stretching her legs.

When she came back, she stood in the open door, the
night sky starry behind her, and the smell of clean fresh rushing night in the air, and said, "God, that'd make a sweet picture, Congreve, you and that little kid in your arms that way."

And then I got mad.

I put the kid down—I didn't hurt her but I wasn't especially gentle, either—and then I stalked to the open door and said: "No fucking way am I going to go through this again, Polly. I don't want anything to do with this kid, you understand? Not a thing."

She knew better than to argue.

She went back and picked up the kid.

She came back to the open door.

I'd jumped down and stood there waiting to lead the way back to Hoolihan.

Polly was pissed. "You think you could hold the kid long enough for me to jump down?"

"Don't start on me, Polly. You know what I went through."

"I love it when you whine."

"Just hand the kid down and get off my back."

She handed the kid down.

I took her, held her, numbed myself to her as much as possible. It wasn't going to happen again.

Polly jumped down. "That Hoolihan is some piece of work."

"Dreamdust."

"That's an excuse and you know it. He would've done that if he was straight. It's his nature."

"Nothing like a bigot."

"I'm not a bigot, Congreve. There're lots of white people just like him. I'm starting to think it's genetic."

"Here's the kid."

She didn't take her right away but put her hand on my arm. "I know how hard it is for you, Congreve, after what happened and all, with the little one here I mean."

"I appreciate your understanding, Polly. I really don't want to go through it again."

"I'll take care of her."

"I appreciate it."

"We're saving lives, Congreve. That's how you have to look at it."

"I hope I can remember that."

Now she took the kid. Cuddled her. Looked down at her. Started talking baby talk.

It was sweet and I wanted to hold them both in the brisk night winds, and then sleep warm next to them in a good clean bed.

When I got Polly and the kid in the skymobile, Hoolihan said, "I heard about what you did."

"Yeah, well, it happens."

"You're a crazy fucker."

"Look who's talking."

"Yeah, but I got an excuse. I'm a warlord. I got to act crazy or people won't be afraid of me."

"I guess that's a good point."

He nodded to the kid inside the bubble dome. "You think you'll do it again?"

"This time I won't have anything to do with her."

"I'd still like to buy that chick."

"No, you wouldn't. She's too tough for you. You want somebody you can beat into submission. You couldn't beat her into submission in twenty years."

He laughed. "She sounds like a lot of fun, man. I love a challenge."

I got in the skymobile.

He leaned in and looked at Polly, who was completely captivated by the small child in her arms.

"I'll see you both soon," he said, wanting to get one more shock in. "You know them little ones never last very long."

Young Doctor Pelham and his number two, Dr. Sullivan, put her right to work.

Polly gave her the name Sarah and fixed her up a nice cozy little room and then proceeded to wait on her with an almost ferocious need.

She also dressed her differently, in jeans and sweatshirts and a pair of sneakers that Polly had dug up somewhere in the basement.

Pelham started Sarah on the most needful ones first, which only made sense. He knew not ever to yell at her or push her—as I'd seen him do with a couple of them—but he was never tender with her, either. To Pelham, she was just another employee.

Polly, Sarah, and I started taking meals together in the staff mess on the lower level.

Polly fussed with everything. Made sure Sarah's food was heated just-so. Made sure her drinking glasses were spotlessly clean. Made sure that with each meal—which was usually some variation on chili—there was at least a small piece of dessert for Sarah.

In that respect, Sarah was a pretty typical kid. She lusted after sweets.

But that was the only way Sarah was typical. Autism is the closest thing I can liken her condition to. She was with us in body but not in spirit. She would sit staring off at distances we couldn't see. And then she would start making a kind of sad music in her throat, apparently responding to things far beyond our ken.

She hadn't been used much before we'd gotten her because she didn't exhibit any of the usual symptoms of deterioration. They start with the twitches and then graduate to the shakes and finally they end up clasping their heads between their hands, as if trying to fight a crushing headache.

After that, they're not much good to anybody.

And after that . . .

I didn't see much of Polly for the next few weeks. Not that I didn't go up to her room. Two or three times a day, I went up to her room. But she was always busy with the kid. Bathing the kid. Fixing the kid's hair in some new pretty way. Singing to the kid. Reading to the kid . . .

A few times I tried it real late at night, hoping that she'd want to lean against the wall with me the way she sometimes did.

But she always said the same thing. "I wouldn't feel right about it, Congreve. You know, with Sarah in the room and all."

I just kept thinking of what had happened to me with the kid before this one . . .

How fast you can get attached . . .

I felt responsible for Polly: I never should have taken her along to Hoolihan's . . .

"Pelham says we can have a holiday party."

"Good old Pelham," I said. "What a great guy."

"You don't give him his due, Congreve. Maybe you'd be more like him if you were responsible for this whole hospital."

"Maybe I would."

She stood in my doorway, natty as always in her nurse's whites.

"You know why I brought up the holiday?" she said.

"Uh-uh."

"Because we need a Santa."

"Aw, shit."

"Somebody found an old costume up on the sixth floor."

"Aw, shit."

"You said that."

"I don't want to play Santa."

"That nice little beer belly of yours, you'd be perfect."

"You haven't seen me naked lately; my little beer belly is even littler now."

I said it in a kidding fashion but I think she knew that there was some loneliness, and maybe even a bit of anger in it, too.

In the three months since Sarah had been here, I'd seen increasing little of Polly.

No more standing-up lovemaking.

Not even the occasional hugs we used to give each other. Sarah was her priority now.

"I'm sorry we haven't gotten together lately, Congreve."

"It's all right."

"No it isn't and you know it. It's just that between my two shifts and taking care of Sarah—"

"I understand."

"I know you think I'm foolish. About her, I mean."

I shrugged. "You do what you think's best."

"You think I'll get too attached to her, don't you?"

I looked at her. "You know how much you can handle."

"She's not going to be like the others."

"She's not?"

"No." She shook her coppery hair. I wanted to put my hands in it. "I think I've figured out a way to let her rest up between the visits she makes. I think that's what happened to the others."

"That doesn't sound real scientific."

"Simple observation. I saw how she was when Pelham

was scheduling her. She started to twitch and shake and do all the things the others did. But two weeks ago I convinced Pelham to let me make up her schedule—and you wouldn't believe the difference."

I saw how excited and happy she looked. She was one damn dear woman, I'll tell you.

"I'm happy for you, Polly. I hope this works out for you."

"She isn't going to end up like the others. That I can promise you."

I stood up and went over to her. I wanted to make it friendly and not sexual at all but I guess I couldn't help it. I slid my arm around her shoulder and held her to me and felt her warm tears on my face. "You'll do just fine with her, Polly. You really will."

We stood like that for a time, kind of swaying back and forth with some animal rhythm coupling us fast, and then she said, sort of laughing, "You know, we never have tried it lying down the way most people do, have we?"

"You know," I said. "I think you're right."

And so we tried it and I have to admit I liked it fine, just fine.

6

A few days after all this, I saw a miracle take place: I was walking down a dusty hall, half the wall hoved in from a Fascist-Christian bomb, when I saw Young Doctor Pelham break a smile.

Now understand, this was not a toothpaste commercial smile. Nor was it a smile that was going to blind anybody.

But it was a) a real smile and b) it was being smiled by Young Doctor Pelham.

He was talking to Nurse Ellen on whom I'd suspected he'd long had some designs, and when he saw me the smile vanished, as if I'd caught him at something dirty.

By the time I reached the nurse, Pelham was gone.

"I think I just had a hallucination."

"Pelham smiling?"

"Yeah."

"You should have been here a minute earlier. He slid his arm around my waist and invited me up to his room tonight. It's the kid."

"The kid?"

She nodded her short-cropped blond head. "The Pain-eater."

"Oh."

"She's the best one we've ever had."

"Really?"

"Absolutely. She did three patients last night in less than two hours. Then she went into surgery with them this morning." She angled her tiny wrist for a glimpse of her watch. "In fact, that's where I'm headed now. Somebody got caught by some Dobermans. He's a mess. I'm not sure we can save him. They've been prepping him for the last ten minutes."

"The kid going to be in there?"

"Sure. She's already in there. Trying to help him down."

"Guess I'll go take a look at her."

I started to turn away but she grabbed my arm. "I want to say something to you, Congreve, and I'm going to say it in terms you'll understand."

"All right."

"You're full of shit about Doctor Pelham."

"You're right. Those are terms I can understand."

"He works his ass off here. He's the only surgeon in the whole Fortress. He suffers from depression because he loses so many and when he can't sleep he spends time with all the wounded and injured. That's why he needs the Paineaters, Congreve. Because he doesn't have anybody else to help him and because he's so damned worried about his patients." She was quickly getting angry. "So I want you to knock off the bullshit with him, all right? The only reason he was mad about what you did was because of the bind you left him in with the patients. Or can't you understand that?"

The funny thing was, I did understand it and for the first time, what Young Doctor Pelham was all about. I guess I considered him cold and arrogant but what I missed seeing was that he was just a very vulnerable and overworked guy doing an almost-impossible job. And it took Nurse Ellen to make me see it.

"He isn't so bad, is he?" I said.

"No, he isn't."

"And he isn't just using those Paineaters because he likes to see them suffer, is he?"

"No, he's not."

"Maybe he feels sorrier for them than I do."

"You're a stupid fucker, Congreve. You know the first three of them we ever had in here?"

"Yeah."

"When they—Well, after they died, he took each one of them out and buried her."

There wasn't much I could say.

"So knock off the 'Young Doctor Pelham' bullshit, all right?"

"All right."

"And one more thing."

"What's that?"

Now she gave me a great big smile of her own. "He's not so bad in the sack, either."

On my way back down the hall, I saw Dr. Sullivan and one of the nurses laughing in a secretive sort of way. They were probably telling jokes about Sullivan's boss, Pelham. It almost made me feel sorry for him.

I borrowed a book from Pelham's library once on the history of surgery. Pretty interesting, especially when you consider that the first operations were done as far back as the Stone Age. Using a piece of stone, the first surgeons cut holes in the skulls of their patients so that they could release evil spirits thought to cause headaches and other ailments.

But over the centuries, doctors had gotten used to slightly more sophisticated methods and equipment, X-rays and CAT scans and scalpels and clamps and retractors and sutures and hemostats and sponges and inverts among them.

And anesthesia.

Before 1842, when anesthesia came into use, all doctors could give patients was whiskey or compounds heavy with opium. And then the operations couldn't last too long, the sedative effects of the booze and opium wearing off pretty fast.

These days, Pelham and all the other doctors in all the other Fortresses faced some of the old problems. Anesthesia was hard to come by.

A few years back, a sociologist named Allan Berkowitz was out making note of all the mutated species he found in the various zones, when he was shot in the arm by a Zoner who robbed him and ran away.

Berkowitz figured he was pretty much dead. The blood loss would kill him if he didn't get to a doc. And the pain was quickly becoming intolerable. The blood loss had also disoriented him slightly. He spent a full half day wandering around in a very small circle.

He collapsed next to a polluted creek, figuring he might as well partake of some polluted waters, when he noticed a strange-looking little girl standing above him. His first thought, given the size and shape of her head, was that she was just another helpless mutant turned away by her parents. You found a lot of freaks in the Zone, just waiting for roaming packs of Dobermans or genetics to take them from their misery.

This little girl made strange sad sounds in her throat. She seemed to be looking at Berkowitz and yet seeing beyond him, too. The effect was unsettling, like staring at someone you suddenly suspect is blind.

He dragged himself over to her and took her hand. A fine and decent man, Berkowitz decided to forget his own miseries for the time and concentrate on hers. Maybe there was something he could do for her.

He took her little hand and said, "Hi, honey, do you have a name?"

And realized again that somehow she saw him yet didn't see him. The autism analogy came to mind.

And realized, also, that she couldn't talk. The strange sad noises in her throat seemed to be the extent of her vocabulary.

He wasn't strong enough to stand, so he gently pulled her down next to him, all the time keeping hold of her hand.

And then he started to feel it.

The cessation of his pain, of his fear, even of a generalized anxiety he'd known all his life.

His first reaction was that this was some physiological trick associated with heavy loss of blood. Maybe the same kind of well-being people noted in near-death experiences, the body releasing certain protective chemicals that instill a sense of well-being.

But he was wrong.

He sat next to the girl for more than three hours and in the course of it, they made a telepathic link and she purged him of all his grief and terror.

He knew this was real because each time he opened his eyes from his reverie-like state, he saw animals nearby doing their ordinary animal things—a squirrel furiously digging a buried acorn from the grass; a meek little mutt peeing against a tree; a racoon lying on his back and eating a piece of bread he'd scrounged from some human encampment.

The wound didn't go away—she didn't heal him—but he felt so pacified, so whole and complete and good unto himself, that his spiritual strength gave him physical strength, and allowed him to find his way out of the Zone and back to his Fortress in Glencoe.

He brought the girl with him.

He took her straight to the doctor at the hospital and told the doctor what had happened and, skeptical as the doctor was, the little girl was allowed to audition, as it were.

They put her in the ER with a man whose arm had been torn off. You could hear his screams as far up as the sixth floor. They were prepping him for surgery.

The girl sat down and took the man's lone good hand.

He was in so much pain, he didn't even seem to notice her at first.

Nothing happened right away.

The strapped-down man went on writhing and screaming.

But then the writhing lessened.

And then the screaming softened.

And the doctor watched the rest of it, bedazzled.

Berkowitz's discovery made it possible for hospitals to keep on functioning. All they had to do was hire Outriders, men and women willing to take the chance of searching the

Zones for more youngsters who looked and acted like this one. And while they were out there, like the Outriders of old, they could also note any gangs of people who seemed headed for the Fortress to inflict great bodily harm.

To date, these were a few observed truths about the Pain-eaters as they'd come to be called:

- Generally between the ages of three and six.
- Generally put out to die by their families because of their mutation.
- Unable to speak or see (as we understand seeing).
- Are generally useful for only a three- to four-month period.
- Afterward, must be sent to Zone 4 for further study. At this stage, *dementia* has usually set in.

They could be used up, like a disposable cigarette lighter. They could absorb only so much of other people's pain and then that was it. A form of dementia set in. Fortress North-western had a group of doctors studying the used-up ones. By doing so, they hoped to increase the chances for longer use. There was a finite number of these children and they were extremely important to the survival of all Fortress hospitals.

There were two other observations I should note:

- Extended proximity to these children has been known to make human beings overly protective of them, leading to difficulties with hospital efficiencies.
- Extended proximity to these children has led to difficulties with normal human relationships.

I thought of all this as I stood in the observation balcony and watched the operation proceed.

The man who'd been attacked by the Dobermans was a mess, a meaty, bloody, flesh-ripped mess.

There would have to be a lot of plastic surgery afterward and even then, he would always be rather ghastly looking, a D-movie version of Frankenstein.

There were six people, including Pelham, on the surgery team. Even though he didn't have the equipment he needed—or in truth, the ability to completely sterilize the equipment he did have—Pelham tried to make this as much like his old surgery days as possible. There was the large table for instruments; the small table for instruments; and the operating table itself.

Above the line of her surgical mask, I could see Dr. Sullivan's beautiful eyes. Disapproving eyes. She obviously felt she should be in charge here, not Pelham.

They started cleansing the man's wounds, the surgical team, with Pelham pitching in. Surgeons were no longer stars. They had to do the same kind of work as nurses now.

The kid sat in a chair next to the operating table, holding the hand of the patient.

He was utterly tranquil, the man. The kid had been working with him for some time now.

The kid and the patient faced me, as did the surgery team.

I spotted Polly right away, behind her green surgical mask. She was supposed to be helping with the cleansing but she spent most of her time glancing at the kid.

You really do get hooked into them, some kind of dependence that you ultimately come to regret.

But then she was snapped back to the reality of the operating table when another nurse nudged her roughly and nodded to the patient.

Polly needed to clean a shoulder wound.

She set to work.

And just as she pulled her attention away, I saw the kid do it.

Go into a spasm, a violent shudder, ugly to see.

And then I knew how foolish all Polly's talk had been about resting the kid so she didn't ever get used-up the way all the other ones did.

I got out of there.

I didn't want to be there when Polly noticed the kid go into a spasm, and realize that all her hopes had come to nothing.

7

The argument came three days later. Even two floors up, you could hear it.

I was walking up the stairs to my own room when I heard the yelling and then heard a door slamming shut.

Eighth floor, two down; eighth floor being Polly's. I decided I needed to check it out.

Pelham was in front of Polly's door. So was Nurse Ellen. They were speaking in low voices so nobody except Polly could hear them. Then Dr. Sullivan appeared, swank even in her dusty medical smock.

"What's going on?" I said.

Pelham frowned and shook his head. Of late I'd been nicer to him and was surprised to find that he'd been nicer to me, too.

He walked me down the hall, away from the door, to where a small mountain of rubble lay beneath the smashed-out windows.

Dr. Sullivan and Nurse Ellen stayed by Polly's door.

"Have you talked to her lately?"

"Not for a couple of days. She keeps pretty much to herself."

"That's the trouble. Herself—and the kid."

"I know."

"The same way you got, Congreve." For once there was sympathy in his voice, not condemnation. "Have you seen the little room she fixed up for the kid?"

"Uh-uh."

"It'll break your heart. Polly's convinced herself that she's the kid's mother."

"What's wrong with that? We're all pretty lonely here."

The frown again. But the dark eyes were sad, understanding. "She won't let us use the kid."

"Oh, man. Then she really is gone on her."

"Far gone. Maybe you can help."

"Not if she's this far along. You get hooked in."

"The same way you did."

I nodded. "The same way I did."

Nurse Ellen was getting mad. Raising her voice. "Polly, we've got a ten-year-old boy down there who was shot by some Zoner. We have to operate right away. We need her, Polly. Desperately. Can't you understand that?"

"Let us in," Dr. Sullivan said in a voice that implied she expected to be obeyed immediately.

But the door didn't open.

And Polly didn't respond in any way at all.

"She said the kid has started twitching," Pelham said. "You know what that means."

By now, Nurse Ellen was shrieking. "Polly, we have to have the kid and we have to have her now!"

"C'mon, Congreve," Pelham said. "Try your luck. Please."

"Then you two go back downstairs."

"We don't have long. The boy's lost a lot of blood."

"I'll do what I can as soon as you two leave."

He wasted no time. He collected Ellen, went to the EXIT door, and disappeared.

"They're gone, Polly."

"You can't talk me into it, Congreve."

"Polly, you're not being rational."

"And you are?"

"There's a little boy downstairs dying."

"Well, there's a little girl in here who's dying, too, and nobody seems to give a shit about that."

"She won't die. She's got a long way to go."

"You know better than that. You know how they are after they start twitching. And getting headaches."

"She'll be all right."

"I can't believe you're talking like this, Congreve. After what you did and all."

"They don't have any choice, Polly. They'll come and take her from you."

"I've got a gun in here."

"Polly, please, please start thinking clearly, will you?"

Three of them came through the EXIT door now, two men and a woman. The men were nurses. The woman was an intern. They all carried shotguns.

They were in a hurry.

They swept up to me and forced me to stand aside.

They meant to get Polly's attention and they did.

No warning. No words at all.

Two of them just opened fire. Pumped several noisy, echoing, powder-smelling rounds into the door.

Polly screamed.

The kid was making frantic animal noises.

"You going to bring her out?" one of the male nurses shouted.

"No!" Polly shouted back.

This time they must have pumped twenty rounds in there. They beat up the door pretty good.

"We're coming in, Polly!" the second nurse shouted.

Pretty obviously, she didn't have a gun. Or she would have used it.

Because now they went in. Booted in the door. Dived inside the room. Trained all three shotguns right on her.

She had pushed herself back against the corner in the precious pink room that she had turned into a wonderful bedroom for a little girl.

The girl was in her arms, holding tight, all the gunfire and shouting having terrified her.

Polly was sobbing. "Please, don't take her. Please don't take her."

She said it over and over.

But take her they did, and without any grace, either. The moment Polly showed the slightest resistance—held the kid tight so they couldn't snatch her—one of the nurses chunked Polly on the side of her head with the butt of his shotgun.

I grabbed him, spun him around, put a fist deep into his solar plexus.

Not that it mattered.

While I was playing macho, the other two grabbed the kid and ran out of the room with her.

I dragged the lone nurse to the door and threw him down the hall.

Then I went back and sat on the small pink single bed where Polly was sprawled now, sobbing.

I sat on the bed and let her hold on to me as if I were her daddy and knew all the answers to all the griefs of the world.

8

I was sitting up in my room, cleaning and oiling all the weapons, when Pelham showed up, knocked courteously—I told you we were trying to be nice to each other these days, Nurse Ellen's irate words taking their toll on me—and said, "Polly took the kid in the middle of the night and left."

This was two days after the incident at Polly's door.

"Maybe they just went out for a while."

"She took food, two guns, and some cash."

"Shit."

"I've got a woman downstairs who won't see tonight if I don't get that kid back."

"Damn."

"I know how much you like Polly, Congreve. I like her, too. But I have to—"

"—think of the patients."

"I'm sorry if you get tired of hearing it."

I sighed and stood up. "I'll go get her."

"She tried to start the skymobile. Smashed in the window and then tried to hot-wire it."

"She isn't real mechanical. On foot, she won't be hard to find. Unless something's happened to her already."

I tried not to think about that.

"You have to hurry, Congreve. Please."

Took me two hours.

She was up near the wall in what had formerly been a public rest stop. There were three semis turned on their sides in the drive, the result of the initial bombing, and they looked like big sad clumsy animals that couldn't get to their feet again.

Apparently, the rest stop had been pretty busy at the time of the bombing because from up here you could see the skeletons of maybe a dozen people, including that of a family—mother, father, two kids.

When I first spotted her, she was sitting on a hill, resting, with the kid sitting next to her.

She heard me about the same time as I saw her.

She stood up, wiped off her bottom from the grass, picked up the kid like a football, and started running.

There was a deep stand of scrub pines but they weren't deep enough to hide her for long. I waited till she came running out of the trees and then I put the skymobile down not far away and started running after her.

She was in much better shape than I was. Even holding the kid, she was able to stay ahead of me for a good half mile. I stumbled twice. She didn't stumble at all.

We were working up the side of a grassy hill when her legs and her wind gave out.

She just dropped straight down, as if she'd been shot in the head, straight down with the kid still tucked in her arms, straight down and sobbing wildly.

I stood several feet away and said nothing. There wasn't anything to say, anyway.

Pelham took the kid away from her and then put Polly up in one of the observation rooms in a straitjacket. He wouldn't let me see her for a couple of days.

By the time I got up there, she was a mess. She had a black eye from me having to wrestle her into the skymobile, and her coppery hair was shot through with twigs and dead flowers and her face was streaked with dirt. It was as if she'd been buried alive.

I took a straight-backed chair and sat next to her.

"You fucker."

"I'm sorry, Polly."

"You fucker."

But there was no power in her voice. She was just mouthing words.

"I'm sorry I got you involved in this. I never should have taken you along to Hoolihan's that day. I was being selfish."

"I don't want to live without her."

"You have to stop thinking that way, Polly. Pelham doesn't have any choice. He has to use Sarah for the sake of the patients."

"She's near the end."

"You need to get on with your life."

At one time, this room had been small and white and bright. Now it was small and dirty. The only brightness came from the kerosene lantern I carried, its flame throwing flickering shadows across Polly's face, making her look even more insane.

"Pelham's a fucker and Ellen's a fucker and you're a fucker. You're killing that little girl and none of you give a damn."

A knock. Just once. Curt.

The door opened and Pelham came in. He walked noisily across the glass-littered floor.

He stood next to me and looked at Polly in her chair and her straitjacket.

"You're doing better today, Polly. You're verbalizing much more."

"You're killing that little girl, doesn't that matter to you?"

This time her voice was heartbreaking. No curses. No anger. Just a terrible pleading.

"Another few days and maybe we'll be able to take off the straitjacket."

He was breaking her, the way cowboys used to break horses. By keeping her in this room long enough, in the straitjacket long enough, alone long enough, she would eventually become more compliant. She would never again be the fiery Polly of yore. But she would be a Polly who was no longer a threat to the hospital.

At least that was Pelham's hope.

"Would you like some Jell-O, Polly?"

But her head was down.

She was no longer willing to verbalize, to use Pelham's five-dollar word.

He nodded for me to follow him out.

"You get some sleep, Polly," Pelham said. "Sleep is your friend."

I took a last look at her.

No matter how long Pelham kept her in here, she would never forgive me and I wasn't sure I blamed her.

I followed him out.

9

That afternoon, over coffee, Pelham made me talk about it again and I resented it but I also understood that he was simply trying to help Polly and I was the nearest equivalent to Polly in the hospital.

Eight months ago, the hospital in need of another Pain-eater, I'd taken the skymobile over to Hoolihan's and bought myself a kid.

I got hooked. I wasn't even aware of it at first. The simplest explanation is that the kid became a substitute for my daughters. When she'd get back from downstairs, from consuming the pain of the patients that day, I'd find myself rocking her to sleep with tears in my eyes.

Soon enough, I saw her start to twitch. And then the headaches came. And night after night she made those same muffled screaming noises in her throat.

And Pelham, it seemed, was always at the door, always saying, "We need her again. I'm sorry."

And all I could do was watch her deteriorate.

"I know you hated me," Pelham said. "And I'm sorry."

I nodded. "You didn't have much choice."

He sipped his coffee. "So what finally made you decide to do it?"

"I guess when you started talking about her future and everything. How she'd be studied and tested so that we could get a better grasp on how to make the future ones last longer. 'New, Improved' models, I guess you'd call them."

"Unless things change a whole hell of a lot, Congreve, we're going to need even more Paineaters in the future. And better ones."

"I guess that's what I was against. I don't think we have the right to use anybody that way. We get so fucking callous we forget they're human beings, and incredibly vulnerable ones."

"So you killed her."

"So I killed her."

That's what the nightmares were all about. Seeing little Michelle sleeping in my bed and creeping up to her and putting the gun to her chest and pulling the trigger and—

"I loved her," I said. "I felt it was the right thing. At least at the time. Now, I guess, I can see both sides."

"I really am going to let Polly go free in the next week or so. I just hope she's as rational as you are."

I sighed. "I hope so, too. For everybody's sake."

"We're doing the right thing, Congreve. The god-damned Christians took out half of Russia and China. We have to rebuild the species, what with all the mutation taking place. We normals have to survive. I don't like what we're doing with Paineaters but we don't have any choice. It's just survival is all."

He clapped me on the shoulder and went back to work. He looked exhausted, but then he always looked exhausted.

10

She didn't get out in one week or two weeks or three weeks. It took four weeks before Pelham thought she was ready.

Mostly, she stayed in her room. They brought her food because she didn't go down to the mess. She was not allowed to see Sarah.

I stopped by several times and knocked. I always identified myself and always heard her moving about in there. But she would not acknowledge me in any way.

One day I waited three hours at the opposite end of the hall. I knew she had to come out eventually. But she didn't.

Another day I found her room empty. She was down the hall in the bathroom, apparently.

I hid in her room.

When she came back, I surprised her. Her face showed no response whatsoever. But her hand did. From a small holster attached to the back of her belt, she pulled out a small .45 and pointed it at me. I left.

A week after this she went berserk. This happened down

in the mess. She was walking by and saw people staring at her and she went in and starting upending tables and hurling glasses and plates against the walls. She wasn't very big, and she wasn't very mighty, but she scared people. She wandered, sobbing and cursing, from the mess and went back upstairs to her room. After a while, Pelham went up to see her. He decided against confining her again.

II

"She's near the end. The spasms—I can barely stand to look at her. She won't last past another couple patients."

This was Pelham in his office two weeks after the incident with Polly in the mess.

Dr. Sullivan, lean, hungry, and gorgeous as ever, sat to the left of Pelham, watching.

"Can you get ahold of Hoolihan?"

"Sure. Why?"

"Get another one lined up."

"She's that close to burning out, huh?"

Dr. Sullivan said, "Dr. Pelham is right. A few more patients at most. Sarah takes on trauma and grief and despair and frenzy as her own. She is a very small vessel. She can't hold much more. The situation is actually much more urgent than Dr. Pelham is letting on."

A deep, bellowing hornlike alarm that signals Pelham that ER has a patient very near death rumbled through the ground floor of the hospital.

Pelham and Sullivan were off running even before I got out of my chair. I followed.

"Used some kind of power saw on him," one of the techs said as the three of us reached the ER area.

Indeed. His neck, chest, and arms showed deep ruts where some kind of saw had ripped through his flesh right to the bone. He wasn't screaming. He was unconscious.

"Get surgery set up!" Pelham shouted after one quick look at the man on the gurney.

"Things are just about ready to go," the tech said.

"We need the Paineater, then," Pelham said.

"She's in there, too," the tech said, "but she's not doing real well. You know how they get near the end—all the shaking and shit."

Five minutes later, we were all in surgery. One of the techs was sick today and I was asked to assist, as I did on occasion.

Operating table and instruments and staff were prepared as well as could be expected under these frantic conditions.

And Sarah was in place.

She sat, staring off at nothing, holding the bloody hand of the man on the table. Her entire body shook and trembled— and then went into violent seizures that would lift her out of her chair.

The screams in her throat kept dying.

"Your job is to watch her, make sure she stays linked to the patient," Pelham told me.

I went over and sat next to her. Just as she held the patient's hand, I held her free one. I kept cooing her name, trying to keep her calm.

She'd peed all over herself. The deep sobbing continued.

The operation started.

The patient was totally satisfied. You could see the pleasure on his face. Sarah was cleansing him not only of his physical pain but of all the grief and anxiety of his entire life. No wonder he looked beatific, like one of those old paintings that depicted mortal men looking on the face of an angel.

One thing you had to say for them, Pelham and Sullivan worked well together—quickly, efficiently, artfully. You'd never know they hated each other.

They had started doing the heavy-duty stitching when the rear door of the operating room slammed open.

I looked up and saw her there. Polly. With an auto-rifle. Face crazed and streaked with tears.

"You're killing her and you don't even care!" she screamed.

She worked left to right, which meant that Pelham was the first to die and then all the staffers standing next to him. This gave Sullivan and a few others the chance to hide behind the far side of the operating table.

By now I had my gun out and was crouched behind a small cabinet.

She kept on firing, trying to hit Sullivan and the others where they were hiding.

"Polly! Please drop your gun!"

If she heard me, she didn't let on. She just kept pumping rounds at the operating table, hoping to hit at least a few of them.

I started to stand up from my crouch.

She must have caught this peripherally because she suddenly turned in my direction, still firing, as one with her weapon.

"Polly!" I screamed. "Put it down!"

But she didn't put it down, of course, and then I had no choice. I put a bullet into the middle of her forehead.

She managed to squeeze off a few more shots but then her gun clattered to the floor, and soon enough she followed it.

Silence.

And then Sarah was up and tottering over to the fallen body of Polly's.

Sarah knelt next to her and made the awful mewling noises in her throat—the saddest sound in her entire repertoire—and then she was touching Polly's face reverently with her tiny white hands.

We all stood around and watched because we had never seen this before. Paineaters took on all the physical and psychic pain of others. Here was a Paineater who had to take on her own pain.

After a time, Sarah still kneeling there rocking back and forth and twitching so violently I was afraid she might start breaking her own bones, I went over and picked her up and carried her out of the room.

12

There was a funeral for Polly the next day. Some fine, sincere, and very moving things were said.

Nurse Ellen announced that Dr. Sullivan would now be in charge of the hospital and that people should now come to her with any questions they had.

Afterward, I put Sarah in the skymobile and got ready to take off.

Dr. Sullivan came over to say good-bye. "The doctors at the school will be very interested in this one especially. Studying the effects of her own trauma. With Polly."

Sarah had made no sound since I'd carried her from the operating room yesterday. She just sat there in the throes of her shaking and jerking and trembling.

"I appreciate you doing this," Dr. Sullivan said. "I know you don't think we should prolong their lives or their suffering. But it's necessary if we're to survive."

"That's what Pelham said."

She smiled her beautiful icy smile. "Well, at least he was right about something."

It took three hours to find the school, a rugged stone castle-like building that had once been a monastery sitting in the middle of deep woods.

"Well, this is going to be your home for a while, Sarah," I said.

I'd tried not to look at her. The spasms were really getting to me.

Survival, Pelham had said.

I started circling for my landing, finding a good open area near the west wing to put the machine down.

And that's when the cry came up in her throat and her hand reached over and grabbed mine.

She shook so violently that I couldn't keep my hand around hers. Tears filled her dead eyes.

By now a couple of the docs below had come out and were waving to me. They knew who I was and what cargo I brought.

I waved back—or started to.

I pulled the machine up form the landing I'd started and swung away abruptly from the school.

I could hear them shouting below.

That night, in the mess, Dr. Sullivan came over and sat by me. "I really appreciate you taking her over there this afternoon."

"No problem."

"You doing all right?"

"Doing fine."

"I'm looking forward to working with you, Congreve."

"Same goes for me."

"Thanks."

Then she was off to do some more PR work with other people she felt vital to her new post as boss.

Being tired, I turned in early.

Being tired, I slept at once and slept fine and fast, too, until that time in the middle of the night when everything is shifting shadow and faint, disturbing echoes. I was awake and that meant I'd think back to this afternoon.

I'd tried to do it fast. I'd landed and carried her out of the skymobile and set her down on the grass and put one bullet quick and clean into the back of her skull. And then I held her for a long time and cried, but the funny thing was I wasn't sure why I was crying. For her. For me. For Polly. For Pelham. For the whole crazy fucking world, maybe.

And then I buried her and stood over the little grave and said some prayers and a feisty little mutt from the forest came along and played in the fresh dirt for a time. And I thought maybe she'd have liked that, little Sarah, the way the puppy was playing and all. And Polly would probably have liked it, too.

Darkness. Shadow. My own coarse breathing. I didn't want to think about this afternoon anymore. I just wanted sleep.

"You look tired," Dr. Sullivan said cheerfully at mess next morning.

"Guess I am kind've."

"You're going to see Hoolihan today, aren't you?"

"Uh-huh."

She looked at me hard then. I hadn't been properly enthusiastic when she brought the subject up. "You know how important this is, don't you, Congreve? I mean, for the whole species. Just the way Pelham said."

"Right," I said, "just the way Pelham said."

Three hours later I fired up the old machine and flew over to see Hoolihan.

This one's out of sequence. I've saved it for last for a special reason.

The late Karl Edward Wagner was a writer, editor, and physician. This, I believe, is his last story. We discussed it shortly after he sent it to me. I told him it wasn't exactly what I'd had in mind when I asked him for a short medical thriller, but I liked the damn thing too much to let it go. He said, Fine, we'd talk about it some more after he got back from England.

We never had that talk. He died suddenly within days of his return.

Karl has been eulogized extensively by all the major names in the horror genre, but even more so by the minor names and no names. The reason for such an unprecedented outpouring of grief? Karl edited an annual called *The Year's Best Horror* in which he took special pains to seek out cutting-edge fiction by unknowns and bring them to national attention. He wasn't impressed with reputations; he wanted what he considered the best, most provocative horror fiction and to hell with marquee value.

But that was other people's fiction. Here's the last piece of Karl's own. It's not a thriller; in fact, I think it's probably more truth than fiction. (I'll let you guess who the psychiatrist might be.) And I think Karl let more of his humanity slip through than he'd ever done before.

A damn shame the title was so prophetic.

FINAL CUT

Karl Edward Wagner

No one gets well in a hospital.

Dr. Kirby Meredith had forgotten who had said that to him, but he hadn't forgotten the words. He was a prematurely aging attending psychiatrist at a large hospital in Pine Hill,

North Carolina. He had graduated from the medical school here, gone through his residency, attained his present senior status. Talk was that he would go a long way, perhaps chairman of the department when the time was right.

Dr. Meredith was a nonintimidating, rather dumpy man of thirty-something, with sandy hair and gray in his frizzy beard. He wore the same striped ties he had worn for years, button-down collar shirts, and cotton Dockers. Still wore tight black leather dress shoes, and he pulled on a rumpled tweed jacket whenever he thought the occasion called for it: weekly court commitment hearings, held here at the center; patient's family inquiring as to family member's progress. Shrinks do not wear white. Bad for patient rapport.

He hated wearing ties. If he ever set up in private practice, it would be T-shirts and maybe a sweater. A cardigan. No, just the T-shirt. Or some jogging sweats. Not that he ever jogged. Assume the air of informality. Patient at ease. Dream on.

Dr. Meredith had just completed his rounds, was making medication adjustments to his charts, making mental notes regarding his students and staff, and considering journal club that evening, where he hoped his residents finally would be brought up-to-date on lithium therapy. There was a fine line between maintaining a manic-depressive and killing him, and the foreign resident who had confused q.o.d. with q.i.d. was going to speak at length upon the subject. In broken English.

"Dr. Meredith." The nurse knew better than to interrupt him needlessly, and Meredith felt the tension. "He says he's your cousin, and it's urgent."

"Thank you." Meredith picked up the phone. He shouldn't be receiving personal calls here, unless from his wife or daughter. He worked hard, did not like to be interrupted. Once at home, he could find time for friends and family.

"Kirby!" said the voice over the phone. "It's your favorite cousin, Bob. I got a problem, maybe. Janice told me how to reach you at the hospital."

"What's the problem, Bob?" Meredith thought Cousin Bob sounded drunk. He'd rarely seen him sober. Bob Breenwood lived about half an hour's distance from Pine Hill and ran a small hardware business in a small town. They got together regularly to go fishing. Bob was always drunk. His wife and staff ran the business.

"Just started vomiting. Blood. Can't stop it."

Meredith froze for a moment. "How much blood?"

"I don't know. I was cooking a steak on the charcoal grill, and then it just started."

"Is it bright red, or is it sort of like dark and clotted, like it's coming from your gums or sinuses, and you've maybe swallowed it and choked it up?"

"It's bright red, and there's more of it coming up. All the time. Oh, shit! I got to hit the toilet!"

Meredith was very firm. "Have your wife call 911. Emergency. Get over here without delay. You're likely bleeding to death from ruptured esophageal varices. Do it now. I'll be here. For you. There's no time to waste. You'll be dead in an hour."

Possibly putting it a little too strong, but Meredith phoned 911 himself, with frantic details. Maureen Breenwood had already called. Meredith hovered about the Emergency Room, getting in the way, while explaining why an attending shrink was in the way. He was well liked, and the staff were ready when the ambulance arrived.

Bob's hematocrit was down to 10, for someone who liked

to take down record lows. Typed and cross-matched, the units of blood finally flowed into his arm. He did not go into shock, by some miracle. A balloon was inserted past his esophagus, reducing the bleeding, and his blood pressure finally stabilized at 105/90 from 60/45. He should have been dead.

Dr. Meredith observed, but stayed out of the way. He wouldn't want two or three other shrinks all giving therapeutic advice as he interviewed his patient, and he respected professionalism. Instead he made frequent visits to Maureen, who had left the waiting room for the chapel, and reassured her as she spoke with the priest. Dr. Meredith was an atheist, but therapy was therapy. Janice was coming over to be with her.

Cousin Bob was fully stabilized by three in the morning and off to Intensive Care. Dr. Meredith checked Maureen into a nearby hotel and promised to phone if there were any complications, then returned to his office in the psychiatric wing and fell asleep on his couch.

Meredith woke up about seven, very groggy but too concerned to go back to sleep. He brushed his hair and brushed his teeth, washed his face and sprayed his armpits, put on a fresh shirt and tie from his file cabinets. He wondered why he bothered to pay a monstrous mortgage for their home. He phoned his wife to see if she might stay with Maureen a few hours while Ashley was at school, and to say privately to Janice that things weren't going well—she knew that—and that he'd be home for dinner on time—she doubted that. Hell. This hospital *was* home.

Dr. Meredith knocked back a cup of coffee at the administrative office, had another, tossed a buck into the coffee fund. He hated coffee. About time for morning rounds, and then he had group at eleven. He wished he were as young as his med students, or even the residents. Youth and enthusiasm. Hell, he wasn't that old. He wished he had learned to play an electric guitar. Joined a rock band. Better the devil that you know. He poured another cup of coffee, then went to rounds.

Bob Greenwood was asking for him from the Intensive Care Unit as soon as they removed the balloon from his esophagus. Meredith delayed an outpatient appointment and went to see him instead of taking a late lunch. He wasn't hungry.

Cousin Bob was a year and a half older than Meredith, something he wouldn't let Meredith forget when they went skinny dipping together and Bob was growing hair on his crotch and Meredith was too young. Much later, Bob got him laid for the first time, double-dating in Bob's family's Nash Rambler with the fold-down front seat and a friendly high school girl and a convenient cemetery.

Meredith sat down on one of those uncomfortable plastic chairs at the bedside. Bad practice to sit down on the bed.

Maureen was sniffling, holding Bob's hand. She was a stout brunette with acne scars, but a good cook, which is why Meredith reckoned Bob had married her, because she couldn't keep house and the rest was none of his business.

Bob was as chunky as his wife: blue eyes, blond hair, rather short, no tattoos. Meredith had always thought them a good match. Happy, harmless couple. He was waiting for dozens of clueless offspring to appear.

Instead.

"Maureen," said Bob. "Could you let me talk to Kirby in private? Just for a few minutes. After all, he's a shrink."

"Sure." Maureen left the room.

Cousin Bob glanced around the Intensive Care Unit. There was fear in his eyes. Understandably.

"Liver's gone, they say."

Dr. Meredith had read the charts. "Always a chance for a repair. This is 1973, after all."

"Kirby, they're saying I'm just a drunk. I don't think they really give a damn."

"I'm here for you. I'm staff."

"Did you know that I had TB years back?"

"No. You never told me."

"Friend of mine got it doing time in some shithouse reform school. We'd pass cigarettes and beers back and forth. They found some spots on my lungs after he'd been diagnosed. Put me on their two-drug therapy. Public health shits coming by to make sure I took all my pills. Isoniazid and something, I forget. Took them for ten years or so at their lawful command. Turns out that the combination wipes out your liver long-term."

"Shit." Meredith was familiar with the situation, but could think of nothing more profound to say. He wished he'd known about Bob in time.

"So now I'm here with a trashed liver, wiped out by the best medicine you can offer, told that I'm an alcoholic, serves me right. And they want to operate. Womak procedure, I think they call it. What do you think? I'm ready to walk."

Dr. Meredith had read his cousin's chart. "Well, for whatever reasons, you are in liver failure, and you're bleeding internally. Very badly. It will start again and maybe not stop. I'm a shrink, and your surgeon can explain it far better. Basically they'll remove your spleen and the region of your stomach and lower esophagus where these varices—knotted-up blood vessels—lie. The liver can take a lot of abuse, and only a small portion need recover. There's work on liver transplants. I don't see it happening soon, but you're buying time."

"Then you think I should do it? The surgery?"

"I don't see any real choice. I mean, if you start bleeding again . . ."

Bob grabbed his hand, weakly. "Kirby, I'll go for it on your word."

It was a nonelective case, and surgery was under way by lunchtime the following day. Meredith bought a stale ham sandwich from a machine, munched on it, phoned his wife. She wasn't home. He fumbled around his desk and found some Maalox. By the time he'd had sessions with a few patients, it was growing dark and Cousin Bob had made it through surgery. Meredith spoke to him in the recovery room. He phoned his wife. She wasn't home. Meredith went back to his house. He microwaved a low-cal dinner, ate part of it.

Bob seemed to have come through it all very well. Maureen was at his bedside. Meredith persuaded Janice to visit with her when Janice could spare the time.

"I had a dream, Kirby," Bob told him two days postop. "I'm not sure it was a dream."

"Do you want to talk about it?"

"I'd climbed out of my bed, pulled out the IVs. I was fumbling my way along all these corridors. Lost. Just trying to get out. Go home.

"I was somewhere in the basement—I don't know how. I pushed open a door, thinking it led out. Only I was in the hospital morgue. Two doctors were doing an autopsy on a man. I think the man was me. I must have fainted, but I remember someone taking me back to my room. I'm afraid, Kirby."

Dr. Meredith considered. He decided to be reassuring. "Near-fatal illness. Major surgery. Anesthesia. Pain medication. Not an uncommon sort of nightmare. Just rest and let your body heal. Just ask the nurse to call me if you have any more bad dreams."

He examined the charts, just in case, and found nothing out of the ordinary.

All of this was at the end of June. July brought in a new crop of interns, freshly graduated from med school and eager to excel. Dr. Meredith lost a few of his residents, gained a few more, none of whom seemed promising, but that was his task—to bring them around. When he closeted himself in his office, he studied travel brochures.

Cousin Bob was now five days postop and starting to take semisolid foods.

He choked on the cherry Jell-O. Maureen pounded his back and shouted for help. By the time the nurse arrived, Bob's breathing passage was clear, but the spasms had opened some sutures, and this was causing pain and some bleeding. The nurse called for an intern.

The intern had only just arrived at the medical center, knew nothing about his patient, saw the postop abdominal incisions and fresh bleeding, obvious severe pain—and ordered a liberal injection of morphine to quell pain and agitation. He hadn't thought to check the charts for liver function, but he had been told that the patient in 221 was a hopeless drunk. Whatever. Who cares.

Cousin Bob died before Dr. Meredith could rush over from the psychiatric wing. Janice came to be with Maureen. Meredith followed the body to the basement morgue. There would be an autopsy, although it was obvious to most idiots in white coats that a patient with minimal liver function had been massively overdosed.

"Shit! He's back again!" The chief pathologist was breaking in another pale and trembling med student. Meredith suspected he enjoyed this sort of thing or he'd leave this to residents.

"What do you mean?"

"Patient stumbled in here a few nights back. Guess he just couldn't wait."

"Nothing in his chart about that."

"One of your patients? Well, orderlies don't like to report a fuss when there's no harm done."

"No harm done."

"Looks bad for the hospital."

No one ever gets well in a hospital.

Dr. Meredith wandered from the basement morgue, seeking his office.

The oppressive walls soaked with pain and rage pressed down on him. He thought of a thousand Cousin Bobs—slowly, painfully killed by the best efforts of modern unfeeling medicine. No one ever gets well in a hospital.

Tomorrow he would clear out his office.

Tomorrow couldn't come soon enough.